A TEAM OF SIX

THE UNSANCTIONED ASSET SERIES BOOK 6

BRAD LEE

ISBN: 978-0-9899547-0-9

PART 1

TUESDAY

1

PREY

The six men blundered along the jungle trail with little regard for stealth.

Retired Navy SEAL Alex "Axe" Southmark stalked his prey.

The noise of the men ahead of him, the glow of their flashlight beams through the foliage, and their lack of discipline allowed him to stay farther back than he normally would have while tracking an enemy.

These guys aren't military, Axe thought.

That didn't mean they weren't dangerous—or up to no good. The suspects had been on one of the area's most popular trails for over a mile, walking across, alongside, and up a shallow riverbed. They would soon reach the turnaround point above a popular waterfall.

The men angled off the riverbank and up a small hill. The lush jungle glowed deep green in Axe's night vision goggles, occasionally flaring out if he looked directly at the distant flashlight beams.

If Axe remembered his map correctly, they would soon pass above a narrow, forty-foot-tall gorge the river ran through before it opened into a series of pools.

Why hike here at zero dark thirty?

The trail was easy to follow, especially by flashlight, but the beauty of the scenery would be wasted in the dark.

And what possible terrorist target could there be out here?

The intel had to be wrong.

Haley, his intelligence analyst partner, was as close as the earbud in his left ear, though she managed the operation from a small conference room in Virginia.

After several more minutes of walking, one of the men spoke, a quiet murmur ahead. Axe couldn't make out the words—only the tone. The tango sounded frustrated.

Axe risked moving in. There wasn't much cover in this area, just skinny trees, eafy ground cover about knee high, and medium-sized boulders off the side of the trail. To his left, he sensed the dark openness of the gorge.

If I can catch what they're saying—or hear their language—maybe it'll give me a clue to who they are and what they're after.

Careful step by careful step, Axe drew closer, a lifetime of similar missions allowing him to move like a shadow in the night.

A second voice responded to the first man, his tone patient.

The voices stopped as Axe closed in.

Damn.

They must have resolved whatever they were debating because the group moved on, making less noise than before but still plenty for Axe to pinpoint exactly where they were.

He'd moved in close. Following now might risk exposure. One false step and they'd hear him. He wasn't worried about being seen. If they'd had night vision goggles, they wouldn't have been using the flashlights.

I'll give them a few extra seconds. They're not getting away.

Axe held back long after it was safe to follow. He couldn't explain it, but every fiber of his being told him to keep still. He stood motionless next to several thin trees ten feet off the trail, controlled his breathing, and extended his senses, trying to understand why his gut told him to wait.

His hand inched to the sat phone in his pocket and lowered the volume to zero. He needed to hear over Haley's breathing—and didn't want the slightest noise to escape the earbud and give his location away.

Although he didn't see or hear anything, Axe sensed a presence nearby.

No—not one. There are two people.

The whole group was no longer bumbling through the jungle. Two of them had held back and were moving expertly toward him, inch by inch.

They know I'm back here.

He had suddenly gone from hunter to prey.

2

TACTICS

Outside San Germán, Puerto Rico

Axe's threat assessment skyrocketed as he sensed the two men closing in.

These aren't the poorly trained yahoos I thought they were.

Haley had been right all along. She may not have known exactly what they were doing on the island—hence his mission—but her assessment was correct. The men stalking him were dangerous and quite probably up to no good, even if they hadn't done any harm so far. Hiking at night might be odd, but it wasn't illegal or a plot against the country. There could be an innocent explanation for this all.

Yeah, right. Still, time to bug out.

He wasn't here for a confrontation. His mission was to follow the suspects. To observe and report—unless the men turned out to be terrorists. Then the gloves came off, and he could do what he did best: Take care of the problem in any way necessary.

His rules of engagement were clear. He couldn't shoot or otherwise harm people who weren't trying to harm him, the United States of America, or its people.

Not that it mattered much. He didn't have his normal short-barrel M4. He'd been on a photography trip on a nearby island when Haley had asked him to help follow up on a concern she had about potential terrorists in Puerto Rico.

The pistol he took everywhere—even on vacation—wouldn't be effective at a distance against well-trained enemy fighters.

And in place of the usual plate carrier with ceramic armor he'd wear on an official mission, underneath his shirt tonight, he had only a light ballistic vest that he'd packed on a whim.

It was better than nothing, but if the men stalking him had rifles and decided to shoot, he'd be in trouble.

For another few seconds, Axe had a slight advantage. He'd held back and was farther away than he bet they believed.

The men drew closer. They moved with a stealth that rivaled—or surpassed—his own abilities.

How long have they known I've been trailing them?

Axe pushed aside the concern over his abilities and stepped back, using every bit of experience to move silently, at one with the night and jungle.

He would hide until the men gave up looking for him and moved on— or presented as a threat so he could take them out.

His NVGs showed a group of trees growing tightly together on the other side of the path, toward the gorge. Their trunks twisted and entwined, forming both small and large gaps between them. He could hide behind the trunks or slip into the dark folds and disappear.

Axe concentrated on his movement. He had to move faster than the tangos—but still silently—to get into his hiding spot before they got close enough to see him through the thin cover.

He placed one foot, testing the ground before settling the rest of his weight on it.

A pause, then he shifted forward and repeated the process with the other leg.

One careful step at a time.

Behind him, a pebble moved. One of the men had stepped onto a loose rock.

They're closing in.

Axe kept moving.

For two minutes, the deadly slow-motion cat-and-mouse game continued.

Axe moved.

The men behind him moved.

As he carefully stepped across the trail, Axe had to face the facts. The men were gaining on him.

They're better than I am. I'm not going to make it to the tree.

He had to change tactics.

A jumble of head-sized boulders lay just off the trail among the low jungle plants.

With a last look at the group of trees fifteen feet ahead—which might as well have been a mile—Axe eased to the ground, settled face down among the ground cover and rocks, switched off the NVGs, and went dark.

During sniper training years before, he had developed the ability to fade away. By shutting down his thinking and drawing into himself, he could become nearly invisible with only the thinnest concealment.

He used the skill now, letting go of the concern that he'd be easily noticed if the men had night vision goggles.

Laying among the boulders and leaves as the two men closed in, Axe vanished.

3

LUCK

Central Analysis Group Headquarters
Conference Room C
Alexandria, Virginia

Haley had the connection with Axe piped through the high-end speakerphone on the round conference room table, though the device was on mute. Only she spoke with her partner while he was on a mission. He didn't need to have several voices in his ear while downrange, but Haley wanted everyone to follow along. If Axe needed something fast, they'd all be able to get on it without her having to repeat the request or explain the situation.

She adjusted the noise-canceling headphones on her ears, careful not to make a noise the microphone would pick up, and tried not to worry. Axe was extremely resourceful. He'd been in situations much worse than following unknown men through the jungle in Puerto Rico. Still, she couldn't ignore the bad feeling that had crept in a few minutes earlier.

He's good—and lucky, Haley thought. *But everyone's luck runs out eventually.*

Across from her, Nancy bit her lip. The older woman's medium-length gray hair was frizzy due to DC's spring humidity.

As one of the two senior analysts, Nancy had participated in the direct-action ops the group had run in the past, but never in real time, monitoring via coms. Her nerves were getting the best of her.

Being in the office, powerless, is harder in some ways than being in the action.

Nancy glanced at her, eyes questioning.

Haley shrugged in silent reply.

Like I know what's happening.

Axe had gone silent forty-six minutes earlier as he left his vehicle. The suspects had parked at a popular tourist destination—a hiking trail to a scenic gorge with a shallow stream and waterfall. He was hiding his rental car off the road and would follow them.

Dave, the other senior analyst, sat to Nancy's right. They were a couple and had been for years, but they didn't let on at the office. Like Nancy, he was in his mid-fifties, his black beard flecked with more gray every week, it seemed. His dark eyes and skeptical demeanor couldn't hide his growing concern.

He clicked at his laptop. A map showing the trail to the waterfall, marked with Axe's estimated location and daytime tourist photos of the area, appeared on the huge wall-mounted TV monitor.

Haley nodded her thanks. If Axe needed help, she might be able to vector him to a landmark or otherwise point him in the right direction.

Her boss, Gregory, leaned against the wall behind her, observing. As usual, his longish gray hair was perfectly styled. With his fashionable black frame glasses and tailored suits showing off his developing muscles from working out with the president, he seemed like a combination older-brainiac-manager-turned-gym-rat.

This was her op to run. He was there for support and advice, along with the authority to escalate the operation if Axe discovered an impending threat.

Marcus, the newest member of their small team, fidgeted to Haley's right, his dress shirt's cuffs rolled up to his elbows, revealing thin yet muscular dark arms. Fifteen minutes earlier, he'd unknotted the snazzy navy-blue bow tie and unbuttoned the top button of his shirt, giving in to the stress and trading fashion for comfort.

Marcus had wanted to go all out, with drones, spy satellites, and a full team of SEALs backing up Axe. Nancy, Dave, and Haley had suppressed their amusement. Their tiny organization only had access to those resources in the case of an impending threat against the country, not for tracking a group that could be terrorists—or drug traffickers, common criminals, or ultrarich insomniacs who liked to trek through the jungle at night.

Haley's hunch about the men relied almost entirely on guesswork and supposition. The intel had been iffy, as usual.

In general, bad guys had gotten wise to the incredible resources the United States had to uncover their plots. They kept off comms and the internet, using the tools only when absolutely necessary.

At first, Haley hadn't put much into the weak gut instinct that had led her to ask Axe to cut his vacation short by a day and get to Puerto Rico. If he hadn't already been in the area, she would have sent an alert to the local police.

But a small, nagging sense of uneasiness convinced her to take action.

Her path to sending Axe to Puerto Rico had started with the report of a Russian spy ship off the coast of Hawaii, thousands of miles away from Puerto Rico. But after piecing together several small bits of intel, she had an idea that a group of bad guys might be using a small yet luxurious yacht in Puerto Rico for... something.

She had a perfect track record of taking scraps of unrelated information and uncovering threats no one else in the vastness of America's intelligence apparatus had any inkling of.

I'm going to be wrong one of these times. Is this it?

But Axe had gone silent, which had to mean something.

She stared at the speakerphone, willing Axe to provide a whispered update. Being in the office was certainly safer, but sending a person into harm's way and waiting while they did their job was definitely stressful in its own way.

Come on, Axe. Come on...

4

BAIT

Outside San Germán, Puerto Rico

Axe lay with his cheek in the damp dirt off the trail, eyes closed.

The two tangos closed in.

He willed his heart to slow, his breathing to quiet, and his body to sink into the earth.

One man walked along the trail to Axe's side; the other was closer to the gorge. They moved so quietly that Axe had trouble tracking them, but it became easier to hear and sense them as they neared.

The one by the trail closed on Axe's position. As long as he didn't hear, see, or otherwise sense Axe, he would pass only a few feet to the left.

The man stopped.

Axe remained frozen, at one with the ground.

Does he see me?

The suspected terrorist was three feet away, standing at the level of Axe's waist.

Is he waiting for me to surrender?

Axe resisted the impulse to move.

This isn't over.

He'd had instructors during sniper training stand nearly on top of him and not notice he was there—at night and in daylight.

Axe kept his mind blank and his body completely relaxed. His energy wasn't contained—it was nonexistent.

He simply wasn't there.

After what seemed like an hour but couldn't have been more than a few seconds, the man took a careful step forward, then another and another.

The one to Axe's right did the same.

They're advancing on the group of trees.

A few seconds later, there were several dull *pops* as the men fired suppressed pistols into the darkness of the trees' intertwined trunks.

They're not using night vision goggles—and they think I'm hiding in there.

Just like he'd planned.

The shooting stopped. Leaves moved, and pebbles bounced. It sounded like the men were patting the ground near the tree.

They're feeling for my body.

He had a chance. The men had fired first. He could shoot back now, taking both out while they were distracted looking for his lifeless body in the folds of the entwined tree trunks.

No—not yet.

He trusted his instincts, honed over fifteen years of nightly combat missions and several operations with Haley since he'd retired from active duty.

Something wasn't right.

Axe put himself in the men's situation.

They were being followed by an unknown person. They don't have NVGs or rifles—only silenced pistols.

He must have given himself away somehow while on the road, trailing their SUV. They must have noticed and pulled into a trailhead to lead him to a remote location far from help or curious eyes.

They made noise and used flashlights to lure me in—and I fell for it.

He pushed the disappointment in himself into the box all difficult feelings went into while on a mission. There would be time for dealing with them later—and for learning important lessons for next time.

The men had argued loud enough to draw him closer.

Then they sent half the group ahead, making a racket.

Leaving two men behind to find and kill him.

No.

That part didn't feel right.

What if there were more guys in the group?

He'd seen four men leave the small but expensive yacht in San Juan Harbor that Haley had sent him to watch. He had dropped back after identifying their vehicle, not wanting to risk following too closely.

There could have been more men already in the SUV, or they may have picked others up when they were briefly out of my sight on the busy, twisty roads.

That would leave one or more tangos out there in the jungle somewhere.

They might be hanging back, waiting for me to make a break for it.

If Axe moved now, he might be shot—or worse, captured and tortured to provide intel they wanted.

They'd want to find out who I am and why I'm following them.

Now wasn't the time to move.

"He who is prudent and lies in wait for an enemy who is not will be victorious."

He stayed in stealth mode and waited.

5

GONE

Yuri had been a professional soldier for ten years in Russia's Special Operations Forces.

He was treated and paid much better now as a freelance mercenary.

The money partly made up for the humidity of the jungle. He preferred cold temperatures or, if necessary, the dry heat of the desert. It wasn't even summer yet, and the jungle's relatively mild temperature had him soaked in sweat.

He'd taken a risk by splitting up the group of mercenaries under his command. The entire mission would be at risk if this gamble didn't pay off. But protecting the two civilian hackers with only one of his soldiers wouldn't matter if the man who trailed them wasn't dealt with.

Whoever had discovered and followed them was good—no doubt about that. Only bad luck had revealed him. A sharp turn in the road had offered a glimpse back the way they'd come just as the man's car—lights off—had traversed an opening in the thick foliage.

No one in their right mind drove with their headlights off on the island's poorly kept roads—unless they were trailing a target, wanted to stay undetected, and were either desperate, suicidal, or had night vision goggles.

It had to be the night vision goggles—which meant a professional.

But at the moment, it seemed the man had disappeared.

Where is he?

Yuri had ordered a stop at the tourist hiking trail, gotten everyone out, and lured the man into a trap.

The flashlights would negate some of the advantages of the pursuer's night vision goggles, causing flaring and forcing the man to look away or be careful how he used them.

When one of the hackers—a nerd who had never hiked a mile in his life—had complained about the exertion, Yuri reassured the man and hoped their follower was closing the distance to listen.

His two best warriors had doubled back.

The trap had then been sprung—but the man had slipped away somehow.

He has to be here.

There was no place to hide except the group of small trees that had grown together, leaving gaps among their trunks. As his men searched the dark spaces but came up empty, then picked up their spent bullet casings —feeling along the ground for them in the dark—Yuri had to face the facts.

He's not there.

Yuri scanned the area, his eyes well accustomed to the darkness. After so many years as a soldier in Russia's ill-equipped army, he could see nearly as well at night on his own as the enemy could with their fancy goggles.

All he needed was a sliver of moonlight—like tonight—or the stars to see by.

Nearby, there was nothing out of the ordinary. Rocks, some type of low fern, various other jungle plants, and thin but tall trees.

He couldn't have slipped by us.

Still, there was no sign of the man who was slowing down his time-sensitive mission.

Where are you?

6

HUNCHES

Haley heard gunfire.

That had to be suppressed pistols shot nearby.

Only Gregory had picked up on the significance of the odd sound over the long-distance sat phone connection. He moved from his position against the wall and sat next to her at the table, not saying a word.

My thin hunch was correct—these are bad guys.

What hadn't been established yet was what kind of bad guys they were. They weren't necessarily terrorists.

They could be drug dealers for all we know.

Axe hadn't so much as grunted, so he hadn't been shot at least.

He's amazing at what he does, but he's not a superhero.

If he had been hit, he would have made noise—and shot back.

Unless they shot him in the head and he died instantly...

She couldn't—wouldn't—go there.

Axe would be fine. He had to be. She'd never forgive herself if one of her hunches got him killed.

7

PATIENCE

It took Axe several seconds to figure out what the tangos were doing by the tree. Finally, it dawned on him.

They're picking up their spent brass. Who are these guys?

They were nearly silent in the darkness, had gone straight to the only hiding place around, fired first and inspected the area afterward, then took the time to leave no trace of their suppressed gunfire.

They were well-trained pros—or well-led, at least.

The more he considered it, the more the latter made the most sense.

They have orders. Someone is managing them.

Having the insight didn't make his current situation any easier or change his strategy. For now, all he could do was wait and hope they made a mistake.

All I need is an opening.

Yuri didn't move or acknowledge his men in any way as they returned up the trail to rendezvous with the two computer hackers and the fourth member of the team.

They'd done exactly as he'd ordered—except for killing the man who was supposed to be hiding in the folds of the tree trunks. Now they fell back on the contingency, which Yuri had planned only out of an abundance of caution.

The man stalking them was not likely to be a police officer. Police, especially the island's local force, weren't trained well enough to disappear like this man had.

No, the man they hunted had to be military. Top-tier, too. No average soldier would be able to hide from them.

This led him to concerning conclusions.

Either a mistake has been made, our communications have been compromised, or there is an informant.

How else could they have been targeted?

Those considerations were for later, though. In a while, his men and the hackers would return along the path, making noise and using their flashlights as before. They would walk right past Yuri's hiding spot.

If he was still out there, the soldier would emerge from hiding to trail them.

Yuri would shoot, wounding him if possible—to extract information about how they had been discovered—or killing him if necessary.

Then again, shooting to kill from the start might be the best approach with this level of opponent.

All Yuri had to do was give the enemy the chance to make a mistake.

8

GAMES

Outside San Germán, Puerto Rico

Axe held his position in the thin cover off the trail.

Several people passed within ten feet without a clue he was there.

He didn't dare move his head to look, but from the footsteps, it sounded like three warriors escorting two people who were unfamiliar with moving quietly in nature.

They drew me in with those two as bait—and I bought it.

He'd thought he was dealing with amateurs when he'd been tailing a fire team of four experienced soldiers and two civilians.

Who are the civilians, and why are they so important?

No one comes along on a mission who isn't absolutely necessary.

He'd have to figure that out later—or pass it along to Haley once he could safely speak.

Three soldiers passing by meant one—the leader or most experienced man—was still out there, watching and waiting for Axe to make a move.

That's when he'll try to capture or kill me.

It came down to timing. Axe had to follow the group and find out what they were up to.

As soon as he moved, though, he'd reveal himself to the warrior hanging back and risk getting killed.

Does the last man have a mission besides me?

If he was the team leader, he would want to be with his troops and the people they escorted.

If he was a sniper, killing Axe would be the only mission that mattered.

The two tangos by the tree had used suppressed pistols. Would the last man have a rifle?

Axe had too many questions and too few answers.

I'll have to risk it.

Axe waited until the men were long gone.

Nothing moved in the jungle besides small animals and the faint gurgle of water over rocks from the gorge.

Timing. It's all in the timing.

He risked the tiniest movements, slowly tensing and releasing his muscles to prepare for what he had planned.

Axe had been to Puerto Rico years earlier on vacation—and studied for this mission on the short flight to the island, looking at pictures of the cities and most popular beaches to prepare for a multitude of different possibilities. He had memorized all the main roads and had familiarized himself with many of the tourist attractions, both those in the towns and the fabulous hiking areas in the outskirts, like this one.

The island had many waterfalls. They were a huge draw for tourists.

The memory of one picture in particular gave him hope. It had shown a gorge, like the one nearby, viewed from the shallow water of the river below. Along the side of the gorge in the photo, long vines—or maybe roots—fell over the side of the tall cliffs, hanging nearly all the way down to the water.

He couldn't remember where and when the picture had been taken.

Were the vines at every waterfall cliff? Could they be seasonal? Had they been torn away by people using them to swing into the water?

Doesn't matter. If they're gone, a forty-foot drop won't kill me.

But it sure as hell would hurt and could injure him badly.

There's no other way.

Yuri waited, growing more frustrated.

No one is this patient, this good.

He had overreacted.

The man trailing them must have been a curious local and turned back before Yuri sent his men to capture him. It was the only explanation that made sense.

Yuri didn't move from his prone position, pistol covering the area downhill from him—just in case—but his thoughts turned to how he would make it to the predawn rendezvous on the beach with his men.

Axe felt it. The time had come. Anyone watching and waiting would be having second thoughts, doubting themselves, and wondering what went wrong with the two separate traps.

Now!

He exploded to his feet, sprinting full tilt toward the edge of the cliff thirty feet away, his daily weight-training, cardio, and running paying off.

As long as he doesn't have a rifle, I'm fine.

Yuri only stifled his gasp of surprise with instincts honed over decades of fighting. A boulder and chunk of the jungle floor had magically come alive seventy-five feet in front of him. Before he could take a shot, the man—it could only be the one he had given up on finding—was farther away, rushing toward...

The ravine.

He fought the desire to shoot—and to follow—forcing himself to remain still.

You win another round, but the game is not over yet.

There were no gunshots, though he might not hear the tiny pop of a suppressed weapon while running.

No bullets whizzed by or hit him.

All good news. He'd taken the enemy by surprise.

Now, if I can survive this next part...

Axe flung himself off the cliff.

His momentum carried him across the gap as he fell, arms wide open in front of him as if he were going in for a hug.

His face slapped against something.

He grabbed at it, his hands closing on a slippery, rope-like vine—or tree root, he still wasn't sure—and held tight, sliding in a barely controlled plummet into the darkness.

His forward momentum caused him to swing, then slammed him into the rock wall. The sat phone in his pocket crunched, silencing the soft sound of Haley's breathing in his ear.

Suddenly, his hands held only air. The root had ended.

He fell, arms flailing desperately to catch hold of another one and slow his descent.

He plunged into the river. The water cushioned his fall just enough to prevent injury, though his feet slammed into the sandy bottom of the shallow river. His knees would feel it tomorrow.

At least I didn't break my legs.

Axe waded through the waist-deep water until he was under a small overhang, protected from anyone above shooting at him.

He had bought himself a few minutes and improved his tactical situation, but he was in a narrow canyon with only two ways out: downstream or upstream.

The tango would be hurrying to the downstream side of the canyon to block Axe's pursuit of his team.

Or he might edge farther down the trail to set up another ambush.

Axe looked up, wondering.

Is he crazy enough to attempt my stunt?

He turned on the NVGs, and the narrow, dark canyon was bathed in the familiar green glow. Axe found it comforting.

To his right, the water flowed from the small waterfall farther up the trail.

Or the tango could be a sneaky bastard and try to rush me from there.

Axe drew his pistol and waited.

The chess game continued.

Your move, asshole.

9

MOVE

The only logical choice for Yuri was to rush down the trail and ambush his talented opponent as he exited the gorge.

He debated making a surprise tactical move and sneaking up on his target from upstream but discounted it quickly.

Sometimes a head-to-head fight is best. I'm faster, and my approach is easier.

Trading stealth for speed, he hurried down the trail.

He had to be careful. No one worked alone. Since there hadn't been any other movement nearby, he could only assume the man's partner—or team—would be staged farther along the trail or at the trailhead.

I hope they are not as well trained as this one.

If the man had only one partner, Yuri's men were likely fine. They would manage against one enemy.

If there was a full team of three others, though, his men would face a challenge—especially considering they had the added duty of protecting the hackers.

Since he'd heard no sounds of battle, he hoped his team had gotten away clean to continue the mission.

Yuri slowed as the trail sloped and turned toward the river. He brought up his weapon, the suppressor still on.

No need to alert any locals with the sound of gunfire from the jungle.

The opening to the gorge was just ahead. Yuri walked carefully from rock to rock, once again moving silently, putting his years of experience to work.

It was darker here. Higher up the trail, there had been fewer trees to hide the stars.

He slowed further. Movement attracted the eye.

The man should be coming any second, Yuri hoped. He didn't relish entering the canyon to stalk an enemy who could disappear at will.

The darkness at the edge of the canyon wall changed nearly imperceptibly.

There!

He squeezed the trigger twice.

10

PAIN

The bullets slammed into Axe's chest at the same moment he fired at the tango standing along the streambed. With no suppressor, the noise of his shots echoed off the canyon walls.

Axe staggered backward. The back of his head slammed into a sharp chunk of rock protruding from the rest of the canyon wall.

He collapsed to his knees in the shallow water next to the wall, dazed.

In the green glow of the night vision goggles, the stream and canyon were blurry. Axe blinked, willing his mind and eyes to get it together and function properly. He struggled to his feet, careful of the low section of wall he'd backed into, and kept his pistol aimed at the entrance to the narrow canyon.

His head pounded, but he wouldn't need to see perfectly to kill anyone rushing toward him.

His chest was on fire from the impact of the bullets. It hurt like hell but didn't feel like the rounds had penetrated the Kevlar.

The vest caught the bullets.

It had saved his life, but it didn't prevent the agony of the bullets' impact. If the tango also wore armor or a vest, they were in the same situation—in pain but still in the fight.

Did I get him?

11

PLAY OUT

Central Analysis Group Headquarters
Conference Room C
Alexandria, Virginia

The satellite phone connection had been out for less than three minutes, but to Haley, it felt like hours.

It's technology—shit happens. Calls are dropped all the time.

And if Axe was on the hunt or in contact, he wouldn't call back until he could do so safely.

"Check the sat phone network," Haley called out, eyes never leaving the speakerphone on the table. "Make sure there's no outage."

On her right, Marcus clicked on his laptop. "No problems reported."

Damn it! I should be there backing him up.

No—she wouldn't debate that with herself again. After the last mission in Los Angeles, she'd made a monumental decision: No more fieldwork for her.

On her left, she sensed Gregory's concern without having to look at him.

"We have to do something!" Nancy whispered.

Haley searched her mind for a solution and came up empty

She agreed with Nancy in principle. Sitting in the office monitoring an operation, seconds felt like hours, and hours seemed like days.

Out in the field, though, hours could fly by in an instant. And the last thing she wanted when she was on an operation, fighting for her life, was to be bothered by desk jockeys half a world away.

Haley took a deep breath, released it slowly, and looked at her team. "We are. We're letting it play out."

12

CHOICES

Outside San Germán, Puerto Rico

Axe waited, grateful for the time the enemy was taking. His head felt better every minute, though his bruised ribs would ache for days.

After what seemed like an eternity, he quietly waded back into the shallow stream and emerged on the far bank. Any well-trained enemy would expect him to emerge in a different place than before, but there were only three choices: the left bank, the stream itself, or the right bank. Axe didn't want to be stuck moving slowly in the water, and he wouldn't risk reappearing where he'd been a minute or two ago, so the far side was the only choice.

He crept forward, ready to fire again.

He saw nothing. No movement, no enemy.

Axe slowed until he was barely inching forward, a mere shadow in the darkness.

As his angle improved, he checked the far bank of the stream where the tango had been last, just in case his first two shots had done the job.

A crumpled form lay sprawled on the ground, face up, feet toward Axe.

Axe put two more bullets into the body to be sure. The tango twitched but didn't roll away or return fire.

Still moving carefully, scanning the surrounding area for an ambush, Axe closed in slowly.

———————

The pain had faded as Yuri's body went into shock.

Two new bullets slamming his body reignited the fire.

He lay on the sandy bank of the stream where he had fallen when the enemy's shots had pushed him off his feet.

He didn't have long to live.

He willed his hand to move, to lift the pistol and shoot the figure approaching across the stream, but his body didn't respond.

Yuri had been raised believing the United States was the enemy.

It seemed somehow fitting he should now die at the hands of an American, on the man's own soil.

As the darkness took hold, his last thought was on the mission.

May my men succeed—and help bring America to its end, once and for all.

13

CLUES

Axe knelt over the enemy. The man had been a worthy adversary.

Rest easy, brother.

With his fingertips, he gently closed the man's eyes.

The man's pockets contained no keys, wallet, maps, or other paper. Just two spare magazines for the pistol and a small, high-tech smartphone of a brand Axe didn't recognize. Axe took it all. Maybe the weapon could be traced or the phone hacked, though he couldn't unlock it using the man's fingerprint or face scan.

Axe pulled off the NVGs and shone his small flashlight on the man, searching for clues. His Caucasian face was round and full.

Axe pried open the dead man's mouth.

Bad teeth and rudimentary dental work.

The man's clothes were similar to Axe's: dark hiking pants, hiking boots, and a loose black shirt, all name brands and relatively new.

A common pistol with an uncommon—but easily hidden—suppressor. No ballistic vest, no NVGs. Both would be difficult to explain away if discovered.

The men were undercover and didn't want to get caught with things the average tourist isn't supposed to have.

Removing his backup comms from a cargo pocket, Axe wasn't surprised when the saturated cell phone refuse to boot up.

Water resistant isn't the same as waterproof.

It would probably dry out and work again, but he couldn't use it to take a picture of the man's face or fingerprints.

I'm not carrying him back to the car, either.

Axe once again studied the man's face, committing it to memory. If his buddies returned to get him before Axe got the authorities here, Haley could connect Axe with a sketch artist to draw a likeness of the man. They might be able to get to the bottom of who he was and why he was in the middle of Puerto Rico with a team of warriors, escorting two men who clearly weren't used to sneaking around at night.

He left the soldier where he lay. It was time to attempt the impossible and track down the five others who had a huge head start.

They're the targets now. I can go in shooting with no qualms at all.

With aching knees, bruised ribs, and a dull throb in the back of his head, Axe flipped down the NVGs and started back to the car as fast as he could without blundering into yet another ambush.

14

SPIDER AND DIABLO

Outside Yauco, Puerto Rico

Spider, as he was known in the hacker community—and as he insisted on being called in real life—forced down the need to be carsick all over the driver's head in front of him.

We have to be almost there.

Although he'd demanded the front passenger seat and cited his motion sickness, the soldiers had ignored him. One soldier drove, and another navigated. The third sat on the far side of the rear bench seat, which was more spacious since the team's leader—Yuri—had stayed behind.

Next to Spider, his buddy and fellow hacker Diablo seemed to be handling the evening much better than he was.

They turned off the poorly paved main road onto a graded gravel one. A few miles later, careful navigation from the soldier with a map in the passenger seat brought them to another turn onto a rutted dirt path. It felt like the jungle was swallowing the SUV as they crept along.

We could walk faster than this—though I've had enough hiking for one night, thank you.

He hoped this site would pay off. The last one had been a bust. There was no security camera—the one thing he and Diablo needed to achieve this part of the mission.

His nausea threatened once more, forcing him to choke back bile as it rose in his throat. "Are we almost there?"

The soldiers ignored him.

"We're the essential part of this mission," he said to the soldiers in English, as required. One of the mission parameters dictated they never, ever spoke Russian, despite it being their shared language. "You understand that, right? Basically, you work for us!"

He knew he'd pushed too far the moment it came out of his mouth. The warrior on the far side of Diablo leaned across the SUV. With a massive, scarred hand, he pressed the button to lower the window. Humid air flooded the vehicle.

As Spider looked at him questioningly, the man slammed the side of his fist into Spider's stomach.

The shock and pain of the strike overwhelmed Spider's willpower. He turned his head just in time to spew his dinner—greasy pizza picked up by the men hours earlier—out the window.

The warriors chuckled, including the driver—Lev—who had been the number two man but was now in charge after Yuri had stayed behind.

"We don't work for you," the man who struck him—Pasha—said in slow, careful English. "You don't work for us. We work together for a single purpose, yes?"

"Yes," the rest of the men in the car agreed—even Diablo.

"Yes," Spider said softly. They all hated America and its arrogance. They were all equal.

For now, at least.

He and Diablo used to sit in air-conditioned comfort and penetrate system after system. It was a toss-up as to which group could do the most damage to America and the West: the soldiers or the hackers.

But the future is in our hands—the hands of the cyber warriors.

Tonight's hacks, if they found what they needed, would open doors the Americans didn't suspect. Spider didn't know much of the plan and didn't want to. It was enough to know that his actions would cause Americans great pain.

"I apologize," he said after a moment.

"Apology accepted," Lev said immediately, slowing the SUV. "We are nearly there. For a while, we take orders from you. What is next?"

Spider glanced at Diablo, and both grinned with excitement. Now was their time.

"Just like the last site," Diablo said. "We need to find a security camera and go to it without being seen."

With a nod, Pasha slipped out of the vehicle.

Five minutes later, he returned. "There is a mobile construction trailer with one security camera on the corner, pointed at the door. A red light is on."

Perfect!

Although it meant another trudge through the dark jungle, Spider and Diablo happily exited the vehicle on the man's side, carrying their computer backpacks. They followed him carefully as they bushwhacked, flashlights off, trying their best to move as quietly as he did but failing miserably.

Pasha stopped them inside the tree line and pointed at a small beat-up work trailer, dark and still in the wide clearing where the dirt road ended. In the starlight, with no light pollution around to inhibit their night vision, Spider could make out the bars on the lone window and a thick horizontal bar adding extra strength to the door.

The security camera's tiny red light shined like a beacon in the night.

The area had the feel of an active workplace deserted for the evening.

Just like the data suggested.

The local power company was spending millions repairing, replacing, and upgrading the area's power lines that had been damaged or destroyed during the past years' hurricanes. This outpost was a combination storage depot and coordination work site for the region. Given the local population's frustration and disappointment with the pace of the work and frequent power outages, the security measures were not unexpected.

Exactly as hoped.

From their small backpacks, Spider and Diablo removed state-of-the-art laptops—American-made, naturally.

Spider used his to look for the first, most obvious opening in the computer network on the Wi-Fi router broadcasting its signal from inside the trailer.

He glanced at Diablo and nodded.

These people will never learn.

Given that the site's workers were laborers and possibly a manager or two, the lack of proper cybersecurity didn't surprise him.

It took only seconds to break in.

As soon as he was in, Diablo went to work.

Several popular security cameras had a known flaw. Although difficult to infiltrate over the internet, in person, an experienced hacker could break into the camera as long as its software hadn't been updated, or "patched."

This one hadn't been updated. With a little effort, know-how, and special hacking software, Diablo soon had access to it.

Spider used the access to send a small computer program to it—a virus that would infect the security camera. The virus would then travel along its connection to the power company's old computer in the trailer, used for tracking hours, equipment, and supplies.

Once it infected that system, it would go to the company's main server, a large computer at the corporate headquarters in San Juan, which was very well defended from outside attacks but vulnerable to assault from inside its own network.

Finally, the virus would use the internet connection of the company's main computer to seek out any other power company systems it was connected to, spreading the infection as it went.

By morning, their tiny virus would be in power company computers across the United States of America.

How many, they wouldn't know until each was contacted over the internet and checked. Some—probably many—would have updated their systems, locking the virtual doors that the virus needed to gain access.

That, however, was a job for another team.

The power company in Puerto Rico was understaffed, underfunded, and overwhelmed with the daunting job of continually replacing and repairing the physical infrastructure that was pounded by storms and hurricanes each year.

They didn't have the time or the expertise to completely secure their systems.

If the hackers were correct, this was the opening they needed.

Thirty seconds later, they closed their laptops and slid them into their backpacks.

Spider tapped the warrior's arm. Pasha hesitated, throwing them a questioning look and pointing to his watch before shrugging and leading them quietly back to the SUV.

"It is done?" Lev asked as they climbed into the vehicle. He caught Spider's eyes in the rearview mirror.

He can't believe it.

"Yes," Spider answered. "Their security was easy."

"How can it be?" Pasha asked.

"They can explain again on the way," Lev said as he started the vehicle and began backing out the long approach path.

Spider and Diablo had both explained how a security camera connected to the internet, whether via satellite, a fiber connection, or a simple phone landline, could be used to upload a small computer program.

"The computers at the power company are protected from attack over the internet. The one in the trailer, too," Spider said, trying a new approach. These soldiers rarely worked with computers and had a difficult time grasping even the basics. "Like a strong wall around a village. The security camera is like a secret gate in the village wall, long forgotten. We sneak in through the gate. Now we are inside the village and can do what we want."

The three warriors were nodding now.

They get it.

"But we do not care about this island's power plant," Pasha said.

"True. But..." He thought for a moment. "The village is connected by a path to another village. The second village doesn't guard the entrance from the path to the first village. They guard only their main gate."

Do they understand?

"Once we are inside the first village via the secret gate," Lev said, "we can go from village to village."

"Yes," Spider said.

"All villages?" the driver asked.

"No," Spider admitted. "Many. Not all. Some villages guard their entrance from the path. Some don't, thinking the people from the other villages can be trusted."

"Or they do not want to spend money posting guards—and do not want to slow traffic to and from their village," Diablo added, getting into the simplified explanation of cybersecurity.

They had reached the road and were able to turn the SUV around.

"The next location?" Lev asked, deferring to Spider. The night was young, and there were other vulnerable facilities on the island that could only be exploited on-site, not over the internet.

"Yes," he said, his car sickness forgotten after emptying his stomach and with the excitement of the successful hacks.

"The next village and gate," Pasha said. "With these, we will harm America?"

Spider nodded. "Yes, very much."

THE BIRTHDAY

Lux View Marina Tower
Penthouse—Floor 35
Dubai, United Arab Emirates

Abdul Khan Dagari settled into the comfortable chair at the table on the balcony, relishing the quiet part of the day as the sun came up. Inside the penthouse apartment, his office awaited. If everything went to plan, today would be the last of the peaceful mornings.

He adjusted the traditional *thobe* worn in the region. The ankle-length linen garment was a bit lightweight for the cool of spring, but he didn't mind. The temperature was welcome; in a few weeks, the daytime highs would soar, and the balcony would only be bearable this early in the morning.

He soaked in the incredible opulence that came with this lifestyle: the views, the servants, the travel. So different from his home village in Eastern Afghanistan or even the larger cities.

A part of him detested the money wasted on the apartment and furnishings. One of the twelve custom-made sofas in the five-bedroom, seven-bathroom home could lift many people in Afghanistan out of poverty.

The sterling silver knives and forks to serve a dinner party of thirty-six could greatly improve the lives of an entire region.

This wealth is a necessary evil.

He needed all of it to maintain the lifestyle, to convince the world he was who he pretended to be.

The view from the ten-million-dollar, eleven-thousand-square-foot penthouse apartment was as spectacular as every other part of this life of incredible luxury. From this balcony—there were four, one on each side of the building—the emerald green of the Persian Gulf, with its engineering marvel of Palm Jumeirah Island, gleamed in the bright sunrise.

The island's seven-star hotel, where he often enjoyed business lunches and met with other men of stature, jutted into the sky but was dwarfed by the building he occupied.

A delicate cough from a servant interrupted his reverie. "Malik," he said quietly, using the term for the respected elder or head of a tribe. Abdul had earned the honorific through his acts of leadership and bravery on and off the battlefield over his fifty-five years.

The servant wore the smart three-piece suit of the household's chief butler and used two hands to carefully hold out a bundle of dark cloth about the size of a small shoe. "This arrived moments ago."

The butler's dark eyes tried but failed to hold back his terror—and revulsion.

Abdul didn't take the offered package. "Put it in a box, and wrap it nicely with paper." He didn't fight the grin that spread across his face. "And a bow—it must have a bow. The paper should be colorful... with balloons, perhaps. Make it suitable for a birthday."

The servant—Samoon—was an older man of about seventy, originally from a village near Abdul's own. If not for the position as Abdul's butler with its plentiful and nourishing food, relatively easy life, and access to quality health care, the man would have been dead years before.

Samoon nodded once and waited for the next instructions. Every "gift" needed a recipient.

"Inform Jamil that there will be two for coffee this morning," Abdul said.

"Yes, Malik," Samoon said, backing five steps before turning and hurrying away.

Abdul enjoyed the view while wondering about the operation in Puerto Rico and relishing the mayhem he would soon unleash on the unsuspecting United States of America.

At 6:30 on the dot, the sliding glass door opened. Jamil, a tall man of medium build, with dark hair and a trimmed beard, fifteen years younger than Abdul, pushed a small silver serving cart onto the balcony, careful to not disrupt the two bone-white china cups on saucers or the tall china coffee pot on the starched white linens.

His high-collar, knee-length button-down tunic was perfectly white and unwrinkled, as were his white cotton pants. His sturdy black work shoes shined, all courtesy of the household staff member dedicated solely to keeping the rest of the servants impeccably attired.

"Welcome, Jamil!" Abdul said, standing and gesturing to the table. "Please, join me. I understand it is your birthday."

What a delightful coincidence.

Jamil nodded, his eyes flicking left and right like he suspected a trap. "Yes, Malik," he said. His voice was a quiet, frightened whisper.

Guilty. No doubt.

Jamil didn't move. "Sit, sit," Abdul said, gesturing again. "It's not every day you turn forty. It is forty, isn't it?" he asked, as if he could be wrong.

Even if he had been, Jamil wouldn't dare contradict him.

"Yes, Malik," Jamil said, moving slowly to the second chair at the small round patio table.

Abdul himself stood, set both coffee cups on the table, and poured first into Jamil's cup before serving himself. The piping hot coffee steamed in the cool air.

Abdul smiled reassuringly at Jamil as he returned to his seat. "It is long past time I join the staff in celebrating milestones. You will have a small gathering tonight after work with the others, no doubt?"

Jamil nodded, his thin lips pressed tightly together as he sat up straight on the front edge of his chair.

Abdul sipped his coffee, burning his mouth, and set the cup down to cool.

Jamil said nothing and didn't touch the coffee in front of him.

Moments later, the butler returned with a beautifully wrapped square box with a cheerful red ribbon tied in a perfect bow. The white paper had small colorful balloons, streamers, and a rainbow of confetti.

Abdul nodded. Samoon moved the untouched coffee cup and saucer to the side and placed the box on the table in front of Jamil.

Jamil studied the box, his eyes squinting in confusion as he looked from it to Abdul and quickly back.

"Stay," Abdul told the butler, who had already taken three steps backward. He stopped instantly, placed his hands behind his back, and stared into the distance.

"We come from the same region," Abdul said to Jamil. Without conscious effort, his voice had quieted and turned colder. "You understand the importance of this," he said, gesturing with his hand at the apartment, the patio, and the view. "Of my mission."

The staff didn't know of the changes that were to come, but they understood Abdul's importance at home in Afghanistan, along with his growing influence in the United Arab Emirates and the wider region. They saw important men from all parts of the Middle East come and go for coffee, meetings, and meals.

They knew Abdul was a man of great respect and power.

That should be enough, but for this one, it is not.

Jamil's lips quivered. He took a breath, preparing to speak, but Abdul silenced him with a raised finger.

The man had been brought from Afghanistan two years earlier to serve as a general household laborer. He came from a poor but trusted family.

In the past months, the butler had informed Abdul that several sterling silver forks had disappeared. He had no suspects.

"You know my aversion to surveillance cameras and other electronic devices," Abdul continued. "But as a temporary measure, one was installed in a storage closet. Do you know what it discovered?"

Jamil nodded. His face flushed red as he looked down at his lap.

A second later, Abdul caught the unmistakable smell. The man had lost control of his bladder.

Disgusting. I will have to get a new chair.

Out of the corner of his eye, Abdul saw the butler's desire—his duty—to hurry and clean up the mess. Abdul didn't need to speak. Samoon would stay in place until released—or until he dropped from exhaustion, even if it meant voiding his own bladder and making an additional mess.

"Please," Abdul said. "Open your present. Then you may clean up and return to your duties. You must finish on time so you can celebrate tonight."

Jamil's hand shook so much it could barely grasp the end of the red ribbon to pull it, but he eventually managed. He hesitated at tearing the expensive paper for a moment before turning the box over to gain access to the small pieces of tape holding the paper together on the bottom.

The contents inside *thumped* as he flipped the small box.

The butler flinched at the sound.

Jamil had the paper off. With another *thump* from its contents—and a second shudder from the butler—he turned the box right side up and removed the cover.

He glanced again at Abdul, his eyes narrowed in confusion at the package inside, bundled in old dark fabric.

"Hurry! Unwrap it," Abdul urged with a smile.

With still trembling hands, Jamil unwound the fabric. A final tug separated the fabric from its contents, leaving the servant holding a woman's delicate hand, freshly severed at the wrist.

The day seemed to stand still as the younger man froze, both of his hands cradling the smaller one, his eyes glued to his gift.

Finally, Abdul spoke, explaining the situation. "You are valuable to me. I do not have time to train a new staff member. Nor do I wish to take the risk of introducing an unknown person into my operation. And, of course, an 'accident' here might bring unwanted attention."

He frowned. Over the past few years, workers' rights and safety had somehow managed to encroach even in this country.

"Questions would be asked. Bribes would have to be paid to eliminate any concerns. I do not need that. Your wife, however..." He trailed off. Jamil likely wasn't hearing him, anyway.

A long length of rough twine pierced the palm of the hand and formed a loop. Abdul idly wondered if the hand had been threaded prior to the severing last night, but he realized he didn't care enough to ask the butler to find out.

"This will serve as a reminder to you and the rest of the staff. You will not steal or otherwise go against me. You are to wear your wife's hand around your neck, close to your heart, while at work for the next twenty-four hours, except for when you service the fifteenth floor.

"Tomorrow morning, after serving coffee, give it to Samoon. He will dispose of it. Now, you are excused. Get cleaned up and return to work."

With a nod from Abdul, the butler hurried forward, bundled up the box, paper, and bow, and nearly ran backward into the penthouse.

Jamil staggered to his feet and carefully slipped the twine around his neck. His skin had gone pale, matching the color of his wife's hand. He bowed and stayed bent slightly at the waist, nodding once in Abdul's direction without raising his eyes. Backing slowly into the house, the hand swung forward and back, lightly thumping his chest with each step.

Abdul smiled.

Jamil would be forever changed—and he would most certainly never steal again.

Watching such a life-changing scene is an incredible gift.

Over the coming days, Abdul looked forward to giving the United States of America opportunity after opportunity to have its own life-changing moments.

16

HACKERS

The view from the fifteenth floor of the office and residential tower could have been one perk of working in Dubai—if anyone cared about the scenery.

No one did. Every man in the room sat focused on an ultra-high-resolution computer monitor, preferring technology to the incredible beauty of real life outside the windows. There was no time to take in the emerald-green waters of the Persian Gulf or the vast wealth surrounding them.

Data filled their screens as the viruses inserted into computers on the island of Puerto Rico spread.

The workspace occupied one half of the fifteenth floor. The other contained their spacious quarters: luxurious private bedrooms, a living room with a pool table and big-screen television, plus a dining area and kitchen stocked daily with delicious homemade meals.

The office was ridiculously large for the eight computer experts. They sat at glass desks grouped in the center of the room.

No cleaning crew visited the office. The men cleaned up after themselves, emptying the trash cans of the endless energy drinks and the incredible variety of Western junk food, from chips to candy bars, which a tall, bearded servant delivered daily to the kitchen.

The men worked twenty hours a day or more, slept when they had to, and never left the floor.

They were too busy preparing for their mission—and they weren't allowed, anyway.

The men had been handpicked for their hacking skills and desire for more: more challenges, more action, more results.

The main advantage of working for the company: Together, they were about to wreak havoc on the United States of America.

There were no politicians to hold them back.

No concerns about going too far.

They had been unleashed, which is what had finally convinced each of them to leave Russia and work for DPC.

The office was quiet, as usual. The air conditioning hummed occasionally, competing only with the sounds of the computers' fans and aluminum cans returned to the glass desks after long sips of caffeine.

Although the desks were close together, the men barely spoke—they used a group chat for all to see.

Rapture: *San Juan Power Plant—we're in.*

Shark: *Yes!*

A few minutes later, the others reported to the group chat.

Atom: *I'm into a power plant in Michigan!*

Haze: *What about the one near the prison? Or the prison itself? It would help.*

Silver: *Nothing yet.*

Nightowl: *Damn!*

Freak: *We need that one.*

The nicknames were based solely on hacking ability and personality. None of them matched the outer appearance of the men, especially not their leader. He looked like a blond ferret with large eyes and a pointy nose and face, but he called himself Wolf. He had personally recruited each of the young men away from their positions in Russia's premier hacking collective unofficially working for and controlled by the military.

The others looked like the late-teens, early-twenties geeks they were: pale from more than a year of not being in the sun, thin arms and legs but chubby around the middle from junk food and lack of exercise, and glasses from sitting at computers for hours on end.

Wolf's desk faced the other seven hackers.

He smiled at the responses on the group chat and typed his own reassurance.

Wolf: *Don't worry. The virus will spread. More will come.*

The prison they worried about had been added to their hit list last night.

Wolf had explained there was no guarantee it could be breached, but his boss had been adamant. The prison had to be hacked.

Wolf monitored the group chat while reading about the prison they had to have access to by tonight, local time.

Cutting power to the facility by shutting down the power plant feeding it would be a start, but backup generators would kick in.

They had to find a way to gain access to the facility's controls.

So far, their usual tricks had failed.

The prison's security system was invulnerable to outside hacking.

They'd tried social engineering by impersonating an IT help desk employee and calling the prison about a made-up computer issue. Wolf's English was flawless, and he had only a slight accent, nearly undetectable.

It had gone nowhere. They would try again in a few hours when the prison's morning shift started.

There has to be something.

Every system had a vulnerability. It merely had to be found and exploited.

Which led him to his in-depth background research.

In the past fourteen hours, he had become an expert on the Maryland facility.

He finished another article about the prison and clicked to page sixty-three of the search results. The next story described the many opportunities for the inmates to learn, grow, and reform themselves while incarcerated, which made him shake his head. Prisons in Russia weren't like this.

Wolf bit his lip as he read. The prison had a large saltwater aquarium in one of the buildings housing prisoners. The inmates could see the fish from their communal space.

When it was first installed, trustees—trusted prisoners who had freer access—tried to maintain it. Fish died, which upset the inmates.

An outside firm was hired to manage the huge tank.

Wolf's fingers flew on the keyboard, quickly finding a link to the company that kept the prison's collection of fish alive. The company provided the service for free as part of a community outreach endeavor.

The security of outside vendors was often much more lax than the systems they were connected to, making them a frequently exploited tool for hackers around the world.

He pushed back his chair and stood. "Listen," he said.

Immediately, he had all the hackers' attention.

"The target is Seabreeze Aquarium Supply in Cumberland. They monitor and care for the prison's fish tank. It has a remote connection to a thermometer and other sensors. Get inside this company."

The hackers nodded their acknowledgment and went to work.

"Once we have access," he said, "we will connect to the sensors in the tank and use them to get inside the prison's main system."

He addressed the hacker nearest him on the right. "Rapture, when they accomplish this," he said to a pimply nineteen-year-old, "you will inspect the system and customize a virus that will do what we want on command. I will work with you."

Wolf smiled. "Time is short, but I know we can do it. If you have questions or problems, ask for help. This is no time for egos, yes?"

The men nodded, not looking up from their computers.

Wolf typed his instructions into the group chat. A few didn't listen well and did much better with written directions.

Sitting back, he bit his lip and hoped they had time to complete this last-minute mission.

If we do this, we will be heroes.

17

THE ENEMY

Axe drove the back roads, searching for the dark SUV with the tangos in it, but it was a big island.

This is hopeless.

His head throbbed. The severe concussion he'd suffered on the oil-drilling platform off the coast of Venezuela months ago had left him susceptible to head trauma.

His knees, already abused from years of active duty, ached from slamming into the streambed.

And every breath he took hurt his ribs from where the bullets had hit the ballistic vest.

While hiking back to the rental car—after realizing there wasn't an additional ambush set up—the adrenaline from the fight had worn off, letting in the pain.

He could function; it just wasn't pleasant.

The only easy day was yesterday.

He'd been in a minor battle. He wasn't bleeding, and nothing was broken. He'd been in worse shape after heavy training days back when he was on the Teams.

The years are catching up to me. I'm definitely getting too old for this.

Staying in shape didn't stop the aging process or the cumulative effects of injuries from fifteen years of nightly punishment, running and gunning, jumping out of hovering helicopters and off roofs, and hiking with heavy gear.

He had to face facts. Although he hated to admit it, even to himself, the tangos in the jungle tonight had been better than him. Straight up. They weren't quite as good as Axe's active-duty Team buddies, but they were close. They were experienced, hardened warriors who knew how to move smoothly and silently, communicate plans and orders without speaking, set up an effective ambush, and plan an operation that would have taken out most people.

It had only been because of his experience and gut instincts that he'd managed to survive and kill his adversary.

If I hadn't been wearing the ballistic vest, or the tango had had a rifle instead of a suppressed pistol, I'd be dead.

Axe blocked out his concerns and discomfort, putting them aside to deal with when there weren't more bad guys to track down.

He spent a fruitless hour driving slowly toward the nearby small town of San Germán, searching for any sign of the tangos' SUV.

Maybe I should just wait by the trailhead for when they come back to pick up their man.

That could be his last-resort plan. Although if he were in their position, there would've been a secondary rally point the dead guy would have gotten to on his own.

Probably by stealing my car once I was dead.

Instead, Axe stopped outside a closed bar on the main street of San Germán. It had a light on inside.

He parked and pounded on the door until a gruff voice inside announced in Spanish that they were closed.

"Homeland Security," Axe called. "I need to use your phone."

The man inside cursed him in Spanish and refused to answer the door.

Axe removed two damp twenties from his wallet and slid them through a tiny gap under the door. "One minute on the phone."

For a second, Axe thought the man was going to refuse—and keep the money. But the door cracked open. A lanky middle-aged guy looked him over, along with the fake Homeland Security identification Axe held up.

Despite Axe's overgrown, shaggy black beard with a few gray streaks creeping in, the badge was enough for the man to let him into the bar. It was dim and stank of spilled beer—fresh and old.

A minute later, as Axe stood at the far end of the bar and held the receiver of the landline phone, Haley answered his call.

"Hey," he said, settling onto a barstool. "I'm fine—calling from a bar. Phone problems."

"Copy," Haley said, sounding relieved. "What happened?"

"Long story—we can debrief in full later. Those guys I was following made me. I'm not sure how yet." He tried to keep the frustration out of his voice but failed. "They set up an ambush, and I almost blundered into it. One EKIA," he finished, hoping the bartender, cleaning beer glasses in the sink and pretending not to listen, didn't understand the acronym for "Enemy Killed In Action."

The bartender's head snapped up, his eyes wide.

Guess he does.

"Dealing with their team leader put me behind, and I lost the tail. They could be anywhere now. And I don't have a clue as to what they're doing here."

The bartender gave up all pretense and just stood behind the bar, watching and listening.

"Hold on," Axe told Haley. He turned to the bartender. "What's the most important thing on the island?" he asked.

Thankfully, the man took the question seriously. He thought for a moment, then answered. "Power. And fresh water."

Axe nodded. "Power and fresh water," he repeated to Haley. "Better wake people up, get them out looking."

He described the SUV, the number of people in the group, and what the dead guy by the creek looked like, which reminded him.

"Oh yeah, and send someone to the trailhead. There's a dead guy on the right bank of the river, about a mile and a half upstream."

While Haley gave directions to her team, Axe pulled more damp money from his wallet. "One hundred dollars to rent your cell phone until morning," he said, holding out the money to the bartender. "And I need a brand-new plastic trash bag."

"This a scam? Or are you really Homeland Security, and there's a dead guy in the jungle?"

"Unfortunately, this is all real."

"Well, hell." He pulled out a cell from the back pocket of his jeans and handed it over. "Keep your money." He retrieved a new trash bag from under the bar and gave that to Axe, too.

Axe put the tango's pistol, magazines, and cell phone in the bag and knotted the top.

The bartender told Axe the phone's passcode and number, which Axe relayed to Haley. "I'm leaving a weapon and a cell phone taken from the dead guy at this bar," he said, passing along the address and details the bartender gave him. "Maybe they can be traced."

"We're on it," Haley said. "Gregory is calling the governor of Puerto Rico. I'll get someone to the bar to pick up the items and start digging or get them to us. The locals will harden the sites supplying power and water and go from there."

"I'll be out looking for the tangos," Axe said. "Call me if you need me."

They hung up. Axe entrusted the plastic bag with the bartender, thanked him, and promised to make sure the cell phone got back to him. Then Axe hurried out to drive the back roads of the island.

He pushed down his mounting concern. He had little hope of finding the men who could now definitely be called the enemy, whether they were actually terrorists or not. They'd figured out he was following them, staged an ambush, and shot him. They were up to something big—something worth killing for.

Over many years, the island had suffered much at the hands of mother nature.

It didn't need terrorists messing with it, too.

He'd keep searching until Haley needed him somewhere else, but he had a bad feeling in the pit of his stomach. Puerto Rico was beautiful, and its people were kind, but that didn't make it a good terrorist target. At most, it had to be a stepping stone to what the tangos were really after.

Something's coming—and I'm in the wrong place to stop it.

18

CONTINGENCIES

Central Analysis Group Headquarters
Conference Room C
Alexandria, Virginia

After Axe's report confirming Haley's hunch, the night flew by. While the others made trip after trip to the coffee pot in the small office kitchen, Haley plowed through her work with a large bottle of diet soda to keep her awake.

With a well-placed call from Gregory to the governor of Puerto Rico explaining the situation, they had more police officers mobilizing to look for the SUV Axe had described, as well as the suspects.

Unfortunately, there were far more officers than there were vehicles.

And it was the middle of the night. People took time to wake up, organize themselves, and get out on patrol.

Maybe we'll get lucky.

Pitahaya Beach
On the south shore of Puerto Rico

The sky lightened, but dawn was still at least an hour away.

Spider, Diablo, and the three soldiers stood on the beach. They'd left the SUV backed into the jungle and hiked yet another mile. Only the success of the night's computer hacks made all the walking Spider had endured remotely bearable.

Lev, the driver of the SUV and second-in-command of the group, waded into the water as a small black dingy motored quietly toward them, steered by their small yacht's captain. "It is time."

Spider and Diablo raised the backpacks containing their precious laptops over their heads and followed the soldiers into the water.

"Shouldn't we wait for him?" Spider asked.

Vlad shook his head. "Yuri is either dead or on the run. Either way, we leave. There are contingencies for him. Come," he said, gesturing at the boat as it coasted to them.

Spider looked at Diablo. They both shrugged and climbed into the boat, careful to keep their backpacks dry.

The captain swung them around to return to the luxury yacht where they'd spent the past week. It had dropped them off in San Juan, where Vlad had procured the car. Now it was here on the south shore of the island, waiting for them.

"Contingencies?" Spider asked. "What about for us—Diablo and me? What if we had needed to escape or hide? Were there contingencies for that?"

The three warriors tried to hold back their chuckles and failed. They laughed as if he'd told them the funniest joke ever.

I don't get it.

He looked at Diablo, whose eyes were wide. But Spider still didn't catch on.

"Their contingency was to kill us and leave us behind," Diablo whispered.

Spider's heart pounded as he realized the truth of Diablo's explanation.

Can I jump overboard and swim for it?

"Don't worry, my friends!" Vlad said, his laughter fading but a smile still on his face. "You were successful, and we are escaping. You will live."

He seemed sincere, but Spider had to wonder.

What if the people behind this operation need to erase their tracks?

PART 2

WEDNESDAY

19

RISK

"Are we happy?" Special Agent Grant Monroe, in charge of the Secret Service advance detail, asked his right-hand man.

"We're... okay," Special Agent Lukes said, all business.

Monroe had worked with Lukes for eight years and trusted him completely.

If he says we're happy, we're solid. But "okay" doesn't cut it.

The two men stood on a rooftop helipad—the main one of the three on the ninety-acre compound making up the resort. It all rested on top of a flat mountain, with views overlooking a desert valley and other mountains as far as the eye could see.

"There are a lot of reasons to be happy," Lukes said. "First, the country is solid. Not anything like a democracy, but the leader is a few years into the gig after the last guy died. He takes care of his people with decent social programs and a good business environment. No real dissent or unrest to speak of."

Lukes gestured to the two-lane road curving up the mountain far below them. "Second, the approach. Inland, there's one road that curves like a damn snake. Easily defended at every turn if need be. Gated access at the bottom and another security gate at the top. No unauthorized visitors that way."

They turned and looked south.

"Then there's the cliff," Lukes said.

The main hotel building where they stood was one hundred yards from the edge of a cliff that dropped hundreds of feet down to the valley far below.

"What about rock climbers?" Monroe felt stupid asking, but it was his job to be thorough and take nothing for granted.

Lukes didn't laugh or roll his eyes. "The rock is loose—horrible for using as hand- and footholds. Plus, the locals have roving patrols: three teams of two along the edge of the cliff, twenty-four hours a day. Night vision goggles and a K-9 for every shift. They rotate off every thirty minutes to stay sharp. No one's getting in that way."

"The mountains?"

Two miles away to the east and west were mountain peaks, lower than the flat mesa where they stood.

"Manned outposts on each with more roving patrols," Lukes answered. "Both are also slightly below the hotel elevation. No sniper shot to the hotel itself."

Monroe nodded. He agreed with the assessment.

"The rest? You have concerns." He had them, too.

Lukes frowned. "Definitely. There's a lot of ground to cover," he said, gesturing to the dusty mountain outside the lush grounds of the hotel. "But they have a fence—very secure itself, plus it's monitored with plenty of security cameras and patrolled with more K-9 units and guards. Anti-aircraft missiles are manned and ready; we secured permission to have our men embedded with the crews during the time the vice president is en route, on-site, and exiting." He shrugged. "It's as secure as the White House or Camp David. Maybe more so.

"But"—Lukes held up his hand to list the drawbacks of the location—"they're not allowing any helicopters. They'll have a full no-fly zone over the entire country aside from the attendees' planes into the local airport. The VP will have to travel by motorcade from there. Not horrible, but less than ideal. Also," he said, holding up a second finger, "we don't control the space. We're relying mostly on the Omani government and military to lock it down." A third finger went up. "All the other leaders and attendees will have their own armed security. That's a lot of weapons in close proximity to the VP."

Lukes held up a fourth finger. "Finally, we'll have a smaller team with the VP than I'd like. A backup team will stay with the caravan to guard the vehicles, and there will be more people in the assigned bungalow—that's where I'll be monitoring the situation. For close protection, the VP will have two of his usual agents near him, but the man will want his space, so they'll be too far away to interfere if someone wants to take a shot."

They'd argued long and hard for the usual large team of personal protection agents with the VP the entire time of the planned three-day summit but had been denied. All dignitaries and leaders were allowed only two men with them. A limited number of others could be stationed in rooms on standby or to be rotated out in shifts, but the usual number of men and women stationed in the immediate vicinity of the vice president wouldn't be allowed.

At least we got the bomb-detection K-9 unit to sweep the area.

"We'll have a doctor, spare blood, and plenty of gear, but…"

The Secret Service could bring pistols only—and so could the rest of the attendees' security details.

Monroe was fine with that. His men and women were better trained—and better shooters—than any terrorists or rogue security personnel.

They'd watch like hawks and protect the VP.

"Emergency exfil?" Monroe asked. He knew all the answers; it was all in the report, and he'd read it twice. But going over it again, out loud, with his second-in-command never hurt. In the past, they'd uncovered holes in their plans by talking through the security arrangement.

"An additional quick reaction force available at the airport thirty minutes away."

"A lot can happen in thirty minutes," Monroe muttered, spinning in a slow circle. He took in the dry, dusty mountain landscape contrasting with the fountains, grass, and lushness of the resort grounds. "The remoteness and difficulty of approach cuts both ways. If enough bad guys get in, it's nearly impossible to get anyone out alive."

"The good news is the place is a fortress, custom-built last year with exactly this type of event in mind. It's already hosted several heads of state from the region. It's the go-to meeting place for wealthy businessmen, politicians, and vacationing dignitaries from around the world. They've had zero attacks or threats."

Lukes flicked his eyes around, making sure they were alone and couldn't be overheard. "Besides, it's Champion," he whispered, referencing the code name for the new vice president, who had been a former college football star. "It's not Grizzly," he joked. "Grizzly" was President Heringten's code name, chosen for the man's ferocious nature.

"Stop it," Monroe said with fake severity. They took the job of keeping every protectee safe very seriously. He appreciated the dark humor but couldn't encourage it—at least while on the job.

Losing the vice president would be horrible. He wouldn't let it happen on his watch, but his old friend was right. The country could lose another VP. The president—especially this president, who garnered the respect of the agents because of his military service—was far more important.

Monroe was satisfied. Lukes was mostly happy. They'd stay on station, familiarizing themselves and the entire team with the fortress oasis resort and ensuring nothing changed in the meantime. The vice president's normal close-protection team had been here the day before and had headed back to the United States to pick up their man. They'd return with him and stick close during the first afternoon and evening, rotating out with Lukes and others for the next two full days of mixers, meetings, and negotiations.

"So a manageable risk?" Monroe asked.

"As manageable as we can make it," Lukes said.

20

PREPARATIONS

Lux View Marina Tower
Floor 15
Dubai, United Arab Emirates

"We're working on it, but we are not ready," Wolf argued. He stood before his boss's desk, making his case. Merely being this close to him made Wolf's heart rate increase and his palms sweat.

The tall, muscular man in Western clothes had black eyes, a long, straight black beard, and a weathered face. He rarely blinked. Wolf had seen him smile only once—an inhuman, terrifying expression that still featured in Wolf's nightmares.

Fourteen months before, when they had met for the first time, he had introduced himself to Wolf as "George."

George could not be his true name. He was from Afghanistan—or maybe Pakistan. Wolf couldn't be certain based on George's skin tone, facial structure, and accented but fluent English. Somewhere in that region, though, certainly.

Wolf had no doubt the man had tortured and killed.

"We need one more day," Wolf explained, standing his ground. He had been given complete control over the electronic hacking side of the operation. His decisions were supposed to be final.

"I understand," George said. Only his lips moved. His stillness was uncanny, as was the mildness in his voice. "This is not my preference or decision. Certain events require the timeline to be adjusted."

"What events?" Wolf asked. Maybe a hacking solution could buy him and his men the time they needed.

"We have received word," George continued, "our target is being moved. He will arrive at the prison this morning—local time." George paused. His eyes seemed to burn into Wolf's. "Can you complete your part of the mission?"

In every life, there are small, defining moments. Wolf knew this was one of his. If he said yes and the hack didn't go as planned, his life would be over—but not until long after he begged for it to end.

No one had hinted at a price for failure in the operation, let alone torture and death. As far as the rest of the hackers knew, this entire organization was funded by a Saudi—or another Middle Easterner—with very deep pockets and a hatred for the United States of America.

That's what Wolf had been told and what he had passed on to the others when he recruited them, offering access to incredible resources—money for themselves, and freedom to finally use their hacks—when he enticed them away from the state-sponsored Russian hacking collective. They journeyed to Dubai and set up shop, planning on a one- to two-year mission.

The hackers knew they'd be wanted criminals if they succeeded.

None of them had considered what would happen if they failed.

Once Wolf had more direct contact with George, he realized how large the stakes were.

The other hackers didn't interact with George. They might see him come and go, but he never spoke to them.

If they had, they might have gotten the same, unshakable feeling Wolf did.

If this fails, we die... slowly.

He wasn't entirely convinced they would live even if the operation succeeded, either.

"It would be better if we had more time. We have a solid lead, but it may not work," Wolf said.

George sat immobile, staring and waiting.

Here goes.

With a sigh, Wolf nodded. "We will have some control."

George's face rearranged itself in a gruesome smile.

Wolf forced himself not to shiver.

George nodded, still smiling. His eyes were the same cold blackness as always. "And the rest?"

"We are ready. But again, more time would be helpful. Every hour gives us more access."

Wolf had a sudden insight.

He and I are in the same situation.

George also reported to someone.

Does that person scare him as much as he scares me?

Wolf shuddered, thinking about what type of man would frighten George.

"Prepare to launch the attacks," George ordered. "I will coordinate with you once I receive final approval."

Wolf nodded, though George's statement hadn't been a question. "We will be ready."

"That would be best," George said, causing Wolf's blood to run cold.

21

THE SECRETARY OF STATE

The Grand Ballroom
The Grand Central Hotel
New York City, New York

United States Secretary of State Hank Elias Wilson hated staying in New York City. He'd much rather fly in from DC early in the morning and go directly to the United Nations via helicopter or motorcade.

Sometimes, though, it didn't work out. The president disliked the idea of tying up traffic and pissing off the voters of the country's largest city.

Plus, the press had to be fed red meat from time to time, which meant the occasional press conference, like the one he'd finished earlier.

"We're ready when you are, Mr. Secretary," Martin, one of the agents of the Diplomatic Security Service—DSS—security detail, said from slightly behind him.

Hank finished jotting some notes on a legal pad, put the pen in his breast pocket, and handed the pad to a nearby aide.

It was time for the short motorcade trip to the United Nations building where he had meetings the rest of the day. He was finally making progress on a number of fronts: Russia's reluctance to lower the price of their oil; Iran's ongoing nuclear ambitions; North Korea's erratic, threatening behavior; and a brewing dangerous trade war with China as they worked at displacing the United States as the world's largest superpower. He even had the damn Taliban at the negotiating table, working them on human rights in general, women's rights in particular, and convincing them how they'd have to govern to be welcome in the world of civilized nations.

All that, and there were the final preparations for his trip with the vice president later in the week for the Middle East Peace Summit.

The press had dubbed Wilson "America's Master Negotiator."

His superpowers were talking and listening.

People knew he played fair and that President Heringten took his advice to heart.

He could sit in a room with people and, more often than not, emerge hours—or days—later with at least an understanding, a kernel of an agreement.

Although nothing could take the place of America's armed forces, peace through negotiating was often a lot cheaper and didn't cost lives.

"Let me just hit the bathroom, then I'm ready," Hank replied. His stomach had felt off since his early morning jog and workout in the upscale hotel's workout room, which had been opened especially for his use and guarded by the same men now surrounding him.

As always, he was escorted to the bathroom. He had to wait outside while Martin cleared the room of threats.

"All clear, sir," the agent said, exiting the men's room.

At least they let me take care of business in peace.

The men's rooms of the world and his bedroom were the only two places he was ever alone these days. Coming from a background as a business executive, he was no stranger to constant meetings and ever-present aides and other staff, but the added security component that came with the job had surprised him.

While he was fourth in the line of succession for the presidency, and his security coverage was nearly as extensive as President Heringten's, he hadn't expected this level of sheer supervision when he'd agreed to take the job.

Hank used the urinal, then stood before the mirror, washing up. His hair had gone full white—not gray—over the past few years. His wife claimed he looked distinguished.

At least I'm not balding.

He grabbed a paper towel from a neat pile on the counter to dry his hands and blinked as his world wobbled.

Weird.

Swaying unsteadily, he placed a hand on the marble bathroom vanity and took a steadying breath. One of the staff had caught a cold late the previous week and had to be ordered to stay home. She'd wanted to come in and work, but no one needed those germs spreading.

Damn—I must have caught it anyway.

He'd either power through or hole up in an office, take some medicine, and minimize his exposure to others until he was in the clear.

No matter what, though, his work had to go on, even if he had to switch to phone or videoconference. He had too many irons in the fire and was too close on several negotiations to take any time off.

Feeling steadier, he wadded the towel and tossed it into the trash, reliving his glory days as a college basketball player.

Swish. I should have gone pro instead of finishing my business degree.

What would life have been like as a professional basketball player?

I wouldn't be negotiating with world leaders and having meetings with the president of the United States, that's for sure.

He got two steps toward the door before he felt himself fading. Instead of collapsing in a heap, he lowered himself to the cold marble floor of the men's room. Before he could call out, he dropped the rest of the way and lost consciousness.

The role of a special agent in the Diplomatic Security Service took a specific type of individual with two competing attributes. Agents had to be patient. There was a lot of standing around. Plus, the protectees were important people. Their schedules ruled. If they needed to stay in a location to extend a meeting or finish making notes, the DSS made it happen—as long as it didn't compromise the life or security of the protectee.

Agents also had to be aggressive, going from understanding, diplomatic people behind the scenes to assertive, take-no-prisoners action in an instant if a threat presented itself.

Martin and the rest of the team of men and women constantly balanced the dual roles.

Standing outside the door to the hotel's main-floor restroom, Martin subtly checked the second hand of his watch and held back a smile.

Must be number two.

The distinguished Secretary Wilson would be mortified to learn his security detail had a working knowledge of his normal bowel movements, including frequency and how long each particular task took.

Mid-morning wasn't the secretary's normal time for a BM, but when you had to go, you had to go.

Or he's hanging out in there, shooting hoops with the towels to unwind or get a few precious seconds to himself.

A month earlier, Martin had made the mistake of quietly poking his head into the men's room and caught the older gentleman attempting a three-point shot with a paper towel, much to both of their embarrassment.

As much as he wanted to avoid a repeat of that moment, protocol was protocol. No location was one hundred percent invulnerable.

Martin rapped his knuckles once on the heavy wooden door and pushed it open. "Mr. Secretary?"

Shit!

The seventy-year-old man lay on his side a few steps from the sink, arm stretched to the door.

"Weigh anchor!" Martin yelled into his radio as he rushed into the bathroom. "The lobby men's room. Weigh anchor!"

The unusual code phrase for the protectee being down would cause an immediate reaction.

The security posture would harden.

Nearby agents would converge on the bathroom door and hold the area, weapons drawn.

By the time Martin had his fingers to Secretary Wilson's neck—thankfully finding a strong pulse—two other agents crashed into the men's room.

"He's alive but unconscious," Martin called.

"Heart attack? Stroke?" one of the other agents asked.

"I can't tell."

The nearest hospital was only three minutes away—without sirens.

As much as Martin wanted to pick the man up, carry him to the secure SUV, and motorcade the few blocks, potentially saving the Secretary some embarrassment if the only problem was the flu, dehydration, or regular old exhaustion, they couldn't risk it.

"Bring up the ambulance and prep for immediate departure," he said into the radio.

"I see the medics. Ten seconds," one of the agents called as he stood holding the door open.

The DSS medics raced in with a gurney and took over, checking the secretary's vital signs as they prepped him for transport.

"Secure the area," Martin said, stepping back and forcing himself to turn away from the medics working on Secretary Wilson. "No one sees this—no press, no hotel employees. Kill the security cameras. We can't keep this a secret, but I don't want video of the man on the nightly news. And inform the White House: Secretary Wilson is alive but unconscious. He wasn't shot or attacked, but we don't know what's wrong with him."

22

BOOM

Haley went through the flight manifests and radar logs from Puerto Rico's airports but found nothing.

The tangos on the island had vanished, pure and simple.

They're still holed up there, or they left on a boat.

The boat seemed likely—the same way they had arrived.

Unfortunately, she didn't have the resources to track every small vessel in the area.

The unknown men had gotten away.

Haley felt the frustration well up. She'd had a hunch and pulled Axe away to check it out.

I should have committed to the mission and put the whole team on it.

The problem was the amount of chatter and threats popping up lately. There was too much to sift through.

There were rumors out of China about their development of new weapons systems.

Credible evidence surfaced of an unlikely truce between rival gangs in large cities across the United States.

Suspected Russian spy ships were reported off the coast of Hawaii, which is what had led to her hunch about the suspicious men and activity in Puerto Rico.

And, as always, there were constant cybersecurity probes and minor breaches of government systems, along with ongoing ransomware and computer viruses aimed at private and public companies.

Haley's inbox overflowed with odd tidbits of alarming rumors and wild theories funneled to her from their various sister organizations on Gregory's direction, dating back months ago.

Most of the threats wouldn't amount to much. It took real skill, money, resources, and guts to attack the United States of America—physically, at least.

It had gotten more difficult lately via computer, too, as the United States learned the hard way about computer attacks and spent more money on cybersecurity.

Effective attacks came mostly from state-sponsored groups, whether they were officially acknowledged as such by China, Iran, North Korea, or Russia, the big four cyber enemies of America.

Haley was overwhelmed—and her direct-action team of Axe, Mad Dog, Johnboy, and Tex was too small to fly around the world investigating every loose end she found.

Nancy and Dave joined her at the conference room table, bringing their laptops. Marcus joined the impromptu meeting a moment later.

"What have you found?" Haley asked her team.

There was a moment of uncomfortable silence before Dave spoke. "Nothing on our end. We just don't see the strategic benefit of the island of Puerto Rico."

Nancy nodded her head, causing some of her flyaway hair to spill onto her face, which she brushed back with her hand. It made Haley brush her own blond hair back behind her ear.

"Nothing against the place," Nancy said. "I'm sure it's lovely. But it's been hit over and over with hurricanes. Just when they get halfway back to normal, it's hurricane season again, with additional destructive storms. There isn't any infrastructure critical to the United States. Protecting the people is obviously essential, but there are easier, more populated soft targets than that island."

"There's a military base, but if our enemies were targeting us, I'd look to the military prison in Guantanamo Bay, Cuba," Marcus said. "There's no indication of any suspicious or suspected activity there, though."

Dave jumped in before Haley could ask a question. "There's a decommissioned nuclear plant in Puerto Rico, but all the fuel—the nuclear material and everything associated with it—was sent to the mainland of the United States. There's no radioactive material to steal."

Her team had been at it all night and done a stellar job, but they were all still missing something. They weren't any closer to figuring out the puzzle.

Haley thought it over for a second. "The men Axe followed—and the one he killed—were there clandestinely for a specific reason. Let's dig deeper. Expand your searches. Get creative. We can't just sit back and wait for something there to go *boom*. That's not how we work."

23

THE VOW

Lux View Marina Tower
Floor 14—Kitchen and Staff Areas
Dubai, United Arab Emirates

Jamil returned to the Tower long past the time he should've been off work.

The ever-present building guards at the main-floor employee entrance had checked his ID and allowed him inside despite the late hour, ignoring him once they determined he was on the approved list for entry.

They weren't repelled by him, unlike Malik's guards and his coworkers earlier in the day.

When they had noticed his wife's hand hanging around his neck, he'd instantly become a pariah. No one wanted to be seen talking or even looking at him.

He had become virtually invisible.

The guards on Malik's penthouse floor looked at the hand and instantly turned away, as if seeing him for any longer than necessary would make his misfortune, thieving ways, and punishment fly off of him and descend on their lives.

The rest of the day, they'd only glanced his way long enough to note the dangling hand before literally turning their backs on him.

Even Malik, as Jamil served him lunch, tea, and dinner, refused to look at or acknowledge him.

Jamil had removed his wife's hand, leaving it in his locker while he emptied the trash on the fifteenth floor, delivered the prepared meals to the refrigerator there, and restocked the energy drinks and snacks for the mysterious young men who lived and worked there.

After work, his planned birthday celebration—dinner at one of the cafés in front of the hotel that served as their apartment building—hadn't been canceled.

Instead, no one showed up.

Jamil had sat alone at the large reserved table, ate dinner by himself, and slunk back to his tiny room before deciding to return to work.

Not that he'd been in a celebratory mood anyway.

His plan to steal small items from Malik and send more money home had backfired spectacularly, and instead of ruining his life, he had destroyed his wife's.

On the fourteenth floor, which consisted of much of the staff area serving Malik's penthouse and the men who lived and worked on the fifteenth floor, Jamil hurried down the corridor to the male employees' locker room.

Even though it wasn't forbidden for him to be at work now, it was unusual. But Jamil couldn't stay away. Not tonight.

Not with all that had happened.

Opening his locker, he delicately took his wife's hand in both of his.

Fighting through tears, he whispered to her, hoping somehow, she would feel his words in her heart across the miles between them.

"I am sorry, my love. I have failed you. Us."

He sobbed quietly for a minute, cradling the hand to his heart.

"I can do nothing now," he continued after looking around to ensure he was alone. "But I promise you. Someday, I will make this right."

Jamil put the hand back on the top shelf of his locker. He stripped off his plain pants and T-shirt, changing into the work uniform hanging neatly in the locker.

Finally, he picked up the hand and placed the twine around his neck, feeling the reassuring presence of his wife's hand thump against his chest.

He closed his locker and walked to the elevator, then used his security keycard to take it to the penthouse floor.

As the doors opened, the guards across the wide hallway—different than the ones from earlier in the day—had their rifles pointed his way.

They both stared at the hand around his neck for a moment before looking away and ignoring him.

He did busy work, wandering the halls and rooms of the massive home.

Anything to keep his wife close to his heart for a while longer before he had to give her hand to the butler for disposal.

As he worked, he planned.

A Pashto proverb reverberated through his mind incessantly.

Revenge is sweeter when served cold.

24

THE MALIK

Lux View Marina Tower
Penthouse—Floor 35
Dubai, United Arab Emirates

George—whose real name was Gogol, which none of the hackers needed to know—forced himself not to stare as the elevator doors opened quietly. The penthouse level's gold trim and Italian marble floors beckoned, but it took a moment to force himself to step from the elevator into the hallway.

A dark-haired household servant in the standard white uniform kept his head down, eyes on the floor as he walked by the opening doors. Gogol didn't register what he looked like. His eyes focused only on the severed hand dangling from the servant's neck on a piece of thick twine.

This had happened once before in his village back in Afghanistan. The man must have been caught stealing, and a loved one had been punished in his place. Given the size and shape of the hand, Gogol guessed it was a wife or grown daughter.

The dangling hand is a lesson to us all. Failure is not an option. Nor is betrayal.

There was an air of supreme discomfort in the hall. The two security guards standing on the opposite side of the wide hallway, fingers near the triggers of their AK rifles, kept their eyes on Gogol, carefully ignoring the servant working late and pushing through a door down the hall.

As he hurried down the hallway in the opposite direction, Gogol wondered at his own ability to dispense justice as his brother did. He could frighten the young hacker, Wolf, but he was unsure he could be as ruthless as his brother.

That is why he is Malik, and I am his helper.

Abdul was only two years older, but by being the eldest son, he was and would always be the special one.

Both Abdul and Gogol had helped their father and the other men of the village fight the Russians when they were very young, carrying ammunition, relaying messages, or serving as unsuspected lookouts and spies.

They had grown up to fight the Americans and then, at times, the Taliban.

Both had killed, but only as warriors attacking other fighters.

Neither had harmed women, children, or noncombatants.

Today, because of Abdul—Malik—that would change.

His brother would do anything to accomplish his goal of punishing America—and Russia—for invading Afghanistan.

Between the two conflicts, millions of Afghan men, women, and children had been displaced, wounded, or killed.

In all wars, civilians are caught in the middle.

But for the invaders, only their soldiers died.

Now, America would finally discover what collateral damage felt like.

Soon after, if all went to plan, Russia would learn as well.

Given what was at stake, was cutting off a woman's hand to teach a lesson overly harsh? And considering what had been done to his country, did killing and wounding women and children matter?

Or do the ends justify the means?

It wasn't his decision. Abdul was the leader. As the second son, Gogol only followed and did as he was ordered.

He cast aside his concerns as he walked the long hallway until reaching the third door on the right. Gogol knocked once and pushed open the door to face four more guards, all alert and ready to defend Malik—the term for a respected elder and leader.

Abdul used the large room, which had once been a bedroom, as a sitting room outside his office, with two plush couches facing each other across a large coffee table and other small seating areas, including a cozy corner with a leather recliner, reading lamp, and small end table stacked with books—nonfiction about warfare and the history of the Middle East.

Gogol walked across the room, his feet silent on the plush carpet, his movements watched the entire time by the guards. Outside, past the small balcony, the dark water of the bay contrasted with the many sparkling lights of the vibrant desert city beneath them.

He opened a heavy wooden door on the far wall and entered a small den, leaving the spectacular nighttime view behind.

Despite being nearly midnight, Abdul sat in a leather executive chair behind a glass tabletop that served as his desk. His frame was as muscular as Gogol's, his face just as ravaged by the sun and the wind. Their beards were similar, but Abdul's was longer, with a few flecks of gray while Gogol's was still black. He wore a beige *thobe* along with a white *ghutra* —the traditional headscarf worn by men in Dubai and the rest of the UAE. A black headband held it in place. He looked not only like the successful businessman he was but also… regal.

Truly, he is Malik—the leader.

Gogol preferred the feel of Western clothing and knew he fit in better with the hackers in pants and button-down dress shirts.

The room contained only the desk, Abdul's chair, and a plain folding chair facing the desk. The plain white walls were bare—if there had been bookshelves in the room, they were gone.

A china tea set with two cups sat on the corner of the desk.

Abdul nodded at Gogol but kept writing with a pen on a piece of paper. Several others, face down in a stack on the desk, had already been filled.

A large silver ring with a stylized depiction of the triangular head of a viper, the most dangerous snake in Afghanistan, adorned his middle finger.

"Tea?" Abdul asked.

Gogol poured them each a cup and sat down in the chair, waiting patiently.

Abdul finished his note, placed the paper face down on the others, took a sip of his tea, and nodded again.

Gogol took that as his cue to report.

"Malik, the team on the island of Puerto Rico was successful," he started. "Their virus is spreading, and the hackers gain more access every minute." He hesitated. "One man did not make the rendezvous and is feared dead."

"Dead or captured?" Abdul asked.

He doesn't care about the man—only the mission.

"He would not have allowed himself to be captured."

"He is Russian, as I ordered?" Abdul asked with an edge in his voice.

"Of course," George said.

"Then it is not a problem either way."

"Agreed. It may be helpful, in fact. I have the team on it to make sure the information is hard to find but accessible eventually."

Abdul continued to sip his tea. "There is more. What has you so pleased?"

"The United States secretary of state was rushed to a hospital in New York."

Abdul sat forward, his lips in a cruel smile. "It worked? Against all odds?"

"It appears so. Of course, we don't know if it was a lethal dose," he said, hedging his bets.

"How was it done?"

"Water bottles in the refrigerator of the hotel's private gym were replaced overnight with tampered ones. He took one and drank. The rest were removed after the Secretary worked out and before he collapsed."

"Well done. Enough money silences everyone's ideals."

"Not everyone, we hope," Gogol said.

Abdul conceded the point. "Yes. Continue."

"The last-minute addition to the mission isn't fully ready. They have asked for more time but plan to have at least something by tonight."

"There is no more time," Abdul said. "Neither of us likes this, but we do what we must. If they are not ready, the mission moves forward. The soldiers will have to handle it all themselves."

"In that case, success isn't guaranteed."

Abdul pondered for a moment before shrugging. "The effort is the mission. Success is preferred. If not..." he said, trailing off.

As long as we put on a good show, no one will be blamed for the failure of a last-minute, ill-advised demand.

"And the rest?" Abdul asked.

Gogol was on more solid ground. "A mix of systems. No single hack has been one hundred percent effective. Two or three years ago, the plan would have been devastating. The world has learned, however, and more systems have decent security. Our attacks will be impactful. Hundreds, maybe a few thousand, will die. It is ready—I recommend today. The longer we wait, the more chance the systems may be patched or our infiltration detected."

Abdul smiled and raised his teacup in a toast. "Do it. It is almost lunchtime in New York City. Perfect—for the pedestrians."

"As you command, Malik," he said with a bow. "It is finally time for our revenge."

Gogol kept his misgivings about targeting civilians hidden, hoping Abdul couldn't read him as well as he had earlier.

He stood from the plain metal folding chair, backed away, and left Abdul sitting at his desk, sipping the tea.

The ends justify the means.

25

CARNAGE

Wolf stood behind his desk facing the rest of the hackers, eyes switching from monitor to monitor.

The desk had been rearranged. Four additional monitors crowded the space. Nightowl, a hacker in his early twenties—the second oldest after Wolf and the unofficial second-in-command—sat at the desk in Wolf's place, taking over his system.

Each monitor had eight boxes—views from security cameras across the United States. A combination of busy intersections in New York City's Time Square, Philadelphia's City Center, and the Loop in Chicago, along with Los Angeles, Houston, Omaha, Phoenix, Denver, and of all places, a small city in the center of the country called Des Moines.

The brief had been specific: No area was to be spared. Smaller cities and those not on the coasts were to be equally impacted.

All of America must feel the pain of the attacks.

For the hackers, that just made it more challenging—and fun.

"Wait…" George said from Wolf's left.

It was the first time George had entered the main hacker room. All the Russian hackers were on their best behavior. No one joked in the group chat. No energy drink cans were tossed in the wastebaskets from a distance. They all sat poised at their computers, studiously avoiding staring at the scary presence in their midst.

It was the middle of the night in Dubai, but none of them cared.

"We don't have to find the perfect time," Wolf whispered into George's ear. He disliked being so close to the man, but the idea of embarrassing him in front of the rest of the group was worse. "The software will do the work for us. That is the beauty of it."

Instead of completely reprogramming the safety features of the assisted driving software of modern cars, the team had found a way to make the cars do the opposite of what they were supposed to do.

By changing the underlying code governing the safety systems, they essentially turned the collision-avoidance safety systems into collision-seeking systems.

Believing the emergency update was a new safety measure, cars and trucks across America would switch from slowing down when near obstacles to speeding up; they would aim at other vehicles, buildings, and pedestrians instead of swerving away from them.

A simple algorithm created and uploaded by the hackers would assist each vehicle's computer in determining which nearby objects to steer—and accelerate—toward.

While the hackers couldn't control individual vehicles, the cars' computers were about to turn each one into an unmanned, multi-ton missile seeking out the closest, most vulnerable target.

Wolf had briefed George extensively on the ins and outs of the brilliant hack, but the dangerous man's forte wasn't computers.

George's eyes never left the screens. He only shook his head and pointed a finger upward.

The rumor, discussed in hushed tones among the hackers, was that the man controlling the entire operation either lived or worked in the skyscraper tower. George's finger appeared to confirm it.

"Ready…" George said, his voice soft.

Wolf thought he caught a touch of… what?

Sadness? Regret?

He had to be imagining it. George was a stone-cold killer.

The main screen showed pedestrians crossing streets and strolling on sidewalks. Across the country, the weather was warm and sunny.

"Almost… Now!" George said.

Nightowl, sitting at Wolf's computer, touched one key.

The single press on the keyboard sent commands over the internet and halfway around the world to a computer in Oregon, two in Detroit, and another in Oklahoma.

Those computers received the command as if it had come through proper channels. To each, it seemed as if a programming manager had entered final approval to execute a new patch—an update—to the driving safety features of their cars.

In the blink of an eye, each system sent out emergency over-the-air software updates the hackers had already stored inside the computers.

Nearly two million new vehicles, electric, hybrid, and gasoline-powered—built within the past eighteen months and equipped with state-of-the-art self-driving and assisted-driving technology—received the software update over 4G and 5G cellular networks.

Many vehicles were parked in garages, in lots, in driveways, or along streets.

They processed the new instructions but didn't move. Security features the hackers hadn't been able to overcome prevented them from starting and shifting into gear.

Some vehicles in motion accepted the emergency instructions but didn't alter their behavior. Their code had extra security overrides preventing updates from executing while moving; their systems had to reset while parked before processing new features.

At Wolf's workstation, Nightowl opened a small window displaying the number of vehicles in motion that had accepted the patched "safety" features.

The green digits updated in real time, increasing as the vehicles reported to their manufacturers' servers, which in turn forwarded the data to the hackers.

13,014

78,833

154,907

584,810

846,998

A silence hung over the hacker room, different than the day-to-day quiet when the men typed into their chat stream. This was the quiet before the storm.

On the screens, life continued in America for several seconds.

Just another day…

Then the carnage began.

26

MAYHEM

Lux View Marina Tower
Floor 15
Dubai, United Arab Emirates

Wolf's team had struggled to hack the traffic control systems and cameras of every large- and medium-sized American city.

All were locked tight, resisting their best efforts.

They were forced to rely on other methods to witness the effects of their hacks: doorbell cameras, security cameras at various shops and commercial buildings, and cameras on freeways and at busy intersections, where television and other news organizations were given access to provide up-to-the-minute traffic reports.

What they saw on their screens thrilled them.

In New York City, spring tourists packed the midday streets in the area of Times Square. They strolled in crosswalks, stood on corners taking selfies, and marveled at the billboards.

New Yorkers ignored them, hurrying back to work after lunch.

Both groups filled the sidewalks up and down Sixth, Seventh, and Eighth Avenues, Broadway, and along Forty-Second Street.

Taxis, trucks, and passenger cars clogged the area.

Newer vehicles with automated and assisted driving features weren't prevalent, though seven had been visible in the hacked security cameras around mid-town Manhattan.

Two showed up on Wolf's screen at the same time.

Both were traveling south on Seventh Avenue in heavy traffic.

One, the second car back at a red light, accelerated. Its powerful electric motors could normally take the vehicle from zero to sixty miles per hour in 3.5 seconds on an open road.

With a bright yellow four-door taxi in front of it, however, the car served more as a battering ram than a missile.

The electric car surged forward, smashing into the rear of the taxi.

Airbags inflated in both cars from the violent impact.

The taxi careened into the crosswalk, hitting six pedestrians.

Their bodies flew into the air, sideways into the intersection.

Three were hit by another taxi driving eastbound on Forty-Second Street.

The electric car continued forward, pushing the first taxi into the second.

Inside the electric car, the updated safety protocol calculated the next "safe" direction: toward the large group of stunned pedestrians on the southeast corner waiting to cross Forty-Second Street.

With the taxi out of its way, the self-driving feature directed the wheels eighteen degrees to the left and accelerated.

It carefully steered around concrete safety barriers designed to protect pedestrians and rammed into the group at forty-seven miles per hour.

Several people were mowed down, turning into living speedbumps as the car continued onto the sidewalk.

Others were hurled into the air, landing on the ground or striking the building on the corner with sickening thuds.

The car impacted a streetlight pole on the left. The computer, detecting hundreds more pedestrians farther down the sidewalk, scraped between the heavy pole on the right and the building on the left.

Some alert pedestrians—New Yorkers and tourists alike—jumped clear of the car barreling toward them.

Others were stunned at the unexpected sight of a car driving on the sidewalk, speeding faster with each passing second. They were mowed down.

A few people died immediately from the high-speed blunt-force trauma of getting pummeled by the car. They were the lucky ones.

Several others were flung down the sidewalk only to be run over by the tires or dragged under the car's body.

At Fortieth Street, the car powered through the picture windows of a restaurant on the corner, where it ran over late-lunch diners, punched through a thick oak bar, and came to rest, wrecked, halfway through the wall leading into the kitchen.

Wolf watched in awe at what they had done.

The other vehicle with assisted driving no longer showed on any of their camera feeds. He could only imagine the destruction.

We did it! Our hacks worked.

Across the many computer monitors, cameras displayed more and more destruction. The same scene played out across the United States, in large cities and small towns. No one was safe.

One window showed the corner of North State Street and West Madison in Chicago. Black smoke filled the intersection, and flames leaped up a building.

"Our car hit another car. It hit two more," Nightowl said as Wolf leaned in to see the small window among the others on the man's screen.

"Something caught on fire," he said, more to himself than Wolf.

In full-color, high-definition video, the scenes looked horrific. As proud as he was at their success, Wolf was glad none of the cameras had sound.

Watching was enough.

27

ALBANY

Albany, New York

Just outside of Albany, Bob sped south on Interstate 87. The speed limit dropped from sixty-five miles per hour to fifty-five there, but people who drove the road regularly knew that once they were past the speed trap where the State Trooper often sat after morning rush hour, they could drive as fast as they wanted.

Besides, everyone sped there. The only reason to slow down was the curve in the road approaching the twin bridges spanning the narrow Mohawk River.

Bob didn't bother to muffle his groan of pain. He'd scored an urgent root canal appointment at a dentist's office in Albany after a week of suffering, downing over-the-counter pain pills, and rubbing his gums with numbing cream.

He took the wide curve in the interstate doing eighty, though it felt like sixty. His new electric car cruised smoothly and silently. The vehicle's assisted-driving technology allowed him to sit with his hands on his legs while the car steered, though he wasn't comfortable enough with the technology yet to trust it completely. He paid attention, ready to take over at a moment's notice if the thing acted up.

An alert popped up on the large display screen with a ding.

Emergency update installed.

He loved the car. New features could be installed over the air whenever necessary.

Traffic was light at this time of day. Rush hour was long past. The only vehicle nearby was a school bus ahead of him in the slow lane, packed with older kids. A sullen teen in the back of the bus looked out the rear window and flipped him off.

Bob laughed despite the pain of his tooth and gave the kid a thumbs-up as he started to pass.

Just like me at that age.

The car jerked right—hard—and slammed into the rear of the bus, just behind its back tires.

What the hell?

Bob grabbed the steering wheel as the teen's face appeared at the side window, eyes wide.

The back of the bus shook.

The car jerked right, crashing into the bus again. Bob's hands twisting the steering wheel had no effect.

He wasn't in control.

The powerful dual electric motors of the car, combined with its momentum, fought with the bus's greater mass.

The car won. Pushing against the rear of the bus caused it to pivot even as the driver must have slammed on the brakes.

Past the point of no return, the school bus tipped onto its right side, the teenager's expression going from shocked to terrified in slow motion as Bob stomped on the brake and twisted the steering wheel one direction and the other, all in a fruitless effort to make the nightmare stop.

Teenagers flew around inside the bus as it spun.

Its momentum carried it at the low barrier at the side of the bridge, where it hit, slowed, then crashed through and slid foot by foot over the edge, toward the dark water below.

Bob sat in shock, his throbbing tooth forgotten, knuckles white on the steering wheel, foot holding down the brake pedal.

Stop. Please, please, stop.

This had to be a dream, right? A nightmare from the pain. He'd wake up in a sweat any second.

Wake up, wake up, wake up!

The car picked up speed, hitting one-hundred-eighty miles per hour as it flew down the interstate, quickly catching up to cars, minivans, and semis heading south through Albany.

28

SIOUX FALLS

Sioux Falls, South Dakota

Lucy dropped her son off at school late—again.

"It's okay, buddy," she said, trying to console the eight-year-old. The kid loved school for some strange reason—she had hated it. "Mommy will call the office. They'll understand. No problem."

He put on a brave, fake smile and nodded. "Bye, Mommy. Will you pick me up?"

"Of course, kiddo. Right on time today."

His face betrayed his disbelief.

"I will!" She had gone for a tone of grown-up assurance. It had come out as a defensive plea for understanding and forgiveness.

I don't care if I have to quit one of my jobs, but from now on, I do better.

She never wanted to see that look on her little man's face again.

"I love you, Mommy," her son said, making her heart melt.

"Love you, too, buddy."

He jumped out, shut the door of the newer car carefully—the elderly neighbor lady had let them borrow it this morning when their old piece of crap wouldn't start again—and ran toward the school's front door.

If she waited, she'd be able to see him enter his classroom, the first room on the left, past the elementary school's main office. But she only watched until he got buzzed in through the outer and inner doors, waved, and put the car into drive a second after a quiet chime came from the dashboard.

The car hesitated for a second.

That's strange. Is it out of gas?

It wouldn't be like the neighbor lady to leave the car on empty. She was more like the kind of person who never let it fall below the halfway mark.

Before Lucy could give it more gas, the car turned right, mounting the school's wide sidewalk as it surged forward.

It mowed down the carefully manicured flower garden the second grade students fussed over.

It deftly adjusted course to avoid the stick of a tree planted by a "graduating" third grade class last year.

While she fought the steering wheel, stomped on the brake, yanked on the gear lever, and called it every curse word she knew, the car crashed into the block wall of her son's classroom.

An airbag deployed.

Her head smacked into it, bounced back, and came forward again to rest against it.

She sagged, stunned by the impact but aware enough to give thanks that whatever had happened, the old school's solid construction had stopped the car from making it through the exterior wall.

She blinked and tried to figure out what was happening as the car's tires spun, the vehicle surged backward, missing the tree again, and took another run at the wall, impacting the same spot as before.

This time, the front end made it through.

Her screams competed with those of the students in the classroom as the car backed up again to repeat the process.

She locked eyes with her son as he stood in the doorway to his classroom, and the car sped forward one last time.

29

SCOTTSDALE

Scottsdale, Arizona

Maddox had been in too many close calls with idiots to take chances on his motorcycle.

He no longer wove through traffic during rush hour like he did when he was younger.

He wouldn't dream of not wearing his helmet and the 360-degree camera mounted on it that recorded every second of every ride. It had been the second best investment for preventing road rage and hassles from people. When drivers noticed the camera, they backed off, gave him the space they would a car, and generally let him be.

Or maybe it was the black full-size 9mm pistol holstered on his belt.

Arizona was an open-carry state. As long as the weapon was in plain sight, there were few restrictions.

Maddox wanted it out in the open. The best deterrent to bad behavior from cars and trucks, on the freeway and city streets, was the pistol. No one who saw it bothered him.

Given the camera and the pistol, then, he was surprised when a new-model white pickup sped up from about a half mile behind him and closed in fast.

He was in the center lane, cruising five miles per hour over the speed limit on his day off, heading out of town for a quiet ride up to Payson—

maybe see if there was any snow left on the mountains. If it got too cold, he'd turn around, stop and grab some lunch, then head home before dark.

The truck raced toward him.

Dude, there are two other lanes. Pick one.

He could sense this was going to be a problem.

He looked right, signaled, and smoothly pulled into the right-hand slow lane.

Damn it, come on. Live and let live.

He didn't understand some people's problems with motorcycles. Sure, some guys—and gals—gave riding a bad rap, racing each other or flying along at unsafe speeds, risking everyone's safety. But drivers of cars did that, too. Assholes were assholes, no matter what their ride.

The Scottsdale Road exit was coming up. Maddox debated getting off there, if only to use the off-ramp to get clear of the white pickup before going through the stoplight and getting back on the freeway.

The truck had moved into the right lane and was nearly on top of him.

Without signaling, Maddox swung right onto the off-ramp.

The truck came after him, not slowing. If anything, it had picked up speed.

Maddox gunned it, the bike's powerful engine rocketing him forward right as the pickup tried to ram him.

What the actual—

The pickup matched his acceleration, closed, and clipped his tire.

Maddox flew, the bike flipping behind him.

The landing hurt as his leg snapped.

His leather riding pants and jacket saved his skin as he slid on the rough concrete of the off-ramp, coming to a stop at the edge of the road against a concrete barrier.

The truck skidded to a stop at the bottom of the off-ramp.

Oh, man, I got this all on camera. You are so going to pay, dude.

Maddox lay his head back, grateful to be alive, and took stock.

Aside from the pain in his leg, bent at an odd angle, he was bruised and battered but alive.

That's a frickin' miracle. Good, clean living.

The truck's engine screamed as it reversed up the off-ramp—directly at him.

Maddox pulled himself toward the concrete barrier at the side of the road, planning to dive over it to safety, but the pain from his leg made him realize he'd never make it before blacking out.

There was no other choice. He pulled the pistol, took aim, and started firing.

His first shots only hit the truck.

Halfway through the mag, he got lucky. The driver slumped forward.

Maddox hated the idea of taking the driver's life.

But better him than me. Self-defense. The guy deserved it.

As Maddox lowered the pistol, both relieved and horrified by what had happened, the truck kept coming. It didn't slow or swerve off-course.

Maddox aimed at the tires and only stopped when the magazine emptied and the back wheels of the truck ran him over.

30

STAGE TWO

Lux View Marina Tower
Floor 15
Dubai, United Arab Emirates

Wolf watched with wide eyes as crashed cars and trucks in cities across the country filled the screens.

One window showed a highway outside Atlanta, Georgia. An eighteen-wheeler dangled half off a bridge. A crumpled minivan and two cars sat wrecked nearby.

In suburban Los Angeles, eight electric cars pulled away from their charging stations and drove straight into stores at the nearby high-end strip mall.

As people fled the stores, other cars coming into the parking lot accelerated right at them, running them down before aiming at other stores and vehicles.

Near Phoenix, two cars sped through railroad safety arms and rammed a passing freight train. A tanker car exploded, whiting out the view from the security camera they had hacked.

Wolf was jolted back to the room by the strong hand of George on his shoulder.

"Now," George said. His eyes seemed heavy and filled with regret.

I must be imagining things. He should be excited by the destruction.

"Stage Two," George said, his voice firm and cold.

Wolf cleared his throat and nodded. "Launch Stage Two," he said to the room.

At the main workstation in front of them, Nightowl typed a command into the computer. The other hackers did the same with their pet projects.

As simply as that, they unleashed more hell on the United States of America.

31

THE LOBBY

Central Analysis Group Headquarters
Conference Room C
Alexandria, Virginia

For a second, Haley thought the crashing noises came from her dream.

A moment later, she was on her feet, pistol in hand.

She'd been sound asleep, head down on the desk of her cubicle in the bullpen—the warren of cubicles used by the men and women of the Central Analysis Group.

As the fluorescent overhead lights flicked off and the dim emergency lights kicked on, she sprinted toward the door to the workspace. Adrenaline flowed through her body as her mind struggled to figure out what could have caused the noise.

Are we under attack?

Her coworkers popped up from their cubicles like meerkats, heads turned toward the heavy, locked door that led to the lobby of the building with its security contingent.

Wayne is out there on duty today.

Her favorite security guard—who didn't give her crap about her pistol and the smaller backup one on her ankle—was a retired Marine who was still tough as nails.

As long as he's alive, he won't let anything through.

A small security video monitor showed the destruction in the lobby. Two cars—she recognized one as a swing shift analyst's fancy new luxury sedan—were wedged against the far wall. Dust or smoke filled the space.

I should call—

Gregory appeared at a dead run from the hallway leading to his office.

"Two cars in the lobby," she called to him, noting the pistol in his hand, pointed at the floor.

When did he start carrying that?

"I don't hear any gunfire," she added.

She picked up the phone, praying Wayne would answer. Through the haze in the lobby, she couldn't make out the security desk with the men who guarded the building.

Please don't let them be dead.

"No answer," she said as Gregory stopped next to her, barely out of breath.

He surveyed the scene himself.

"Accident or attack?" he asked.

Haley shook her head and shrugged. Her gut didn't give her an indication either way.

Gregory turned to the analysts. "Prep your systems," he yelled, his normally quiet voice filled with power. "Protocol D-1. D-1," he repeated. "When you're finished…" He paused, looking again at the scene of the lobby on the monitor. "Prepare for immediate evacuation from door number 3."

Protocol D-1 entailed initializing special software on each analyst's laptop.

If anyone attempted to log in to the computer and didn't input the proper system password the first time, the software would instantly wipe all data from the hard drive.

Door number 3 was in the back, down the hall, past Gregory's office. It opened onto the secure parking lot with a secondary guard post.

Every analyst followed their training and reacted immediately, bending to their computers and initializing the security procedure software.

"Somebody grab Haley's laptop," Gregory yelled. "Marcus! Get over here."

Another analyst from the back waved that he had Haley's computer as Marcus sprinted toward them, his bowtie and dapper outfit looking out of place with him running at full speed. He had his laptop in hand, still open as it booted up the D-1 protocol software.

"Your backup piece," Gregory said to Haley, his hand out.

Haley looked from him to Marcus, eyebrows raised.

"He's a crack shot. Right, Marcus?"

Marcus looked embarrassed but nodded. "I enjoy my time at the range," he said. Checking his laptop screen, Marcus closed the lid and tucked it under his arm.

"No, give that to someone to carry," Gregory said, gesturing to the nearest analyst, who took Marcus's computer and slid it into a book bag along with her own.

Haley bent and reached under her khaki pantleg, pulled the smaller 9mm pistol from its holster on her ankle, and handed it to Marcus. He expertly checked it, confirmed a round was loaded and ready to fire, and held it safely at his side.

"What's the plan?" Haley asked.

"I trust Wayne and his crew," Gregory said. "If they're alive, they'll handle themselves and any intruders. We're going to escort all the analysts, support staff, and the IT team away from the building via door 3. We go across the parking lot and take cover in the next building."

Their building sat on a large plot of land with a bigger parking lot than they needed. A six-foot chain-link fence topped with barbed wire surrounded the land.

Other buildings, housing private companies that required tight security, including high-tech businesses, investment firms, and several medical research businesses, shared the ninety-acre office complex.

He paused and looked at Haley.

He's asking if it's a decent plan.

"What about the back fence?" she asked.

There was only one way onto their grounds—through a guard gate at the front entrance to the parking lot.

Given the destruction in the lobby, anyone guarding the gate has to be dead.

She shook off her concerns for the men and women in the security detail, who she greeted every day as she came to work.

"Up and over. Where there's a will, there's a way."

Haley raised her eyebrows but nodded. "We can throw jackets over the top," she said. "Assuming we're not being shot at," she added under her breath.

"You're likely the best shot," Gregory told her. "You'll lead. Marcus, you're on the right of the group. I'm on the left. Assuming there's a guard still alive back there, he'll help out. Questions?"

Haley and Marcus shook their heads.

"Let's get people to safety," Gregory said, before turning to explain the plan to the rest of the group.

32

THE HACKS

Lux View Marina Tower
Floor 15
Dubai, United Arab Emirates

Atom, a twenty-year-old hacker from a suburb of Moscow, clicked on his mouse repeatedly, commanding wastewater treatment plants across America to go haywire.

Smaller municipalities around the country often didn't have the budget, know-how, or manpower to keep their cybersecurity measures up to date.

Thanks to a virus sent by the hackers who had visited Puerto Rico's wastewater treatment facility, he had access to several dozen plants on mainland America—along with the one outside San Juan.

One by one, he shut down the processing of wastewater—and the computer systems that controlled the plants.

The on-site computers locked out the staff operators and gave no indication that anything had happened.

To anyone in a control room, all systems were green.

Atom giggled, thinking of what would happen soon.

Depending on the volume of waste and the size of the plant, at some point in the next few hours, the facilities would reach maximum capacity.

With the systems not functional, the waste would eventually back up into peoples' homes and businesses.

Things were about to get disgustingly messy in several dozen small towns across America, and there was nothing anyone could do about it.

Rapture, sitting to Atom's right, had a more immediately impactful hack ready to release.

With several clicks of his mouse, the fire and smoke detection systems in thousands of office buildings across the country suddenly went crazy.

Like the hack of the self- and assisted-driving vehicles, it flipped the response to the opposite of what it should be.

If no fire or smoke was detected, the fire alarms tripped.

Blaring sirens came on. Strobe lights flashed.

Tens of thousands of small sprinkler heads erupted in the ceilings of board rooms, corner offices, and floors filled with cubicles, spraying water over every inch. They drenched papers, computers, and people as they fled in panic.

In some buildings that had vehicles crash into them, fires started—but the fire control systems failed to activate. The fires burned, spread, and killed.

Shark, to Atom's left and the closest to the window with its stunning view even this late at night—which he didn't care about—typed and clicked on his computer.

He had seen an American movie as a child in which a young man his age played with a train set. He'd been envious and had vowed to one day have one of his own.

That day was today.

In train rail yards across America, switches flicked, directing trains onto incorrect tracks.

The men and women in control rooms for five of the country's major train companies would see nothing amiss—until trains started crashing into each other.

In the next row back, behind Shark, it took Haze less than thirty seconds to bring America's oil and gas infrastructure to its knees.

Over the past year, he had patiently hacked into oil and natural gas terminals in Louisiana and Texas.

Now, with a few commands, Haze shut down their critical operational processes.

As soon as the commands hit the computers of the various companies at the ports, no products could be loaded or unloaded from ships or trucks. Pumps stopped working, and the computers controlling the systems crashed.

America's gas and oil exports were finished. Wherever the energy products were at that moment, they'd stay until the system could be debugged and brought back online. Which wouldn't happen—ever.

With another click, Haze locked the entire system down. Only he could reverse the process.

He wasn't finished. He logged into another computer system and entered a short command.

Seconds later, over six thousand miles of pipeline, supplying more than sixty percent of the fuel supplies east of the Mississippi River, stopped flowing.

Within a day, gas stations up and down the east coast would run out of gas—and there would be no more coming.

Panic buying, hoarding, price gouging, and fuel shortages would soon follow.

There would be chaos.

He rubbed his hands together with joy at a job well done. Finally, he could hit Americans where it hurt—in their ability to travel freely.

Let them see what it is like to struggle, fear, and go without.

33

THE FIRE

Central Analysis Group Headquarters
Alexandria, Virginia

As Haley led the group of analysts, support staff, and IT crew down the long hallway, Gregory popped into his office. Seconds later, he returned wearing a small backpack.

He has a go bag? Smart man.

Her already high opinion of him went up several more notches.

"Ready?" he asked.

"I want you and me to switch places. I'll cover the left flank—closest to the parking lot and front entrance. You lead everyone to safety."

Gregory frowned as they continued down the hall to the rear door. "I know that look. What do you have planned?"

"I'm going to get to my SUV. I have an arsenal in there. And if anyone's having trouble with the fence, I can drive over and ram it."

"Copy. Just—be safe, okay?"

Haley nodded. "You know me."

Gregory gave an exasperated sigh as they reached the back door. "Yes, that's why I said it."

The video monitor on the wall next to the door showed the backdoor guard standing in his small, bulletproof hut—basically a double-size phone booth with a stool, a phone, and a small security camera monitor. He held an M4 at the low ready.

Beyond the security station, nothing moved in the empty back parking lot.

Gregory pressed the comm button. Onscreen, the man answered his phone immediately.

"Door 3," the guard said.

"It's Addison. Have you heard anything from the lobby?"

"No, they're off comms. The lobby is full of smoke or dust, and there are two cars inside. No movement. But the front gate is fine. Are we under attack?"

"That's what we wondered," Gregory said. "No gunfire, so maybe it's just an accident?"

"The guards at the gate reported they let the two swing shift vehicles in—properly ID'd. One guard is on his way across the parking lot to the building to check out the lobby."

Gregory looked at Haley. "What do you think?"

"No gunfire or follow-on attack makes me lean toward an accident. Unless…" She had a horrible thought. "If the cars are packed with explosives that haven't gone off for whatever reason…"

Gregory nodded and pressed the talk button on the intercom. "We're preparing to exfil the entire staff, just in case. I'll take point. You cover our rear."

"Copy. Come on out." The man exited his tiny shack and moved forward, weapon up and ready to fire.

"Everybody ready?" Gregory called back.

The long hallway was crammed with analysts with laptop bags, along with support staff and the small IT department members. There was nodding and a feeling that getting hell out of the building had to be a good idea.

"Let's go," Gregory said.

Haley exited, her pistol up and ready, and moved away from the back entrance, covering the group as the rest of the staff sprinted across the back parking lot.

The spring sun felt warm and welcoming on her face.

At least the attack isn't during a blizzard or rainstorm.

With the last of the people exiting the building, and no gunshots, helicopters attacking, or explosions, Haley whistled, gave Gregory a wave when he looked over, and took off for her SUV sitting on the front side of the building.

She didn't make it.

One look at the destruction of the building's lobby made her veer in that direction.

I've got my pistol—that's good enough for now.

The weapon wouldn't work well if she had to engage an enemy at a distance, but a few minutes after the first crash from the front of the building, it didn't look like a follow-on attack was coming.

It has to be car bombs—or an accident.

The light gray smoke she'd seen on the security monitor had turned dark, almost black.

Fire.

One of the front-gate guards was on his walkie-talkie as she ran up.

"We're thinking car bomb," she said as she reached him.

"Us too."

"Has anyone come out? Any word from Wayne?"

"No, and no."

Haley holstered her pistol. "I'm going in."

"Miss Albright," the guard started, then stopped. He'd seen the look on her face. "Be careful," he said instead of trying to talk her out of going in, which is what she figured he'd been about to do. "I'm handling getting ambulances and fire rescue here, then I'll be right behind you."

She nodded and ran to the building, plunging through the car-sized opening in the front of the lobby and into the smoke.

Flames licked at the back wall.

Two vehicles—a newer black truck, and the red sedan her coworker had picked up the week before—were smashed against the rear of the building where they'd come to rest.

She went to the security station first, but it was empty.

The smoke got thicker as she moved further inside. The heat was intense.

"Wayne! Wayne! Friendly coming in!" she yelled at the top of her lungs.

The sprinkler systems hadn't come on.

This whole place is going to burn.

34

CATASTROPHE

Outside of Pittsburgh, Pennsylvania

John was still young—only sixty-five. He'd been working on trains for his whole career.

With only three months to go before retirement, he was grateful for each day but ready to leave. It was time to fulfill promises he and his wife had made to each other to travel the world and enjoy the retirement they'd waited so long for.

He had a bit of a tummy—who didn't, at his age? His wife had one, too. They'd walk off the weight on the cobblestone streets of all the European cities they were going to visit. Sixteen days, four countries; they had the tickets booked, the hotels picked out.

The trip of a lifetime, his wife had been telling all their friends.

His eyes were drawn to the tracks ahead.

That's strange.

The tracks curved, running parallel to another set. An optical illusion made it look like another train was on his tracks, not the ones next to his like it should be.

No!

He acted on instinct, hitting the emergency brake valve, knowing it was much too late.

As the distance rapidly closed, he locked eyes with the conductor of the other train. The horror on the man's face was a mirror of his own.

I shouldn't have waited until retirement to take that trip.

"I'm sorry, Marsha," he whispered, filled with regret.

Ten excruciating seconds later—both far too much time and not nearly enough—he pointlessly braced himself for the impact and closed his eyes.

He pictured his wife's face and whispered her name one last time as the two trains collided.

35

CRIES

Omaha, Nebraska

Life had gotten easier as the twins grew. Now eight, they could play together without supervision for a while. All Cindy had to do was listen. If they were quiet, she had to wonder what they were up to. But as long as they incessantly were telling each other, "Okay, but watch this!" she could get a few things done around the house.

Of course, when they had the flu, it was twice as hard. They spiraled downward, each one trying to out-awful-ize the other and show her he was the sickest, that he felt worse.

Could only one of them ever get the flu at a time? No.

Today they were upstairs in their room, home sick, reading in their beds. They were probably faking being too ill to go to school, but as long as they weren't obvious about it, she'd let them stay home now and then.

Cindy snuck up the stairs to check on them. If they were really under the weather, they'd be asleep after the tomato soup and grilled cheese lunch she'd made.

If they were awake, playing games or doing anything other than reading, she'd make them get up and help her fold laundry.

As she slowly opened their bedroom door, the smart speaker in the nearby bathroom erupted at full volume.

It took her a second to make sense of the sounds coming from it.

Her eyes widened at the moans of pleasure.

"Mommy, what's that?" one twin said, yelling to be heard.

No, no, no!

Her other son giggled and whispered to his brother—or tried to. "It's like…" She thankfully couldn't hear the rest as she dashed into the bathroom and ripped the power cord from the wall.

They can't know what those sounds are yet, can they? They're only eight!

The speaker went quiet, but the one in the kitchen, directly below the twins' bedroom, remained on.

So did the one in the bedroom she shared with her husband.

The noises rang through the house.

She ran to the bedroom as she heard her husband's voice calling her name over and over.

Diving across the bed, she yanked the device from the nightstand, silencing the damn thing.

From the kitchen, directly under the twins' room, came the sound of her voice calling his name, both of them in the throes of passion from one night a few weeks earlier when the twins had been at their grandparents' house for a sleepover, allowing Mommy and Daddy a rare and much-needed date night.

"No!" She ran back to the hallway and rushed down the stairs toward the kitchen as the sounds continued, their cries of pleasure blaring.

Three doors down, Mrs. Clarno stared at her smart speaker with wide eyes. A moment before she had been enjoying a symphony.

Now, somehow, she was listening to the nice couple with the twins have sex.

"Computer, volume down," she yelled, but the machine did nothing. She tried again, but the sounds continued to play at full volume.

Pressing the little button on the top didn't turn it down, either, which was a shame. She wouldn't mind listening, but not this loudly.

She chuckled as she left the kitchen and went into the living room. The wall blocked enough of the sound that it no longer hurt her ears, but she could still hear just fine.

For a moment, she wondered if she heard the sounds coming from other homes on the street, but she shrugged it off. That would be impossible.

"Good for you two," she said. "Hope you don't get another set of twins, though."

The sounds changed. Mrs. Clarno realized she was no longer listening to the young couple.

"That's Mrs. Vigliati," she muttered. The man had called her by her first name with a smile in his voice.

Mrs. Clarno settled into her rocking chair facing the window so she could watch people coming and going in the neighborhood.

"But that is not Mr. Vigliati," she said. She saw Mr. Vigliati some mornings at dawn when she walked around the block and he drove his fancy car to work, where he spent all his time. They exchanged waves.

While she'd never heard Mr. Vigliati in bed, she was positive it wasn't him making those noises with Mrs. Vigliati—at least, not according to Mrs. Vigliati. This man's name was Kevin. Her husband's name was Alan.

Staring out the window, Mrs. Clarno rocked and listened as the show continued, trying to put faces with the sounds coming from her speaker as the voices changed again.

36

THE STAIRS

Downtown Salt Lake City, Utah

When the fire alarm went off with its piercing sound and flashing lights, Laura's coworkers on the twenty-fifth floor stood from their desks, looking around at each other to figure out what they should do.

Her thoughts immediately turned to 9/11 and those poor people who couldn't get out of the towers.

Salt Lake City was a world away from lower Manhattan, but she wasn't going to be a victim.

The sprinkler system kicked on seconds later, showering every inch of the floor and ruining all the computers.

I'm out of here.

Laura called to her closest friends and waved them to the emergency stairs.

By the time she made it to the fifth floor, she was spent.

But no one was caring for the poor older man rubbing his left arm and slowing down everyone behind him on the stairs.

"He's having a heart attack! Get help!" she cried.

People rushing down the stairs flowed around them as she helped him collapse into the corner of the landing.

Laura held his hand, waiting for the fire department that never came.

When the light went out of his eyes, she felt for a pulse, knowing he was gone.

She picked herself up off the cold cement floor, said a quick prayer, and continued down.

At least he wasn't alone when he went.

37

SPRING BREAK

South Beach, Miami, Florida

South Beach wasn't yet officially in the midst of the massive Spring Break throngs it would see in a few weeks, but there were plenty of other college kids to hang out with on the beach during the day, dance and drink with all night, and hit on every moment in between.

Mike played the odds. Offer enough young ladies a smile, turn on the charm, buy the most likely prospects drink after drink, and sooner or later he'd land one.

Or two, or three.

So far, he'd struck out. All he had to show for it was a wicked sunburn, a hangover that wouldn't quit, and a credit card bill he would be paying off for a year.

But it was only Day Two. Plenty of time.

He woke up—or maybe he had passed out—under a rented beach umbrella he'd splurged for to keep from making his beet-red skin worse and in the hopes that a few of the pale midwestern ladies nearby would join him under it.

They hadn't, insisting on renting their own a few down from his.

Mike's beer-soaked brain told him there was a brand-new car resting where the ladies and their beach umbrella had been.

I must be drunker than I thought.

It took several seconds, a lot of blinking, and a few sips from the lukewarm can of beer next to him to realize the people dancing and screaming, having a great time, were actually frantically trying to get the attention of some of the many police who constantly patrolled the area.

Others he had thought were working on a sand sculpture he now realized were trying to dig underneath the car, which was really there, near the ocean, hundreds of yards from the street.

He staggered to his feet, drained the can for courage, and ran to help.

38

THE OIL

Missouri River, North Dakota

The oil kept coming.

With the valve closed, there was nowhere for it to go.

The weakness in the pipeline would have never been a problem except for the abnormal pressure.

The pipeline burst, allowing the oil to flow unrestricted into the Missouri River.

Hundreds of miles away, an engineer sat at his workstation, trying to get back into the system.

It wasn't just him. The others that worked nearby—hell, in the whole damn place—were locked out as well.

Everyone was worried. If there were problems, they wouldn't be able to stop the flow of oil or manage the situation.

It could be worse, though.

He still had access to the display panel, and all his systems showed green.

39

THE BUS

The rides in the autonomous minibuses had been a novelty the first few times. It looked weird, having an empty driver's seat and steering wheel that moved on its own, all behind a locked plexiglass barrier. But the results spoke for themselves. The system had been running for months and had a perfect safety record.

Since the small buses served the downtown area, Jessica had started taking them to run the errands demanded by her bosses at the firm.

As an intern finishing college, she didn't have a lot of disposable cash. While the firm reimbursed her for expenses, it took thirty days after the end of the month to get the money—an eternity when she had to stretch her limited dollars.

The autonomous minibuses were a trial program and—at the grand price of free—fit perfectly into her budget. She could hop on, go a mile, and hop off to get whatever done the firm needed.

A quick jog across the street to the return bus got her back to the office quickly—and people had noticed. Important people.

The other interns took the time to walk and enjoy the spring weather when they had an errand. It was a chance to take an unsupervised break.

Her manager had asked her to stay a few minutes late this afternoon. Jessica had to get back to her off-campus apartment to study but had agreed. The full-time job offer she'd coveted after graduation was coming today. She just knew it.

When the driverless bus sped up, she welcomed it. Anything to get back quicker and continue to impress the bosses.

When it swerved into a group of pedestrians waiting to cross the road, she screamed.

When it smashed into a busy fast-food sandwich shop and came to a sudden halt amid flying lettuce, tomato, bacon, pickles, and cheese, she flew out of her seat and crashed against the front windshield, no longer worried about getting back to the office... or anything else.

40

GOING ROGUE

Through the smoke in the lobby, a figure staggered toward Haley.

"Wayne!" She raced ahead, stopping as she got to him. He was carrying the obviously lifeless body of one of his security team over his shoulder.

"I'm fine," he coughed. "They're gone—the cars hit them. Jared is ahead about fifteen feet—on the other side of the truck. Gotta get him out. Can't let him burn up."

"You're wounded," she said, eyeing the man's dangling left arm. White bone stuck out of his forearm.

He followed her gaze and scowled. "I'll be fine. Check on the drivers. I just came to and haven't gotten to them yet. And get Jared."

"Got it. Go. Hurry—this place is going up."

He resumed his way to the parking lot, staggering under the weight of his colleague, while Haley ran forward. Jared, a young guard with a crewcut, lay in a heap to the left of the truck.

Definitely dead.

She went to the door of the truck.

The living before the dead.

More of the back wall had caught fire. Flames leaped in the air.

"Duane," she yelled, recognizing the swing shift analyst. He lay bleeding against the driver's side window, but he didn't look dead.

Haley drew her razor-sharp knife from the horizontal sheath at the small of her back, hidden under a fleece jacket, and carefully opened the door of the truck several inches.

Duane groaned, an agonizing sound, but at least he was alive.

She used the knife to cut the seat belt instead of fighting the tension on it. After returning the knife to its sheath, Haley opened the door the rest of the way.

Duane tumbled out of the truck, onto her shoulder, in an imperfect but manageable firefighter's carry.

Haley staggered before getting her feet securely under her.

At least he's skinny and light.

The hours of working out in the office gym paid off as she marched back the way she'd come.

She passed Wayne, who was going back in.

"I didn't get to the car or Jared," she called.

"I'll get them." Wayne looked horrible, but like every Marine she'd ever met, she knew he wouldn't stop until he was dead—if then.

The front-gate guard helped her lower Duane to the ground.

When she started to run back inside, despite the smoke being thicker than before, the guard ran with her.

"You don't have to—" she started.

"Yes, I do," he said. There's still Mr. Jeffries in the electric car, right?"

"I didn't see him," she said as they ran, "but he must be there."

More walls—and the high ceiling of the lobby—were on fire.

The heat was nearly unbearable.

Smoke filled Haley's lungs with every breath.

I will never quit.

She and the guard made their way toward the red car. In the smoke, something moved on the ground.

Wayne!

The older Marine sat on his rear, using his legs to push himself back toward the front door, then heaved with his good arm, pulling the body of Jared a few feet before repeating the move.

"Help him get Jared out of here!" she said to the guard.

She fought her way through the smoke, crouched over to avoid the worst of it.

Closer to the ground, she smelled the gas leaking from the truck.

That's not good.

When she eventually reached the car, she looked in horror at the face of Jim Jeffries, an analyst she knew only well enough to say hi to when their paths occasionally crossed. He was in his early sixties, close to retirement age.

The red electric car he'd saved for, and had only owned a few days, was wrecked.

His bloody face looked at her through the driver's side window, barely visible through the lobby's thick smoke. His eyes were wide with panic.

He yelled something that she couldn't make out over the noise of the fire that seemed to surround her. The meaning, however, was clear. He was trapped.

They locked eyes as Haley reached into her pocket.

"Lean away," she yelled at the top of her lungs.

When she first started working with Axe, after he had rescued her from the kidnappers who were going to torture and kill her, she'd rolled her eyes at some of his suggestions. When he'd given her the exceptional fixed-blade knife to carry at the small of her back, she'd gone along with it because he meant well and the gift touched her, though the idea of wearing a knife like that every day, even at the office, seemed excessive to say the least.

The next gift, that same night, had been a high-quality folding knife for her pocket.

"Come on," she'd said, thinking he was joking. "Two knives. Isn't that a bit... paranoid?"

He'd repeated one of his favorite SEAL slogans: "Two is one, and one is none."

"Besides," he'd said with a shrug, "have you ever tried to break a car window? The butt of the other knife might get it done, but the folding knife has a special tool for it."

She'd almost made a joke, but her first time in the field had been filled with mayhem, death, and destruction. Axe lived in the space where danger lurked, waiting for the unaware and unprepared.

She yanked the knife out of her pocket, swung hard, and slammed the small, sharp butt end against the glass.

It shattered, allowing smoke to pour inside.

Jim already had the seat belt undone, so she got him to quickly crawl out of the broken window, helping as much as she could.

Together, they ran out of the lobby.

Hacking and coughing, they stood far from the building with Wayne, the bodies of his front lobby team, and the gate guard.

Sirens in the distance announced the fire department's impending arrival.

They're too late. What took them so long?

The police and fire should have been at the front gates within a few minutes of the accident—or whatever it was. The Central Analysis Group was completely undercover; only high-up security officials in the United States government knew they had an office building, let alone where.

The CAG wouldn't get special treatment from the police or fire departments, but still. The response time was much slower than expected.

This doesn't add up.

Inside the lobby, the gas tank of the truck finally erupted, blowing debris high into the air and out into the parking lot.

Jim Jeffries stood bent over next to her.

"What happened?" Haley managed to get out between coughs.

"I don't know. A malfunction, maybe? I was about to park in my normal space when the car took over and wouldn't let me turn. For a second..."

"What?"

"It paused, like it was trying to figure out where to go. Then it aimed at the lobby of the building, right in front of me about a hundred yards away. I went from zero to max speed in a few seconds, full out. I had my foot on the brake, but nothing happened. I ran straight into... Oh, no, no, no!"

Jim let out an anguished cry and threw up on the asphalt of the parking lot.

He must have run over one of the guards.

She put a hand on his shoulder and squeezed lightly, letting him know he wasn't alone.

"I saw the truck," Wayne said, sitting near her on the ground, his voice rough from all the smoke he'd inhaled. "Same thing. He was in the next row over from Mr. Jeffries and about to pull into a spot. The truck slowed, stopped, then came straight at the building."

Two analysts going rogue? Not very likely.

"Two vehicles—one gas, one electric—manufactured by different companies, and they both go off the rails at the same time?" she mumbled, thinking out loud.

"Sounds like damn Chinese hackers to me," Wayne said. The bone sticking out of his arm looked gruesome—and painful. "Or maybe Iranian. North Korean? Somebody."

"Yes," she said slowly. "That's exactly what it could be."

41

PEOC

It had been a frustrating day so far, as many of them were for President James Heringten.

A frustrating four and a half years, really.

Things were a lot simpler when I was a SEAL.

Daily workouts in the basement weight room not only helped the sixty-one-year-old president stay fit—they also reduced his stress and let him deal with the daily ups, downs, and bullshit of the job.

The weightlifting hadn't prevented his dark hair from going gray little by little. At this rate, he realized, he'd have a full head of white before he left office.

He still radiated power, though. The workouts helped with that. He saw it in the eyes of his staff, the advisors, and the leaders he met with—foreign and domestic.

That alone was worth the sweat and pain of the gym.

He had won reelection for a second term, but the country was deeply divided. It took a great deal of time, negotiation, and political capital to get even the most sensible measures through both houses of Congress.

Everyone needed their ego stroked or wanted to fabricate a fight they would later claim to have won so their constituents back home viewed them favorably.

No matter who they were or where they were from, the next election was always right around the corner.

This brought James to a meeting in the Oval Office with his senior economic advisors on the twin couches before him and standing around behind them. Their aides stood and sat along the back wall of the historic room, taking notes at least a few would find a way to leak to the press, his enemies... or both.

Which ones aren't loyal? he wondered. *Who's just in it for the book deal when I leave office?*

He tuned back in as one of the economists—a man who wasn't at all as brilliant as he thought himself to be—finally summed up his policy proposal.

"And that is why, Mr. President, I recommend—"

Two of the doors into the room—from the left side, leading to his Chief of Staff's office, and the one to the main hallway, where his secretaries sat—burst open without even a polite knock. The aging economic advisor was so startled, the legal pad with his carefully prepared notes flew into the air, pages fluttering.

Secret Service agents flooded the room, many with pistols drawn but pointed at the floor.

"Everyone stay where you are," the first agent through the door called as they rushed in.

His voice was commanding; the president himself didn't budge from his chair until the man continued. "Mr. President, we need you to come with us immediately."

Two agents stopped on either side of the chair and lifted the president to his feet. For a moment, James thought through the items in his morning briefing, hours before. There had been nothing about a security drill.

The truth hit him in the gut as he stepped away from the chair, each of his arms locked in a tight grasp by the agents next to him.

This is not a drill.

"PEOC?" he asked, pronouncing the acronym as "pee-ock." It stood for the Presidential Emergency Operations Center, a room under the White House. It looked like a nicely appointed executive office, a smaller—and safer—version of the White House Situation Room.

It was actually a bunker designed to keep him safe in the event of an emergency facing the country or the world.

Men and women swarmed around him, forming a human shield. The wall of agents moved him toward the door.

One of the lines from the SEAL ethos, his—and many other men's—north star, came to mind.

"I lead by example in all situations."

"Stay calm, people," James called over his shoulder as he was rushed from the room. "Do what the agents say, and I'll see you on the other side."

The stunned and scared faces of the economists, other advisors, and their assistants were the last thing he saw before he was through the doorway.

This is going to be a highlight of the books they write, assuming we all live through whatever's happening.

In the hallway, more agents ranged ahead, some with pistols, others with M4s. Instead of being pointed at the floor, every weapon pointed downrange, ready to shoot.

It was pointless to ask the agents around him for details. They wouldn't know. Their role wasn't to advise him or help him understand the crisis. They focused on protecting the leader of the free world and getting him to safety.

The irony was not lost on him that, had it not been for a few crucial choices, his life might have gone a different way. Instead of being the protectee, he might be one of the men with a weapon out, rushing down the hallway in the White House, willing to sacrifice his life to save the president's.

42

REPORTS

James Heringten stepped through the door into the PEOC, leaving the mass of Secret Service agents behind.

Inside the cramped room, a few of his national security team were already present. They leaped to their feet.

James waved them back into their chairs. "What's happening?"

"We're under attack, Mr. President," the director for the National Counterterrorism Center (NCTC)—Samuels—said.

"How? And by whom?"

That the NCTC director had answered likely meant it was a non-nation-state, but James's thoughts turned first to the country's enemies.

Is it the Chinese? The Russians? Or have the North Koreans finally done something so stupid we have to blow them to hell?

"Reports are coming in, sir," the FBI director said. "We're trying to make sense of it. All of the damage is in the United States. Nothing military has been harmed. Preliminary reports make it look like we've been hit by a massive cyberattack, but we're not sure. There may be…" He trailed off as an aide handed him a piece of paper.

"A cyberattack? Aimed at what?"

They wouldn't have rushed me down here for a mere cyberattack.

The FBI director's face had gone paler than his normal pasty white. He opened his mouth to speak, stopped, and licked his lips before getting the words out. "Sir, if this is correct, there are several issues. First, it seems like many—maybe all—newer vehicles with any sort of assisted-driving capabilities, from full self-driving to assisted lane-changing, have been compromised. Sir... they've been turned into guided weapons. Think directed car bombs and suicide attacks on a massive scale."

James tried to parse the information. "How many vehicles are we talking about?"

"Unknown, Mr. President. Hundreds of thousands. Some—perhaps many—are safely parked in garages and parking lots. The ones on the road, however, are..." He glanced down at the note as if he couldn't believe what was on it. "Sir, instead of avoiding hazards like pedestrians and other vehicles, they seem to be actively targeting them. They're mowing people down, Mr. President. Others are ramming buildings."

At the end of the table, Samuels hung up the phone from the call he'd taken while the FBI director spoke. "Mr. President, we're also getting reports of train collisions and derailments."

"They're blowing up our trains and tracks?"

I swear I'm going to destroy the infrastructure of whatever country is behind this.

"It may be more cyberattacks, Mr. President. They seem to have done something to our switching, monitoring, and control systems."

"What about the air traffic control system?" James asked, quickly making the leap. At this time of day, there would be a few thousand planes in the air over the United States.

That's thousands of innocent people.

"No reports about airplanes yet, sir."

James thought quickly. "Put a hold on takeoffs as well as all non-emergency landings immediately. If our comms are compromised or they've otherwise hacked our systems—like radar or whatever—we don't want anyone trying to take off or land. Get everyone into holding patterns, and execute emergency procedures to keep them safe up there. Let's keep planes from crashing."

Aides jumped to relay his commands.

"And if you're sure about the self-driving vehicles, get that out to the press. Ask people to stay home, off the roads, and to not drive anywhere unless it's an emergency." He thought it through for a second before continuing. "We'll hold off on martial law or mandatory stay-at-home orders for now. People will pay attention and do the right thing."

I hope.

"What else?" James demanded.

An aide had turned on the large monitor at the end of the room. Squares showed the director of the CIA and the two men James most needed to hear from if this was actually a cyberattack: the Department of Homeland Security director and the director of the United States Cybersecurity and Infrastructure Security Agency (CISA).

"Mr. President," the Homeland Security head started, "I apologize for the delay in joining you. This is definitely a concerted attack on our infrastructure." He nodded at the screen. "Take it away, Larry."

Larry Cooney, the CISA director, was a man of about fifty with a round face and thinning hair.

"We're working on gathering more information for you, Mr. President. As you've heard, vehicles are crashing and apparently driving themselves. Trains have been routed onto the wrong tracks. The signaling system isn't working correctly; trains are crashing into each other and derailing. We're also getting reports of malfunctioning fire alarm systems and other nuisance items that may or may not be related. We'll have more for you shortly."

"What about the power grid? Nuclear plants? Military bases? I want everything on high alert, right now."

"Yes, Mr. President," Larry Cooney said. "We've already sent out the word. The alert level of every sensitive facility around the country was raised in less than three minutes."

Excellent. The effort we've put into training has paid off.

"I want to know who is behind this—and suggestions on how to defend ourselves better now… and retaliate later," James said, adding the last under his breath.

He could make all the demands he wanted, but he understood the reality facing him. If this was truly a cyberattack, the hackers were exceptional. Nation-state–quality.

Which meant they would also be adept at hiding their involvement.

China, Russia, Iran, or North Korea.

It had to be one of them—in that order of likelihood.

All had reason to be upset at the United States of America.

None dared risk open war, hence the attack on America's infrastructure.

They'd better have covered their tracks damn well.

If they hadn't, America's cybersecurity people would find them.

And James would make them pay.

43

ALPHA X-RAY ECHO

North of Richmond, Virginia

Axe circled at forty-one thousand feet in the private jet Haley had arranged to take him from Puerto Rico to the DC area.

Beneath him, the country burned. He saw two trains that had collided head-on and derailed. Smoke came from several of the freight cars.

Crashed vehicles jammed the highways. Several of them burned, too.

The destruction was horrific.

From the plumes of smoke, it looked like a war zone.

What's taking so long to land?

They had been flying in a circle over Virginia for thirty minutes. He had to get down there and figure out how he could help.

He unclicked his seat belt and left the creamy leather seat of the small but fast executive jet, likely on loan from the CIA, which had called in a favor from an executive flight company. No one let on the flight was anything more than a normal charter flying a VIP at a moment's notice.

His ribs hurt, though his knees and head were fine.

Axe hadn't communicated with the pilot or copilot aside from their initial welcome as he stepped onto the plane. That changed as he stooped and poked his head through the open door into the tight cockpit area.

"Hey, guys, what's going on down there?" he asked.

"No idea, sir. Please return to your seat, if you wouldn't mind," the copilot said.

Axe ignored him. "How long until we can land?"

"We're in a holding pattern. The air traffic control system is on high alert due to some... activity... on the ground. No one is landing—or even moving out of the general area they're in now. Everything's on hold, sir."

"Cut the 'sir' bullshit and tell me what's going on," Axe said. "We're all grown-ups here and know the score."

No need to pretend this isn't a plane hired by the CIA or that I'm a fancy executive businessman instead of an operator.

The pilot and copilot exchanged quick glances, and the copilot spoke again. "Right. Looks like the US got hit by somebody. Sounds like some kind of cyber thing, but that's not my specialty. Lots of destruction on the ground—trains and cars at least. The worry is that there's something wrong with the air traffic control system that will go belly up as soon as they try to bring us in for a landing."

"So we hold," the pilot said, finally speaking. "No one wants to topple the next domino and have planes dropping out of the sky."

Axe shook his head, his lips tight.

If I had caught up to the rest of the tangos last night, I might have stopped this.

He stuffed the feeling away.

His next thought was of Haley.

If she hasn't already figured out who's behind the attacks, she's going to need me.

"Listen, guys, you've got to get me on the ground. Long story, but I'm a small part of this situation, and I can help fix it."

Once more, the pilot and copilot exchanged glances.

I bet this is more than anyone usually talks to them—and no spy or operator admits to being anything other than a CEO.

"I get it, but it's not happening, sorry," the pilot said. He sounded sincere. "Besides, no offense, but one guy's not going to make a difference here." He tilted his head out the side window at the many pillars of smoke far below.

If you only knew.

Axe had one card to play—a gift from Admiral Nalen at the end of their first mission during which all flights had been grounded. A "just in case," last-ditch, top-secret method of cutting through red tape.

"Listen carefully," Axe said, speaking slowly, ice in his voice. "You're going to call the tower and tell them you have an X-Ray Delta Bravo Foxtrot Niner and request permission to land."

"What kind of bullshit is that?" the pilot asked.

"Yeah, buddy, we're not doing that," the copilot said, backing him up. "Please, go sit down. We'll get you there as soon as—"

Axe put one strong hand on the pilot's shoulder, the other on the copilot's, and squeezed. Hard.

That'll get my point across.

"Make the call."

The pilot hesitated a second until Axe increased the pressure.

"Fine," he mumbled, rolling his shoulder. Axe eased up.

"Um, ATC, this is Alpha Delta 424. We have an…"

"X-Ray Delta Bravo Foxtrot Nine," Axe said, leaning close to hear through the pilot's headset.

"Alpha Delta 424, this is ATC." The air traffic controller came back before the pilot could continue. "Please observe radio silence at this time. We have no further details. Maintain pattern and hold unless you're declaring an emergency."

"We're going to be so screwed after this," the pilot muttered. He keyed the radio. "Copy, ATC, this is Alpha Delta 424. We have an X-Ray Delta Bravo Foxtrot Niner," the pilot said, sounding ready to get chewed out again. "Request permission to land, over."

There was nothing from the radio.

The silence stretched on without any acknowledgment from the tower.

The pilot turned to glare at Axe. "Hope you're happy. Now that I've made an ass of myself with the tower, why don't you get back to your seat and—"

The radio interrupted him. "Alpha Delta 424, this is ATC. Authenticate, over."

"Tell him Alpha X-Ray Echo," Axe said.

The pilot repeated the words.

"Alpha Delta 424, turn right to heading two-seven-zero. Emergency landing approved, runway zero-two R."

"ATC, this is Alpha Delta 424. Copy. Turning to two-seven-zero for immediate landing on runway zero-two R."

The plane banked hard and angled down.

"I'll go strap in," Axe said, patting the pilot on the shoulder. "Get me on the ground—fast."

"What just happened?" the pilot called over his shoulder.

The plane leveled out before nosing down more steeply, descending fast.

"It pays to have friends in high places," Axe said as he fastened his seat belt.

44

FAVORS

After a quick check of the news playing in the VIP lounge of the airport, Axe pulled out his phone—fully dried out and working once again.

Haley answered on the first ring. "I'm okay," she said, but her voice sounded hoarse. "We don't know what happened yet. I'll probably need you but don't have any leads."

"Copy. I'm south of you—an hour out by car, but…"

"Yeah. The roads are mostly shut down up here. Hang tight. We're working on getting back up and running."

Back up and running?

He wanted to ask, but she was already gone.

As he thought through the situation, he landed on a potential solution. He hated to call in the favor, but his gut told him that whatever Haley needed, if it was on the east coast, staying off the roads would be imperative.

He made the call.

"Tucci Helicopter Service," the gruff voice answered with a distinctive New Jersey accent.

"Hey, brother," Axe said with a grin.

"No. Hell no! Absolutely not. Not again."

"It's Axe," he said, just to mess with the retired Army pilot.

"I know who the hell it is. That's why the answer is no."

"Come on. It ended up okay last time, didn't it?"

After Tucci had rescued Axe and choppered him to a hospital, saving his life and that of billionaire Kelton Kellison, an extremely grateful Kelton had given Tucci plenty of work—until Kelton had lost most of his money and control of his company not long afterward.

"You know how hard it was to get your blood out of my bird's carpet?" Tucci asked.

"I thought Kelton replaced the carpet for you."

"Well, yeah, but still," the pilot grumbled. "Then his money ran out."

"I hear you, but I need you to come get me. I'm in Virginia. How long until you can get here?"

"In case you didn't hear, they might issue a no-fly order. We've gotten hit again. So I gotta ask—are you insane? Check that. I know you're insane. Do you think I'm insane?"

Axe said nothing, waiting out the man's tirade.

"Still there, 'brother'?" Tucci asked, mocking Axe's use of the word.

"I am. And I don't hear helicopter rotors turning on your end."

Tucci offered a long, melodramatic sigh. "You're gonna get my ass landed in jail—or killed. You know that, right?"

"What, you want to live forever?"

"Now that you mention it, yeah, that wouldn't be so bad."

"Just come get me. It'll be fun, I promise."

"Fun," Tucci said, barking out a laugh.

Axe kept quiet. He could picture the pilot shaking his head in resignation.

"Fine," Tucci said with another sigh. "Where the hell are you?"

Axe told him.

"It'll take some time," Tucci said.

"Just get here as fast as you can."

"Where are we going, anyway?" Tucci asked.

"I'll know by the time you get here. And Tucci?"

"Yeah?" he said, wary.

"Bring your shotgun."

45

INTEL

The Presidential Emergency Operations Center
The White House
Washington, DC

James sat ramrod straight in his chair at the head of the long conference table. Advisors filled the seats, speaking on phones, working their laptops, gathering intelligence for him.

Others joined in via videoconference. Their faces filled squares on the large TV monitor on the wall.

For the moment, however, he learned about the extensive destruction of America like any other citizen—via live TV reports.

At his nod, an aide switched the screen away from the block of advisors, most on mute while they spoke on phones or with people in the background.

A national cable news channel replaced them. The network feed showed a scene of several bodies lying covered on a sidewalk in Manhattan before switching to a car inside a fast-food restaurant in Oklahoma. Firefighters were at work trying to extinguish the flames from the nearly destroyed building. In the background, medics hurried to load a stretcher into an ambulance.

An aide muted the television as NCTC Director Diego Samuels

cleared his throat. "Mr. President, we have some fresh intel for you," he said. His face was drawn.

An aide clicked on her laptop. The news show switched off, replaced by a live feed James recognized as coming from a drone.

Dozens of train cars lay on their sides, lining both sides of the train tracks for what might've been over a mile.

Smoke filled the air, and flames consumed several of the freight cars.

"Mr. President," Samuels said, standing at his place on the right side of the table. "This is outside of Pittsburgh, Pennsylvania. Two trains ended up on the same tracks and collided head-on. Preliminary intel reports one was routed onto the track of the other via a switch that we believe was controlled by hackers. Additionally, the monitoring station never saw an indication of a change."

On the screen, a train car blew up, spewing thick black smoke into the air.

"What were those trains carrying?" James asked.

"That's one of the problems, sir. Both had highly flammable—and toxic —industrial chemicals. The governor of Pennsylvania has declared a state of emergency and ordered people in a five-mile radius to shelter in place."

"What can we do?" James said, fighting to keep his voice even and presidential.

"I'm… I don't think there's anything we can do, Mr. President."

James lowered his gaze to the table to give himself a moment to focus. "Fine. Pass along a message to the governor—to anyone managing the aftermath of local attacks—that we're here and ready to offer whatever assistance they need."

"Sir," another advisor said. "Some good news. Our military doesn't seem to be affected. Also, our nuclear power plants haven't been attacked. Police, fire, hospitals, and ambulances seem fine, as does the media," he said with a nod to the television. "Traffic control, air traffic control— basically everything that we prioritized hardening after the EMP and hacking attempts by Stephan Conroy—is solid."

"That's excellent news," James said, "but let's not harp on that. It would be cold comfort to those who have lost their lives today."

"Yes, Mr. President. Of course, sir," the man said, returning to his seat.

If we'd only spent more money on cybersecurity.

Who could have predicted that so many systems were this vulnerable —and that one of America's enemies would dare to hit them so hard?

The Homeland Security director spoke up via videoconference, his face appearing onscreen. "Mr. President, we're getting reports about local water supplies in towns and smaller cities. There is no tap water—no water at all getting to homes or businesses."

"How is that possible?" James asked, then waved his hand. "No, let me guess. The release of water is controlled electronically?"

"Exactly, Mr. President. We're receiving notifications that these smaller locales have lost all control over their electronic switching."

"Manual options?"

"Limited in some, sir. Nonexistent in others."

The two men shared a long look.

We're well and truly screwed if millions of people across the United States suddenly have no running water.

"Sir," the director continued, looking at a note handed to him by his aide. "More news from many of those same localities. It appears that..." He paused, swallowed hard, then continued. "Whoever tampered with the freshwater supplies also hacked the wastewater control systems. No waste is being received at the plants." He read more of the note. "It won't be long before a lot of people are going to find their systems backing up into their homes—and into the streets in places."

"I understand," the president said. "Is there anything we can do about it from here?"

"No, Mr. President. They won't be able to do much until they—or we —figure out what's happened and a way to fix it."

Larry Cooney, the director of CISA, spoke. His thinning hair was a mess from where he'd been running his hands through it, almost literally pulling his hair out. "We're all over it, sir, but so far haven't made progress."

James resisted the temptation to tell him to work harder or faster. The men and women under his command were surely doing all they could. Getting chewed out by the president of the United States of America wouldn't motivate them more than seeing the hundreds of essential systems around the country that were hacked.

"Stay on it. I know you and your people are doing their absolute best," he said instead.

He tamped down his anger and feeling of impotence.

There's only so much I can do.

People assumed the president had tremendous power—which was true.

But until a culprit was identified, the leader of the free world had to sit, watch, and wait like anyone else.

"Reports from around the world?" James asked. "Has anyone else been attacked?"

The CIA director, an older woman with dark skin who looked like a sweet grandmother but had one of the sharpest minds in the room, spoke up from the end of the table, where until now, she had remained quiet. "No, Mr. President. It's only us, as far as we know."

"I understand. Thank you."

James addressed the group, making eye contact with each of his senior advisors, whether they were still on the phones or not. "Put our military on high alert in case it's a first strike. Lock down our embassies around the world. Continue gathering intel. We help where we can. Next, we need to focus on the big picture: who, why, and how. Is the attack finished or ongoing? A prelude to something bigger? You know the drill. Do your jobs. Stay focused. Don't panic. We'll get through this."

46

COFFEE

"Gregory says we carpool somewhere and get back up and running," Haley said to Marcus, Nancy, and Dave as they stood at the edge of the large group of analysts in the back corner of the CAG parking lot. "No new vehicles, though," she added.

Based on what had happened in their lobby and what they were seeing on news reports on their cell phones, any car built within the last two years seemed to be at risk of malfunctioning—or had been hacked, which was the consensus among the five of them, though that hadn't hit the news yet.

Axe had helped her disable all safety features on her newer SUV. She didn't like the idea of a vehicle "assisting" her, especially after taking a weekend tactical driving course.

The rest of the buildings in their large office park had fared better than the CAG building but weren't entirely spared. One of the CAG analysts had climbed the fence and ventured forth, making contact with people from two nearby buildings as they milled around outside. The fire alarms and sprinkler systems on every floor had come on, forcing them to exit—and destroying thousands of dollars of computers and office equipment.

There were no fires that anyone saw.

Wayne—the chief of security—and the two injured analysts whose vehicles drove into the building had been taken away by ambulance, along with the bodies of the dead lobby security guards.

Firefighters continued to spray water on the building, but all but one truck had left for other emergencies.

The remains of the office smoldered. The fire had spread quickly, and the place was a total loss. It would have to be razed to the ground.

The group of analysts, support personnel and remaining guards, plus the IT group, walked to their cars. Those with newer models carpooled with people who had older cars. Everyone pulled out and formed a long line that snaked through the parking lot.

The convoy comprising what remained of the Central Analysis Group crept its way from their former headquarters to drive on streets filled with crashed newer-model vehicles.

They traveled eight miles, gradually leaving civilization farther behind, and turned into the deserted parking lot of a local diner surrounded by empty fields that would someday surely be housing developments, more office complexes, and strip malls.

The Nighttime-Daytime Diner
Suburban Arlington, Virginia

"It's a national security issue," Gregory explained.

The restaurant was a typical suburban diner—not a quaint, old-style, long and narrow chrome affair but a square building with lots of windows, a long counter across the back wall, a narrow area for the counter serving staff, and a back kitchen running behind a wall with a large opening to pass food through.

It had vinyl floors, lots of chipped Formica booths lining the windows, two- and four-top tables in the middle, and large round booths in the back next to the door to the kitchen. It smelled of french fries, strong coffee, and pie.

The coffee shop owner, a short, stocky man with black hair and a white chef's coat, shook his head with an apologetic half smile.

"Sorry. I have to get home and check on my wife and grandkids. We take care of them after school. With all that's happening.... You understand. Besides, I already sent all my staff home to look after their loved ones. You'll have to go somewhere else." He stepped to the glass front door and held it open for Gregory.

So much for patriotism.

Gregory slung his go bag around and reached in the large outer pocket, coming out with a banded pack of hundreds—ten thousand dollars in total.

"Your country needs you," Gregory said and handed the pack to the man.

The owner's eyes got wide. He glanced from the money to Gregory and back.

"Okay," the man choked out.

"I'll have a form for you to sign in a minute," Gregory said. "It says you can't talk about a single thing that happens here. You understand?"

"Yes, no problem," the owner said. "I'll sign whatever you need me to. And I'll make some coffee," he said, stuffing the money into his back pocket, heading into the diner and behind the counter.

I'll have one of the team run a background check, but the odds of the owner of a suburban diner being an asset for a foreign country are pretty slim.

Gregory gestured for everyone to get out of their cars and come in.

We're back in business.

A few minutes later, the IT team upgraded the security for the internet router.

The analysts grabbed tables and counter space and opened their laptops.

One filled mugs with old coffee—the owner didn't have a fresh pot ready yet.

Gregory locked the front door and made sure the "Sorry, We're Closed" sign showed.

He cleared his throat. The intelligence analysts turned to look at him.

"We want leads on who did this to our country," Gregory said. "Our sister agencies will be doing the same thing. They'll use the methods they are best at. We'll use ours: big picture. Where were the flaws—and are they still there? How did this happen? Most importantly, what's next? I want concrete recommendations. I'm going to report to the president soon, and I'd like to give him something he can use. Get on it."

People dived into their laptops while he went to the far corner, near the kitchen, where Nancy, Dave, Haley, and Marcus had commandeered one of the large round booths. They filled the red vinyl bench seat, so he pulled up a chair and joined them.

"I have faith that we'll get to the bottom of this eventually," he started, his voice a low murmur so the others at nearby tables had less chance of overhearing.

Haley was already frantically typing and clicking on her laptop, but he had to hope she was at least partially listening to him. He looked at Nancy and Marcus. "You two—use..." He paused, hating to phrase it like this. "Use Haley's method. Dive deep. Find me a lead."

Marcus nodded and turned immediately to his laptop. Nancy's lips twitched into a grin at his discomfort at telling them to use Haley's unorthodox method of following their gut instincts to gather and analyze the intelligence before she nodded and got to work.

"What about me?" Dave asked.

"Start with the big four: North Korea, China, Iran, and Russia. Give me a probability for which one is the most likely culprit."

"On it," he said and started typing. Dave was great at the big picture, and this type of analysis was right up his alley. He'd been working on a report about Russia he wouldn't say much about. Maybe that would help.

"Haley?" Gregory said, trying to get her attention.

Her gaze didn't flicker from her screen, and she gave no indication she'd heard him.

She's in her own little world already.

"Haley?"

Still nothing. Either she was so deep in the zone that she truly wasn't listening, or her insubordination had reached new heights.

I can't give her the satisfaction of asking again.

"Keep at whatever you're on," he said, knowing the others at the table would see through the directive and understand it for what it was—a way for him to save face in front of them.

47

FIRST STRIKE

The Nighttime-Daytime Diner
Suburban Arlington, Virginia

Haley didn't have her dual large-screen monitors or the noise-canceling headphones, but she dropped immediately into the zone as soon as she sat in the booth at the rear of the diner.

She was vaguely aware of Gregory joining them but didn't pay attention to what he was saying.

Instead, her fingers flew across the keyboard, opening databases. She speed-read the latest reports on the destruction hitting the country.

Where did it start?

No matter how careful people were, they left a trail. Whether it was electronic or physical, there would be a way to find who had attacked America.

The cars seemed the logical place to begin, but she paused as a feeling in the pit of her stomach sent her a signal.

Everyone will look at that. What else happened?

Were the cars going crazy, running over pedestrians, slamming into other vehicles, and ramming buildings actually the first attack?

Haley set a news search in one window and a search of one of the overall intelligence databases in another.

There—that's it.

Her eyes were drawn to one item that appeared on both lists from earlier in the day.

Secretary of State Wilson Rushed to New York Hospital

The headline grabbed her, but the article didn't have much.

The classified intel database had more details, though they still remained sketchy. The older man had held a news conference, gone to the restroom, and collapsed.

At his age, it could be a heart attack from stress or overwork.

The secretary of state had nearly the level of protection as the president of the United States. Harming him wouldn't be easy... but people were clever. A determined foe might be able to reach him with patience, great resources, and luck.

Haley felt the sense of being on the right track.

Somehow, somebody did something to him.

"Who's looking at the nation-states?" she asked, her mind coming back to the diner and the other people at the table.

Gregory nodded at Dave while the senior analyst raised his hand and looked up. "I am," Dave said.

"The first strike wasn't the cars going crazy," she told him. "They hit the secretary of state this morning. We figure that out, we'll be that much closer to who's behind this. Find out what's wrong with Secretary Wilson. Then cross-reference the usual nation-state suspects with who had the most to gain from taking Secretary Wilson off the table," she ordered.

I'm not in charge. I shouldn't order people around.

She glanced at Gregory. "Is that okay with you?" she asked, trying to sound deferential.

Gregory gave her a small, amused smile and nodded.

He sees me trying, at least.

She dived back in, looking at the car attack from the opposite end.

Who couldn't have done this? Who wouldn't dare?

48

THE VOID

The Nighttime-Daytime Diner
Suburban Arlington, Virginia

Haley chugged the tall glass of soda someone had placed on the table. Her eyes focused on the room and her coworkers in the booth as her mind left the river of data she had been swimming in and returned to the real world.

The diner hummed around her, the place packed with analysts. Without their usual cubicles, there were more conversations, more sharing of ideas—and more noise.

She hadn't been aware of any of it.

At her table, she focused on the well-dressed man near her.

"Marcus," she said. Although he was several years older than her, she still thought of him as a kid.

His eyes were locked on his screen, lost in the zone.

"Marcus!" she said, louder.

He looked up, startled.

"Sorry," Haley said. "I need to know everything about Dawson Reite."

Marcus blinked several times as he came out of the zone. "The hacker?" he asked.

"Yes, the hacker. 'Eternal Void' or whatever he goes by."

"'EV' or 'Void' for short. He's in prison."

"I know he's in prison," she said, trying to be patient. "I read your analysis."

One of Marcus's main duties at the Central Analysis Group was writing in-depth analyses about prominent people in the world, from political figures to businesspeople. Anyone who might be of interest in the world as a potential asset, threat, or target based on their influence, abilities, financial situation, ambition, or a number of other reasons got a write-up. Some were one or two paragraphs. Others went on for several pages.

She'd just finished reading Marcus's short report on Dawson "Eternal Void" Reite—and she needed more.

"What isn't in the report?" she asked. "Rumors, innuendo, guesses." She forced her face into a smile, trying to be pleasant while hiding her impatience.

Come on, come on! We've been through this before—you know how it works.

Marcus composed himself quickly and started spitting out facts. "Smart guy, early twenties. Brilliant, really, but in the computer realm only. Doesn't have a lot of common sense. He acts impulsively, and it has gotten him into trouble."

Yeah, I know how that feels.

"He just received a prison sentence for seven years. He's been in custody for the past year for his trial—he was deemed a flight risk."

Marcus checked his computer, switching windows and accessing a report. "He arrived this morning at a medium-security facility in Maryland about two and a half hours from here to begin his sentence," Marcus continued. "Let's see… rumors. No one knows who his parents are. The story goes that his first big hacks were to erase himself from the world's computers. He has an American passport, birth certificate, and social security number that are completely legit, but the rumor is he's actually European and came to the US as a kid."

"Go on," Haley said. So far, she liked what she heard. "Does he have internet access inside the facility?"

"No way. It's a Federal Correctional Institution—a federal prison— and he just got there this morning. Even before today, he wouldn't have had internet access. Certainly not the kind needed to pull off something like this," Marcus said, gesturing at the world around them. "And for the past year, he's been in tighter lockdown—nearly solitary confinement. He hasn't been near a phone or computer."

"Someone could smuggle in a cell phone," Haley argued. "A tablet or small laptop with cellular connectivity."

Marcus shook his head. "Not likely."

"One of the main targets for the attack was electric vehicles from four of the five top car manufacturers," Haley said. She didn't want to let it go. "The initials of his hacker name are 'EV'! He hacked the cars before to steal them. It's how he got caught. He knows them. It fits."

"Stranger things have happened," Gregory said from Haley's left. "If he's managed to bribe some guards or his attorney cooperated, he could have accessed a computer."

"He got caught hacking electric vehicles, but he's done more— allegedly," Marcus said, not arguing with them but providing more context. "Credit card scams, hacking corporate computers and holding them hostage with ransomware, all that—but they couldn't pin it all on him, so they went with the obvious. Having the stolen high-end electric car in his garage certainly helped convict him."

Haley listened while she typed into the secure communication app on her phone. When she finished, she waited a minute, received the reply she was hoping for, and slid the phone back into the front pocket of her khaki pants.

"Here's the big question," she said. "If he had internet access, could he have done all that happened today? Maybe had it all set to go and triggered it from inside?"

Marcus hesitated, started to speak, then stopped. An agonizing ten seconds passed while he bit his lip and stared into space before he shook his head slowly. "The courts took away his internet access while he was on trial. He's been locked up for a year. But even assuming he had a computer and internet access... No. I don't think so."

Haley pressed her lips together, not wanting to believe him.

"But," Marcus continued, "even without direct internet access, if he was just using the telephone, mail, or messages through a shady lawyer, he could have coordinated it with others on the outside."

Yes! That's it.

Haley smiled and offered a surprised Marcus a high five, which he awkwardly accepted.

49

KITCHEN

Haley stood in the diner's long, narrow kitchen, away from anyone who could overhear the conversation. She sucked down another full glass of diet soda the owner had gotten for her before Gregory had exiled him from the kitchen, where he'd been making sandwiches for everyone.

Gregory leaned his back against the prep counter, a thoughtful frown on his face.

"If Void didn't have a hand in it, which I admit is a possibility," Haley said, stopping Gregory's argument before he could make it, "he could point us in the right direction."

Gregory just looked at her patiently, unmoved.

"It's not dangerous," she said, slowing down and explaining her reasoning. "It's a federal prison."

"It's a solid lead," Gregory said, nodding. "Well done. But we'll send the FBI."

She held back a frown and refused to get emotional.

If I stick with the logical reasons why this makes sense, I'll convince him.

"He'll never talk to the FBI."

"He'd talk to you?"

She gave him her "yeah, duh" expression. "Not because of my looks," she said, her voice quiet. "My guess is we think alike. He's going to be attracted to my brain. I bet you good money we get into a duel of the minds."

Gregory shook his head. "How many times have we been through this, Haley?" He leaned forward. "I almost lost—" He caught himself and leaned back. "You can't go."

She stared at him for a long moment, her mind racing, analyzing what he'd almost let slip.

It had to be one of two options. Either he'd almost lost her... or he'd almost lost his job.

He cares about me like he does all his people. It would kill him to lose any of us. But that's not what he means.

"You almost lost your job over what happened in California?" she asked, not wanting to believe it but knowing what her Uncle Jimmy must have gone through, not knowing if she had been captured or was undercover.

She had willingly gotten into a helicopter with Cesar Madris, a billionaire businessman and, at the time, a possible suspect in an attack on the country. For a few hours, she'd been out of contact.

Gregory, Axe, and everyone else, including her adopted uncle— James Heringten, president of the United States—worried she'd been abducted and could be ransomed or tortured for knowledge of America's secrets.

Gregory offered a half smile as he shook his head. "No, I almost lost my mind worrying about what was happening to you. If it had turned out differently, I could never have forgiven myself for giving you permission to go into harm's way."

Oh, he's very good.

She couldn't tell if he was being honest.

Haley stared him down, searching his face for a micro tell that would prove he was lying, along with his aura, energy, or whatever mumbo jumbo people wanted to call the truth behind his words.

There was nothing.

Is that itself an indication?

Her intuition didn't offer any help.

We'll have to revisit this at some point soon—after I get back.

"Besides," Gregory said, "the roads are a mess. It's over a hundred miles away, and every state has issued stay-at-home guidelines while emergency crews attempt to clean up the accidents. You'd never get there."

Haley didn't bother to try to hide a triumphant smile.

"Haley? What do you have planned?"

"We both know you're going to let me go," she said, finishing her soda and handing him the empty glass.

"Haley—"

The drumbeat of a helicopter flying low rumbled through the walls.

"Call the warden and get me in to see Dawson Reite. No monitoring, no guards. And don't worry," she said, her voice rising to compete with the noise of the chopper. "Axe is with me."

She stepped toward the kitchen door but stopped and turned back. "And if Uncle Jimmy ever tries to fire you or hold you back in any way, you tell me. I'll take care of it," she said and headed out into the diner in time to see Tucci's helicopter land in the middle of the road outside the diner.

All the analysts were standing at the windows, watching the dirt and dust that blew in the rotor wash.

Haley left the restaurant, getting another analyst to lock the door behind her. She jogged to her SUV. The giant rear door unlocked as she pressed her thumb to the release. She used a number code to open a large, sturdy locker in the rear of the vehicle.

Her go bag sat, ready, but she paused and eyed the rest of the gear in the box.

As much as she wanted to take the short-barrel M4, it seemed excessive for a helicopter ride to a prison.

Better safe than sorry.

She grabbed the M4 and the bag. Extra magazines were already inside with spare clothes, a plate carrier, a med kit, and assorted other essential gear for heading into battle.

Haley locked everything up, slung the backpack over her shoulder, and carried the M4 across the parking lot to the helicopter.

The side door slid open as she neared.

She ducked inside and closed the door behind her, waving at her colleagues. She smiled as all of them waved back, their eyes wide at one of their own hopping into a waiting helicopter.

For an instant, she felt a little guilty.

Good luck explaining this, Gregory.

She shrugged as she sat down on one of the rear seats and grabbed a headset with a microphone attached to it.

The country has bigger problems than the people of the CAG realizing I'm more than just an analyst.

The helicopter lifted off as she got the headset on. "Hey, Axe. Tucci."

Axe nodded at her with his serious, "we're going to war" look she'd seen so often.

"Haley," Tucci responded, trying to act grumpy at once again being conscripted into helping them. But he didn't fake it well.

He loves getting the call and being back in the action.

"Let me guess," Tucci continued, his eyes front as he expertly brought the bird just high enough to clear the trees and powerlines in the area. "From what I saw from the air, the world is going to hell, and we're on the front lines to save it?"

"You nailed it. Thanks for helping out."

Tucci grumbled again. Haley and Axe made eye contact, both holding back smiles.

"By the way, you brought your shotgun, right?" she asked.

"What is it with you two?" Tucci said. "Of course I brought it. But like I told Axe last time, if you need me and my shotgun, you've already lost."

She got serious again.

I hope it doesn't come to that, but...

"You never know..." she said quietly.

Tucci glanced back and gave her a resolute nod.

"You never know," he repeated.

50

REJOICE

The hackers celebrated.

Finally, their work had real-world, practical effects.

They had all been raised on a steady diet of explanations for why the United States of America was the enemy.

After they'd bought into the belief, it had become hard to know they had the skills and ability to harm America via cyberattacks but weren't allowed to do anything.

Being recruited by Wolf and coming to Dubai had changed all that.

The screens in front of them were proof that they had power.

They had attacked America.

They had won.

And the worst was yet to come.

Their group chat blew up with screenshots of death and destruction, videos of their accomplishments, boasts, and mutual congratulations.

An image of a whole city block on fire with multiple cars rammed into buildings.

Rapture: *Success!*

A picture of a line of dead bodies on the sidewalk outside an office building, their faces haphazardly covered with spring jackets and sweatshirts. Survivors stood over them, crying and waiting for overwhelmed emergency personnel to respond.

Shark: *Unofficial death count so far: 1,108*
Nightowl: *Nice!!!*
Shark: *Will be higher each hour.*

Haze posted a link from a social media site. A mother in the southern United States had live streamed from her bathroom. Pale yellow tiles lined the bathtub enclosure.

Atom: *Look! We did this!!!*

The pure white bathtub was filled with disgustingly dark, scummy sludge.

It reached the top of the tub. For several seconds, it seemed to hold there.

Silver: *Is that it? Did they fix our hack?*
Atom: *No—just wait.*

On the live stream, the drain gurgled. A large air bubble rose to the surface.

The disgusting water sloshed over the side of the tub, onto the floor, and kept coming.

A moment later, the bathmat was overwhelmed.

The homeowner threw white, fluffy towels on the ground to stop the flow as she cried, "Somebody do something!"

"No one can help you, American lady," Atom muttered. His delight mixed with the pleasure of a job well done, along with the satisfaction of having attacked America.

And, way down deep, the tiniest hint of regret. Hacking was one thing. The challenges had thrilled him from age twelve, when he'd first started penetrating Russian systems.

Knowing he had caused the suffering of real people, though, and seeing the results of his actions, gave him pause.

I have done well—but killed no one.

He hadn't helped with the vehicle hacking. That had been the others.

His attack on the wastewater treatment facilities had been challenging and fun, a fitting way to show Americans that they weren't as mighty as they believed. Let thousands of their homes spew wastewater from their toilets, bathtubs, and sinks.

He shook off his mixed feelings.

I have nothing to be ashamed of. America is the enemy. They are getting exactly what they deserve—even the injured and dead.

The hackers hadn't been told of any further plan beyond today's attacks, but they could read between the lines of their additional target list.

Something else was coming.

With any luck, the next part would leave more of America in flames and more of their dead littering the streets.

51

PRISON

"They're going to allow us to land, right?" Tucci asked as they neared the Federal Correctional Institution—Cumberland. The sun was setting over the spring landscape of northwest Maryland on a day Americans would remember forever.

"Outside the perimeter, yes," Haley said. "But you'll need to lift off right away and circle. They don't want a bird sitting outside. Too tempting. It's only medium security, after all."

"They still have fences, razor wire, and locks on the doors, right?" he asked. "It's not like the inmates can just waltz out."

"They have all that, but us dropping in like this is ruffling a lot of feathers. Best to get you out of here. You have plenty of fuel?"

"Yep!" Tucci said with a chuckle and a glance back.

"My credit card filled up the tanks," Axe explained with a frown.

They flew over two ambulances and an old school bus on the road leading to the prison.

Probably filled with the dead and injured.

The area around the prison wasn't as empty as she had thought it would be. There were large buildings that looked like manufacturing plants, warehouses, and farms.

"The prison didn't have any problems related to the hacking, did it?" Axe asked, watching the area as they passed over it.

"Not that I heard before we left," Haley said. "No jails or prisons have been impacted. They're obviously pretty security conscious—physical and cyber. Especially the federal system. I'll check my phone when we land to make sure, though."

"You think a hack of this level can be organized or run from prison?" Axe asked.

"Dawson Reite could have set it up, directed it, or assisted. If not, my bet is he knows who pulled it off. All we can do is shake the tree, right?"

"Copy that," Axe said. He handed his pistol, extra magazines, and two knives to Haley to put in her go bag, wincing as he moved.

"You okay?" During the short flight, he'd updated her on the rest of the details from Puerto Rico, including injuring his head by backing into a rock and getting shot in the ballistic vest, hurting his ribs.

"Fine, just stings a little. I doubt anything's broken."

She removed all her weapons and added them to her bag. Better to leave them in the chopper than have to go through the hassle of checking them before they entered the prison.

"I'm going to drop you off in front of the main building," Tucci said. He handed Axe a radio. "Call me on that when you need to be picked up. If it seems like you're going to be a while, let me know and I'll set down in one of the warehouse parking lots to the south. Save you some gas money."

Tucci brought them in slowly, avoiding flying directly over the egg-shaped grounds of the prison. It had multiple buildings connected by cement paths.

When the helicopter touched down, Haley and Axe jumped out quickly, and Tucci was off.

"Think this will work?" Axe said as they approached the two-story brick building, where they'd meet the prisoner.

"Opportunities multiply as they are seized," Haley replied, quoting Sun Tzu.

"Amen," Axe said. The door before them made a heavy *click* as an electronic lock released. Axe pulled the door open and held it for her.

"I don't know if you've given any thought to strategy, but here's another one by Sun Tzu that might be fitting for today. 'Pretend inferiority and encourage his arrogance.'"

Haley smiled as they waited for a second, interior door to unlock remotely. "I was thinking more along the lines of, 'Prove superiority and encourage his defensiveness,' but we'll see what the man's like."

The door unlocked and they stepped in, ready for the confrontation.

52

PROCEED

The sniper lay buried in leaves just inside the tree line, three hundred yards from the entrance to the prison, invisible. It had taken all day to creep his way unnoticed to the position, but he'd made it in plenty of time.

With the arrival and departure of the helicopter, however, he guessed there was a fifty-fifty chance the mission, finalized at the last minute, would be called off.

Too risky now.

They'd only gotten word of which prison the target would be at the day before and had rushed to the western part of Maryland.

The helicopter meant someone might know about their attack, which was scheduled to launch in twenty minutes.

He keyed his mic and broke radio silence, speaking in English, the language he shared with the mercenary group of former soldiers from Russia.

"The helicopter is gone. Two people entered the building. One man, one woman. The man is a soldier. The woman too, maybe. Over."

"Standby," came the reply from the Russian in charge, his accent thick.

He could stand by. As a sniper, it was what he did.

Warehouse Parking Lot Staging Area
1/2 Mile South of the Federal Correctional Institution

Nestor, the leader of the mercenary group, cursed his fat fingers as he typed the encrypted update and hit send, ignoring the misspellings.

His instructions were clear: Radio silence except in the event of an emergency.

The helicopter's arrival—only minutes before the planned attack—seemed suspicious.

They had time to call the whole thing off. They could ride away together in one of the ambulances, leaving the school bus behind.

The Chinese sniper could sneak out easily as it grew darker. They would pick him up, or he could make his own way to one of the several secondary vehicles staged a few miles away.

It would be easy to ditch the mix of semiautomatic pistols supplied to them and resume their roles as tourists before returning to their home countries until the next person or company needed retired soldiers for less-than-legal work.

Nestor thought he'd have to wait while the client—whoever it was—looked into the situation and weighed the pros and cons of continuing the mission.

He was surprised when the short sentence popped up on the phone's secure communication app.

Proceed as planned.

"We go as planned," he announced over their radio network to the Chinese sniper and the other Russians waiting in the ambulances and bus.

53

DANGEROUS

Wolf and George stood behind Nightowl, the hacker who had taken over Wolf's workstation.

Some of the other young men had finally grown tired of watching the mayhem. They'd left the main office to eat and catch naps. They had another long day in a few hours.

On the large computer monitor, twelve windows showed the live feed from the vast array of security cameras at the Federal Correctional Institution in Maryland. The hack of the aquarium thermometer and monitoring systems had been successful. They were in—and in control.

Every three seconds, the images in the windows changed, flicking to the next batch of cameras.

"There. Hold on that one," Wolf said, pointing to the upper right corner. "Enlarge."

With a few clicks, Nightowl changed the view. Four windows across the top and bottom, plus one on each side, allowed for a larger center window to display the selected view.

A beautiful blond woman who moved like a tiger accompanied a forty-something-year-old man with a muscular build and dark hair—a soldier. His dark beard was bushy and in need of a trim.

As the warrior and the woman entered the lobby of the prison's main building, the man looked directly at the camera and nodded with a polite smile.

Beside Wolf, George stiffened. "That man is dangerous," he muttered.

"You said to continue with the mission," Wolf said. "Should I send an emergency message? There is still time."

George spoke only after a few agonizing seconds. "No. Your control of the technology will make the difference. You will follow this man and make sure he is locked inside a room until the end of the mission."

"I…"

George turned and stared at him with the lifeless eyes of someone who had killed more men than he could remember.

"If they put him in a room, we can keep it locked," Wolf said, praying it worked out that way.

He sat down at the workstation next to his usual one, logged in, and navigated into the prison's system. It would now take more than one person to ensure the mission succeeded as planned.

54

PROFESSIONALS

The Federal Correctional Institution
South of Cumberland, Maryland

The modern facility was impressive in its design, security, and staffing.

Two male guards—muscular and each at least six feet tall—escorted Axe through the metal detector first, making him send the radio through a conveyor-belt-style bag scanner.

Both of the guards checked Haley out as she went through the metal detector, but they were discreet about it.

Haley's boss must have made an impact on the warden who passed along a message to the guards to play nice.

"The warden wanted to greet you, but he had to leave. You just missed him," one of the guards said. "We'll escort you to a visitor room. Your guy will be here soon. They're just finishing dinner," he said, glancing at his watch.

"Have there been any problems with him?" Haley asked as he walked them through more electronically locked doors that clicked open for them as they approached, triggered by other guards somewhere.

The guard shook his head. "I checked the log. He got here first thing this morning, around eight. He was assigned a bunk and clothes, and it sounds like he settled in pretty quick."

"Any problems in general today? Security, fights, unusual behavior?"

He shook his head again. "Not that I've heard. Pretty low-key group here. No one is physically dangerous—not that any of them couldn't be violent, but if they were that bad, they'd be in another facility. White-collar criminals for the most part, though we have a New York mafia boss. He's probably given a lot of orders to kill or hurt people, but nothing that could be pinned on him. He's in here for tax and insurance fraud."

The walls of the long corridor they walked down were painted a pleasant taupe color. The lights were bright without being overpowering. It felt less like a prison and more like a mid-level office building.

"Escape attempts?" Axe asked, eying the security cameras and thinking about the twenty-foot chain-link fences with razor wire they'd seen outside. "Not from Reite, obviously, but others? It seems like you run a tight ship," he added, buttering the guy up but being honest, too. He could tell they took security seriously. They looked like they could handle themselves. Neither of the men carried weapons that could be taken and used against them, though there was likely a locked armory somewhere in case of emergency.

"Most of the people here would love the chance to get away," the other guard said. "These white-collar types probably have money stashed they could access. Almost all of them were held without bail from the start. Too easy for them to skip town. But picking a lock on their cell, sneaking out of one of the buildings, scaling the fence, and racing off to a waiting car? Not these people. If it isn't easy—physically, I mean—they're not doing it."

They arrived at a visiting room. It wasn't large—only about twelve feet by twelve feet—but had plenty of room for a family get-together or meeting with an attorney. The door had a large window with metal security mesh embedded in the glass.

A guard can watch to make sure there's no hanky-panky while still giving the low-risk inmates privacy.

A stainless steel table with benches, like a picnic table, was bolted to the floor in the center of the room. In this room, there was no pretending that guests weren't visiting with an incarcerated person, but other than the stark look of the worn white linoleum floor and blank, pale yellow walls, it wasn't bad.

The room looked clean and, as the lock clicked open, Axe was surprised that it smelled pleasant; lemony from the floor cleaner or surface wipes used on the table, he guessed.

Haley asked the most important question, the one they'd been leading up to. "I know this guy is some all-star hacker. What are the odds he got ahold of a computer or a phone—anything with internet access?"

She leaned in close to the guards and whispered. "I'm sure you two wouldn't do it—you look like straight shooters. But could he have bribed anyone else—kitchen staff, a chaplain, a guest teacher, someone—to get him access this morning? Or had it on him when he arrived?"

Both guards shook their heads. Coming from Haley, they hadn't been offended—she'd played it perfectly.

And they enjoyed a pretty young woman leaning in close and speaking conspiratorially with them.

"No chance," one whispered, taking the opportunity to get a little closer to Haley. "Not here, at least."

"Yeah," the other said, with his own lean in. "If it was cigarettes, small quantities of drugs, I'd say that, unfortunately, it could happen. But not a cell phone or tablet with Wi-Fi; not with that guy. It'd be like giving a gun to the mafia boss. Some things you just don't do."

Haley nodded and smiled her appreciation for the guards' candor. "Got it, thanks."

Axe and Haley stepped into the room. "Sorry, we've gotta lock you in. We'll monitor you from the control room—you two don't look like you need a babysitter outside the door. Other guards will be here soon with your guy. He's already on the way."

"Great, thanks," Haley said as they closed the heavy door.

The lock clicked, and they sat down to wait.

Lux View Marina Tower
Floor 15
Dubai, United Arab Emirates

"No, no, no," Wolf mumbled, watching his screen.

The target, Dawson "Eternal Void" Reite, had been the original architect of the assisted driving software hack.

Wolf had worshipped him from afar for years. His exploits were legendary, though he wouldn't have been on board with what the hacker team had done today. He preferred hacking systems, holding them hostage with ransomware, or stealing from companies to impress women with his genius and ill-gotten gains.

What a waste of talent.

If they'd had him on their side... Wolf suppressed a sigh and forced the thought away but not before a quick dream about being in control of America's military, air traffic control system, or a nuclear reactor located near a large city. If Void had been on the team, those dreams might have been possible.

For tonight's last-minute mission, the intel they'd received claimed that Void would be in D Building's common area, where he could play chess, watch TV, or read.

But on the screen, Wolf watched as two burly guards handcuffed Void, marched him through several security doors, and outside into a waiting SUV.

"They're taking him to the main building to meet with the man and woman," Wolf said. "Should I take control now and lock the man and woman in the visitor room?"

George shook his head. "Not yet. It is too early. We will change the plan."

"It's not too late to call it off."

George shook his head again. "Send a message. The operation continues. This will be easier in some ways. One team will enter the main building, secure Reite, and leave immediately. The rest of the plan remains the same."

"But they'll realize he's the target."

The original plan would have created confusion. With all the inmates who wanted to escape gone in the ambulances and the school bus, including Reite, the primary target would have been impossible to determine.

"That is unfortunate," George said, "but the only other alternative is to leave him in custody or delay the plan, neither of which is acceptable. Send the message."

Wolf used his computer to type into the secure app and hit send. "What happens if they don't see it in time?"

"They will," George said. "They are professionals."

55

FOUR MINUTES

Outside the Federal Correctional Institution
South of Cumberland, Maryland

"Four minutes," Nestor said into the radio, feeling exposed as they neared the prison. The compound and surrounding area were well lit, with many powerful lights on tall posts shining onto the grounds as well as lighting up the exterior area.

The ambulance behind him followed his left turn, passing through the main building's parking lot onto the perfectly paved two-lane road that curved around the back side of the prison complex to the rear entrance.

There, two reinforced gates topped with coils of razor wire, a guard shack housing four guards, and numerous cameras prevented unauthorized entry.

All were electronically controlled, as were the doors to the observation rooms on top of the guard towers around the perimeter.

This will be easy if the client is able to do what they say.

Nestor's phone pinged. He let out an exasperated sigh as his driver, another mercenary, looked over with raised eyebrows.

Unlocking the phone, Nestor read the message, sent a short reply, and keyed his mic.

"Small change of plans," he announced, checking his watch.

The time is tight.

"I will peel off and enter through the front. The rest of you continue. Vehicle 2, take the lead." He quickly sketched out two contingency plans before signing off, then turned to his driver. "Turn around and drop me at the front door. Hurry."

———

Administrative Building
Federal Correctional Institution
South of Cumberland, Maryland

"Who's hurt?" Cartwright, the swing shift supervisor, asked, crunching a carrot. His wife was on another health kick and wanted them both to drop ten pounds before summer.

An ambulance drove up to the door of the front building—right outside the security control room, where he was standing.

On another security monitor window, he noticed a second ambulance and an honest-to-God school bus driving around to the back gate.

"What's going on?" he asked his staff of two techs. "Did the numbnuts try another riot over the food and nobody told me?"

The inmates had gotten it into their heads last month that the food wasn't up to their fine dining standards. Instead of a hunger strike, which would have meant a large dose of sacrifice from each of them, they decided to protest with what could only generously be called a riot.

Basically, they'd had a food fight.

Like naughty children, they'd been sent to their cells and spent until lunch the next day in lockdown. Anyone who hadn't been bright enough to eat at least some of the subpar food went hungry for two meals.

By lunch, there were no complaints about the food.

The real problem had come from the lack of communication among the security teams.

A downside to the current security arrangement was the separation of the facility into exterior and interior zones. The idea from some consultant seemed to be that if something went wrong in either zone, the inmates would still be secure because of a separation of duties.

No matter what happened, whether it be inmates overpowering the guards on the interior or an exterior assault from idiots thinking they could get inside and free their buddy, the facility would be safe.

In practice, the new measure didn't work. It wasn't fully embraced by the staff. The two security groups didn't communicate well. Sometimes the right hand didn't know what the left hand was doing.

"Check in with each of the buildings," he said. "Find out if people are injured."

"Maybe there are hurt people in the ambulances and they're bringing them to our infirmary?" one of the techs suggested. There weren't a ton of new cars with assisted or autonomous driving in the region, but there had been enough to cause some major problems—especially from autonomous semi-trucks that had recently come on the market.

Plus, a train had been switched onto old tracks and derailed nearby.

Along with the water being shut off to everyone in town and their sewers backing up on them, too, the place was a mess. Cartwright was happy the prison had its own water and sewer systems.

He checked his watch. Almost 5:45. Dinner would be over and the inmates in the common rooms.

He had a bad feeling and tossed the half-eaten carrot stick into the trash can by the wall.

"Look alive, people. Alert the back gate, just in case they're sleeping and haven't noticed. Let's take this seriously."

His crew sat up straighter and placed the call.

One of the techs held the phone in his hand and turned to Cartwright. "The phone doesn't work."

56

THE PRISONER

Visitor Room
Administrative Building
Federal Correctional Institution
South of Cumberland, Maryland

"Can you take those off?" Axe asked. The two guards who had escorted the prisoner into the visitor room shrugged and unlocked Dawson Reite's handcuffs.

"Wave at the camera when you're done," one said. They took the cuffs with them to the door, which once again clicked open as they approached and locked after they left.

"You're not cops," Dawson said, rubbing his wrists and sitting on the table's metal bench. Haley and Axe sat across from him.

Axe stayed quiet, letting Haley take the lead.

How's she going to play this?

Dawson wore cheap khaki pants that were about a half size too big for him. A too-small khaki button-up shirt with a white T-shirt under it completed the prison outfit, aside from the white slip-on shoes with no laces.

He looked goofy, like he'd outgrown his shirt but lost weight around his stomach, causing his pants to slip low on his waist.

Otherwise, he seemed like a typical twenty-something. Caucasian, thin face, dark curly hair, and a smart, geeky sense about him. He hadn't shaved that morning. Stubble grew in patches on his face. He seemed surprised to see them... and there was something else, just beneath the surface, that he kept mostly hidden, but Axe couldn't put his finger on what.

He's not nervous. Is he defeated? Scared?

No, it wasn't either of those. He looked tired. Dragged down but trying to hide it.

I think Haley's right again. He knows something.

Haley stared at the kid, giving him an amused smile and raising her eyebrow. "'Eternal Void'?" she asked, gently teasing him about the nickname.

"I know, I know." Dawson sighed. "I was young when I called myself that. After a few years, it was too late to change. Mostly, people call me 'Void' now."

Haley could sense his intelligence. Even as he responded to her question, he was feeling her out.

He knows something.

She felt it in her gut, along with another feeling. A stronger one, tinged with danger.

Her spine tingled. She glanced at Axe, her face still.

He feels it, too.

Axe looked around the empty room. So did she.

They were alone, aside from Dawson.

Axe reached into his pocket and switched on the radio. "Joisey, how copy?"

"Solid copy," Tucci replied immediately.

"Get back here ASAP and circle."

"Copy, I'm a few minutes away."

"Copy. Out."

"What's going on?" Dawson asked.

"Nothing at all," she said.

The dance has already begun.

Axe would handle whatever they both sensed. Her mission was to get the information she needed out of the hacker as quickly as possible.

57

ONE MINUTE

Administrative Building
Federal Correctional Institution
South of Cumberland, Maryland

Nestor glanced at his watch as he approached the front door of the FCI's main building, timing his steps to the second the operation was scheduled to begin.

His hand grasped the metal door handle and pulled the instant he heard the *click* of the lock disengage.

A good sign.

It wasn't proof yet that the plan was working or that the client had full access to the prison's computer systems. The guards inside could have seen the ambulance drop him off before driving away. His paramedic uniform might have fooled them into allowing him access through the first set of bulletproof doors.

The next door also unlocked as he stepped to it.

He kept his head down, avoiding looking at the security camera mounted over the door, though he wanted nothing more than to remove his baseball cap, wave it around, and smile while giving a rude gesture to the men in the security control room.

This beats an armed assault any day.

Cartwright's sense of danger was off the charts as he watched the paramedic waltz through both security doors.

"Why the hell did you click him in?" he asked the tech in charge of the front doors. "That's against every protocol!"

"I didn't! The door opened on its own." The tech clicked on his screen, running a diagnostic. "The system's having a glitch—the phones must be part of it."

"That's not possible," Cartwright said. "You two," Cartwright said to the guards on front-door duty who had escorted the top secret visitors. "Get out there and find out who the guy is."

On-screen, the paramedic stepped through the metal detector. It beeped, and the red light on top of it flashed.

He then read the signs on the wall and turned left, following the arrows down the hall toward the visitor rooms.

One of the guards tugged on the control room door. "It's locked," he said.

"Unlock the damn door—hurry!" Cartwright said.

"I can't," the tech said in a worried voice. He typed on the keyboard, clicked his mouse, and turned to look at Cartwright. "The system has been taken over. We're no longer in control."

Rear Vehicle Entrance
The Federal Correctional Institution
South of Cumberland, Maryland

The Russian mercenary driving the ambulance—Petrov—checked his watch.

Five seconds.

One of the guards left the security hut, taking the initiative.

That's a costly mistake.

The driver frowned. He had hoped to get through the mission without bloodshed. It's what the plan called for, though they had been authorized to use deadly force the moment it was required.

The guard approached the tall, heavy fencing that made up the back gate.

"You're not authorized to be here!" he yelled.

Nosing the ambulance closer to the gate, the driver angled the vehicle to the right. He rolled down the window and leaned his head partway out as if he didn't hear the guard the first time.

"You can't be here!" the guard yelled again.

With a final check to ensure the guard hut door had swung securely closed, the driver stuck his arm out of the window and shot the guard once in the head.

The noise from the unsuppressed pistol was loud in the cool spring evening. It provoked an instant reaction from the guards in the hut. All three immediately drew their sidearms. One reached for the handheld radio mic on his shoulder while the other two rushed for the door.

They came up short when they couldn't open it.

After pushing and yanking, one flung himself at the door, trying to use his considerable bulk to break it open.

The whole hut shook, but the door didn't budge.

In front of the ambulance, the first security gate slid open, controlled by the mercenaries' employer via the internet.

The second gate, fifty feet ahead, did as well.

The mercenary edged the ambulance forward, scooting through the opening with barely an inch of extra space on each side.

He avoided running over the dead guard out of respect—from one warrior to another.

Behind him, the school bus and second ambulance followed, having made up time from dropping off the captain.

"One minute," the driver said to the men in the back.

58

DANGER

Axe didn't think much of astrology, crystals, or tarot cards. People claimed they could see auras or knew the future based on tea leaves or whatever—fine. He had no experience with that one way or the other. People could believe in whatever crazy stuff they wanted, especially if it worked for them.

What he believed in, though, was one hundred percent real. It had saved his life on several occasions.

He could sense danger.

Maybe fear, deadly intent, the thrill of the hunt, and other strong emotions sent some sort of energy waves into the universe. Or it could be pheromones, a higher power sending a warning, or a disturbance in the force, but something happened when danger came knocking.

Most experienced warriors could feel it.

So could survivors of violence or trauma.

And children. They were often attuned to it long before adults knew there was danger.

Axe felt the energy now. Haley did too, though she had her focus on verbally fencing with Void.

Axe's skeptical mind tried to convince him he was being paranoid this time, that nothing could happen to them in the admin building of a federal prison, but he ignored it.

Something isn't right.

A quick check of Void's body language showed him focused on Haley.

He's not the danger.

Which meant the threat was outside the room—or coming for them.

Axe stood, lightly putting a hand on Haley's shoulder, giving her a subtle signal to stay with Void as he moved out of sight of the window in the door and the view of the room it provided.

Whatever comes through the door next is the problem.

Lux View Marina Tower
Floor 15
Dubai, United Arab Emirates

"He's alongside the wall!" Wolf yelled at the computer screen—as if the mercenary captain approaching the door to the visitor room could hear him from half a world away.

Wolf switched screens to compose an urgent text.

George's large, heavy hand on his shoulder stopped him. "Don't distract him now. He is a professional—he will understand the situation."

"But it's one-on-one. If the soldier surprises him—"

"He's armed. The soldier isn't." George hesitated, then spoke again, sounding less confident in the outcome of the confrontation about to unfold on the screen. "And it is not one-on-one," he said under his breath. "The woman is as dangerous as the man."

59

SHOTS

Haley tuned out what Void was saying the moment the door lock clicked open.

Whoever was about to enter the room was dangerous. Whether he was a guard or the warden himself, the person in the hallway meant them harm. She knew it in her bones.

She had only an instant to decide.

Is this a rescue attempt, an assassination to tie up loose ends, or are they after Axe and me?

She threw herself across the table at the shocked Void, taking him backward off the seat and onto the ground.

He grunted at the dual impacts of his body hitting the floor and Haley landing on top of him. His body cushioned Haley's landing.

She rolled off, grabbed his arm, and pulled him behind the end of the table. It offered the smallest bit of concealment, though no real cover from the man coming through the door, gun drawn.

Axe launched himself toward the door before it opened completely.

A man dressed as a paramedic in dark-blue cargo pants, a button-up shirt, and a ball cap stepped inside, pistol tight against his body, angling toward him.

Axe noted the professionalism. An amateur, thug, or even some police officers would have the weapon in an outstretched arm, leading the way into the room with the pistol. The paramedic held his too close to his body to easily knock from his hands.

The paramedic fired as he moved into the room.

The point-blank round caught Axe in the chest.

The Kevlar vest stopped the bullet.

It hit a few inches lower than the round he'd taken from the tango in the jungle less than twenty-four hours before.

Despite the vest, the bullet slamming into Axe's ribs at such close range hurt even more than the two the previous night. It felt like getting hit by a hammer swung at full force by an angry construction worker.

Axe grunted in pain as he rushed the man. Together, they crashed against the door and tumbled into the hallway, fighting over control of the weapon.

Nestor fired again, struggling against the soldier's iron grip on his arm.

The second bullet went wide.

The first had hit home, fired as the man crashed into him—exactly as he would have attacked if their situations were reversed.

The shot should have at least slowed him down.

He must have on a ballistic vest.

There was one sure way to end this quickly...

No vest stops a shot to the head.

Nestor cranked his wrist, only needing an instant. He pulled the trigger, but the dark-haired soldier's head jerked right before the weapon fired, moving out of the bullet's path.

The man pushed hard against Nestor's arm.

His next shot also went wide, penetrating the wall of the hallway.

Nestor grappled, trying to gain the upper hand, but his enemy matched every move and countermove. Finally, the soldier made a mistake, giving Nestor an opening. Taking advantage of the moment, he scored an elbow into the man's damaged ribs, eliciting a sharp gasp of pain.

60

TRAPPED

Visitor Room
Administrative Building
Federal Correctional Institution
South of Cumberland, Maryland

Axe gasped as the tango's strike hit home.

The pain from the blow to his ribs made him see stars.

That hurt! Hurry up, Haley!

He'd given the enemy an opening, knowing there would be a price to pay.

He didn't dare turn his head or even glance toward the doorway to see where the hell Haley was.

As long as Haley had made it to the door before it swung shut and locked, he expected his partner to appear any second now and—

The distracted tango's head snapped back as Haley's foot connected with his chin.

The man collapsed, out cold—at least. Axe had a feeling Haley had broken his neck.

Axe grabbed the man's pistol and found spare mags on a holder hidden under his shirt. By the time Axe looked up again, Haley was in the doorway, calling to Void.

"Let's go," she said. "You don't want to make me come in there and get you."

Axe found the man's cell phone, hoping it could be unlocked by a fingerprint, but the lock screen demanded a code. He tried the still-warm finger, just in case, but nothing happened.

Maybe Haley's IT team can access it.

"Thanks for the assist," Axe called from the floor.

"Happy to help," Haley said. Void stood in the doorway, staring at the tango dressed as a paramedic.

"Is he dead?" Void asked, looking paler than usual.

Axe felt for the enemy's pulse but knew right away he was gone.

No head moves like that on a working neck.

"Dead. Nice kick," he said. "You've been practicing."

Haley had a firm hold of Void's bicep. She stepped away, distancing herself by straightening her arm but not letting go as the hacker bent at the waist.

"If you're going to barf, do it now," Haley said. "Tucci will kill me—then you—if you hurl all over his precious helicopter."

True.

The kid—Axe couldn't help but think of him as a kid now, seeing his reaction to the violence—shook his head and stood straight, eyes fixed on the dead guy.

"You ready to talk?" Haley said. She sounded reasonable, but her voice had a hint of danger underneath it. "Was he here to help or hurt you?"

"I don't know."

"What was the plan?" she said, stepping closer to him. His eyes never wavered from the dead tango on the off-white linoleum floor.

"I really have no idea," Void said. He sounded sincere.

"There's no time," Axe said. "Where there's one, there are more."

His radio squawked. "I'm circling," Tucci called. "Same spot for pickup?"

"Give me a sitrep," Axe said. He led the way back toward the front entrance, pistol up and ready to shoot. Haley followed with Void.

"Looks about the same," Tucci said. "Except... wait. That's strange. The back gate is open—both of them, actually. Interior and exterior. And there's a school bus plus two ambulances parked by one of the buildings, rear doors wide open, headlights on, but no flashing lights. Are you shot up again—you need me there?"

"No. That's not us, for once. It might be a prison break."

"So maybe I stay away from that area."

"That might be best. We're heading to the front doors but…"

"Yeah, I get you."

Exfilling the same way you arrived was never a good strategy.

"Stay out of range as much as possible until we figure out what's going on. You ready for a hot extract?"

"Oh, how I miss those days," Tucci said. Axe blamed the radio for not being able to tell if Tucci was being sarcastic or sincere.

"I don't know why this whole place isn't going crazy with sirens, flashing lights, and guards running everywhere, but it's dead quiet," Axe said into the radio. "Can you alert the local police about a possible well-organized prison break here?"

"Not a problem."

"Great. We'll let you know about the extract. Out."

Wandering the halls took many precious seconds, but Axe finally found the security control room.

A window in the door showed four very frustrated guards—including the two who escorted Axe and Haley to the visitor room—and an older, heavyset man who had to be a supervisor. His face was bright red, and he looked like he was a minute away from a coronary.

Axe tried the handle, but it didn't budge. "Can I shoot it open?" Axe yelled.

The supervisor shook his head. "The glass is bulletproof, and the door and lock are designed to be unbreakable," he yelled through the thick glass.

"What can I do?" Axe asked.

The red-faced man threw up his hands in anger. "Nothing. It's all computer controlled, and we're locked out."

"The front doors?"

"Same. Our radios and phones, too."

Damn. Waiting around isn't an option. If we can get outside, we can get on the chopper and get away.

"You armed in there?"

The man nodded.

"Okay, stay safe. We're going to try to make a break for it with the prisoner—Reite. He's what they want—so we won't let them have him."

Axe didn't wait for a reply or permission. He sprinted back down the hallway. Haley kept up easily, pulling along the thin but out-of-shape

Void, whose pants kept slipping further down his waist, exposing his tighty-whities.

Back at the front entrance, nothing looked unusual or out of place. No tangos waited with rifles pointed at the doorway.

Axe eyed the interior door, the vestibule, and the exterior door.

What the hell—why not?

He reached for the door handle to test it… and the lock clicked open.

"Stick close," Axe whispered.

Pulling the door open, he slid into the entrance area.

"Whatever you do—" he said.

"I'm not going to let it close," Haley said. "I'm with you."

Axe stopped at the exterior door, turned, and looked over his shoulder at the security camera mounted on the wall above the interior door.

The exterior door lock didn't click.

Axe waited.

"Whoever is in control of the system wants this door closed first," Haley said from behind him. "They want us locked in."

"Yep. It's a trap."

"If they let us out…"

"Then it's an ambush, but at least it'll let us know how well prepared they are."

Axe stared at the camera, daring whoever was watching to unlock the door.

Come on. Make it interesting.

Ten seconds later, the lock clicked.

Axe stepped through the door in a flash, paused a half second, and jumped back inside, letting the door swing shut on its own.

A bullet slammed into the metal door, right where Axe's head had been an instant earlier.

He smirked at the security camera, flipped it the bird, and followed Haley back inside.

"We're trapped," he said.

61

D BUILDING

D Building
The Federal Correctional Institution
South of Cumberland, Maryland

Petrov, the second-in-command of the mission, entered D Building's main door as the lock clicked open.

Behind him, the rest of his team had stacked themselves in classic assault entry formation, ready to go.

He yanked the door open. The men raced through.

All the doors unlocked in succession as they neared.

In the main common area, prisoners watched a TV mounted on the wall. Others read books or played cards, chess, or checkers at tables bolted to the floor.

Everyone looked up in shock as Petrov's men swarmed the room.

"Against the wall!" his men yelled at two guards watching over the prisoners.

Their hands went up at the sight of the men dressed as paramedics pointing pistols at them.

"Stay where you are," Petrov said to the inmates.

No one moved—not even the few prisoners sitting in their cells with the metal doors standing open.

He and another mercenary ran up the open stairs at the side of the common area to check the second floor.

Petrov couldn't hold back a smile at the sight.

Several guards stood in the control room overlooking the twin corridors of cells and the open area where the inmates spent most of their time.

They were taking turns slamming themselves uselessly against the door, trying to force it open.

Petrov shook his head at them with a grin. The door would remain locked until the mercenaries' employer allowed it to open.

D Building was his.

Returning to the main floor, Petrov looked around the room at the prisoners who sat perfectly still. The ones in their cells craned their necks to see what Petrov and his men were doing but didn't stand up.

He thought he had his target—an older gentleman sitting alone on a plastic bench, bolted to the floor on the far side of the room. On the other side of a large window, a huge aquarium had colorful fish swimming around inside.

"Mr. Salvatore Burattorio," Petrov called out in the English he'd spent his free time perfecting. Mercenaries with excellent English got paid more.

The man on the bench shook his head at Petrov.

Frowning, Petrov scanned the other prisoners for the New York mafia boss.

There, that's him.

A man with wavy, dyed black hair, held perfectly in place in an old-fashioned, puffy style, put down his playing cards and stood from a table in the middle of the room. He moved smoothly, like a man who took care of himself despite his obvious advancing years.

Three other men around the table, all younger, with dark hair, muscular bodies, and no necks, stood with him.

"Please come with us," Petrov said.

The man's lips twitched in a smile.

"Of course," Burattorio said in the voice of someone from the streets who had spent a lifetime trying to act cultured.

Burattorio moved toward the building's main door, led by one of Petrov's mercenaries. His three bodyguards followed them outside to the waiting ambulance.

Perfect. Part One complete.

An unhappy murmur arose from the prisoners.

"What the hell—take me, too!" a heavyset older man said nearby.

"Why does he get to go?" one chess player asked.

"They're here to break him out, dufus," his opponent answered.

"You can all go soon," Petrov said, speaking above the grumbling.

That got their attention. "Quietly. No violence. You should work together for the escape. Here is the plan. On the count of three, you will all point to a person. This man will be in charge. He will control your escape vehicle. He will organize and lead you. So choose wisely."

Petrov let the instructions soak in before he started counting. "One. Two. Three. Choose now."

Men pointed in various directions. Many pointed at themselves.

A quick glance revealed one man, sitting by himself near the television, had the most votes. He was bald, with a strong, lean body, and wore black-rimmed glasses. His finger marked his page in the middle of a thick novel. He looked like an accountant-turned-serial-killer.

"Why him?" Petrov asked the pointing men.

One inmate spoke. "Jack is the smartest guy here."

Petrov nodded to his men in the corner. They forced the guards up the stairs, heading to the entrance to the locked security room.

"You will be locked inside for your own protection," Petrov called to them. "You will not be killed by us or your inmates—unless you try to escape or fight. If you do, you will all be shot. If you do not resist, the worst that happens is these men escape. Think of your families."

Petrov moved so he had a view of the second floor.

The guards lined up single file in front of the door to the observation room. For a second, when the guards inside seemed ready to rush the door once it opened, Petrov thought he would have to order them all shot. But cooler heads prevailed. They stood back, the door unlocked, and the others filed inside.

The door locked behind them. A few seemed angry. Others looked relieved.

Petrov gestured for Jack, the smart man, to come forward and spoke quietly to him. "There is a school bus outside. There are paper maps of the nearby states on the dash. There is also a briefcase filled with money— small and large denominations—under the driver's seat, with plenty for everyone."

Jack took in the information with ease, his eyes focused and intense. His bald head reflected the overhead lights.

"Abandon the bus as soon as you have other transportation," Petrov continued, reaching behind his back and pulling a pistol from his waistband. "Do you know how to use this?"

"No, I've never had one," the man said in a crisp manner with a hint of a Boston accent. "But I understand in principle. Show me."

"There is no safety. Point, pull the trigger, and people die. There are fifteen bullets. Do not aim it at me or my men."

Petrov handed the gun over. The man examined it briefly, careful to keep it pointed at the floor, then nodded.

"You will wait until my men and I have left the building before organizing your escape," Petrov finished. "Any questions?"

"Is it only D Building, or are the others going free as well?"

"Only this building gets transportation. As soon as the bus leaves the gate, the exterior doors of the other buildings will open, along with any doors keeping inmates contained. The same will happen at the nearby minimum-security campus, too. All prisoners will be free to leave if they choose, but they will do so on foot through the rear gates. Most guards are already locked inside their observation rooms, as are the ones in the guard towers outside."

The man nodded his approval.

"Realistically, how long do we have before we're hunted?"

"My guess is one hour," Petrov said. "Longer if no one attempts to contact this facility and realizes the phone lines are down or comes to investigate."

Sixty minutes after the ambulance left with Nestor and the primary target—Reite—at the front building, the authorities would be informed of the escape. By then, Petrov, Nestor, the mercenaries, the mafia boss, and the hacker would have switched vehicles and would be long gone.

"We will use the time to our advantage," Jack said. He switched the pistol to his left hand and stuck out his right, surprising Petrov. He shook it. "Thank you. I'll do my best to make it hard for them to find any of us."

Petrov followed the rest of his men out the door, leaving Jack in charge of the other inmates. As he climbed into the passenger seat of the waiting ambulance, the burner phone in his cargo pocket—provided by their anonymous employer—vibrated, startling him.

It would do that if...

Nestor had to be dead, captured, or out of commission, making Petrov the new leader.

After unlocking the screen with a ten-digit code, he read his new orders on the phone's only app—a secure communication program.

Urgent: shoot down the helicopter before it picks up passengers.

Another message came through.

Acquire the primary target. Kill the soldier and blond woman protecting him. Take all men except a driver for the ambulance.

62

CARTWRIGHT

Administrative Building
Federal Correctional Institution
South of Cumberland, Maryland

All Cartwright could do was watch from the security room and worry about what this meant for his once-promising career.

Burattorio, the New York mafia boss, though technically only imprisoned for extortion, undoubtedly had the blood of hundreds on his hands. Unfortunately, not one of his underlings or victims had been willing to testify against him about ordering the death or beatings of people.

Although he'd been deemed a nonviolent offender and sent to this medium-security prison, he was truly a dangerous killer.

Cartwright watched helplessly on the video monitor as Burattorio gracefully stepped into the back of an ambulance. The unappetizing food, daily workouts, and the weekly yoga classes by the earnest young people volunteering to help "reform" the prisoners had done wonders for him. He'd lost weight, gained muscle, and looked much fitter than someone his age should.

His three goons—men who had committed white-collar crimes and pleaded guilty to end up in the same facility as their boss—followed him into the ambulance.

A minute later, several paramedics—or criminals dressed as paramedics, Cartwright supposed—climbed in and slammed the doors. The ambulance drove forward before stopping abruptly.

Several of the paramedics jumped out of the ambulance and took off at a run toward the admin building and welcome center, where Cartwright and his men had become prisoners.

That's about the soldier, the blond, and the hacker, I bet.

The ambulance drove forward again, out the still-open double gates, passing the three guards trapped in their hut and the dead body of a guard lying on the ground.

The don is getting away, and the soldiers are coming to save that asshole hacker.

Cartwright would put his money on the soldier and his blond partner despite the bad odds.

Cartwright had lost track of them when they went up the stairs to the second floor of the admin building—there were no cameras up there. He wished he could offer a warning, but the system still had his team locked out.

"What are we going to do, sir?" one of the guards said, breaking his reverie.

What he's really wondering is how screwed we are.

"I don't know," Cartwright said.

The only thing he knew for sure was that as soon as he got out of this damn control room, his next stop was the staff kitchen area. One of the newer guys always brought in donuts, and he was having one—at least.

To hell with the diet.

63

DROP

The admin building's second-story windows, unlike the first floor, did not have metal mesh embedded in the glass, probably as a cost-saving measure. In a minute, Axe would break the floor-to-ceiling window at the end of the hallway—on the west side, far from where the sniper was, he hoped.

Axe unwound the military-spec paracord from his survival bracelet. The tall ceilings of the admin building made the second floor too high to leap from… unless they had to. Haley probably could have managed. His own parachute training would likely keep him safe. But Void's lack of physicality would be the problem, so the paracord to the rescue. They didn't need a twisted ankle or broken leg tonight.

"No cameras, right?" he asked Haley.

"None up here that I can see," she said. "We might surprise whoever's taken control."

"Still need to hurry," he said. He formed a large loop and tied a bowline knot in the cord. "After the loop, this is only fifteen feet," Axe told Haley and Void. "I'll lower you, but you'll have to slip out of it and drop the rest of the way when I run out of cord."

He tied the other end tight around his waist. The cord was too thin to climb down and not long enough to work out a suitable body belay. He'd have to back up and walk down the hallway, using his mass as the counterweight.

Axe handed the confiscated pistol to Haley and slipped the loop around one of her arms. "The building should shelter us from the sniper," he said. "If not, run to the woods. Try to flank him while I draw his fire."

That'll be fun.

He turned to Void. "You're a smart guy, right?"

The hacker shrugged. He looked shocked from the night's activities—and nervous.

"Here's how this works," Axe said. "I've seen this before, and it's important you keep it in mind. You're valuable to them, right? They want to rescue you."

Void shrugged first, then nodded again. The guy didn't know what the hell was happening.

"Yeah," Axe said, "we're not letting them rescue you. Not going to happen. We've been authorized to use deadly force to keep you in custody."

A little white lie never hurt anyone.

Void looked from Axe to Haley and back, his eyes wide.

"The people out there won't shoot you on purpose," Axe continued. "But they don't want us to have you. They're grunts—soldiers—just doing a job. They don't want to die or end up in jail. At some point, they're going to realize it's a lot safer to cut their losses. They'll 'slip' and shoot you 'by mistake.' We'll get blamed for killing you. They'll escape and get paid. They'll be happy to get away…"

"And I'll be dead," Void said.

"Told you he was smart," Haley said.

"You were right, as usual. Actually," Axe said, holding his hand out to Haley, "give me the gun back for a minute."

Her eyebrows furrowed in confusion, but she took the pistol from the small of her back and handed it to him.

"I can't ask you to do this," he told her, just loud enough for Void to hear.

Axe turned to the hacker, holding the pistol at his side, and leaned in close to whisper.

"Most people don't get a choice. Say the word, and I'll end it now. You'll be gone in an instant and save all of us a great deal of time and trouble tonight. No pain, no stress, no bleeding out on the ground in agony later if they decide to take you out. I'll do you this favor and blame it on the bad guys. I've killed before—it's no big deal to me. And no cameras up here, right?" Axe made a show of looking around.

"It's not what we want—we'd prefer your help to figure out who attacked our country," he continued. "But it's up to you. We're very good at what we do. Go along with us, and we'll risk our lives to keep you safe. You can help us later. Or..." He leaned closer, lips nearly touching Void's ear. "Tell me. I promise you'll never see it coming and won't feel a thing. So—do you want to live or die? Decide. Right now."

He better not call my bluff.

"I want to go with you and live," Void croaked.

"You going to do what we say, when we say it? Answer all our questions? No hesitation, no bullshit?"

"Yes," he said, voice cracking. "Yes," he repeated, sounding more certain and in control.

Axe stared into the kid's eyes for a second. "Good man." He handed the pistol back to Haley, who smoothly slid it back into her waistband.

"Stand over there and wait for me," Axe told Void.

He immediately moved to the spot Axe pointed to and stood straight and still.

He's under control—for now.

"Um..." Void said. "One tiny problem."

Already?

"What's that?" Axe asked.

"I have a problem with heights."

"We're only on the second floor."

Void shrugged and blushed red. "Sorry. Can you, I don't know, knock me out or something?"

Don't tempt me, kid.

"You'll be fine," Axe said. "I promise." He turned to Haley. "Ready?"

I hope she knows me well enough to understand I was never going to shoot the kid, no matter what he said.

"Ready," she said, all business.

Axe stood back, bent his knee, and kicked the corner of the window with his heel until it shattered. He used his boot to clear out all the glass.

Moving up the hallway, he stopped when the cord connecting him to

Haley was taut. He nodded and Haley took a small step back. He advanced the same amount.

They continued. Haley stepped backward out the window, legs straight, like she was rappelling down the building.

The cord cut into Axe's waist.

She's put on weight.

He had a flash of the night he'd met Haley and ended up giving her a piggyback ride as he ran along a country road.

"Muscle weighs more than fat!" she muttered, reading his mind.

He walked slowly forward, lowering Haley, until he reached the window opening. Haley hung several feet off the ground.

She slipped out of the loop of rope and dropped lightly to the grass alongside the building.

No one shot at them.

In the distance, to the south, Tucci's helicopter circled.

Axe grabbed the rope, pulling it up as he stepped back into the hallway. Once he had the loop, he draped it under one of the hacker's arms, snugged it up into his armpit, and directed him to the window opening. The kid closed his eyes, trembling, but followed Axe's every instruction to the letter.

"Pretend you're playing tug-of-war," Axe said. "Keep your legs straight."

"It's only the second floor. It's only the second floor," Void chanted, holding back sobs as he walked out the window and down the wall like he'd been practicing all his life.

It took a few seconds of Haley coaching him, but he slipped out of the loop and dropped to the ground, landing in Haley's arms.

Bet that made it easier to jump.

There were still no shots fired.

Axe pulled up the cord. The knot at his waist would take too much time to untie. He coiled the rest of the cord, slipped it into his pocket, and called Tucci on the radio. "Southwest side of the building, outside of the security wire. Be aware there was a sniper, likely on the east side. Come in low and fast."

"Copy. What about the foot mobiles moving from the northeast corner of the grounds, by the inmate buildings?"

Damn it!

"Consider them hostile. You used to be a hot-shit pilot. Let's see if you've still got it."

The only reply was two clicks on the radio.

Axe squatted at the base of the window. He wasn't looking forward to this part. Careful to avoid any residual shards of glass, he clutched the tiny edge of the windowpane and lowered himself outside.

Once he hung from his arms, fully extended, he offered a silent apology to his poor old knees and dropped.

64

TAKING FIRE

Administrative Building
Federal Correctional Institution
South of Cumberland, Maryland

The helicopter came under fire as it screamed in from the west, its skids barely missing the treetops of the woods that extended past the loop road around the prison.

At the last possible second, the bird flared, spun to point south, and hovered six inches above the ground. The admin building blocked the gunfire for the moment until the tangos could move to get a better angle.

Axe and Haley ran full tilt, pulling Void along with them. He kept having to yank up his pants as they slipped down.

They dived into the open doorway of the helicopter.

Tucci lifted off, their feet dangling as they kicked and scrambled to get fully inside.

"Taking fire," Tucci yelled. He sounded angry at his precious helicopter being in combat.

"See?" Axe said into Void's ear. "Told you so! They're cutting their losses. You're expendable now."

The tangos were shooting to bring down the helicopter, not kill Void, but he didn't need to know that.

What's another little white lie to convince him to work with us?

Axe slid the side door closed, doing his best to ignore the treetops scraping the skids as they fought for the safety that distance and altitude would bring.

"We're clear," Tucci yelled a minute later. "Out of range."

Haley got Void strapped into one of the seats. He stared into space, his eyes unfocused, in shock from the night's ordeal.

"Nice flying!" Axe said into the headset as he buckled himself in next to Void. Haley did the same on the far side of the kid.

"Still got it," Tucci said, looking back and meeting Axe's eye with a grin.

The smile faded quickly as warning lights flashed.

Tucci swore and started coaxing the aircraft. "Come on, baby, you've got this. Hang in there for me," he murmured.

The helicopter started to shake, then shimmy.

They started losing altitude.

"We must have taken more fire than I realized," Tucci said, his voice laced with sadness, not fear. "Hold on. We're going down."

65

FREEDOM

"Why aren't we moving?" Salvatore Burattorio asked the soldier dressed as a paramedic in the front seat.

"We wait," the man answered with a Russian accent.

He doesn't speak much English, Sal thought.

"For the others?" he asked. The leader of the group had jumped out of the ambulance a few minutes earlier, calling on the others—except the driver—to follow. Gunfire came a minute later from near the admin building. Sal guessed they were trying to shoot down the helicopter he'd heard.

The driver nodded.

"I understand," Salvatore said.

He wasn't good at waiting. He'd waited years in prison, playing endless games of cards with the boys, working out, and doing yoga of all things. The longer they waited now, the more chance they had of getting caught.

Not going to happen.

"Anthony," he said softly to the largest man of his goon squad, with a nod toward the driver.

Anthony stooped low as he moved to the front of the ambulance, between the two seats, and wrapped his gigantic hands around the throat of the man driving the vehicle.

"You give me your weapon and get out, you live," Anthony said, squeezing. "Anything else, you die, and we take our chances."

The driver didn't have to understand all the words to get the idea. He would pass out from lack of oxygen in only a few seconds.

The soldier slowly drew his pistol from the holster on his hip and placed it on the passenger seat.

"Please," he gasped.

"Sal?" Anthony asked.

"Let him go," Sal said.

Anthony released his grip. "Get out."

The soldier opened the door and tumbled to the ground.

Anthony slid into the seat, racked it back as far as it would go, put the ambulance in gear, and floored it, angling for the back gates, driving them all to freedom.

66

THE AMBULANCE

Administrative Building
Federal Correctional Institution
South of Cumberland, Maryland

Being relatively new to the mercenary business—this was only his second contract since leaving the Russian Special Operations Forces—Petrov didn't know exactly how failing the mission would be received by their employer, but he doubted they would be happy.

At least we freed the mafia boss.

The ambulance roared by on the road outside of the security fence, leaving them behind. For a moment, Petrov thought he'd been betrayed by the mercenary he'd left in the driver's seat, but one look back showed the soldier standing dejectedly in front of the D Building.

The bus and second ambulance followed behind the first, carrying Jack and the prisoners from D Building.

Any minute now, the rest of the prison population would be released to make their escape on foot, ensuring chaos and making the search for any specific prisoner—which was supposed to be Dawson Reite—extremely challenging.

The prison break was meant to provide cover for the hacker's escape—which Nestor had botched.

Can it all be blamed on him, or will we be punished for our failure to shoot down the helicopter before it escaped?

They'd run toward the administrative building, firing on the helicopter, but the pilot had flown expertly. Most of the helicopter's approach and escape had been blocked by the building. They hadn't had the angle to bring it down, though he was certain they'd scored several direct hits.

He gathered the men around. "The mission is over. We have failed. We did what we could. Now we focus on escaping this country."

The men responded stoically, as soldiers do. They jogged toward the back gate, and the former ambulance driver raced to join them.

"We have an hour to lose ourselves in this country," Petrov said as they ran. "We can make it to the secondary vehicles by then. We have cash and alternate identification. We will drive nonstop to the large airport in Georgia and fly home."

He'd get his men free, then deal with the consequences of the failed mission.

Just like that, my promising career as a contract soldier is finished.

67

THE DEBT

Axe already had his hands tight to the chest harness holding him to the seat when Tucci yelled. "Brace!" the pilot said as the helicopter angled in, barely under control.

Axe smelled smoke.

That's never a good sign.

Haley held onto her harness, the backpack with their weapons strapped to her chest. She glanced over at him, and he gave her a reassuring smile.

"This happens all the time," he called.

He'd been in several helicopter crashes.

She raised her eyebrow at him but said nothing.

Void, having the worst night of his young life, sat with his eyes closed, his lips moving.

No atheists in a foxhole—or a crashing helicopter, I guess.

"Are we going to die?" Axe asked Tucci.

"Probably not," he grunted from the front, wrestling with the stick. "But it ain't gonna be pretty. Now hold on."

They hit hard.

The helicopter slid a ways before tipping onto its side.

The rotors snapped with a disconcerting sound.

Axe closed his eyes and joined Void in silent prayer.

Please, not today—and not like this.

Axe stared at the burning helicopter, at a loss for words. Flames leaped high into the air, illuminating the clearing they'd landed in and the woods around them.

Tucci's livelihood burned—and it was all Axe's fault.

Haley was busy working her phone, trying to find enough cell signal to send a text… or at least figure out where they were and how to get to civilization.

Void sat on the ground, hugging his knees and rocking silently.

His fear of heights now extends to flying, I bet.

Tucci stood, shoulders slumped, watching flames consume his helicopter.

"Sorry, brother," Axe said, resting his hand on Tucci's shoulder. "I know how much she meant to you."

Tucci stared at the burning wreckage and didn't reply for several seconds until he gruffly muttered, "You owe me a helicopter."

That's fair, but where am I going to get the money for a helicopter?

It wasn't the time to point out that he would never in his life make enough money to replace the craft. "You got it," Axe said.

I'll worry about how later.

Tucci sighed. "I guess we gotta save the world again first, though, don't we?"

"Well, yeah, sorry. Priorities and all that."

"I get it." He held up the shotgun. "I'm better at flying, but I saved this. And until you come through with my new ride, you're stuck with me. So where do we start?"

Axe kept his expression neutral, hiding his surprise.

We've got a new teammate.

Axe led them away from the crash site—a large clearing in the middle of the woods somebody was turning into a vacation home site.

Sorry about messing up your front yard with the wreckage of a helicopter, Axe thought to the unknown owner of the property.

At the end of the mile-long driveway that cut a path through the trees, they turned south onto a gravel road.

The stars shone incredibly bright in the spring darkness this far from any city.

The first road turned into a potholed but paved two-lane country highway. After more than two hours of walking, Marcus arrived, vectored in from the diner by Haley.

The smell of fresh sandwiches greeted them as they crammed into the older model sedan. Haley offered the front passenger seat to Axe and his long legs. Haley kept Void company in the back seat, along with Tucci.

"No shop talk in front of our 'friend,'" Haley told Marcus as soon as she slammed the door.

"Got it," Marcus said. He handed out the sandwiches and bottles of water, plus a diet soda for Haley.

Everyone ate except Void, stuck in the middle of the back seat between Tucci and Haley. At least he looked better than he had in the helicopter.

Life's been a series of video games and computer hacks until now. Welcome to the real world, Void.

"The roads aren't bad," Marcus said as he changed the destination on his phone's GPS and executed a three-point turn to drive back the way he'd come. "They have most of the accidents cleaned up."

"How many?" Void asked in a quiet, sad voice.

"Accidents?" Marcus asked.

"Deaths," Void answered.

A realization finally hit Axe, and the kid's earlier attitude made sense.

Those are the emotions he's been trying to hide this whole time: shame and guilt.

"We still don't know for sure," Marcus said. "And they're not breaking it down into how many people are dead from the cars being hacked versus the train derailments and other stuff."

"How many?" Void asked again. "Overall?"

Marcus glanced at Axe, who nodded for him to answer the question. "A least a thousand. Probably a lot more," Marcus said.

Void let out a soft, anguished cry, followed by a sob. "Stop the car!"

Axe nodded and Marcus pulled over quickly. Haley had her door open before the car had fully stopped. She stepped out with Void right behind her.

Void leaned over and vomited into the grass alongside the highway.

"There it is," Axe mumbled. "I knew it was coming."

Too much trauma tonight, and the guilt from the attacks finally pushed him over the edge.

Haley murmured into Void's ear and offered him a bottle of water.

Excellent. She can play the good guy.

After a few dry heaves, Void and Haley got back in the car.

"Sorry," Void muttered. He took a deep breath. "My hack... I was only doing it to show the vulnerabilities of the system. I never would have..."

Marcus braked, stopping the merge back onto the road in case Void had to throw up again, but Void waved him on. "I'm fine now."

Marcus sped up and pulled back onto the deserted highway.

It was the first Void had spoken about the hacking he'd done. There hadn't been time to get into it before.

So it actually was him. Score another point for Haley.

"I had to stop when I got arrested," Void said. "I was almost there. But I swear I didn't do this. Or coordinate it. What was done makes me sick," he mumbled.

Marcus slowed the car, glancing back to see if Void needed to throw up again. When the hacker just sat slumped in the seat, Marcus sped up.

Now's the time.

"The way I see it, you have a couple of choices," Axe told Void, turning in his seat as the hacker took a gulp of water and swished it around his mouth. "Help us, like you agreed back by the second-floor window—"

"I want to help," Void said before Axe could finish, sounding sincere —eager, even. "But what's the second option?"

Axe gave him a dead-eye stare, like Void was a piece of meat, a dead man walking. "Your choice, of course."

"I'll help," Void said. "What was done... that shouldn't have happened. I would have locked all the cars down so they couldn't move until I got paid—then I would have provided the info they needed to fix their security hole. Not this. Never anything like this."

Axe nodded, pleased. The kid could be full of crap, but he sounded like he meant what he said.

If we're dealing with hackers, we might as well have one of our own.

Marcus turned on the radio and selected a news station. "The president is scheduled to deliver an update from the Oval Office," he said. "We should listen. Unless..." He glanced at Axe, then back at Void.

"No, let's hear it," Axe said.

It can only help us for Void to see what hackers like him did to our country.

68

THE ADDRESS

The White House Oval Office
Washington, DC

President James Heringten finished the main body of the speech and prepared to wrap up his live Oval Office address.

The room was filled with a three-person video crew, several of his advisors, their ever-present aides, TV lights, a makeup person to keep his face from looking shiny on camera—and smooth out some of the stress lines—and Chad David, his Chief of Staff.

Once again, the United States had been attacked.

On his watch.

It wouldn't matter to anyone—in his party or the other—that it had been Congress that refused his repeated requests over the last several years to strengthen the country's cybersecurity.

Budgets were always tight; there was never enough to go around.

Planes, tanks, and warships were big projects. They were easy to see and employed a lot of people to build.

Spending money on geeks sitting in darkened rooms with large computer monitors wasn't as interesting or easy to grasp as a missile fired from a plane or a new aircraft carrier.

He'd get blamed for the attacks.

He could handle it. It was part of the job.

As was consoling the nation in times of crisis.

Other politicians could—were already—taking potshots at him and those they needed to beat in the next election, politicizing today's horrors.

James had to rise above the rhetoric and take on the much more difficult task of leading the nation.

He started the closing section of the speech. Earlier, he'd explained as simply as possible how unknown people could enter commands on keyboards and harm Americans.

The country now understood the threat computer hackers presented. Too little, too late in James' mind, but it was what it was. They had to move forward from here.

He stared directly into the camera and spoke with full emotion, reading from the teleprompter the words he and the speechwriters had come up with.

"Instead of facing us as adversaries, at the negotiating table or on the field of battle, our enemy cowardly hacked our vehicles. Our water processing. Our homes and offices. Our trains.

"We have been attacked.

"So many have died.

"So many more have been injured.

"Others have been overwhelmed, put out of work, and forced to deal with the aftermath of these hacks.

"Our enemy wants to bring us to our knees, but I say this: America still stands.

"Though injured, we stand.

"Though grieving, we stand.

"Though livid with rage, we stand.

"To those of you responsible, hear this."

The president paused for a long moment. When he spoke again, his eyes were narrow and his voice ice cold. "If you had a part in this, your days are numbered. We are coming for you. This, I promise."

After another pause, his tone softened. "To my fellow Americans and anyone affected by today's attacks, you are in my prayers and all of our thoughts. Words and prayers won't bring back loved ones, won't change the situation, won't alleviate your suffering. But know that you are not alone. The country—and the good people of the world—stand with you. Together, we will get through this."

James paused. The teleprompter displayed the closing words of the speech.

He wanted more.

Speaking straight from the heart, he added an unscripted line.

"We will have our vengeance," he said in his cold voice, followed by a single resolute nod.

This is my promise.

"May God bless you, and may God bless and keep the United States of America," he finished in a softer voice.

James stared into the television camera lens long after the large red light went dark and an aide quietly said, "We're clear, Mr. President."

69

THE LIGHTS

Outside Ashburn, Virginia

After the president's speech, Haley got Marcus's attention and mouthed the letters "SDR."

No one could have followed them by car after they'd been picked up after the helicopter crash, but protocol was protocol.

Marcus doubled back the way they had come, made U-turns, sped through yellow stoplights, and generally made sure they weren't being followed.

Haley relaxed slightly. There were far fewer cars on the road than there would normally be, which made it easy to see that no one was interested in them.

But they still had a long way to go before she could get back to work at the diner.

Marcus brought them quickly up to speed.

"Lots of train derailments," he said, "both freight and passenger trains. There are a lot of people dead and more affected, especially because of the toxic chemicals released from some of the freight trains."

"How did they do it?" Haley asked Void.

"It wouldn't be hard," he said in a sad voice.

"What else?" Axe asked from the front seat.

"No deaths from this so far, but there are several dozen freshwater and wastewater treatment plants offline. It's causing a big problem. People can't last long without fresh water, and there's no solution to it."

"You have to catch whoever is behind this," Void said. "If you get their computers, it will be easy. Otherwise, even I probably couldn't reverse-engineer their hacks."

"Got it," Marcus said. "And finally, the cars. You knew about that part. Thousands—tens of thousands—of newer cars went berserk and targeted people, buildings, and other vehicles. A lot of people were run over. It's pretty gruesome."

Void had started out depressed but fiddled in his seat, getting angrier the more he heard.

"Do you think that's all we'll see, or are there more attacks coming?" Haley asked, mostly talking to Void.

"I swear, my whole attention was on hacking the cars," the kid said. "With the money involved, I knew that not only would my name make history—my hacker name, I mean—but the companies would gladly pay me off to get control back and learn how I broke in so they could fix the vulnerabilities. This whole thing makes me sick. Well," he mumbled. "Obviously. You saw that."

"What's your best guess? Could there be more to come?" Haley asked.

That's the million-dollar question.

"Of course. Nothing is impenetrable. Well, except the military, which you guys have locked up pretty tight."

He filled them in on how he would have approached the various hacks and offered detailed suggestions for ways to fix the problems... and investigate if any other important infrastructure was at risk.

Haley had her phone out, recording his stream-of-consciousness report for the IT geeks at the office—now the diner—to sift through.

"Who was that at the prison? Who tried to rescue you?" Axe said when Void seemed to be slowing down.

"I don't know," Void said.

Sitting right next to him, Haley's shoulder touched his. There was no way he could lie and have her not sense it.

He's a kid playing at being a grown-up. To him, hacking was a fun game—a way to make money and a name for himself. Until it wasn't.

"The president is right," Haley said. "We're going to find the people behind the attack. With your help, I hope, Void."

The hacker nodded quickly.

"Let's hope they're done hitting us," Axe said. "It's tragic, but we will get through this."

There were resolute words of agreement from everyone in the car, including Void.

As they crested a hill and started into Ashburn, Virginia, the suburbs spread out before them.

One second, everything was fine.

The next, all the lights went out.

70

THE PROMISE

Lux View Marina Tower
Floor 14—Kitchen and Staff Areas
Dubai, United Arab Emirates

As usual, Jamil arrived early to prepare and serve coffee to Malik.

He almost hadn't come to work this morning.

Only knowing that his wife's hand awaited for a short while—and what would happen to her in Afghanistan should he desert his employer—got him up, onto the metro, and into the elevator to the servant areas on the fourteenth floor.

He had decided against writing a letter to his wife. How could he apologize for what he had done, for what had happened?

In the end, he hoped she knew how much he regretted his actions.

In the large kitchen where meals were prepared for Malik, the staff, and the young men on the fifteenth floor, Jamil made a pot of coffee.

After his coworkers' reaction to him and his wife's hand hanging from his neck all day yesterday, he welcomed the solitude that came from arriving earlier than the rest of the staff, aside from the day shift guards and Malik's personal butler.

While working late the night before, he had noticed Gogol—Malik's younger brother—arrive on the penthouse floor.

Seeing him had helped Jamil make his final decision. Gogol and Malik had the same blood. They both would have to die for Jamil and his wife to be free and safe.

For now, Jamil was powerless. He could get close to Malik, but though he and the boss were of similar build, Malik had fought and killed. So had Gogol. During the many years of conflict in Afghanistan, Jamil had done exactly what he did now. From the time he was six years old, he had been a servant, cleaning up, running errands, making food, and serving tea.

He didn't have the skill to get revenge.

But eventually, there would be an opening, and he would strike.

He poured the piping hot coffee into the tall china coffeepot, loaded up the silver cart, and prepared to bring it to Malik.

He had another hour with his wife's hand on the twine around his neck. He touched it gently, remembering her face.

Someday, my love, I will make this up to you.

71

BAD NEWS

Lux View Marina Tower
Penthouse—Floor 35
Dubai, United Arab Emirates

"Well done so far," Abdul said, picking up his coffee cup from the saucer, which had been delivered precisely on time by Jamil. His wife's severed hand still dangled from the twine around his neck.

Abdul ignored him, as did Gogol, who sat across from Abdul at the small round table on the west-facing deck, sipping his own coffee.

His younger brother had done well with managing the hackers, and they'd dealt the Americans a crushing blow.

Thousands were injured and dead.

America was in crisis—exactly as planned.

But as much success as they'd experienced so far, Abdul saw his brother had bad news to share.

He waited until Jamil had left with the silver serving cart and the heavy sliding door was closed behind him.

"Tell me, brother," Abdul said. "What is on your mind?"

He had a bad feeling he knew what was coming.

"The prison break failed," Gogol said. "All went to plan until two people, a man and a woman, arrived via helicopter moments before the team's assault. Reite was taken from his cell building to an administrative building housing the visitor rooms." Gogol detailed the change of mission and its ultimate failure. "The captain in charge is dead. The second-in-command is leading the rest of the men to an airport to fly back to their country as soon as possible."

Abdul pondered the situation, not pleased but unsurprised.

This complicates matters.

After two sips of coffee, he had an answer. "The captain—Russian?"

"Yes sir."

"And his men?" Abdul had given specific instructions and expected them to have been followed, but confirming them never hurt.

"Yes sir. All but one. The other is Chinese. All but the Chinese soldier —a sniper—were captured on numerous surveillance cameras," Gogol said. "All are former Russian special forces. They will be blamed."

"Excellent. We did all we could given the difficult, last-minute nature of the mission. Its failure will still further our goals. But…"

I must try.

"Is there anything that can be done to track down Reite?"

"I have all the hackers on it. Whoever picked him up in the helicopter must be part of an intelligence organization. Police wouldn't have those resources."

"Which makes it unlikely we will find him in time," Abdul said with a frown.

Although Abdul didn't understand most of the technology they were using to harm America and had never operated a computer, he could read people. It was his gift. Others could invent the machines. Some could write the programs that made them run or break inside them to do harm. But it took a person like him to run an organization.

To exact revenge.

With his cold, calculating mind and decades of experience, this plan was his chance to lead his people out of poverty and a dead-end existence, paving the way for their supremacy for the rest of the century and beyond.

But he, too, had his orders.

We must at least make the effort.

"Can the hackers find where Dawson Reite went?" Abdul asked.

George hesitated before answering. "I asked the same question. They could by accessing a satellite and using the visual logs to track the man and woman who took him. But," Gogol said, "the satellite hack is a one-time use. The intrusion will quickly be discovered, and they will be kicked out. The vulnerability will be fixed, and we won't be able to use it a second time or on other satellites."

Abdul considered the possibilities and weighed the pros and cons.

"However," Gogol said with a clever smile, "the satellite belongs to Russia, so…" He let the implication hang in the air.

Perfect. If the Americans wonder how they were tracked, Russia will once again be suspected.

"Do it. Tell the remaining soldiers their work is not done," Abdul said. "Make the hackers find Dawson Reite. Get him back in one piece. Kill the man and woman who ruined our plan… and everyone they are associated with."

72

THE FLU

Secretary of State Hank Wilson lay on the hospital bed, the upper part tilted so he could sit up and watch the television mounted on the wall.

"What time was your shift over?" he asked Special Agent Martin, who refused to go home.

"It's not a problem, Mr. Secretary."

"It is if you're too tired to keep me from getting attacked," Wilson said. "Go on now. Get some rest. I'm fine, and you have a lot of other agents here. You did well today."

Hank was thankful there hadn't been any television footage of him being rolled out of the hotel on a stretcher. The rest of the day's events would have easily overshadowed his little trouble, but the news would have used it in their "In other news…" segments to break up the horror of the day's cyberattacks.

Hank just wanted to be left alone. The vomiting was bad enough. The bloody diarrhea—and being helped quickly to the bathroom to handle it—was worse.

The fewer people who saw him like this, the better.

"That's an order," Hank said, though the words came out with none of the force they would have earlier today.

Martin nodded, probably taking pity on him. "Yes, Mr. Secretary. Do you need anything before I go?"

"Just send the nurse in again, please."

"I can—"

"No!" It came out harsher than Hank intended. "Just get the nurse, please."

Quickly, he wanted to add but didn't. He had multiple nurses dedicated to him, and a whole team of doctors trying to figure out what was wrong with him. Martin could send one in on his way out.

The flu, stomach bug, gastroenteritis—or whatever they thought it was this hour—had come on suddenly.

His fault—he wasn't the kid he used to be and had been overdoing it lately. And the flu was going around; one of the staff had stayed home with some kind of bug.

Everyone was overreacting. He'd be fine in a day or two and be able to get back to negotiating various agreements with the North Koreans, Chinese, Russians, Iranians, and the Taliban before heading to the Middle East Peace Summit.

Nothing in the world could keep him from helping the vice president at that historic event.

73

THE CELEBRITY

The Nighttime-Daytime Diner
Suburban Arlington, Virginia

Axe stood outside the small car, glad the drive from the helicopter crash site was over. He reached up, stretching, feeling the pain in his ribs and his aching knees.

It had been a hell of a twenty-four hours, and the mission was far from over. At least he'd get some more food, coffee, and maybe find a wall to lean against for a nap.

The diner was unaffected by the power outage that had hit Ashburn and its suburbs. It was filled with men and women Axe knew to be the analysts Haley worked with, though he'd only met Nancy, Dave, Gregory, and Marcus.

On the other side of the closed blinds covering the windows, shadows hunched over computers and moved around the room.

Haley turned Void over to Axe before going into the diner to check in with Gregory.

"Will you let me help?" Void asked from next to him. "I want to help."

Void had made the point clear on the drive, including through the long stretch of suburbia after the electricity had gone out.

"Help who?" Axe asked, once again searching for tells that might reveal deception or evasiveness. "Yourself? Us? Or the people who attacked the country?"

"I can help you get them. And…" he said after a pause, "if it's not too much to ask, let my actions help me."

The kid had the decency to look sheepish. His black curly hair was a mess, and the prison uniform still made him look goofy with the too-small shirt, too-big pants, and cheap slip-on shoes.

"You're not getting out of this. You're going back to jail."

The hacker's shoulders slumped. "I know. I get that, but I still want to help."

"Why?" Axe asked. He wanted to believe that the kid had seen the devastation of the country and realized his vehicle hack might have been the inspiration for part of it, but he worried that they were all about to get played by a highly intelligent guy who looked like a harmless dork.

Void's lips pressed together, and his eyes burned with anger. He shook his head. "I should tell you I want to help the country. That I feel bad for people, and that's partly true. What I found—the holes in the self-driving systems… I never intended to hurt anyone. That's not who I am. Just the opposite. I wanted to prevent that." Void met Axe's eyes and revealed an intensity previously unseen. "But the truth is, I want to take them down for perverting my hack."

That's real. There's no faking that level of emotion.

"And, you know," he added quickly, "all that other stuff. Helping people."

"It's not up to me," Axe said. "Haley's boss will decide. If he agrees, though… You remember the hallway? When I gave you a choice?"

Void froze for a moment before nodding.

"That would have been quick. Painless." Axe stepped closer, invading Void's personal space.

Dawson took a step away, but Axe kept pace, intimidating him with his closeness.

Axe gestured to the blind-covered windows of the diner and the shadows of men and women working. "You're probably smarter than all these people put together, at least when it comes to computers and hacking."

He moved his head close enough for his lips to brush Void's ear. "Try to pull one over on them—no matter how small, like sending a message or revealing your location—and it won't go quickly and painlessly. I'll take you out back. We'll have a nice, long chat, just you and me. I will hurt you in the most excruciating ways... and places. Imagine never being able to use a computer again. Imagine your worst fears realized." Axe paused, giving Void some time to let his mind consider the possibilities before whispering, "Do we understand each other?"

Axe could smell the hacker's fear as Dawson nodded vigorously.

Axe hid his smile.

Once you convince them you're a monster, they'll believe anything.

Axe escorted Void around the outside of the diner with Haley leading the way.

They went through the back door straight into the kitchen. Three young men dressed in khaki pants with baggy, wrinkled dress shirts and one young woman wearing black jeans with a faded black band T-shirt under a black sport coat waited expectantly, all holding laptop computers.

Haley cleared her throat. "Okay, everybody, this is Eternal Void."

The IT team stood in stunned silence, eyes wide.

No one seemed to care about Void's dopey clothes or mess of black hair. The IT team exchanged excited glances. They looked like they couldn't believe their luck.

They're meeting a celebrity.

The dark-haired woman spoke up. "The Eternal Void? I thought you were in prison."

"I was," Void answered with a boyish grin.

"We broke him out," Axe said.

"Who are you?" one of the men blurted out.

"I'm the guy who was never here." It came out with more force than Axe had intended—along with a dangerous vibe, he realized as the kid took a step back, pressing himself against a prep counter and holding his laptop defensively in front of his chest.

The rest of the IT group looked at Haley for reassurance.

Axe put up his hands and stepped in before she could speak. "I'm on your side, but seriously. You never saw me. The story is that Void here came in on his own—he escaped and found you using super-duper hacking skills. Then he offered to help get to the bottom of this hacking thing. Didn't he?" Axe asked Void with a nudge.

"That's exactly how it happened," Void said in a firm voice with a straight face.

Haley had outlined the working conditions to Void before they walked around the back of the diner, but Axe wanted to explain it to the IT crew himself.

Haley had a reputation at the Central Analysis Group. Her ability to look someone in the eye and make them quake had improved tremendously in the past months. Still, having the law laid down by a dangerous stranger would make the instructions hit home that much harder.

"Under no circumstances is this man to touch a computer," Axe said. "I don't care if it would be easier and faster for him to have his hands on the keyboard or mouse. He explains. You type or click—and only when you understand exactly what will happen when you do. If you don't know, you ask, even if it hurts your ego."

Axe paused, looking each of the four IT crew members in the eye. "Does anyone here have a question—or problem—with these instructions? Because I'm the one who you're going to deal with if you don't follow them to the letter." He let the threat hang in the air for several seconds. "And you really don't want that," he said, just loud enough for them to hear.

The IT crew glanced again at Haley, but she was no help. She looked at them without a bit of reassurance on her face.

One by one, the IT crew nodded at Axe.

"Good," Haley said to them and to Void. "Get to work. Find us the people who attacked our country."

74

THE LEADER

The White House Situation Room
Washington, DC

Just when James thought they had things under control, someone had pulled the rug out from under them.

The power had gone off around the country.

Several power plants that everyone thought were safe had been hacked somehow.

At least they didn't rush me to the bunker this time.

"Come on, people," James said, taking a breath and getting his patience back before continuing. Half of leadership seemed to be setting the correct tone for the situation. A boring day of meetings required a leader deliberately focused on the details; calm competence was needed during a crisis.

"Let's start with what we know, what we suspect, and what we need to understand," James said.

"Mr. President," Diego Samuels, the NCTC director, said, standing from his spot halfway down the right side of the long table that filled the Situation Room. "The attacks have been all cyber in nature. There have been no physical attacks, whether with armed terrorists, planes, or what have you. This destruction has been facilitated entirely via the internet."

"Including the power plants? Damn it, I thought we had those locked down tight."

On the TV monitor at the end of the room, the CISA director cleared his throat and looked down at his notes. His thinning hair was still a mess. "We thought so, too, Mr. President. And yes, those were all done electronically. We, um, don't know how yet, sir."

James let that admission hang in the air for several seconds before moving on. "Who is behind these attacks?"

Samuels, who seemed to have taken point of the mess for now, shifted his weight, fidgeting like he'd rather be anywhere besides standing in the Situation Room and admitting they were all clueless. "That would move us into the realm of what we don't know, sir."

"Best guess?"

An uncomfortable silence filled the room.

No one else spoke. The men and women around the table and on the teleconferencing windows on the TV busied themselves with making notes or examining papers in front of them.

"Anyone," James said. "Don't feel left out. Jump in any time."

His dry tone broke the tension slightly and garnered him small smiles.

"Let me get this straight," James said. "We've been attacked across the country, from the largest cities to the smallest towns. We have more than a thousand people dead from runaway vehicles and train crashes. Our infrastructure is a mess, with cars inside structures, fire sprinkler systems flooding buildings that aren't on fire and not turning on for the ones that are in flames. People's toilets, sinks, and bathtubs are backing up with sewer water."

"Only in several smaller cities and towns, Mr. President," one advisor said from the far end of the table. James glared at him, and the man's face flushed red.

"Those same… smaller cities and towns, you said… don't have fresh water. And among many other issues, a few minutes after my televised Oval Office address, eleven small to mid-size power plants serving millions of people go offline."

He took a breath to once again calm himself. "And no one here can tell me who attacked us, whether we're still vulnerable, or what we can do to retaliate."

We're all exhausted. How can I best lead them?

James stood. Everyone in the room stood with him.

"I know you and your people are doing all you can, as fast as possible.

Keep at it and pass along my gratitude for their efforts, along with the thanks of all Americans. Rotate people on and off shift, whether they want to stop or not. We're not going to fix this in the next hour. Make sure your people sleep—and you do as well. That's an order. A few hours of rest might just result in a breakthrough. Remember, displays of dedication aren't as important as actual results. No one is going to be faulted for stepping away and coming back recharged and better focused."

James looked around the room as the mood changed. People stood taller and met his eye. "I'm going to follow my own orders. We'll meet back here at zero five hundred."

If we make it to morning without another hit.

75

HUNTING

The Nighttime-Daytime Diner
Suburban Arlington, Virginia

Haley hunted.

For the past hour, she had sat at the back booth, close to the kitchen. Day, swing, and night shift analysts crammed into the diner, filling every seat. More had staked out wall space and the prep counters. The owner kept everyone supplied with coffee and sandwiches.

Tucci sat in her SUV out front with his shotgun. He'd volunteered for guard duty along with the evening security crew, who had reported to the diner instead of the burned shell of the Central Analysis Group headquarters.

Nancy, Dave, Gregory, and Marcus at her table; Void in the kitchen with the IT crew; Axe wandering around restlessly... all of it had slipped away as she found the zone.

Her fingers danced on the keyboard, entering searches, making notes, building a clearer picture of what they were dealing with—and up against.

Occasionally, she glanced up to give Gregory orders, only belatedly remembering she needed to ask her boss instead of making demands on him. She'd offer an apologetic smile. He'd shake his head with a look of amusement... and get her what she needed.

Haley's small piece of the puzzle came together relatively quickly.

She didn't need to figure out the big picture. There wasn't time for that. By working together, breaking the problem down into manageable pieces, she hoped they'd have something for Gregory to take to the president by morning.

An expectant, excited energy filled the diner. The other analysts were in the zone as well. Everyone would contribute.

This might actually work.

PART 3

THURSDAY

76

THE CONFESSION

Dmitry, the director of Russia's Foreign Intelligence Service, sat in the last seat on the right side of an incredibly long conference table, joined by two dozen of President Nikitin's top advisors. The group was heavily tilted toward men in military and intelligence, but foreign affairs, economics, and other advisors all waited silently for their president to finally speak.

Dmitry's position was the least prestigious spot—as far from the president as possible.

Have I lost my status?

Dmitry had enjoyed a close working relationship with the president for the past several months.

That appeared to have changed as of this morning.

He has to know I had no hand in the attack on America.

Dmitry would never betray the president's confidence or do anything to go against him. He wouldn't end up like Orlov, his mentor and former director of the intelligence service. He wouldn't allow himself to be put in a position where he would either need to kill himself or face being murdered.

The president, who looked more like a former college professor or an accountant than Russia's latest leader, had been pacing for almost a minute, his face growing more flushed by the second. His thinning dark hair showed his scalp turning red, too. His eyes were squinted, making his bushy dark eyebrows pull together and downward.

Instead of the old, gray corduroy sport coat, dark slacks and, turtleneck sweater he often wore day-to-day when he didn't have meetings with outsiders, the president had on a stylish charcoal-colored suit, light blue shirt, and red tie.

He looked presidential—and angry.

Dmitry had arrived early, prepared for a private audience with President Nikitin, who had taken a liking to him. Dmitry always told the truth, whether the president wanted to hear it or not. For this, the president had welcomed him into his inner circle, using him as a sounding board and a trusted personal advisor.

But instead of the pre-meeting private audience, Dmitry had been ordered to sit at the far end of the table.

Have I been played this whole time?

The president had proven himself to be a wolf in sheep's clothing, allowing the world and his fellow Russians to underestimate him so he could better achieve his aims.

Dmitry may have fallen for the show of trusted friendship despite knowing how intelligent and scheming the man was.

"Unlike so many of my predecessors, I am not unreasonable," the president finally began. His clipped words and tight, angry voice contrasted with what he said. "Grading on a curve, as it were," he said in a softer tone, with a hint of a smile, referencing his college professor look and style.

The men around the table chuckled uncertainly, not accustomed to a president who made jokes at all—let alone about himself.

The president had been struggling to turn the tide of the country from a fading dinosaur in danger of going extinct to a robust, modern, civilized society. The Russia he inherited had been on the brink of a war planned by the previous president, who had meant to invade Ukraine, Latvia, and Lithuania.

Nikitin came to power, canceled the invasion, and looked behind the facade to see a country barely staying on its feet.

He'd cleaned house, eliminating corrupt politicians and military leaders at all levels while scrambling to quietly rebuild—or at least shore up where he could.

Dmitry had helped the president hide the true nature of the "accidents" that befell so many of the corrupt men, keeping the true reason for their deaths from the West, along with the truth of the rot within the country from the rest of the world.

Until President Nikitin had more money coming into the country and more secure alliances, Russia was incredibly vulnerable to attack from without or revolt from within.

If the true nature of Russia's military and economic vulnerability were known, the country—and Nikitin's rule—weren't safe.

"You have all seen what is happening in America," Nikitin continued. "The death toll mounts. Most of their systems might not come back online for a while, from what you tell me," he said with a nod to Leo, the man next to Dmitry. He was also young, in his forties—thinner and paler even than Dmitry, who himself didn't get out into what little sun there was to find during the spring in Moscow.

Leo was a former computer geek who had suddenly found himself in a position of power due to a love of computers and an impeccable family lineage, with a long history of loyalty to the country... or at least its rulers. He looked the part, too. He had fashionable Western-made rimless glasses that mostly disappeared against his face and sharp features, from his nose to a wide forehead—emphasized by his dark hair, which he kept swept back.

"They have been hit hard, Mr. President," Leo said quickly, looking eager to get an opportunity to speak in front of the group of the country's leaders.

"As yet, no one has told me who is behind the attack on the Americans," Nikitin continued. "Or whether we could be next."

The men around the table shifted uncomfortably. Aside from Leo, few had direct experience with computers. They were older, from a different era. The military men were more comfortable with tanks, planes, and rifles.

The intelligence men focused not on computer hacking or stealing secrets via technology but on recruiting spies in foreign countries using blackmail. The country wasn't rich enough for hard-currency financial bribes.

And more than half of the people at the table spent much of their time spying on the citizens of Russia, making sure they didn't rise up against the government.

All—aside from Dmitry and Leo—had grown fat and wealthy from their positions and were much more loyal to the established ways keeping them comfortable than they were to Nikitin.

Only Dmitry and Leo led the charge—such as it was—to recruit and manage a group of hackers officially unaffiliated with the government yet at the same time under its total control.

"I gathered you here to learn whether any of you have a hand in this attack," President Nikitin said as he turned to stare at the men who truly controlled the country.

Dmitry sensed genuine shock from everyone around the table.

"Some of you see war with America as inevitable and have long recommended a nuclear first strike." The president shook his head. "This is madness, of course. But I worry that there may be among you some who saw a cyberwarfare first strike as a way to force my hand—our hands— into a war with the West. A war, I might add, that we are unprepared for and don't need." He paused. "At this time," he muttered loudly enough for all to hear.

The men who had taken the most bribes or stolen the most equipment to sell on the black market were gone from "accidents" they had recently suffered.

There were plenty of men at the table, however, who were corrupt. They had simply been less greedy or more careful in their illicit actions. Everyone, though, guilty or innocent, sat stiffly and stared expressionlessly at the president.

"You will have an opportunity to privately admit your involvement," President Nikitin said softly. "If you confess, the punishment will be swift but fair. You will be allowed to resign. You will keep all your accumulated wealth. Your families will be unharmed, but you will be imprisoned for ten years in what I will tell the Americans is a horrible work camp but will actually be a comfortable dacha along the sea. There will be no retaliation other than this house arrest."

The president's offer hung in the air.

While no one stirred, the air felt charged with electricity.

Those are extremely generous terms to offer a traitor.

Dmitry's mentor—Orlov—had been ordered killed for running an operation against America without telling the president. He hadn't been offered any way out besides death.

"If you do not confess, I will eventually find out your involvement." President Nikitin smiled slightly, but his eyes were cold. "Many of you believe I am too soft to be president. My offer only cements that idea in your mind, I'm sure. However, consider the many men who have resigned, fallen ill, or had unfortunate accidents since I have taken office," he said in a soft, tight voice. "I have been selective. Careful. A few of you may have wondered, but most of you likely have not suspected the truth—I had them eliminated for stealing from or undermining this great country."

Whether the men around the table had suspected the disappearances were more than accidents or not, their mood changed. Dmitry sensed they now understood their supposedly gentle, professorial president was actually a predator capable of anything, as Dmitry had known for months.

"When I learn who is behind this cyberattack, whether it is from my internal security or when the Americans figure it out and tell me, things will not go well for you… or your loved ones."

Nikitin made eye contact with each man at the table, one by one, as the silence and discomfort grew.

"I will see each of you in my office, where you will stand before my desk and confess—or swear on the lives of your friends, family, and all you hold dear—that you had nothing to do with the attack and have no knowledge of who did." He pointed at the man closest to him on his left. "You first. Come."

The president turned and walked away as all at the table scrambled to their feet.

The first man hurried to follow the president out the door to his office.

77

FIELD PERSONNEL

The Kremlin

Dmitry was the last to enter the president's large, luxurious formal office.

"I'm sorry," President Nikitin said, standing and waving him over. "I should have told you my plans, but…"

"You needed it to be a surprise to everyone," Dmitry said.

"Exactly." The president sat and gestured to the chair in front of his desk for Dmitry to join him.

"Did anyone confess?"

The president barked out a laugh. "No, and I believe them. But I made my point." He looked expectantly at Dmitry.

"You are not one to be trifled with?"

"Yes. And things must change. I have eliminated the worst, but every man at the table—except you and perhaps Leo—is corrupt to some degree."

Dmitry couldn't speak for the others but didn't doubt the truth of the president's statement. Men at high levels of power worldwide tended to believe the rules didn't apply to them. They did, however, know how to cover their tracks better than the ones the president had already eliminated.

Drawing himself straight in the chair, Dmitry said, "I will formally state that I did not have a hand in the attack nor knowledge of anyone's involvement."

"If I suspected you in the slightest, you wouldn't be here," the president responded. "And as much as I believe no one at the table today is behind the attacks on America, we need to be prepared for what I fear is coming next."

"Which is?" Dmitry asked. He had his own guesses but wanted to hear what the country's leader thought.

President Nikitin shook his head and didn't answer the question. "Why don't we know more? The hacker collective is under your directive, is it not?"

"It is, sir. Although, for deniability reasons, they are not technically part of the Foreign Intelligence Service. 'Red Bear' is the group's code name. You should be aware that they have been working on hacks similar to what happened in America," Dmitry admitted. "However, we are not to blame in this."

The president nodded. "I understand. My main concern is whether we are the next target of whoever did this. My other worry is the Americans will blame us when—this time, at least—we are innocent."

Red Bear had done plenty of other hacking at the behest of the Foreign Intelligence Service: actively sowing discord in America via social media, probing all infrastructure, looking for openings, and attempting to hack every political figure, no matter how minor. You never knew who would one day go from school board president to mayor of a small city, governor to congressperson, or senator to president.

Russia was far from alone in the matter. The Americans did it, too, along with the Israelis, who were by far the experts at the long-simmering cold cyberwar.

"The problem, Mr. President, is that in the past year to eighteen months, some of the best hackers have left."

"I didn't realize we gave them that option," the president said dryly.

"Yes, well, normally we don't. These are hackers, however. One day they were at work; the next, several were gone."

"Where? To America and the riches of its Silicon Valley?"

"Due to their special skills, they were difficult to track. We lost them initially, but we eventually traced them to Dubai. It may take a while, but we're good at finding people."

"What are they doing there? Working against us?"

"We don't know, sir. They entered a luxury building—very secure—and, as far as we know, haven't emerged."

"How long has it been since you found them?"

"Almost a year, Mr. President."

"You lost the trail."

"No, sir. With respect, I mean. They have not emerged. Our presence in the area is minimal and surveillance in such an opulent area is difficult, so we have not pursued this further. But now, perhaps…"

"Yes. Allocate more resources." The president paused, thinking. "And strengthen our cyber defenses. Take entire systems offline if need be. Insert verbal confirmation into any essential-order framework. I do not want missiles flying or other acts of war conducted because a hacker—possibly one of our very own—presses a button in Dubai."

"Yes, Mr. President."

"Find out exactly where our hackers are, what they have done, and who they are working for. If the opportunity presents itself, question at least one using whatever methods are necessary to get the entire truth."

Dmitry nodded at what the president had ordered—and left out.

"No," Nikitin said with a firm shake of his head. "Do not kill them. They are more valuable alive."

"Sir, we cannot turn them over to the Americans," Dmitry said.

"To prevent a war, we certainly can if needed. But I would prefer to learn all they know about any other vulnerabilities the United States of America might have… and about our own. Though the most important aspect of this all is to convince the Americans that we are innocent and did not attack them. Understood?"

Dmitry nodded. He would manage the mission himself. He stood, assuming the president had finished with him.

President Nikitin held up his hand, stopping him. "I still have a concern. All signs point toward us having attacked America. It may not have been one of the men around the table this morning, but there are others with enough power and connections to make it happen."

He's referencing the many oligarchs who have corrupted our country.

"Given what has happened, what I need is someone trustworthy to handle the situation. Beyond reproach. Above the political fray and not swayed by money, power, or ambition. A person whom I can trust… no matter which direction it may go."

He's describing me.

Dmitry's pulse pounded at the thought of having to go to Dubai instead of managing others. He wasn't field personnel. The president eyed Dmitry with an amused shake of his head. "A qualified field agent."

Dmitry did his best not to sag in relief.

Definitely not me.

Months before, Dmitry's hands had shaken so much holding the syringe he'd been ordered to use to kill Orlov, his mentor, that he and Orlov had been worried he'd stab himself instead.

Orlov had killed himself in part to spare Dmitry that ordeal.

"In this line of work, Mr. President, what you are asking is..." Dmitry trailed off, an item from a few weeks prior popping into his mind.

"Nearly impossible, I realize."

Dmitry recalled a recent report that had come across his desk. He sketched out a plan in his mind and met the president's eyes. "Mr. President, I may have just the person."

78

A GOOD DAY

Chad David, the Chief of Staff to the president of the United States of America, could have walked the three miles from the White House to his townhouse in Georgetown. It would have cleared his head and reduced his stress.

A fast run would have been even better.

Unfortunately, he could no longer walk anywhere but through the halls of the White House. And his only running was six miles every morning on the treadmill.

He also could have easily defended himself from a rare street criminal who might approach him on the way. As a former SEAL, he would have welcomed the chance to mix it up a little.

How many years since my last fight?

Decades, probably. Fights with random people were discouraged while on active duty. While it might seem cowardly to outsiders, SEALs had to be the voice of reason, calming others down or flat-out avoiding conflicts, even if it meant walking away from drunks, idiots... or drunk idiots.

Besides, it was much more likely a lobbyist or businessperson would approach him looking for "just five minutes of your time" to "run a few things by you the president needs to see" than someone would try to attack him on the street.

However, his position required certain protections and security measures. Instead of a pleasant walk in the cool spring darkness, he rode through the quiet streets of DC in the center SUV of a three-vehicle convoy, keeping himself awake by searching the sidewalks for threats, exactly like the two Secret Service agents in suits in the front seat.

It was either that or fall asleep for the nine-minute ride and be embarrassed when one of the agents coughed loudly to wake him up once they arrived outside the townhouse, which he'd only had to suffer once.

For years, Chad had worked eighteen to twenty-hour days, helping James Heringten become—and stay—president. The position of James's right-hand man had started decades before, when they had both been active-duty SEALs. Chad had encouraged James to go into politics and not settle for being mayor of a small town, pursuing instead the position of senator once they both left the service.

"What time tomorrow do you think, sir?" the agent in the passenger seat asked as they turned the corner onto what had to be one of the safest streets in the city since he'd moved in. They pulled up to the front door of Chad's townhouse, the last of the six brick row houses on this side street. When James had first become president, Chad had put all the money he had into purchasing the place within fifteen minutes of the White House.

It looked much the same as when he'd bought it; he'd barely spent more than four hours at a time inside.

"Let's be on the move at zero four hundred," Chad answered.

Just enough time for a three-hour nap and a shower.

He badly needed both.

"Roger that, sir," the agent replied.

It wouldn't be the same man riding shotgun for the return trip, but the message would be passed along, and the SUVs would be idling, ready to leave right on time.

Chad managed to be civil to the agent on duty at a small guard station inside the door of the townhouse, made it to his bed upstairs, and was asleep within seconds of falling onto the mattress, face down, still fully clothed.

As exhausted as he felt, he went from sound asleep to fully awake when the second-from-the-top stair creaked as someone stepped on it.

A quick check of the bedside clock showed he'd been asleep for twenty minutes.

Chad silently rolled off the bed on the far side, reaching for the quick-access gun safe on the nightstand.

"Sir," the nighttime front door agent called from the stairs in his Texas twang. "Sorry to wake you."

Chad rested his hand on the gun safe but didn't unlock it. "What is it, Kenny?"

"Sir, you have a visitor at the door. He's on your list."

Anyone approaching the dead-end street would have been stopped, whether on foot, bike, or car. Only those on an approved list would access his or the other homes on the street. It drove one of his neighbors crazy—an old woman who frequently complained that she lived in a prison—but the rest appreciated the security measures.

"Who?"

"Ted Laurens."

Despite the crazy hours, he'd managed to keep in touch with a few old friends—mostly SEALs, but some civilians, too. Ted was an old high school buddy who lived near Chad's parents in the old neighborhood and looked in on them from time to time.

What is Ted doing here?

It wouldn't be a social call, and Ted, as a manager of an engineering firm, would have nothing to "pass along to the president" or some other bullshit like that.

"Be right down," Chad said. "Let him in, please."

Chad splashed water on his face in the bathroom and took off the suit coat and tie, but he didn't worry about the white wrinkled dress shirt or his mildly offensive body odor before heading downstairs.

Ted perched on the old leather couch taking up most of the living room. He wore jeans and a sweatshirt. His face was pale, and his eyes were wide. Nervous energy radiated off him.

He looks like hell.

"Sorry," Ted said, the word rushing out of him.

"Beer?" Chad asked, heading to the kitchen, open to the living room and only a few steps away in the tiny townhouse's ground floor.

"Whiskey," Ted choked out, like a man demanding the last drink he'd ever have.

"You okay?" Chad asked, knowing the answer. Ted certainly didn't look it. His blondish-brown hair was a mess. There were large bags under his eyes, like he hadn't slept in days.

Chad detoured to a shelf at the edge of the kitchen, took down two glasses and a mostly full bottle of whiskey, and brought all three over to the equally distressed brown leather chair across from the couch and next to the wood fireplace—unused, but stacked with a few nice logs, more as decoration than for a cozy fire on a cold evening.

Chad poured a generous splash of whiskey into Ted's glass and a small amount into his. Whatever Ted had to say, Chad wouldn't be enjoying a drink tonight.

"No, I'm not okay." Ted took a deep breath, staring off into space for a second like he was looking for where to begin before downing the whiskey in two gulps. "Don't freak out," he said in a whisper after making sure the Secret Service agent that normally sat just inside the door had stepped outside to give them privacy. "They said we're being watched." He spoke in a torrent of words, leaning forward, his face intense. "They also said if I didn't get here and do what they asked, they'd ruin my life. It's the hackers from the attack today. They said I had to come to you and give you my phone. They would do the rest."

Chad blinked, taking it in, refusing to succumb to panic.

"Whoa," he said. "Take a breath and start from the beginning."

"I can't. Don't alert the Secret Service. Please." He sounded frantic and desperate. "Here." Ted handed his cell phone and stood. "Unlock it with the code 0-0-0-0. I'll be right back. I'm not supposed to watch or listen," he said over his shoulder as he walked to the kitchen where he opened the refrigerator door, stuck his head in, and started to hum loudly.

Chad shook his head at the bizarre behavior. This wasn't Ted. Ted was steady, not some nutjob prone to making up crazy stories and sticking his head in the fridge.

Chad tore his eyes away from his buddy at the refrigerator and examined the modern cell phone.

If the phone was a bomb, the K-9 on duty outside would have detected it.

He'd always known Ted to be a solid, standup guy. Middle management, happy life. An average, upper-middle-class American living in the suburbs. If he hadn't had some kind of breakdown over the day's cyberattacks and what he said was true, this was extremely serious.

Could this be some practical joke by my high school friends? A security drill by the Secret Service? Or is someone screwing with Ted to mess with me?

The phone beckoned. The only way to find out for sure was to do what he'd been asked.

What the hell? If it blows up, so be it. Today's as good a day to die as any.

79

IN COLD BLOOD

With a quick prayer that today wasn't his day to die, Chad entered the passcode.

Nothing happened for a few seconds, but then the phone came to life. A frozen video image popped up showing an interrogation cell. A man hung from his arms. His wrists were tied, and ropes stretched overhead, out of the frame. He sagged, but his head faced the camera. His hair was long and stringy, his face wet from sweat or water.

A right-facing arrow waited, overlaying the scene. Chad pressed it.

A voice spoke as the video played—loudly—and Chad pressed the buttons on the side of the phone to turn it down with a quick glance at Ted in the kitchen, still humming in the fridge.

"You're going to tell us what you know. It's just a matter of time," a man said from offscreen.

Chad knew the voice. He spent hours a day with the man. Together, they'd been in more scrapes than he cared to remember. The man on the video had always done the right thing and led by example, but Chad had a growing sense of dread that he was not going to like what came next.

Whoever held the camera stepped back, revealing two men side by side in front of the tied-up man. The one on the right was about the same height but had a dark bushy beard and hair and a sunbaked face.

The person directly in front of the prisoner was a much younger James Heringten—former Navy SEAL and current president of the United States.

From James's face and clothing, along with the low quality of the video, Chad guessed it was from a few years before Chad had become a SEAL and went to work under James's command.

"Tell us what we need to know. Right now. No more games," James Heringten said. "Then we'll get you cleaned up and give you some food. This can all be over."

When the man refused to speak, James lashed out, punching the man hard in the gut. The prisoner retched and sagged against his ropes.

The man on the right surged forward and shoved James out of the way, then bent to check on the prisoner.

Chad felt sick to his stomach. The video was horrifying. President Heringten was beating a tied prisoner.

Torturing him for information.

The second man stood and hurried out of the frame. From his body language, Chad got the impression he was getting the prisoner water… or maybe calling for reinforcements to stop James.

Onscreen, James drew a pistol from behind his back, pressed it to the prisoner's forehead, and shot the man.

The video ended.

Chad sat in shocked silence.

In combat, he'd seen plenty of death. He'd killed many people, but never innocent civilians.

And he had never seen anyone executed in cold blood.

His mind raced.

That can't be real. James would never do that. Not in a million years. Not even if the prisoner was the devil himself.

But he held the proof in his hands.

Ted spoke from in front of the refrigerator, startling him. He'd been lost in his thoughts.

"I don't know what's on it, but I have to take the phone back," Ted said, moving to the living room.

"No damn way."

"They locked out my whole company," Ted said. "All of our CAD software. Payroll. Billing. Marketing. Everything. We got a ransomware notice saying it would be unfrozen in the morning. I got an email tonight once I got home."

His face was ashen.

"It said I had to come to you and show you the phone or they would fry the company's data and frame me for it." Tears streamed down his face.

"Let me see the email," Chad said. "Is it here?" he asked, holding up the phone.

"No. It's gone. There's no proof. If I lose my job, Chad—and the company thinks I did this? No one would ever hire me again. I've got bills. The kids need braces. College eventually. There's no way I survive this. And…" He looked embarrassed. "Besides me, they said they'd target everyone I know. Show their secrets to the world, ruin their credit, hack their bank accounts… They'd pin that on me somehow, too."

Ted checked his watch and stuck out his hand. "I have sixty seconds to leave here with the phone."

Chad guessed the hackers were bluffing and Ted had little to fear, but it wasn't worth the risk. If the hackers had control of Ted's phone, the video was deleted by now anyway. Keeping it would do no good and only harm his friend.

Chad handed Ted the phone.

"They said they'd be in touch and to not follow or try to contact me," Ted said. He rushed across the room and out the front door.

Chad stood, thinking through his next moves.

First, find out if what I saw was real. Second…

He'd worry about the next steps depending on whether he'd actually seen his friend and president murder a tied-up prisoner in cold blood.

80

THE UPDATE

"I brief the president in a few hours," Gregory said, addressing his entire team. They didn't need to know the truth—that he'd be leaving shortly for his pre-dawn private workout with the president, where the real briefing would happen. "Let's review what we have so far and go from there."

He stood near the door to the kitchen and surveyed the crowded diner. No one wanted to go home, so he had almost every analyst in the department there. The stale air smelled like old coffee, sweat, and desperation.

Classical music leaked through the kitchen door along with the raised voices of the IT crew and Void, the hacker. Gregory had ordered the music played at full volume to lessen the risk of Void overhearing their discussion, just in case.

"Dave," he said. "You start."

Dave stood from the back booth and cleared his throat. "We believe that the power plant shutdowns across the country—eleven of them—may have been caused by a hack on the power plant outside San Juan, Puerto Rico. The fresh water and wastewater plant hacks in so many cities and towns today may have come from unsecure facilities on the island as well.

A member of the group that may have been responsible for the hack was…"

Dave trailed off, coughed, then continued. Gregory had told him not to reference Axe's involvement on the island. "Authorities recovered his body," he said, omitting any reference to how they'd come across the information. "He was a former Russian army officer who retired and became a mercenary. His home country should be considered, of course, but intel indicates he worked for a variety of organizations in different parts of the world, from Africa to Europe. He did private security, escorting high-value individuals, and some clandestine direct-action missions that we don't have much intel on."

"What about the rest of the group on the island?" an analyst near the door asked.

"No other people were apprehended, though others were seen. All were Caucasian," Dave responded, going off Axe's earlier verbal report. "They were also experienced soldiers, but no other physical characteristics were observed—this is based only on a visual assessment through night vision goggles."

A few of the analysts near the front door flicked their eyes in Axe's direction. When Axe and Haley had returned, Gregory had introduced him as additional security—understandable, given the diner's exposed location. Most had accepted the story. A few others clearly didn't because Axe didn't come across as a typical guard.

Axe leaned against the diner's cashier counter, his arms crossed, intently watching the briefing.

He's like a dangerous, caged animal waiting for a chance to attack.

"We're trying to track their arrival at the island," Dave continued. "It looks like they came via a small private yacht; it might be a charter. I'll send you the information and assign a few of you to help me back-trace it as well as find out where it may be now."

"The Russians had a spy ship off the coast of Hawaii recently," another analyst said. "Could it be them?"

"That's certainly a possibility," Dave said.

It looked like Dave wanted to say more, so Gregory waited. After a few seconds, however, Dave glanced his way, nodded, and let Marcus slip out of the booth before he sat down.

Marcus started with the elephant in the room—or rather, the hacker in the back. "Dawson 'Eternal Void' Reite is in the kitchen," he began with a nod to the nearby door. "He has admitted to spending months—up until his arrest on unrelated charges—hacking the top car manufacturers' assisted and autonomous driving features."

The room broke out into quiet murmurs of surprise and anger. Most had seen Haley's dramatic departure via helicopter, but their return with the hacker had been more subtle.

"I did the in-depth analysis of the man," Marcus continued. "Based on what I discovered then and what I've learned tonight, I believe there is a likelihood he is telling the truth about the hacking… as well as his claim that he had nothing to do with the actual attack earlier today."

The discussion resumed. This time, his people didn't attempt to keep their voices down or disbelief in check.

"Keep it together," Gregory said. "Let Marcus finish."

Marcus held up a hand. "He has been in custody for a year and offline the entire time. He claims that others might have accessed his work. He bragged about it online to several other hackers and admits they may have learned enough from him to recreate some of his efforts… and take it further. He's working with the IT team to track those hackers and discover if they are behind the attacks."

More grumbling followed. Usually, Gregory could count on his team to be quiet, professional, and subordinate. But the attacks earlier today had everyone on edge, and emotions were high.

"Allowing him to work with us is my call," Gregory said. "If anyone has a problem with it, you can see me later… when you hand in your resignation."

With that, the team quieted down immediately.

"Any indication from him where this may have originated?" an analyst asked after a few seconds. "Were the people he bragged to part of nation-state hacking groups, individuals, or what?"

"He's not sure," Marcus said. "That's one of the things he's working on. We hope to know more soon. If anyone can get us that intel, it's him. That's all we have so far."

Marcus sat down on the bench seat of the booth as Gregory turned to Haley, wondering what she would say.

I should have taken her outside to hear her report first.

Time was tight, though. Every moment counted. He was living on the edge and prayed Haley would behave herself—and that whatever she had to say wouldn't cause a scene.

"Haley?" Gregory asked. She shook her head and gave him a look.

She doesn't want the whole room to hear her report.

"All right. Take what you've heard and run with it. Compare it with the angles you're working. Share your analysis in the group chat. Keep digging."

He walked slowly back to the booth, his eyes on his most talented analyst.

All right, Haley, what are you up to?

81

THE INTUITION

The Nighttime-Daytime Diner
Suburban Arlington, Virginia

Dave sat in the round back booth of the diner, close to the kitchen, and resisted rubbing his temples. He stared at his small laptop screen, ignoring Haley across from him, Marcus to her right, and Nancy to his left.

Other analysts filled the diner, working to research the country's attacks.

After he and Marcus had presented their initial findings, Haley had declined to give her report and announced to the booth she needed a few more minutes.

Dave glanced at her before dragging his eyes back to his screen, wishing he could ignore what he'd come up with but hadn't mentioned to the group in his initial report.

The data and interpretation didn't fit in with the current mission, but after finishing the initial research into the dead operator in Puerto Rico, he'd returned to this analysis anyway... and wasn't happy with where it had led.

For the past several months, he'd been feeling like the odd man out. Haley's intuition-based approach to analysis had uncovered—and stopped —several attacks on the country. No one could argue that.

Nancy had taken to it like a duckling to water.

Marcus, the newest member of their inner circle, had as well.

Dave still preferred logic—connecting the dots with reasonable assumptions based on intel—not guesswork.

Logic didn't care or feel.

Facts were facts.

But they could be interpreted. Hell, that was his job. Data could be considered from several different viewpoints.

He got paid to take a data point and present possible meanings and outcomes. Careful thinking, along with enough other data, produced a relatively consistent conclusion. Give a team of experienced analysts the same information and, nine times out of ten, they'd get to the same place.

Logic could also be harsh. When it led to an unpopular conclusion that no one else had discovered, whether from a lack of data or incompetent analysis, it could be a bitch.

He rubbed his beard, redirecting his train of thought for a few more seconds. Anything to not deal with what he'd discovered.

The bushy winter beard didn't work in the warmer weather. To him, it wasn't spring until he had to get the clippers out.

Maybe I should shave it off.

It had been decades since he'd had a smooth face. The idea of changing so drastically appealed to him, as did eliminating the spreading gray hairs, which were rapidly replacing the black ones.

Those have to be caused by Haley.

Thinking of her brought his attention abruptly back to his current dilemma. He had to face the truth.

It all comes down to one thing. I don't want to look like a fool.

Then again, he could handle the possibility if it meant protecting the country.

And logic didn't care about his feelings.

But would Gregory?

Dave didn't have to worry about Nancy. She was with him. They weren't married and might not ever be. They both liked their current arrangement, and their families didn't seem to care there had never been a wedding. Why rock the boat?

He snorted quietly and glanced around self-consciously. No one looked—they were all focused on their work.

If I'm correct, this could be a tsunami wave that rocks the biggest boat around: the ship called the United States of America.

The safe play was to present this to Nancy first.

He glanced over at her and frowned again. She was hard at work, in the zone the way Haley had shown her, hunting by intuition.

His gaze went back to his screen. Tabbing through the windows, he glanced at each once again. The signal intelligence reports. Human intelligence, including dozens of statements from reliable assets, along with rumors and half-truths from flakey sources.

Other screens showed satellite imagery, NSA electronic intercepts, and economic reports.

A gigantic spreadsheet he'd been working on for weeks filled another window. It had come together over the last few hours, the final pieces falling into place.

Another look at Haley, chewing her lip on the other side of the booth, made him sit back and bite his own lip hard enough to draw blood.

He didn't want to do it, but he had to ask the question he hated most.

What does my gut tell me about this mess?

The data led to a logical conclusion.

And his intuition agreed.

It's real.

He had to tell Gregory soon, along with Nancy, Marcus, and Haley. It might be the piece of the puzzle they all needed.

He'd write up a summary while others, including many of the other Central Analysis Group analysts, looked at the raw intel and tried to find flaws in his process.

As long as Gregory didn't ask the specific question Dave didn't want to answer—or think about too closely—he'd be fine.

82

THE ANALYSIS

The Nighttime-Daytime Diner
Suburban Arlington, Virginia

Gregory glanced at his watch again. He had to leave soon.

Come on, Haley.

He cleared his throat, loud enough only for the analysts at the booth to hear.

Haley raised one finger without looking up from her screen.

"I need what you all have now," he said.

He had the attention of the rest of the table. Haley eventually tore her eyes away and met his, looking thoughtful.

"I realize it's too soon to have an in-depth analysis," he said, speaking softly. Other nearby analysts might be able to hear, but they'd ignore the conversation. Most wore earbuds to help them focus, anyway.

"The president is going to want a best guess. I'll ask you what he's going to ask me. First impressions—who is most likely behind this?"

Nancy and Marcus sat silently.

Haley and Dave spoke at the same time.

"China—framing Russia," Haley said.

"Russia—framing China," came from Dave.

They smiled at each other and chuckled.

Nancy and Marcus looked from one to another like they were watching a tennis match.

Haley spun her laptop to him first. Dave hesitated a second, then slid his across the booth to her.

Each sat glued to the other's research, analysis, and conclusions.

Gregory watched and waited.

The seconds dragged by.

Gregory sighed loudly, hoping to speed up the process. The morning workout time with the president was the right place to share his team's intel privately. It meant he could avoid the mess of having to offer the group's rather unorthodox method of data analysis as a formal report instead of what it was: an informed hunch by his core group of Haley, Nancy, Dave, and Marcus.

After a few more minutes, Haley looked up, glanced at Gregory, and bit her lip.

A minute later, Dave looked up at her and nodded.

"Impressive," they both said at the same time.

"Seeing this…" Haley started. She looked at Gregory. "I think Dave is right. It could be Russia."

"I was about to say the same thing about your analysis," Dave said, his voice quiet but firm. "Russia could be behind it, but it also might be China wanting us to think it's Russia."

Damn it!

"All right," Gregory said, resisting the need to run his hands through his hair but giving in to the desire to remove his glasses and rub his tired eyes. "Both of you, take me through it. Dave, you go first. Tell me why you first thought it was Russia framing China."

83

THE PAPER TIGER

The Nighttime-Daytime Diner
Suburban Arlington, Virginia

Gregory wasn't easily shocked, especially after working with Haley for the past few years.

But by the time Dave finished presenting his conclusions, he could barely believe his solid, dependable, straight-shooting senior analyst had come up with…

Something Haley would report.

"Before we even address the current situation, let me get the gist of your analysis straight," Gregory said, crossing his arms and leaning back in the booth.

Dave leaned forward, a grim but resolute expression on his face. He'd detailed what he'd been working on over the past weeks that had come together after the day's attacks.

His impressive research remained on his laptop screen, pointed at Gregory. They had spoken as quietly as they could, but gradually more and more of the nearby analysts had listened in. Gregory didn't care.

If he's right, we're all going to be working on this in a few minutes, anyway.

"Months ago, you predicted Russia was hours away from invading Ukraine, Latvia, and Lithuania, right?"

Dave nodded but said nothing.

"It didn't happen. For whatever reason," Gregory muttered. He didn't have to say more. Dave and Nancy must believe, as he did, that Haley and Axe had something to do with stopping that attack. His money was on bribing the Russian president's helicopter pilot or ground team to land hard.

Maybe they'd somehow compromised the president's security detail—buying or threatening them—and the crew had simply broken the man's neck in the helicopter, blaming it all on a rough landing.

Or Haley and Axe could have somehow sabotaged the helicopter, though he couldn't see how they'd accomplish that.

When it came down to it, he didn't want to know. They had been off-grid long enough to handle a secret mission. He wouldn't ask. And Marcus didn't need to hear the slightest hint about any of it.

"But now you're saying Russia's military is in tatters?" He stopped and softened his tone. He didn't want to come across as a hard-ass. He wasn't that type of manager. "Your logic is sound. But you haven't addressed the big problems: how, when, and why? It makes no sense. Why be less than a day away from a major offensive if they didn't have the logistical support, men, or materiel to accomplish the mission? And how does it tie into the cyberattack on our country?"

"I'll need the rest of the team to dig into those questions," Dave answered. "Perhaps presenting my conclusion was premature," he said with a pointed look at Haley. "And this could still be wrong."

"No. If there's anything we've learned from Haley," Gregory said, "it's better to get the data out to the right people early. Minutes save lives."

Something bothered him. It took a second, but he put his finger on it.

He's not telling me everything.

"Returning to the problem at hand—what data made you start down this course of inquiry and then continue to pull it together tonight?"

Dave's body language shifted subtly, but Gregory caught it. He fought to keep the smile off his face. A spark of recognition passed between them, which was all the acknowledgment Gregory needed.

He followed a hunch—which drives him crazy, and he doesn't want to admit it.

"We keep hearing of the many Russian generals and other men, up and down the chain of command, having fatal 'accidents' or suddenly resigning," Dave said.

"The rumor is that President Nikitin has been cleaning house and consolidating power," Dave continued. "It makes sense, given his moderate nature and lack of a strong base of support. He wants powerful figures gone and replaced by his people. But what if that assumption is incorrect? What if it's disinformation? If he wants a better-prepared, more modern force focused on cyber warfare? He may believe it's the only way to stop America from steamrolling his weakened empire. The attacks today"—he glanced at his watch—"yesterday, rather, could have been a first strike, which Russia has been obsessed with since the start of the Cold War."

Gregory nodded. The assumption was sound, though it would need to be investigated further.

"Now you, Haley," Gregory said. "Lay it out."

84

THE CONCLUSION

The Nighttime-Daytime Diner
Suburban Arlington, Virginia

"While Dave investigated the dead body from the suspected hacker group in Puerto Rico," Haley said, "I dealt with his belongings."

Haley took a breath, flicked an apologetic look Gregory's way, and went for it.

"Based on what I found, Dave's analysis, and other factors, I believe we can rule out North Korea and Iran. My initial working hypothesis was that the Chinese are attempting to frame the Russians. Now," she conceded, "after Dave's analysis, I'm not sure."

Although she normally liked hunting on her own, letting her intuition guide the search, brainstorming with the others had become another way to put the pieces of the puzzle together.

I may finally be turning into a team player after all.

Researching the attack on the secretary of state had gone nowhere. There were too many people who held grudges against the United States who feared Secretary Wilson's negotiating abilities. Haley was left with combining her own research—and hunches—with the data provided by the rest of the team.

"It's the little things that had me thinking China is to blame," she started. "Yes, the guy in Puerto Rico was a retired Russian special forces captain. But the phone was a brand-new Chinese model. The app they used to communicate isn't on the market—it's custom. Our sister agency that analyzed it reports it's very sophisticated and, even though it's in a common programming language, they claim it 'feels' Chinese. They say they can tell what type of programmers work on software based on a lot of things—they lost me after a while, but they were pretty convincing."

"You think the Chinese hired Russians as part of the false-flag operation," Marcus said, "hoping that if they were caught, we'd blame Russia instead of them."

"But they made mistakes?" Nancy asked. "By providing them with the wrong phone?"

"That's my working hypothesis. Look at this screenshot." She turned her computer toward him. "It's from a security camera at the edge of the prison campus where we rescued Void—almost a mile from the main building."

She had dug it up during the last several hours. The owner of the building had made the footage available to local law enforcement in their efforts to find and capture the one-thousand-plus escaped prisoners from the medium-security facility.

A short, thin figure, dressed in a dark brown jacket and khaki-colored pants, stood near a tree. He carried a long gun—a sniper rifle—nearly as tall as he was.

"This barely caught him moving from one tree to another. It's zoomed in a zillion times; the warehouse had a lot of break-ins and kids tagging it with graffiti. They invested in a kick-ass security camera setup. Any typical system wouldn't have caught this image."

"Looks like a short Bigfoot," Marcus mumbled when she turned her computer so they all could see.

Haley frowned. "The resolution isn't good, but the computer says there's an eighty-four percent chance the man is of Asian descent."

"Eighty-four? From that?" Marcus asked.

She nodded. "And a sixty-two percent chance he's Chinese."

Nancy stared at the screen, shaking her head. "What if it's the North Koreans or Iranians hiring Russians and using Chinese tech to throw us off the trail? Or Russians using the Chinese phone to frame them?"

Haley nodded. "It could be. That's what makes this all so challenging. At the end of the day, though, we have to look at the facts in front of us. We try to weigh the probabilities and come up with a report." They locked eyes. "A recommendation."

"And what is your recommendation?" Gregory asked, looking first at her before turning to the rest of the group at the booth. "Once again, your best guess?"

Gregory turned to look at the rest of the nearby analysts, who had given up any pretense of not eavesdropping. "Anyone?"

Haley spoke for the table—and the room. "It's inconclusive, sir. We just don't have enough to offer a conclusion with enough confidence to take action."

85

THE VAN

Not another one, Tucci thought, slipping out of Haley's SUV.

A van slowed as it neared the diner's driveway. He waited as it signaled and drove slowly across the parking lot toward where he'd backed the SUV into the parking space closest to the diner's front door.

The bright headlights illuminated him—and the shotgun he held ready in his hands.

The weapon had scared away the last half dozen cars that had arrived. They'd all seen the diner lit up and hoped for a meal and maybe some company during this time of chaos and confusion.

The van slowed to a crawl, coming forward a few more feet before stopping.

In the glare of the headlights, Tucci could only make out the dark shape of the driver rolling down the window to ask a question.

"We're closed," Tucci called. He had a feeling of impending danger.

No one stops to chat with a guy holding a shotgun.

When the van didn't immediately shift into reverse and start backing up, Tucci raised the shotgun to his shoulder, taking aim at the man in the driver's seat.

That should get the point across.

The driver raised his right hand in surrender…

The way he moved made Tucci take a quick step to the left—just as the driver fired a pistol in his left hand as it cleared the window.

A bullet snapped past Tucci's head.

Tucci pulled the trigger of the shotgun, obliterating the van's windshield and the driver inside.

"Contact front!" Tucci yelled at the top of his lungs, moving for cover behind the SUV while keeping the van in his sights.

The van continued forward at a walking pace, the headless driver at the wheel, but no one else fired from inside.

86

THE KITCHEN

The Nighttime-Daytime Diner
Suburban Arlington, Virginia

The unmistakable sound of a pistol firing, followed immediately by the boom of Tucci's shotgun, made Axe react on instinct.

Even as Tucci bellowed "Contact front," Axe had Haley's M4 pointed at the front door next to him.

"On the floor now!" he yelled at the analysts. A few were already dropping off their stools and chairs, but out of the corner of his eye, Axe noted others were frozen. "Get down right now!" he yelled again. "Haley, cover the back door and Void!"

He sensed more than saw Haley move from the back booth, through the swinging metal door, and into the kitchen.

Axe resisted the temptation to race to her assistance.

She's more than capable of handling herself. Still...

"Marcus, back her up," Axe called. "Gregory—to me."

The sound of vehicle engines racing closer competed with gunfire from the CAG security personnel Axe had placed on the roof.

At least two vehicles speeding toward us.

Gregory slid along the polished linoleum floor, coming to a stop next to Axe in front of the cashier counter and drawing his pistol like he knew what he was doing.

"Cover the door. I'm going outside," Axe said, making sure Haley's boss could handle the task. "Don't lock the door in case I need to get inside quick."

The older man seemed focused and unafraid as he nodded. With his longish gray hair and fashionable glasses, he didn't look much like a warrior, but Axe was happy to have him as backup. "Copy. Be careful."

Axe reached up, turned the key stuck in the lock, and quickly pushed the front door open, slipping out smoothly.

Haley burst into the kitchen, gun pointed at the diner's back door.

The IT team had their computers lined up on one of the kitchen's prep counters. Void stood behind them. He'd been directing their actions, which had come to an abrupt stop a second before.

They had techno music playing with a pulsing beat. "Kill that music," Haley ordered.

"What's going on?" one of the geeks asked, his eyes glued to Haley's pistol.

"They're here for me again, aren't they?" Void asked. "Who—"

"Get inside, all of you," Haley said, yanking on the metal handle of the large walk-in freezer.

On the roof, the CAG security team kept firing, intent on stopping something headed their way.

"Is that gunfire?" the woman tech asked as they jumbled forward, bumping into one another in their haste to follow Haley's orders and get inside the relative safety of the freezer.

Haley ignored them, watching the back door.

"Coming in behind you," Marcus called softly from the swinging door to the restaurant.

"Come ahead," she called back just as quietly.

The door swung open slowly and Marcus entered, her backup pistol in his hand, pointed safely at the floor.

"We're making progress," Void whispered as he hurried past her. "Don't let them get me, okay?"

"Don't worry," she said, her voice cold. "They won't."

87

THE WAKE-UP

The White House
Washington, DC

Chad paced the floor in the president's everyday office. The Oval Office, immediately next door, was used for meetings and more formal occasions, but James Heringten preferred to get his reading and day-to-day work done in this room.

Chad reached the wall and spun, cracking his knuckles and considering his options while he waited for his friend, mentor, and commander in chief to come down from the Residence on the second floor.

Am I doing the right thing?

As his Secret Service detail had rushed him back to the White House after his brief meeting with Ted, Chad had reviewed the video over and over in his mind.

He'd also considered his duty.

His first loyalty lay to the country and the Constitution.

But a very close second was James Heringten.

He owed the man his life, his career, and many of his abilities. James had taken him, the newest young officer on a SEAL Team, under his wing and over the years trained him, saved his life, and put him in the White House as the right-hand man of the most powerful person in the world.

Chad had helped James every step of the way, acting as a sounding board, strategist, and political advisor.

They were a team—and they worked very well together.

What happens to one of us happens to both.

Chad thought the best plan would be to go straight to the Justice Department or the FBI with what he'd seen.

The cover-up is always where a bad situation gets worse.

But he had some wiggle room because he doubted the video was real. He didn't know how it had been faked—the voice and face on the tape were clearly that of a younger James Heringten. But without the phone containing the video, he had nothing to show to the authorities.

That gives me an out.

He turned again, his polished black dress shoes making no noise on the plush rug, and resumed his pacing.

Come on—how long does it take him to get down here?

Chad checked his watch. It had only been a few minutes since he'd arrived in the building and called the Residence, waking up the president and requesting a meeting in this office.

His mind naturally thought in terms of strategy and tactics. He didn't want to discuss this in the president's private quarters. The situation was too important. If an investigation were to follow, the office was the place for a meeting.

Anything else looks like a cover-up.

He'd also wanted to avoid the more formal Oval Office next door.

This room would be perfect. If, God forbid, the president authenticated the video, Chad could...

What? Have the Secret Service arrest their protectee?

Chad shook his head and spun to pace in the other direction again. If the video was real, the president wouldn't need to be arrested. They would call the vice president, get him here, and President Heringten would resign, effective immediately.

It's the only way, right?

Chad didn't dare send agents or police to Ted's house. If the hackers were watching, it might trigger the cyberattacks they'd threatened.

He'd ask the Secret Service or FBI to very quietly look into Ted's situation once he dealt with the president. If the hackers were true to their word, they might leave Ted alone since he had done all they'd asked.

Or they might be bluffing.

The door opened a few minutes later, and President Heringten walked in, looking like he'd just woken up, wearing worn jeans, sneakers, and a gray sweatshirt. "Am I going to need coffee?" he asked as he stood in the doorway.

"Yes, Mr. President."

"Somebody get me some coffee, please," he said and closed the door. "What's up?"

Chad hesitated. This wasn't the first—or tenth—time Chad had woken the president and gotten him down to the office straight from bed. But it was the first time he didn't know where to begin.

"It's bad?" the president asked.

"Very."

"Shit. Well, 'The only easy day was yesterday.'"

Chad nodded grimly.

He has no idea.

88

THE CONFRONTATION

Chad finished recounting his evening to President Heringten, who had sat stone-faced through the entire story.

They both took sips of their coffee, which had barely cooled enough to drink. The story hadn't taken long—there wasn't much to tell.

"Damn camcorders," President Heringten muttered.

Chad's stomach dropped.

Oh my God. It actually happened.

"The video is real, but it's not true," the president said as if reading Chad's mind. "I was there. It's my voice. But the video has been altered. I wasn't the one who shot the prisoner. I was the other guy, the one who tried to stop it and went for help. The faces and voices have been swapped."

Chad kept his face neutral. He wanted to believe him, but "The other guy did it" was the oldest excuse in the book.

"Can we prove it?" Chad asked, hoping the president had a way out.

"I filed a report immediately. The videotape was confiscated. They told me it would be erased. The interrogator—the guy who pulled the trigger—had connections in that country's government and couldn't be exposed. I haven't checked, but the initial report should still be there." He stared into space, thinking. "The host country could have switched out the tape, planning on using the original footage as insurance or future blackmail. 'Look what the Americans made us do'—something like that. Or maybe someone wanted to use it against the guy who shot the prisoner. Or..." the president said, trailing off.

"What?"

"There were rumors, suspicions, that some of the locals played for several sides. We always wondered which men were still loyal to the previous regime... and its allies."

"Including Russia."

"Yes. Including Russia."

"'The enemy of my enemy is my friend.'"

"Always."

"What about other people who were there?" Chad asked. "Anyone who could corroborate the true events?"

"Three other SEALs were in the room. They're dead—unrelated to the incident in question."

"The interrogator?"

"The murderer was well connected, which is why this all went away. I'll get you the details."

"Did you tell anybody immediately afterward what happened? Write in a journal, call home? Is there anyone to—I hate to use this word—testify on your behalf?"

"No. Only the report. It's Top Secret or above, I'm sure, but we can find it. If we want to go that route."

"What do you mean? We have to. We'll need it to prove your innocence."

President Heringten sighed. "The video is never seeing the light of day. It can't. I took an oath to protect the country from all enemies, foreign and domestic."

"You are not an enemy."

The president shook his head. "You don't see it yet. If the video gets out, I am a danger to the country. And isn't that the definition of an enemy?"

"But the report—"

"Doesn't matter," the president interrupted. "In our polarized country, half the people would defend me whether they believe I'm guilty or not. The other half would want me out of office. Again, whether they believe I'm guilty or not. Either way, I'm screwed. I'd have no political capital.

Everything I do will be overshadowed by the video. If we need to hit Iran militarily? 'President Heringten Attacks Iran to Distract from Scandal.' If we want to raise or lower taxes, fix whatever needs to be fixed... no matter what I propose, it goes nowhere. And that's here in the US. Imagine what happens in the Middle East when they see this. 'Current American President Killed Innocent Prisoners.' There would be protests at least. Riots. Attacks on our consulates and people. Saber-rattling, demands for concessions, apologies, and reparations... Again, that's even if we have solid proof the video is fake." President Heringten smiled grimly and shook his head in resignation. "You were thinking this is blackmail? No— it's to force me out of office. Tonight, my presidency ends." He reached into a drawer and removed a single sheet of paper, setting it on his desk.

He's going to resign.

"Wait. There has to be a way. We could go public," Chad said, grasping at straws.

"Wouldn't matter."

"If you resign, you'll live in disgrace."

He shrugged. "But America will be protected." He tapped the pen on the desk, thinking. "There's a small chance whoever is behind this just wants me quietly gone. If I resign, the video might not be released. I need an excuse. A good reason to leave office—besides the fake video."

Chad frantically thought of ways to stop James from moving forward but had nothing.

"I could cite my health," James said, thinking out loud. "Say I'm turning over the reins to our new, young vice president."

He looked around the room and sighed tiredly. "It wouldn't be the worst thing in the world," he muttered, "to get away from the stress, the negotiating, the bullshit—all of it." James waved his hand at the office.

"Staying damages not only me but the office of the presidency," he said, his voice strong and face once again resolved.

"So you're going to take one for the team?" Chad asked, trying to hold back the rage in his voice.

No, this is wrong!

89

THE FIGHT

The White House
Washington, DC

Chad shook his head, desperate to make the president see reason.

"It's the only way," James said and started to write on the paper.

Chad didn't think through his argument. He spoke from the heart—to hell with the consequences.

Chad exploded. "It's not the only way. It's ringing the damn bell!"

The words hung between them.

In the initial basic SEAL training program—BUD/S—a large brass bell awaited the candidates who wanted to quit and end the misery. All they had to do was ring the bell three times to signal they were giving up.

They would be whisked away, dried off, warmed up, given coffee and food... and a trip away from their dream of becoming one of America's elite warriors.

At every point, candidates were encouraged to make it easy on themselves.

"Just ring the bell and it all gets better," the instructors would say. "You don't have to put yourself through this. There's no shame in admitting you're not cut out for this program."

Every day, many men would give up.

Most classes graduated only about twenty percent of those who entered the program.

Those were the men who could face the challenge.

Who had the mental, physical, and emotional fortitude required to serve the country at such a high level.

Who could be counted on by their fellow SEALs—and the United States of America—to never, ever give up, no matter how bad things got.

There was little worse than accusing another SEAL of quitting—giving up when the going got tough.

President Heringten's eyes narrowed in anger... but he stopped writing.

"You want me to risk my career, my good name, and, more importantly to me, the reputation of the office of the president?" James asked.

Chad nodded and softly repeated a paragraph from the SEAL ethos. "I will never quit. I persevere and thrive on adversity. My Nation expects me to be physically harder and mentally stronger than my enemies. If knocked down, I will get back up, every time. I will draw on every remaining ounce of strength to protect my teammates and to accomplish our mission."

James added the next line in a firm voice, barely above a whisper. "I am never out of the fight."

Chad nodded.

Come on. We can do this.

"What's their endgame?" James asked. "Why show you the video? Did they guess I'd resign?"

"We can figure those things out—if you're willing to fight."

"We'd have to be careful, or it could blow up in our faces," the president said slowly.

"Yes sir," Chad said, not seeing a solution but willing to hang onto the slimmest hope for a better outcome than James's resignation or the destruction of his presidency.

He hesitated to suggest it, but he dived in. "Gregory Addison—and your niece—may be able to figure a way out of this for us... if you're willing to tell them about the videotape."

Several seconds went by as the president stared at the paper on the desk, already filled with a line of writing. "I stop the moment this threatens the country or the office of the president, agreed?"

Chad nodded.

That's it. Fight!

Finally, James tore the paper into tiny pieces. "Destroying presidential records is probably the least of our problems at this point, don't you think?" he asked. James swept the bits of paper into a pile and off the desk into his palm. He passed them to Chad to dispose of.

"The video came from the hackers responsible for the cyberattacks yesterday," James said, working the problem. "Russia has repeatedly probed us. Could they be behind all this?"

"President Nikitin may be sharper and more aggressive than we thought," Chad said. "The video could be a warning shot across our bow to not retaliate for yesterday. 'You strike back, you're done.' That sort of thing. But for what purpose?"

James nodded. "Our intel has shown they're making a big move in the Middle East. We've made our displeasure known all around, but after Iraq, moving into and then abandoning Afghanistan, hitting Bin Laden in Pakistan, and our chaotic relationship with Saudi Arabia and other countries in the region, we have a lot less clout today than we did in the past."

"Maybe they don't know that," Chad said. He thought for a minute, then added, "What if they're desperate? If they really needed something from the Middle Eastern countries? A slowdown in oil production so they can get more money? Selling more of their tanks and weapons to their allies?"

James nodded. "We have no intel to support that—which doesn't mean much. We haven't had great sources there in a while. Of course, it could be simpler than that. The new president could just be making a push. Flexing his muscles to show off to his countrymen and the world."

They sat in silence, considering the situation. "A lot of questions and few answers," Chad muttered. "What about the upcoming Middle East Peace Summit?" Chad said, blurting out the question before he'd fully thought it through. "With Secretary of State Wilson sidelined, the VP will be out of his depth. If you resigned, Vice President Cabreran would stay home to take over. No strong American presence is at the summit."

"Could it be that simple?" James asked.

Chad and the president had been dismissive of the summit, thinking it would be a meeting filled with speeches condemning the United States and promises among Middle Eastern countries to work together and strengthen ties. All that would last until the parties returned home and went back to badmouthing each other and threatening the destruction of Israel, the USA, and each country's traditional enemies.

The president had respectfully declined the invitation to attend and asked the new vice president to go in his place with Secretary Wilson.

The VP and Wilson would play the role of stoic punching bags, letting everyone blame the region's problems on America.

In the background, they would mingle, make promises, and work to advance America's interests. It might not do much good, but reminding their allies—and enemies—of America's power and prosperity wouldn't hurt.

"We have roughly twenty-four hours until the vice president is scheduled to leave for the summit in Oman," Chad said. "We can figure this out."

James rolled his shoulders and cracked his neck.

Chad kept his face neutral, but inside he felt intense relief.

I know those moves—they mean he's ready to go into battle.

"Now that we've talked," James said, offering Chad a nod of gratitude, "my intuition is screaming at me that the only way out is to confront this head-on."

90

FATE

Petrov, the new commander of the mercenaries, sprinted across the parking lot toward the back of the diner at full speed. He hadn't run this hard, this fast, for this far, since his days as a trainee in Russia's special forces boot camp.

Gunfire came from the rooftop of the suburban restaurant, directed at the cars racing toward the diner from two directions.

So far, no one had shot at him.

Even the best soldiers struggle with covering their boring sector when the action is elsewhere.

He felt bad about the men he'd ordered to drive the cars. They would be dead soon—if they weren't already.

Even when they died, the straps on the steering wheels would keep both vehicles on target. The wedges holding the accelerators to the floor turned them into missiles.

Only the most disciplined guards would avoid leaving their posts to help prevent the cars from impacting the building.

The crack of a sniper rifle meant another guard on the roof had likely fallen thanks to Petrov's Chinese comrade in the tree line hundreds of yards away.

He's probably the only one who survives this mission.

They'd been on their way to Georgia to fly home, but the damn mission burner phone had buzzed before they'd gotten far, ordering them to hole up and await further instructions.

Details eventually followed. The target had been moved to a restaurant in the middle of nowhere—at the edge of suburbia in Arlington, Virginia.

The orders were for a suicide mission.

Assault the restaurant. Secure the hacker unharmed. Kill everyone else.

Petrov had been close to ignoring the text, tossing the phone, and not mentioning the change of plans to the other men when a series of buzzes made him check the phone one last time.

What it showed made his heart stop.

A photo of his beautiful wife and child filled the screen.

A picture of his elderly parents came through next.

Other pictures of happy, smiling people followed.

Petrov assumed they were family members of the other men on the mission.

The implication couldn't be clearer. They either did their jobs, or their families suffered.

As he neared the back of the diner, Petrov slowed only enough to keep from harming himself as he slammed into the wall. He panted, taking a second to catch his breath while he looked around. He saw no defenders, only his fate—the diner's dented back door, painted a deep blue.

The scuff of a shoe on pavement made Petrov spin to face the left side of the diner. "Don't shoot—it's us," a voice whispered in Russian.

"Come," Petrov replied softly in English.

They made it.

He thought he'd have to assault the diner alone and surely die.

With his two remaining comrades, they might have a chance.

They didn't have to speak. They had agreed on the plan before the assault.

Arranging themselves in the proper order, they signaled their readiness.

All three knew their chances of survival were slim.

At least our families will live.

91

THE RIGHT THING

The Nighttime-Daytime Diner
Suburban Arlington, Virginia

Haley didn't allow the sound of an explosion from the front of the diner to distract her attention from the back door.

Come on, let's get this over with.

She felt calm and focused.

'The only difference between fear and excitement is experience.'

She didn't think the quote was from Sun Tzu but couldn't remember where she'd heard it. It must have been Axe.

"Ready?" she whispered.

"Ready," Marcus replied from behind and to her right.

She crouched low, pistol pointed at the back door, her body mostly shielded by the counter.

"Just like at the range," she said.

She didn't doubt his skills, but shooting a living person wasn't easy.

Especially if they were shooting back.

The gunfire from the roof slackened.

It'll be now.

Gunshots came from the back door. The tangos had made it to the building and were shooting out the lock.

The rest happened in the blink of an eye.

The door flew open.

A man dressed as a paramedic but carrying a pistol launched himself inside. His eyes locked onto Haley's.

He turned, the weapon lining up with her.

She put two bullets in his chest and another in his head before he could pull the trigger.

Before his lifeless body could fall, three other shots rang out from Marcus.

A second man slammed against the door before his body slid to the ground.

Three more shots came from outside.

Nice shooting, Axe.

He must have come around from the front to shoot any other tangos before they could come through the door.

"Clear outside," Axe called.

"One second," Haley responded. "Moving," she added for Marcus' benefit. She didn't know how jumpy he was and didn't want him shooting her when she checked on the tangos.

Staying low, she crept to the door and poked her head around the corner for an instant before drawing back. She didn't expect to be shot at, but it paid to be cautious.

They're both dead.

Neither could be alive with holes in their heads.

Peeking around the corner for longer this time, she assessed the damage to the men's bodies as well. A pool of blood grew on the floor.

"All clear inside," Haley said in a loud voice. She stood slowly, looking back at Marcus. "You okay?"

His eyes bore into hers as he nodded.

I know that expression.

She'd seen it in the mirror time and again, every morning when she washed her face. It was the look of someone who had taken a life.

"Can I come to you?" Axe called.

Haley checked with Marcus again. He'd lowered the 9mm and stood straight. He seemed alert and in control—if a little overwhelmed.

"Come ahead. Mind the blood," she added.

The geeks.

She moved to the walk-in freezer, holstering her pistol, and knocked three times. "It's Haley," she said as she slowly opened the heavy door. "It's safe."

What she saw made her proud.

All four of the IT team crowded into the far corner. Void couldn't be seen.

They're shielding him with their bodies.

"Well done," she said. "You can come out now… but there are dead guys by the door. Don't look—or keep it together if you do."

Marcus had come forward and stood over the dead tangos.

"Nice shooting," Haley said quietly as she joined him.

He nodded but didn't speak.

"You did good," she started, trying to remember what Axe had said to her in New York and New Jersey what seemed like ages ago when she had killed for the first time. But she drew a blank.

What would I have wanted him to say?

"You saved lives," she whispered. "Mine, yours, Void's, the team's. I know it's not easy to hear, but you did the right thing."

"I'll be okay," he said, equally quiet, and she believed him.

92

THE SHOTGUN

The Nighttime-Daytime Diner
Suburban Arlington, Virginia

Gregory crouched at the front door of the diner. The pistol he hadn't fired felt good in his hands. Back in the day, he'd gone to the range a few times per month. As the years slipped away, though, and he moved up the management ladder, the trips had dwindled, then stopped.

"There's still at least one out there," Axe said as he crouch-walked across the diner. He had slipped out the front and come in through the back. One look at him, and Gregory could tell he'd killed an enemy.

"A skilled sniper," Axe said, kneeling next to him. "But I don't think he'll stick around."

"How do you know?"

Axe shrugged. "I wouldn't. The mission is blown. Unless they have more guys and are prepping an ambush for when we leave, he's the last man standing. He stopped shooting when the cars blew up. He was a distraction to cover the others' approach from the back. His job is done; he'll exfil."

After a second to consider the warrior's words, Gregory nodded. "How many?" he asked softly. Axe would know what he meant.

"We lost one," Axe said. "A guard on the roof. Two more are injured.

They need to be dropped off at a good hospital right away. They won't make it to the base."

Gregory would grieve for the security detail later. For now, they had to get out of here—and he wanted to know how Axe had figured it out. "How did you know I'm moving us to the joint base?" The sprawling military base that served the area was less than an hour away.

"Where else?" Axe said as he prepared to venture outside.

"I should have moved us there from the start," Gregory muttered. The death of one of his security team and the injury of the other two were on him.

"No. They wouldn't have let you on base then, and you know it," Axe said. "You're doing great. Now, get your people together, pile them into vehicles, and let's get out of here before the bad guys figure it out and manage to send reinforcements."

With that, the warrior once again slipped out the front door.

What he said is true. In the middle of the attacks, there's no way they would have let us all onto the base.

"We're leaving in five minutes," Gregory announced to the team. "Stay low. Gather up your stuff and use the restrooms. We've got a drive ahead of us, and we're not stopping."

———

Axe took in the scene as he crawled out of the front door.

Two cars burned near the diner. One was at the curb in front. The other blazed at the side entrance to the parking lot. Both had been stopped by overwhelming gunfire to their engines.

The van with the dead tango in the driver's seat had come to rest against the concrete wheel stop next to Haley's SUV. The van's back doors were open, a testament to Tucci's thoroughness in looking for other tangos —and his bravery in taking on what could have been a vehicle full of the enemy, ready to gun him down.

Tucci stood in front of Haley's SUV, the shotgun in hand.

"You okay, brother?" Axe asked as he joined the pilot, still scanning the road that ran in front of the diner.

"Yeah," he said gruffly, though Axe detected a hint of strain in the word.

He's been in combat. Hell, he might have been in more scrapes and taken more fire than me. But the first kill, up close and personal, always takes a toll.

While Tucci might have launched a missile here or there, he had been first and foremost a pilot. Others had done the killing while he did the flying.

Axe held back from offering any advice or other words of support. Instead, he dropped his hand onto the man's shoulder and offered the only words Tucci needed. "Thank you."

Tucci nodded, took a deep breath, and cleared his throat. "You were right. The shotgun came in handy."

93

THE ASSET

For Ekaterina, former Russian spy, assassin, and operator, the dreary day was perfect. Barely above freezing, with a leaden sky and an off-and-on drizzle. It felt like snow tonight. Tomorrow at the latest.

This is a proper spring.

The endless sunshine of Los Angeles, where she'd spent too much time on her last assignment, could bake in the inferno it was.

Not a day went by when she didn't think of what she could have done differently on the failed Los Angeles operation.

I could have walked into that coffee shop, shot the blond woman in the head, and walked out.

But no, the dark-haired American operator had identified her from the start.

I should have started shooting and taken my chances.

Or at the hotel, during the rooftop assault where all her men had been killed, she could have run up the stairs to the roof, next to the cartel soldier, and shot everyone in sight, including the target—or died in a blaze of glory.

As much as she enjoyed her tiny cabin and self-determined retirement, a small part of her regretted escaping the life on the down note of a failed mission.

Still, she had summer to look forward to—a short growing season to get in a tiny garden, weed and nurture it daily, and put away vegetables for winter.

And she had plenty of books to keep her company. Her read pile on the rickety shelves was finally equal to her to-be-read stack on the floor next to her cot.

She'd had breakfast, stretched and did body-weight exercises, cleaned the small space, and had a light lunch. Finally, she could spend the rest of the day and night reading.

After adding a few logs to the fire, Ekaterina settled into her wooden chair, put her feet on the ottoman, and picked up the latest thick book—a classic American thriller from the eighties she'd been too busy killing people around the world to read back then or since.

A smile touched her face as she opened the decades-old book and started to read. It would be amusing to see what the author had gotten wrong—and right—about life in the then-Soviet Union.

Before she reached the end of the first sentence, a knock came from the cabin's front—and only—door.

She hadn't heard a car nor someone approaching on foot, but anyone coming in the daytime—and knocking—posed no threat.

With a finger marking page one in the book and the hope this wouldn't take long—some neighbor seeking vodka or a friend to talk to, she figured —she twisted in her chair. "It is open. Enter."

Sharp, fresh, damp air blew in, followed by a thin man in his forties, looking like Moscow. He wore an air of professionalism and competence like a shield to hide his true feelings, which were crystal clear to Ekat.

He's petrified.

The intruder wasn't a local; she knew all the people in the small village already. He reeked of the city and the civilization she had gone to extremes to leave behind.

The man was from her old life, if she could call the time from only earlier this year her "old" life.

Scared Mr. Moscow moved deliberately, stepping inside and closing the door. He made no sudden moves, trying to hide both his fear and how cold he was.

He must have parked a mile away and walked to keep me from bolting... and he's not a man used to walking in the cold.

"Come warm yourself," she said with a sigh and turned back to the fire. The logs crackled, and the flames danced. She heard him walk slowly, giving her as wide a berth as the small room allowed, and she smiled.

He's more afraid of me than I am of him.

That was easy. If they wanted her dead, she wouldn't have woken up this morning. And the man now warming his hands by her fire wasn't a killer.

"So, you found me," Ekaterina said. She refused to put the book down in the hope that this—whatever this was—would be over soon, one way or the other. "Are you proud of yourself?"

Antagonizing him shouldn't be hard. He was so on edge, one false move on her part might bring a sniper shot through her lone window, ending things quickly instead of in a long, drawn-out punishment that Moscow likely felt she deserved—and which she entirely expected.

Still, she had a minuscule shred of hope.

Perhaps they only want to debrief me on the Los Angeles mission.

Ekat smiled to herself again. Despite her decades as a killer, a tiny part of the dreaming little girl she used to be remained.

"I meant to complain," she said. "I haven't been receiving my pension."

The young man's face twitched, and he fought back a smile. He said nothing, only kept rubbing his hands in front of him.

He's too young for this job. Too innocent. Or maybe I'm just old.

It had been many years since she'd been innocent.

"Aren't you a little young?" she asked after growing tired of waiting for him to speak.

His smile faded. "Yes, definitely," he said, turning so his back was to the fire and he could look her in the eye.

With his haunted expression and tired eyes, he didn't look so young anymore.

"But my predecessor..." he started.

"Ah." She understood. "You received a sudden promotion after he had an unfortunate accident? An open window, a slip on spilled tea, and a fall out of a three-story building?"

She had facilitated several similar accidents like that in years past.

"He took his own life at his dining room table," her visitor said, no longer looking at her.

"Before you had to do it," she said.

It wasn't a question, and they both knew the answer.

"I've been playing this game for decades," she said, "since long before you were born. I hope you don't expect me to go the same way just to spare your feelings."

Each generation is weaker than the last. This one wouldn't have lasted a month in the eighties.

"No," the young man said. "At least, I hope not."

The look in his eyes showed he had more mettle than she had previously thought.

"Why don't I make us some tea?" he said, moving to the kitchen without waiting for permission. "And I can explain the situation."

She didn't have a second chair—she didn't need one—so when the tea was ready, he returned to the far side of the fireplace, facing her.

He took a sip of his tea, his eyes never leaving her face.

He's going to tell the truth.

The knowledge put her on edge and alarmed her more than anything had in years.

A log sparked in the fireplace. The man startled, then took a deep breath, calming himself. After another small sip of the tea, he began. "First, my name is Dmitry."

She nodded. "And next?"

"We are in trouble."

"We?" she asked, not trying to hide her amused smile.

Dmitry offered her a nod in recognition of her perception and his error. "Russia is in trouble."

"Russia... or the Foreign Intelligence Service?"

She enjoyed toying with him.

This is fun.

She detected the tiniest hint of annoyance on his face.

He wants to get the story out... and I keep hindering him.

"Russia." He meant to hurry on, but she broke in yet again before he could.

"The true Russia? Or the rich oligarchs and their cronies who bleed the country dry?"

"Russia," Dmitry said again, his voice firm.

I believe him.

The man was wide open. If he had the ability to hide his true thoughts and feelings, he wasn't using the capability.

This time, he waited for her to speak.

In her heart, she knew which way this was going.

After a few seconds of first arguing with herself, then feeling exasperated for still having a pinch of caring left for the country she had given so much to, she let out a heavy sigh.

"Tell me more," she said.

94

THE VANISHING

Lux View Marina Tower
Floor 15
Dubai, United Arab Emirates

"The people at the restaurant left an hour ago," Wolf said as George approached his workstation. "We hacked cameras on streets a few miles away and saw vehicles go in every direction. They know we found them and are too difficult to track now. We do not know where the hacker is or if he was in one of the vehicles. He could still be at the restaurant."

"No word from the team on the ground?" George asked. He'd been away a short while, disappearing as he occasionally did to report their progress to whoever was in charge of the operation.

The men in command must be close. He's never gone very long.

The rumors were probably right. It would make sense to keep the entire operation in one building, and there were plenty of businesses and apartments in the eighty-five-story skyscraper.

Wolf shoved down his curiosity. Knowing who led the operation could be detrimental to his health.

"No word," Wolf replied.

"Reports of being attacked?"

"No."

"Police? Ambulances?"

"None. No reports of gunshot victims on their news programs."

George grunted, frustrated. "Not good," he said. "Ideas?"

He doesn't want to report a failure, even though the latest plan to capture Void was a long shot.

Wolf gave himself a few seconds to think through the problem.

It depends on Void.

"Does the hacker want us to find him?" he asked.

"That is a good question," George muttered. "But no, I do not believe so."

95

THE CONDO

High Pointe Downtown Condos
Arlington, Virginia

"We're guests here," Haley told the IT team and Void as they filed past her. "Try not to touch anything you don't have to."

I sound exactly like my mother.

Faced with hackers able to track their moves, Haley had taken drastic measures, not knowing who was after them or what their true capabilities were. After all, their enemy had found the team at the diner, likely by hacking a satellite, finding the burning helicopter crash site, and monitoring the route they took.

After the body of their security teammate had been carefully loaded into one of the analyst's SUVs at the diner, the entire team had rushed outside as one, climbed into their vehicles, and scattered.

Their instructions were to randomly drive, doubling back, making sudden turns, and using parking garages, overpasses, and rural areas to lose themselves from surveillance: traffic cameras, security cams on businesses and homes, or satellites.

After at least an hour of evasive driving, they would meander their way to the joint military base in Maryland. By then, Gregory would have them all cleared to enter and a workspace ready.

Everyone would go to the base except for the core World Intelligence

Agency of Haley, Nancy, Dave, Marcus, and Gregory himself, along with Axe, Tucci, the four shaken IT team members, and Void.

They would drop off the grid.

Gregory had made a call, which led to another few, ending with a very wealthy businessman with security clearance because of... something—Gregory didn't share all the details—who called the concierge and security team at a luxury skyscraper in downtown Arlington, just across the Potomac River from DC. The businessman gave the team access to his home—well, one of his several homes—for as long as they needed.

No questions asked.

Through the floor-to-ceiling windows of the luxury condo, the views of the city were incredible. Though it was the middle of the night, enough lights were on in other buildings to make the downtown area look magical. People in a few cars went silently about their business on the street hundreds of feet beneath them.

The condo took up the entire twenty-third floor, aside from a small entry area with the building's elevators. There were hardwood floors, granite countertops, and neutral beige tones. Artwork lined the walls. A balcony with a table jutted from one side of the kitchen—on the south side of the home—where a small breakfast table sat. It was a cozier option than the long formal dining table occupying the far side of the massive kitchen. A stylish box housed an emergency fire escape system with two harnesses. They could be connected to bolts on the wall to automatically descend safely to the ground in the event of a building fire.

Rich people think of everything.

The refrigerator was fully stocked with drinks, and the cupboards had all the staples they might need for an extended stay. The only thing missing was fresh food, but the owner had assured Gregory that they could have whatever they needed delivered and put on his bill.

Must be nice to have this as merely one of your houses.

They snuck up the elevator exactly on time—when the security cameras from the parking garage to the twenty-third floor were briefly switched off for "scheduled maintenance."

They wouldn't get caught on camera by hackers halfway around the world, or wherever they were. And with any luck, the crazy rush away from the diner would overwhelm anyone with satellite surveillance access.

"You five are confined to the kitchen, the living room, and the bathroom in the hall," she told the IT team, who had already commandeered the twelve-foot-long dining table, accessed the Wi-Fi, and helped themselves to energy drinks from the fridge.

Tucci sat on a stool, his shotgun lying on the kitchen island, keeping his eye on Void.

The hacker was in his element, directing all four geeks at once in their efforts to track down the enemy.

Our enemy. They're likely his friends—or at least his peers.

Haley didn't know whether to trust Void, but she'd had a quiet word with the IT team before they rushed into her SUV; Void still wasn't allowed to touch a computer.

Nancy and Dave took the far end of the table and jumped back online, continuing their hunt for clues by mining the databases of the nation's intelligence agencies.

"Axe?" she called. He'd separated from them as soon as they entered the condo to do a security check.

"In here," he called from a hallway that she guessed led to the primary bedroom.

"Everything okay?" she asked. There had been a strange note to his voice.

"All clear," he said, though he still sounded off.

She found him halfway down the wide hallway, standing in front of a framed picture, four feet wide by six feet tall. It showed a mama bear in a forest clearing, standing on her hind legs, sniffing the air. Behind her, a row of cubs followed. Dawn sunlight perfectly lit the group.

It was one of Axe's art photographs that had sold at his first gallery show in Washington.

"Amazing picture," Haley said, admiring the image.

Axe nodded and rubbed the thick beard on his face.

"You okay?"

"First time I've seen one of my pictures on display in someone's house," he said. "Weird feeling." Axe shook his head and turned to her. "This floor is secure. I'm going up to see how the access is from the roof." He still had her short-barrel M4 slung on his shoulder. "You good here for a while?"

"Yes. I need to sleep, but I'm going to take another shot at some analysis. Tucci's keeping an eye on the IT team and Void. I'll get a nap in a bit. You, he, and I need to stay fresh. I have a feeling this isn't over."

"Me too. Not by a long shot."

96

THE BUG

Haley fought through the fog of exhaustion. She'd been awake for two days straight but couldn't let go and rest.

I'm missing something.

A trip to the refrigerator for diet soda gave her a chance to stretch her legs. Instead of pouring from the large bottle into a glass and returning to the near end of the table, which she'd claimed for herself, she sighed wearily and brought the entire bottle back with her, sipping straight from it as she walked.

Gregory had disappeared into one of the bathrooms to change into gym clothes. He had a short drive to the White House to work out with the president—and update him on the little they knew.

Instead of diving back into her computer, Haley detoured to the tall windows and stared at Washington, DC in the distance. She couldn't make out the White House from her vantage point, but it was less than three miles away.

She took another deep swig of soda and resisted letting out a loud burp. For a second, her tiredness combined with tilting her head back to chug the desperately needed caffeine made her dizzy. Putting a hand on the thick, cool glass window, she steadied herself. Twenty-three floors above the ground was a horrible place to have a sudden bout of vertigo.

Vertigo...

Her intuition screamed at her to pay attention even as her exhausted mind reached for the thread... and it slipped away.

Damn.

She'd almost had it. If she could retrace her steps mentally, it might return.

Staring out the window, she waited, hoping.

Nothing.

The soda bottle screw top went back on. She spun and speed-walked to the refrigerator.

"Haley," one of the geeks called, "I think—"

"Not now," she said, cutting him off without glancing his way.

She put the soda back in the empty spot on the door of the refrigerator, closed it, and repeated her process from a minute before.

Door. Soda bottle. Top. Sip straight from the bottle.

Turn, holding the cap in her hand. Walk to the window.

Tilt her head back and chug.

Resist the temptation to belch loudly.

No vertigo this time.

What causes vertigo?

It was something she should know.

Vertigo was a type of dizziness.

Dizziness can be caused by a few issues but most often by an illness affecting the inner ear.

I'm fine. Tired, but not sick.

Why had her intuition flashed when she'd had a head rush caused by tilting her head back, being exhausted, and standing too close to a window hundreds of feet above the ground?

This isn't Russia, where a few generals "accidentally" fall out of windows.

The soundproof windows didn't open here, though the door to a small balcony off the kitchen did.

Her gut told her she was on the wrong track.

Nancy mumbled something to the rest of the team as Haley stomped back to the refrigerator and repeated the entire process.

She's telling them to leave me alone.

Nancy's intuitive abilities had been improving over the last several months.

Does she feel it too? Or does she just know me well by now?

The refrigerator. The bottle. The window. Gulp after gulp of the soda.

She had drunk half the two-liter bottle, and the fog in her mind lifted little by little.

No dizziness this time.

Dizziness. Inner ear problems.

The secretary of state's head cold?

"Is the secretary of state still in the hospital?" she asked, more to herself than any of the others.

What made me think of him?

"Yes," Marcus said from the table. "They're treating him for a stomach bug."

Stomach, not head.

But she was on the right track. She could feel it.

Haley didn't dare move and break the spell.

"He got the bug from a staffer who was sick, right?" she asked and took another swig of caffeine.

A few more seconds went by before Marcus replied again. "That's correct. A staffer had to be sent home a few days before. She wanted to keep working, but she obviously was fighting off a cold."

"How did they know that?"

You may suffer through a head cold, but no one brags or shows off their stomach bug.

It took longer for an answer, which came from Nancy this time. "The report says... Here it is. Runny nose, cough."

"Does the Secretary have any of those symptoms?"

Haley didn't have to ask. It all clicked. Her original instinct had been that someone had gotten to the secretary of state, causing him to collapse. Dave had investigated earlier, but it hadn't led anywhere.

On the same day as a massive cyberattack, the secretary of state succumbs to the flu so badly he collapses and is rushed to the hospital?

She didn't like the "coincidental" timing.

But how would anyone get to the Secretary?

In her final year of college, hoping for a job at the CIA or a similar agency, she had devoured all she could about intelligence gathering and analysis, spies, terrorism, assassinations, and tradecraft.

Russia is highly skilled at killing its enemies—especially in ways very difficult to detect.

In recent years, people "accidentally" fell out of windows or supposedly took their own lives.

But in the nineties, things were different. Russia was more subtle back then. More careful. More devious.

"Call the staffer," Haley said. "Home, cell, whatever. If she doesn't answer, send the FBI to interview her. Confirm her symptoms. Someone else call the hospital and find out if the Secretary has the same symptoms."

He doesn't.

"I'm not sure they're going to tell us that, Haley," Dave said.

"Gregory!" Haley yelled. "We're going to need your authorization for some medical tests on the secretary of state."

A few seconds later, Gregory hurried in. He wore gym shorts, running shoes, and a sweatshirt.

Haley held up her finger, asking him to wait while she drained the rest of the soda.

The burp came out louder than she intended but felt so good.

"The secretary of state doesn't have the flu or a stomach bug. He's been poisoned with polonium-210."

Gasps came from the table behind her, but Haley couldn't tell if they were from Dave, Nancy, Marcus, or the geeks.

Gregory's eyes sought hers, and they shared a look.

"Dave was right all along," she said, screwing the top back on the empty soda bottle. "Russia is behind the attacks."

97

THE GYM

The President's Exercise Room
The White House
Washington, DC

Gregory took a last gulp of coffee before entering the president's private workout room. Over the past several months, he had started looking forward to the morning workout sessions with Admiral Nalen and the president. He'd bulked up, felt—and looked—better than he had in years, and found himself more energized than ever.

Except for mornings like this, when he'd been up all night on the latest crisis facing the country.

At least the president won't have had much sleep, either.

Warning bells flashed in his mind as he stepped into the small room. Admiral Nalen wasn't there, which wasn't unusual. As Gregory had formally taken over his role of supervising Haley and Axe's "extracurricular" activities, Nalen had stepped away to support his new girlfriend, Senator Woodran, and work on some sort of secret project.

The president, however, had already arrived—early. He had the barbell across his shoulders with several heavy weights on each side, squatting slowly before exploding upward with a fierce grunt. His gray Navy T-shirt was dark with sweat, and his face was red.

Although the president never gave much away, he let his guard down in the weight room. The way he worked out often revealed his mood.

He's stressed, angry... and worried.

"Got started without you," the president said as he lowered himself again. He stood, finishing the squat, and backed up to let the bar rest on its support rack.

Gregory stripped off his light jacket and started a slow jog on the treadmill to warm up.

The president came over next to him, using a small towel to dry his sweaty face. "We'll do everything we usually do. But this is far from an ordinary day," the president said, his voice quieter than usual.

More alarms went off for Gregory.

With all the Top Secret plans we've discussed in this room, now he's speaking softly?

Gregory pressed the button on the treadmill to pick up his pace, feeling some of the fatigue slip away. He had so much to tell the president, but the man was on a roll and not ready to be interrupted.

"I originally recruited Nalen to be available if I ever had a problem I couldn't entrust to the CIA, NSA, or other, more bloated bureaucratic intelligence agencies," the president started. He shook his head with a chuckle. "Of course, Nalen being Nalen, and Axe and Haley being who they are, the team took on a life of its own. With you on board, doing what little anyone can to manage Haley, it all came together. You've saved the country repeatedly. But now it's time for the World Intelligence Agency to go back to its roots. I hope you have another miracle ready. You're going to need it this time."

Gregory pressed the stop button on the treadmill and slowed to a walk. He was as warm as he needed to be—especially given his lack of sleep and what promised to be a less intense workout than usual if he had to remember details and orders from the commander in chief.

"Most of my team has relocated to the joint military base in Maryland and are hard at work tracking leads on the hackers who attacked us, Mr. President. And I have several unofficial preliminary reports for you. I'm not sure how much capacity we have... unless you want us off the hunt?"

Gregory couldn't imagine the president would want to take Haley and the rest of the CAG team away from searching for the perpetrators of the cyberattacks, especially given the head start they had with Dawson "Eternal Void" Reite in their custody and helping them.

The president nodded. "We can get to that. What do you have for me?"

"Haley is convinced Secretary Wilson has been poisoned with polonium-210," Gregory said from the motionless treadmill.

"What the...?" the president said, trailing off, at a rare loss for words.

"Tests are being conducted now. We'll have the results in a while— early this morning," Gregory said.

The president watched him, eyes narrowed. "Let me guess. There's more than that bombshell?"

"Yes, Mr. President. Dave—one of my senior analysts—is convinced that Russia's military is a paper tiger. In his view, it is falling apart at the seams and barely functioning. He believes the former president was unaware of the actual situation and that President Nikitin, being a more thorough and pragmatic leader, discovered the disaster he'd inherited."

"Go on," the president said. "I can see you have more."

"Yes, sir. Dave has also done a deep dive into the Russian economy and warns that it is in dire straits. He predicts record-high inflation, a plummeting of the value of the ruble, and great hardship for the average person if nothing is done."

Gregory let the revelation sink in for a moment before adding the kicker. "If Dave is correct—and I believe he is—Russia is on the brink of economic disaster and potentially unable to defend itself. It is in a carefully concealed fight for its life."

The president nodded slowly as he digested the intel. "That tracks right along with what I was discussing with my Chief of Staff an hour ago."

"I have others in the team checking the raw data and his conclusions now—including Haley," Gregory said. "But my gut tells me that, against all odds and despite all the other intelligence agencies singing from a different hymnal, he's right on the money. The cyberattacks may have been a first strike, one designed to go as far as possible, do us an incredible amount of damage, but not be directly attributable to them. They don't want war—especially if my analyst is correct. They may want us distracted and focused on the homeland instead of projecting power around the world."

The president hung on his every word but didn't seem surprised. "This is making more and more sense. I figured there wouldn't be conclusive proof of who attacked us," the president said. "With the sophistication of the cyberattacks, I would be incredibly surprised if we ever find the hackers—at least with enough evidence for a retaliatory strike. I'm sure the other intel agencies and the military will formally tell me just that in a few hours. But your analyst might be right. It would explain a lot. If Haley is also right, they messed up using polonium-210. It leads right to Russia. It's a strategic error."

"It's not confirmed yet, sir."

"I understand. It's just…" The president looked away and wiped his face with the towel again.

He's stalling.

Gregory had never known the president to beat around the bush. He could be subtle, but he never drew things out.

This can't be good.

98

THE IDEA

"What is it, sir?" Gregory asked. Standing on the treadmill put him an inch above the president, but he didn't want to step down and break away from the conversation.

"You're the only other person in the government to hear about this, aside from my Chief of Staff—Chad—who brought it to me. Use your discretion on who you tell. Understand?"

Whoa. This must be big.

"Yes, Mr. President."

"Do you know what a 'deepfake' is?"

"Yes, sir. A video altered or falsified using computer technology. The visuals, audio, or both can be changed to make it look like people did or said things they wouldn't normally do, or did them in a different location, for example. Thankfully, the technology isn't good enough yet to make completely convincing fakes. So far, they've appeared... off. It's easy to sense they aren't real. But one of my analysts recently wrote a report. By the next election cycle, she's predicting we'll have to be extra vigilant about them."

But they had almost two years until the midterms and three until the start of the next presidential election.

The technology is going to make it a nightmare. People are too easy to fool.

The president waved Gregory over to the squat rack and helped him change the weights to lighter ones, all without speaking more on the subject.

Where is he going with this?

Gregory backed up to the bar, lifted it off the rack, and squatted, focusing on his form while preparing for the bad news.

The president was a stickler for doing the movements correctly to avoid injury as well as get the maximum benefit and, if it wasn't done right, would critique the form. This time, Gregory sensed he was waiting to avoid springing the news on him and ruining his set.

Once Gregory racked the bar, the president finally spoke. "Someone has perfected the deepfake technology and is blackmailing me."

Gregory stared at the president, praying he was joking, but the look on his face showed how serious the situation was.

"I understand. Can I see the video?"

"No. It was shown to Chad last night and immediately taken back. He was told it came from the hackers. They want to keep it from being examined and proven fake. Would that be possible?"

"I... I'm not sure, Mr. President. I'm not an expert on the process. Quite possibly. The technology exists to prove falsified or altered photographs by digging down to the pixel level—the tiny dots that make up a picture. Apparently, there are discrepancies or artifacts—something like that—if a photo has been changed. I don't see why it couldn't be done with video as well."

"Beyond a reasonable doubt?"

Gregory caught the micro-expression on the president's face, along with the slight change in tone.

"Reasonable doubt" is a very specific phrase.

Gregory didn't speak for a moment. His fatigue had vanished. The lack of sleep didn't matter. He focused all his brainpower on the conversation.

This is a historic moment.

If, in the coming days and weeks, he and his team were successful in whatever the president was going to ask him to do, this would be one of the monumental moments in his life.

If they failed, this morning's conversation in the surprisingly cramped weight room in the basement of the White House would be discussed in a trial, congressional hearing, deposition, a Top Secret inquiry—or at all of them.

"What does the altered video show, Mr. President?" he asked softly.

"It shows me interrogating and beating a bound prisoner."

He and the president locked eyes. The president looked defiant and...

Thank goodness.

Innocent.

But there's more.

"What else, sir?" he forced himself to ask, not sure he wanted to know.

"On the video, the person with my face and voice then executes the prisoner by shooting him point blank in the head. But I swear I didn't do it." He paused, then gestured at the barbell. "Rest time is over. Do your next set while I explain."

Gregory stood frozen, processing what he'd heard. It went beyond bad. Any American service member killing a prisoner would make the United States look horrible, let alone a man who went on to become president.

A video like this, fake or not, could tear apart the country if it came out... and would result in worldwide protests against America and its military.

On autopilot, he backed to the bar, lifted it, took a step forward, and started his set while thinking through what he'd heard.

"Don't lean that far forward. Head up," the president said, critiquing his form.

How can he focus on the minutiae of proper body position for his workout partner's squat at a time like this?

The answer came immediately, even as Gregory adjusted his back and head to do the move correctly.

He's a former SEAL and the president of the United States.

He'd also had more time to process the information.

Gregory's mind refused to focus on the weightlifting, which made the last few reps that much harder.

Once he'd finished, he felt better prepared to address the problem.

This is solvable. Maybe.

"The technology and the skills to do this aren't available to the average person with a laptop," Gregory said, thinking it through. "But it's used in Hollywood more and more. A few actors have died while filming movies. Actors with similar body types and movements finish the required scenes, and the filmmakers make it look like the original actor. And certainly, the hackers would have access to the proper tools and time to learn the techniques."

"The tricky part here is that the event happened," the president said with a frown. "A prisoner actually was executed. We're debating accessing the highly classified report that I wrote immediately after the event."

That alone is bad enough.

"Where did the original video come from?"

"One of the host country's interrogators had gotten a camcorder. They were relatively new at the time. The tape was confiscated, but someone must have swapped it out or made a copy."

"Who's behind this, and what's their plan? If they wanted to ruin you, they could've just released it to the press. So obviously they want something. What are their demands?"

The president shook his head. "That's part of the concern. There were none. The person who showed Chad the video was an old friend who was blackmailed into showing it to him. The hackers had complete control of the company he works for and claimed they were going to frame him for crimes. There's a small possibility he simply forgot to deliver the message."

"Under that scenario, Mr. President, I would think he would make passing along demands a high priority."

"Yes, Chad, and I agree," the president said. "Just…"

"Holding out hope."

"Yes." The president leaned against the treadmill. "It has to be the Russians—though even with the polonium-210, it will be difficult to pin on them. If we get close, they'll say it was a rogue element in the government. My working theory is that they want to neuter us ahead of the upcoming Middle East Peace Summit. If I resign, the VP doesn't go to the summit. The Russians point out how chaotic America is, how uncertain it would be to work with or trust us during this time of turmoil. They sweep the field, make favorable deals in our absence, and move up several rungs on the power ladder. Nikitin cements their connections in the region while our power fades. If they are as desperate as your analyst believes, the cyberattacks, deepfake video, and poisoning of Secretary Wilson make sense. They may need the peace summit to get out of the hole they're in."

"Yes, it makes sense, Mr. President," Gregory said.

"Would the VP retaliate or attack Russia right after being sworn in as president?" President Heringten asked, not giving Gregory time to answer. "No, they'd get away with this like they got away with annexing Crimea."

"It's entirely circumstantial," Gregory said, "but in essence, it's what Haley and the rest of my team came up with... without knowing about the videotape, obviously."

The president nodded to himself. "It fits. Russia is to blame. Now, what do we do about it?"

Gregory stared at him, wondering if the question was rhetorical or if the president wanted a tactical or strategic suggestion.

Since he didn't have any specific insights, Gregory stayed quiet.

"We have to throw a wrench into their plans," the president muttered. He began to pace the small room, forced to do an about-face after only a few steps in each direction.

After a half minute, he stopped, a cold smile forming on his face.

"We have to attack," he said.

The idea caught Gregory entirely off guard.

"Attack, Mr. President?"

President Heringten leaned in, speaking barely loud enough for Gregory to hear, and sketched out his idea.

When he finished, Gregory stared at him, speechless.

Now I know where Haley gets her aggressive approach to life. She must have picked it up from her adoptive uncle.

Pulling himself together, he sought the right words—and came up short.

"You can't do that," he said. "Mr. President," he added belatedly, then backpedaled. One doesn't simply tell the president of the United States of America he can't do something, even if he can't. "I mean, um, Mr. President, that wouldn't be advisable. The plan is risky, to say the least."

President Heringten smiled, looking amused at Gregory's consternation. "I can do it, and I will."

They stared at each other for several seconds while Gregory considered ways to talk the man out of his intended course of action.

When nothing came to mind he thought would sway the president, Gregory nodded.

This is going to be interesting.

"How can we help, Mr. President?"

99

PROPORTIONATE RESPONSES

The White House Situation Room
Washington, DC

"As you were," James said as he stalked into the Situation Room, waving at the men and women inside to resume their seats. All his typical advisors had made it to the White House for the early morning meeting—except Gregory Addison, who was on his way to the condo to meet with Haley and the rest of his small team.

"I want an update on the secretary of state the moment it comes in. Is that understood?"

"Yes, Mr. President," an advisor said immediately.

I have to take a breath, calm down, and not start World War III here.

The country had been attacked the day before. People hadn't slept much, if at all—including him. Being short and jumping ahead wouldn't serve anyone.

Gregory's analysts have to write their report and distribute the hypothesis to the other intelligence agencies before I can act.

It would take time.

So would the tests required to determine if Secretary of State Wilson had truly been poisoned with polonium-210.

James had to act like he wasn't one hundred percent convinced Russia was behind the attack.

He leaned back in the leather desk chair as if he had all the time in the world and didn't want to launch an invasion on a possibly defenseless Russia.

"When—if—we discover who was responsible for the attacks yesterday, tell me the options for retaliation," he said.

The chairman of the Joint Chiefs of Staff stood and addressed the question. "There is no precedent for this, sir, aside from the attacks of 9/11. Pearl Harbor would be an obvious comparison, except we knew who did that. We don't know—yet—who was behind the cyberattack."

James nodded as the man returned to his seat. James looked at Diego Samuels, the director for the NCTC. "Anything to add, Mr. Samuels?"

"As you know, Mr. President," Samuels said, "after a terrorist attack, we aim to take out those responsible. However, past attacks—9/11 and others—have been perpetrated by terrorists, not nation-states." He paused and gave a nod of his head, acknowledging a hard yet painful truth. "Or at least without obvious help from their host countries. We've turned a somewhat blind eye in recent years because no one wants to fight in more countries, especially in the Middle East."

There were nods around the table at that, including from James.

I don't want war, either, but if we go, we'll be all in. No half measures.

All he really needed to do here this morning was set the stage for what he might have to order later today or tomorrow: a retaliatory attack on Russia.

Going after a country with nuclear weapons is quite a bit different than invading a technologically backward Middle Eastern country like Iraq or Afghanistan, as my predecessors did.

"With terrorists, we've hit back with a 'proportionate response,'" James said as if thinking out loud. "What could that look like in this case?"

The chairman spoke again. "Mr. President, we don't yet have an idea who did this. Perhaps brainstorming is a bit prema—"

"Humor me, please," James said, cutting him off.

"Yes, Mr. President." The military man glanced across the table at Samuels.

The NCTC director spoke. "If a nation-state is behind this, Mr. President, and we have proof—"

"If we have proof, we go to the United Nations," James interrupted. "Let's discuss having a reasonable certainty."

"Yes, sir. At that point, we would likely recommend hitting back the same way we were attacked. But—" Samuels hesitated, "and of course, this would be your final call, sir—I would suggest avoiding the death toll that has befallen us. We could cripple certain industries and make their technological lives very difficult, depending on the country."

The mood in the room had turned. The tired advisors had probably anticipated a morning briefing where they all reported on the devastation that had hit the country while confessing that none of them knew who to blame.

People were on edge now.

They wonder if they're going to have to talk me down from launching attacks with little or no proof.

James had read plenty about the events of past conflicts, including the run-up to the invasions of Iraq and Afghanistan.

Good people with honorable intentions had made tough calls—some right, some wrong.

Others with their own agendas had pushed for actions that history didn't look back on favorably. Today, people judged them harshly for it.

Intelligent advisors had argued for and against the actions that were ultimately taken.

Through the fog of war and the lenses of worldview, the United States had expended its time, treasure, and—most precious of all—the lives of its warriors in the pursuit of punishing those responsible for 9/11 and other terrorist attacks.

Am I destined to repeat the several mistakes and few successes of the past?

James would only go to war if, in his heart, he knew it was the right thing to do.

His mood cooled.

'Slow is smooth, and smooth is fast.'

If the SEAL slogan was good enough for hunting the enemy on the ground, it could be used well in the realm of war planning, too.

As with his plan to thwart the deepfake attack, knowing the enemy but pretending not to—not acting when or as expected—would be a worthwhile strategy.

'Mystify, mislead, and surprise the enemy.' Sun Tzu nailed it hundreds of years ago.

"Any chance the attack didn't come from a nation-state or a group sponsored by one?" James asked after a minute of thinking. "A group of hackers seeking revenge against America for... whatever they're upset about lately?"

"Highly unlikely, sir," the CISA director said. "This has all the appearances of being a highly organized, well-funded, well-managed endeavor. Hackers—individually or in groups—aren't known for that combination. The hard truth, however, is that we may never have enough conviction to recommend a retaliatory strike."

"I understand," James said. "I know you have reports to give, and I'm ready to hear them. But while that happens, I'd like you all to instruct your staff to look into the following, if you haven't already."

The advisors had pens in hand, ready to make notes of his demands.

"I'd like 'proportionate responses' prepared, focused on cyberattacks and minimizing casualties, especially civilian. I need them for these countries, in this order of priority.

"Russia.

"China.

"Iran.

"North Korea."

James paused. He didn't care about the last three—only Russia.

If the tests come back that Secretary of State Wilson was poisoned with polonium-210, I'm sending Russia back to the Stone Age.

He couldn't let his team know that yet, though. For now, he had to play the role and wait, hoping he wasn't about to go from a cold to a hot cyber war.

Any type of conflict, whether tit-for-tat cyberattacks or limited physical strikes, could escalate quickly.

I don't want to be the president that goes to war with Russia. But if they keep messing around, they're going to find out what we're made of.

"Now," James said to his advisors, "let's hear what else you have for me."

100

THE PROBE

Lux View Marina Tower
Penthouse—Floor 35
Dubai, United Arab Emirates

"Our computers are being probed," Gogol explained. Once again, he had made the journey from the fifteenth floor to the penthouse, passed through Abdul's security, and sat before his brother.

They were inside the small secure office having afternoon tea. His brother's dark, piercing eyes narrowed. "What does that mean—for the computers to be probed?" Abdul asked.

"Someone is hunting us—tracking the hackers via the way they use the internet."

Abdul nodded. "You expected this."

"Yes. Many people are looking for our trail. The problem is that someone has found us, which we did not anticipate. It should have been nearly impossible. The hackers believe it to be a higher caliber talent than the Americans have available. A freelancer, perhaps, or…"

"Dawson Reite."

"The hackers believe he may have been forced to work for the Americans."

"Or he's helping them," Abdul said, half question and half statement.

"Yes. It would be in his personality to do so, according to the hackers again."

"Will he find us?"

Gogol shrugged. "They've done what they can, which is good enough against anyone the Russians or Americans have. Against Dawson, however, they say it's only a matter of time."

"Are they able to reverse the process? Do they know where Dawson is?"

"Yes, they are working on it now and assure me it's possible. Again, a matter of time. A race to see who finds the other first."

"On a battlefield, when the enemy probes the defenses, they learn much… but so do the defenders."

Gogol nodded, knowing exactly what his brother was thinking. "There is still no word from the mercenaries sent to attack the restaurant. I assume they are dead. But we have the team from Puerto Rico on a boat in the Caribbean. They could fly to America—unarmed—and attempt to acquire new weapons quickly, which would be difficult but not impossible. I suggest we send them to be on standby. If the hackers prevail, there may be another opportunity to retrieve Dawson—if you deem it necessary."

Gogol didn't know all the details of whom Abdul spoke with about the overall mission or took orders from, and he didn't want to. But somehow rescuing—or abducting—the hacker from America was important to the plan.

Abdul stared into space for several seconds before speaking again. "Where, approximately, is Dawson Reite?"

"Likely near Washington, DC. The probe is coming from the east coast. If it is Dawson, he stopped his work when our team hit the restaurant, then resumed less than two hours later, which would put him in or near their capital city."

Abdul nodded slowly. "I am not at liberty to tell you more," he said, "but we must make every effort—every effort," he repeated, "to safely rescue Dawson unharmed. Send the soldiers." He paused. "Have them kill the two hackers they have with them, cut up their bodies, and leave them in the ocean. Their work is done."

"As you say, Malik," Gogol said.

He stood and backed from the room to work at "rescuing" Dawson Reite.

101

SECRETS

The condo's hallway bathroom was bigger than his bedroom, and Axe felt foolish huddled in the far corner with Gregory and Haley.

The shower ran at full blast, as did the water in the sink.

I hate this spy crap.

There was nearly zero chance the apartment's owner had any of the rooms bugged, but Gregory had insisted on this extreme precaution.

Judging from his expression, it must be some kind of huge secret he has to share.

Gregory looked drawn and stressed—more so than usual, that is. He ran a hand through his hair, disturbing it more. Its disarray showed the long hours and lack of sleep; the product that normally held it perfectly in place had clearly failed. Long gray strands jutted from above his ears, making him reach up again in an attempt to smooth them down.

"This goes no further than the three of us," Gregory said. "It doesn't exist unless you hear otherwise from me. Is that understood?"

Axe exchanged a brief look with Haley as they both nodded.

"The president is being threatened… or blackmailed," Gregory continued. "He's not sure which. His Chief of Staff was shown a video purporting to be the president executing a bound suspected terrorist during interrogation. It's a deepfake—computer generated to appear authentic. The video itself is real, however. The president was there, but he tried to stop the shooting. He didn't do it."

Axe kept his face still and didn't bother to look at Haley this time. He kept his entire focus on Gregory.

He's telling the truth. Or, at least, the truth as he understands it.

"Where and when?" Haley asked.

"During the president's time as an active-duty SEAL. I didn't ask where, though I assumed it was Iraq."

"I need a copy. We can debunk this," Haley said.

Gregory shook his head. "He wasn't provided with a copy."

"What's the payoff?" Axe asked. "What do the people behind this want?"

"That wasn't provided, either," Gregory said. "But he thinks it, and the attacks yesterday, may revolve around the Middle East Peace Summit. The best guess is what Dave and you brought up, Haley. Russia is making a big move. They slam us domestically, tie up the president by making him focus on repairing America, get him spun up by blackmailing him—or get him to resign—while they go to town in the Middle East."

"Risky," Haley said with a frown. "Complicated. It's not like them."

"My personal thought," Gregory said, "is that someone in their government forced President Nikitin's hand. He's not a powerful figure, though many of the old guard have 'accidentally' died over the past few months. If an inside group could make yesterday's attack happen, they might force him to move forward whether he wanted to or not. A form of a coup. 'Do what we think is best… or you're next.'"

"President Heringten should resign," Axe said, ignoring Haley's sharp intake of breath.

"He's ruled that out for now," Gregory said.

"What if he did it?" Axe asked, not willing to let it go. "What if it happened exactly as shown on the video? Things got out of hand, tensions were high… Maybe it was an accident."

The three of them considered the question.

"Uncle Jimmy wouldn't do that," Haley eventually said, but her voice lacked conviction.

Gregory nodded but kept silent, letting Axe and Haley work it out.

"Remember, we're not the president's private army," Axe told Haley. "I told you when we first met, I'm not in this for your uncle Jimmy—or any president. I serve the United States of America. Going after whoever did this is fine with me—as long as we believe there's a reasonable chance President Heringten is innocent."

"I get it," Haley said. "I do. He's innocent—and the people behind this are still gunning for us."

"Does your gut tell you that?"

"Yes, and it makes sense. There are no coincidences. This has to be the second punch. And there's another one coming—a big one."

"So it's all made up? A true deepfake video?" Axe wanted to believe, wanted to think a SEAL wouldn't do something like that, but there had been bad apples in the community before. The SEAL ethos said, "Uncompromising integrity is my standard. My character and honor are steadfast." But that hadn't stopped a few nutjobs from abusing their status and power.

Heringten probably didn't do it... but what if he did?

Axe didn't want to be on the wrong side of the battle—or the law—and enable a cover-up.

"I don't know," Haley said, interrupting his thoughts. "Let's go find out. If it's him, if he did this, we step back and let the chips fall where they will. We can take it to the press or do whatever you think is best. Let's go shake the tree and find out the truth. At the same time, we'll also figure out what else is going on."

Gregory nodded, and they both turned to Axe. Checking out Gregory's face, Axe's skin tingled.

He's holding something back.

"This isn't the time for games or secrets," Axe said to Gregory, his voice hard. "What aren't you telling us?"

He's acting like I do when I disappear into sniper mode.

Gregory shook his head. "That's all I have for you at this time."

Axe stared him down with a look that made tougher men than Gregory go pale and do whatever Axe wanted them to. And while Axe detected a tiny tremor from the spy chief, Gregory said nothing.

"Why tell us this part if you can't tell us everything?" Haley asked in a tone much friendlier than Axe's, though it still had an edge.

"I needed you to know so you can better analyze the situation," Gregory said. "And I knew you'd tell Axe the first chance you got, no matter what I asked," Gregory said with a smile. "I promise you have all the pertinent information for the moment. At some point soon, I'll be able to say more, but not right now." He spread his hands. "That's the best I can do, directly from the president of the United States."

Axe nodded. That he could respect.

When the commander in chief gives a direct order, that's the ballgame.

"So what now?" Haley asked.

"We go back to the group and figure this out," Gregory said. "Are we good?" he asked, looking at Axe.

Axe checked his gut. He didn't like Gregory holding out on them, but his intuition said it wasn't related to the president's guilt or innocence.

I can live with this for now.

"We're solid," Axe said. "Let's get to the bottom of this so I can go kick some ass."

102

THE DECISION

Haley wondered if Void was petrified, overly caffeinated, or having the time of his life.

The hacker stood at the head of the table, sipping an energy drink and looking twitchy. Six empty cans, stacked one on top of another, made a precarious tower next to him.

How long before he bumps the table and knocks them over?

She resisted the part of her that wanted to channel her mother and make him throw his trash in the garbage.

Tucci snored on the couch in the nearby living room, a great rumble that threatened to knock over the cans if it got much louder.

The sun was about to come up. A hint of color crept across the sky seen through the tall condo windows.

"Go ahead, Void," she said. "What have you found?"

"Your guys are great," he said, speaking fast. "Guys and girl, sorry," he said with a quick nod to Kaylin, the lone female IT specialist.

All four beamed with pride at his compliment before remembering their professionalism and masking their feelings.

"We've been examining the hacks and back-tracing the data packets from yesterday," Kaylin said from her spot at Void's right side.

"English," Axe muttered from his seat at the kitchen island.

"We're following their electronic trail," Void said. He looked happy to have the opportunity to explain.

Haley moved her finger in the air, signaling Void to keep moving. "I'll catch him up later if he needs the details. Get to the good parts."

"I think Russia is behind the hacking. They probably piggybacked onto my original approach based on what I let slip in chat rooms. I recognize some of their work," Void said.

"You can do that?" Dave asked from the side of the table. "Like seeing digital fingerprints?"

"Not exactly. It's more like..." Void faltered.

Kaylin jumped in. "It's a feeling of sorts. You can see how they approach a problem. It's hard to explain, but it's there. Like an artist recognizing the brush strokes from another painter's work."

"Where are the hackers?" Axe called. "That's what we need to know."

He doesn't have much patience for intelligence gathering and analysis.

"This is the really interesting part," Kaylin said. "The attacks didn't originate in Russia, China, North Korea, or Iran."

"I know those are probably your best guesses as to who's behind this," Void added. "We're still narrowing it down—they electronically tripped all around the globe, covering their tracks—but from what we can tell so far, the source is the United Arab Emirates—Dubai or Abu Dhabi." He paused, shrugged, and hedged. "There's a small chance it's Qatar or Bahrain."

"We just have to make sure it's not a red herring," Kaylin said. "We'll keep looking."

"It could be Russia basing a team in the Middle East for plausible deniability," Marcus said from the side of the table.

"If I was to get on a plane right now to go hunt them down," Axe said, "where would you send me?"

"I don't know yet," Void said. He put a fist to his chest and let out a soft burp.

"Best guess?" Axe said.

Uh-oh, he's got that tone of voice. He's tired of sitting around.

Haley nodded at Void to answer as best he could.

Void bit his lip and thought for a moment. "Dubai," he said quietly. "Best guess right now. We'll know more in a few hours. Less," he said, turning to look at Haley, pleading with his eye, "if you give me access to a computer. It's so slow telling them what to do." He composed himself and covered. "They're doing great, though, like I said. It just takes longer."

She shook her head. "Not a chance."

"Haley?" Axe called. "A word?"

Here we go.

"Get back at it. Find us a lead," she told the geeks as she followed Axe into the hallway. Gregory pushed his chair back and wearily came after her.

"You want to go to Dubai so you can shake the tree," Haley said to Axe. "I agree." She turned to Gregory. "Can we get him over there?"

Gregory nodded. "I can work something out. Stick with the classic— freelance photographer on a time-sensitive shoot for a last-minute magazine article or something. It'll be enough."

Axe was shaking his head. "We."

"What?" she asked, playing dumb. She knew exactly what he was saying.

"We need to get to Dubai. Someone else can babysit the nerds."

"Geeks," she corrected automatically, her mind on his argument.

"What's the difference?"

"They prefer geeks. Nerd is derogatory. Don't worry about it. What matters is that I can't go with you."

It took all she had to say it. She refused to look at Gregory, not wanting to see his reaction.

"Haley, we've saved the world multiple times. You can literally do whatever you want, and no one will stop you." Axe pointedly glanced Gregory's way before turning back to her.

"I... I'm stopping me."

I can't believe I'm saying this, but it's the right thing. I feel it.

Axe's gaze seemed to peer into her soul. "Mad Dog and Johnboy are on a contract and can't break away. No one guessed we would need them again this soon. Mariana is busy," he said the word carefully, "with Kelton. Admiral Nalen is in love with Senator Woodran and working on a long-term project for us. It has to be you."

"Axe," she said, speaking from the heart. "I would love to go. For this mission, though, I'm needed here."

It took a toll, but she stuck to her decision.

I'm not going out in the field again. Not after Los Angeles. My work is here, at a computer.

The seconds stretched in silence as they stared at each other.

Haley prayed Axe would understand her decision and support her.

"Throw a little Haley magic their way?" Axe finally asked with a smile.

He gets it—and we're good.

She chuckled and shrugged. "Whatever I can help with."

Axe offered her a fist to bump.

"Fine," he said. "Back to being a team of one." He turned to Gregory. "I need a very fast plane."

103

THE PROGNOSIS

New York General Hospital
New York City, NY

"What's wrong with me?" Wilson croaked as he swam out of the fog dulling his brain. He felt like a truck had slammed into him, sent him flying down the road, then sped up to run him over. He was weak and dizzy.

"You're in the Intensive Care Unit," a woman said. She had a kind but matter-of-fact voice. "The doctor will be— Here she is."

Another voice, also female, spoke from the other side of where he lay. "Mr. Secretary, I'm Doctor Pearl. At the insistence of President Heringten, we tested your urine and blood for alpha-emitters." The doctor paused. "You have a very high amount of radionuclide polonium-210 in your body." Another hesitation. "It appears you've been poisoned with polonium-210."

Although Wilson felt horrible, he could still read people. The doctor's voice had gone from matter of fact, like the nurse's, to trying to hide her concerns.

She's afraid.

"Am I going to live?" he asked.

"It's too soon—" the doctor began.

"Just tell me," he interrupted. He didn't have the finesse he normally used in negotiations. There wasn't time. He felt himself slipping.

"I don't know, Mr. Secretary. We're doing everything we can."

As he faded, he dimly noted the sudden yelling from the two women near him and an influx of people into his room.

Then it all went black.

104

THE FEELING

"This doesn't feel right," Haley whispered.

The dining room table was bathed in the warm spring morning sunlight.

Axe had left a few hours before.

Haley had taken an hour-long nap while Tucci guarded the home, but she had woken a few minutes before and sent Tucci back to bed—this time into one of the many bedrooms, where his snoring wouldn't bother the rest of them.

Across the condo, Void sprawled on one of the sofas in the enormous living room. He snored softly, making a noise like a dolphin.

Around him, the IT team occupied plush leather recliners—and a love seat, in Kaylin's case—and the second couch. All had been sound asleep for an hour.

Gregory stirred at the long dining table next to her. He'd had his head on his crossed arms, face down on the table, taking a nap.

He blinked his eyes repeatedly and sat up.

"Sorry," Haley said. "I didn't mean to wake you."

"Yes, you did," he said, his voice rough.

Nancy and Dave were in a bedroom, all pretense that they weren't a couple gone.

Marcus was in a third bedroom.

None of them had wanted to sleep, but Gregory had ordered it when the IT team, along with Void, nodded off one by one at the table.

Haley shook her head, trying to convince herself, but she wasn't able to let go of the terrible thought.

I was wrong.

"It's not Russia," she said to Gregory, who rubbed his eyes and stared at her like he would be happy to never see her again.

"Why do you—" Gregory's secure cell phone buzzed before he could finish.

"Hold that thought," he said.

He picked up the phone and read the text. "Damn," he muttered. He shook his head at her. "You were right. Again. How the hell do you do that?" he asked, more to himself than her.

"It was polonium-210?" she asked as he put his phone back in his pocket.

Gregory nodded. "I doubt anyone else would have thought to look for it. It was a massive dose. Secretary Wilson died a few minutes ago." He raised an eyebrow. "Still say it's not Russia?"

Haley hesitated.

I was right about the polonium-210. Why am I second-guessing myself?

"It all fits, Haley. Do you realize how hard it is to get polonium-210? The FBI can't figure out how exactly he might have been poisoned, but they will. Eventually, it's all going to come out. This level of polonium could only be produced in a Russian nuclear reactor. The FBI will trace it back to Russia—they'll even figure out what facility. This is a state-level material and tradecraft, not some former goat-herder-turned-terrorist with stolen C-4 explosives in his underwear on an airplane."

"I know, and I agree. It's sophisticated. High-level. But with…"—she nodded to the bathroom where they'd had the conversation about the president's deepfake video—"all that's going on," she said to cover, just in case any of the geeks were faking sleep and could hear her whisper from all the way across the room, "it almost makes too much sense. If that makes sense."

Gregory sighed, took off his glasses, and rubbed his eyes again. "It doesn't. Not when I'm this tired. Spell it out for me, Haley."

She didn't know if she could put it into words. "Okay," she said, scooting her chair at the head of the long table closer to Gregory's on her left, facing the sunny, perfectly blue sky out of the floor-to-ceiling windows of the condo. "I agree. All the signs logically point to Russia. But it feels wrong. Let's track this. You know the president well. What do you think he's going to do now that the Secretary has died?"

Gregory put his glasses on and picked up a can of energy drink, shook it—empty—and set it down. "He's going to want to attack Russia, and I can't say I want to hold him back."

She started to speak again but Gregory held up a hand. "Hold that thought. I can barely keep up with you on a good day. If you're going to start mentioning hunches and gut feelings, I need more caffeine."

He pushed his chair back quietly, went to the refrigerator, and came back with two energy drinks in tall, thin cans for him and a brand new two-liter bottle of soda for Haley.

She accepted it gratefully, opened it, and chugged while Gregory did the same with the first of his drinks.

"Okay," he said. "Better. Hit me with the Haley magic. Convince me."

"Do you think..." she said, trailing off and giving Gregory a look, "will deter the president?"

I know Uncle Jimmy. If he decided not to resign, he won't let the deepfake video stop him from doing what's necessary.

"No, if he's convinced he knows who attacked the country and killed Secretary Wilson, he'd deal with it no matter what might happen to him personally."

"Exactly. If you and I know that, why don't the Russians?"

Gregory looked out the window and took two more gulps of the energy drink while he thought.

"It has the opposite effect," Haley said in a voice so quiet she could barely hear herself, referencing the deepfake video. "It doesn't hold him back. It pushes him toward action."

Yes, this feels right.

"I was wrong before. All signs point to Russia, but it's not them. Russia is being set up to take the fall. Someone wants us to attack them."

Gregory finished the last of the drink and immediately opened the other.

Haley had a temporary pang of regret.

I sure don't make this easy on him.

"Wake up Nancy, Dave, and Marcus," Gregory said after taking another long gulp. "We need to go back to square one."

"And you have to tell the president not to retaliate against Russia," she said.

"I will, but he's not going to listen to me. He's hot to go on the offensive."

Haley nodded.

"You'll have to make him listen. Maybe we'll find the clues, or Axe will shake something loose in Dubai. But we need time. You can't let him attack Russia."

105

STEP BY STEP

The White House Situation Room
Washington, DC

James held up his hand for quiet, and the chatter around the room died down immediately. "What do you have, Samuels?" James asked, though he suspected he already knew just from the look on the CISA director's face. The man had taken point on the entire operation, though technically several others could have muscled their way to being in charge.

At least everyone is playing nice for once.

"Mr. President," Samuels said, "Secretary of State Wilson has died of heart failure. The doctors believe that he may have ingested a lethal dose of polonium-210."

The rest of the room sat speechless at the news.

"May he rest in peace," James said quietly. He waited a moment, said a silent prayer, then nodded at the FBI director to speak next.

"In my mind, sir, this greatly increases the probability Russia was behind not only the Secretary's death but also the attacks on our country," he said.

"Explain," James ordered, more for the sake of argument and the general discussion in the room.

"This is a nearly perfect way to poison a person and get away with it," the FBI director continued. "Given the Secretary's age and recent exposure to the flu, no one would have thought to test for polonium-210. They—whoever it was, sir—would have gotten away with it if it weren't for you."

Every person at the table had to be wondering how the hell he had known to order the tests for polonium, so James addressed the elephant in the room.

"I'm not psychic, people—I received intelligence indicating a possible connection and ordered it followed up on."

There were grim nods all around, except from the director of the CIA, who busied herself with note-taking, not meeting his eyes.

They should have caught this—or at least suspected.

At the end of this latest crisis, he had to find a way to streamline the intelligence services, reduce their fear of going out on a limb, or somehow get more people up to Haley's level.

I can't keep relying on one or two people to have all the good ideas.

"It will take some time," the FBI director continued, "but I believe we'll confirm the polonium-210 used to kill Secretary Wilson came from Russian nuclear reactors. They are the only ones that still produce it."

James nodded. "I agree. Let's assume it came from Russia."

That tracks with what Gregory and his team—including Haley— suspected.

"That doesn't prove they're behind it, though," James said.

To me, it does, but let's see what people have to say if I act unconvinced.

"No, sir. However, it would be virtually impossible for anyone else to get ahold of the polonium. Russian soldiers, no matter their rank, may sell diesel fuel, rifles, and spare tank parts on the black market, but Russia has their nuclear plants and weapons locked up tight."

"Could a country like China coerce a worker into smuggling polonium-210 out?" James asked.

"Doubtful, Mr. President. The Russians are very proud of their nuclear power and weapons. Only their most trusted workers have access."

"Could they have shared it with another country?"

"Like Iran, sir?"

James nodded. "Or Syria. Maybe North Korea? There are plenty of people who could use a good way to kill a highly placed individual without it looking suspicious."

"It's possible, sir," the CISA director spoke up after a nod from the CIA director. "But the more my people dig, the more they believe Russia may be behind the attacks yesterday."

"This is news to me. Explain."

"Yes, sir. I received a report since I've been here." He gestured at a laptop. "To summarize—my computer people can get a sense of the person behind certain hacks. The best I can explain it without getting too technical is an analogy from World War II. Radio operators—telegraphers—learned to identify who was sending a message based on nearly imperceptible hesitations and, well, the style in how they tapped out the Morse code. It's not equivalent, but that's one way to look at it. My team says that the computer code they've uncovered has predominantly Russian identifiers all over it."

"'Predominantly?'"

"Sir, the Russians likely attempted to disguise their work by using other identifiers—that's what my team says."

"How sure are they? Would they go to war with Russia over these identifiers?"

The director of CISA coughed nervously. "I... I haven't asked, Mr. President. I assume they would hedge and say it's above their pay grade."

James nodded with a small smile. "Of course. Continue. What else do we have?"

In the back of his mind, James debated telling the men and women in front of him about the deepfake video.

There were several good reasons to disclose it—and a few not to.

Not yet... Maybe once we have more information.

Would his hidden enemy make the video public?

What did they expect him to do—or not do?

His gut told him the video was meant to make him either resign, turning the country over to the vice president, or hold back, to hesitate and not order a response to the cyberattacks on the country yesterday—and the assassination of Secretary of State Wilson.

They guessed wrong. I'm not resigning, and the video makes me more likely to retaliate, not less.

James had long ago grown accustomed to making incredibly difficult decisions based on limited intelligence. Part of him hated retaliating against the likely culprit—Russia—without knowing more.

Still, it was what he had to do.

He couldn't let the threat of the video coming out deter him from what was best for the country.

"Take me through what we could do to Russia in response to these attacks," James said. "Step by step."

It's time for payback.

106

THE LIES

Wolf had slept, showered, and eaten one of the prepared meals restocked daily in the residence area's kitchen.

Now he once again stood behind one of his young hackers, supervising the next phase of the operation.

The ever-intense George stood at his shoulder.

"Have the Americans fallen for our tactics?" George asked. "Are there rumors? Conspiracy theories?"

"Many theories," Wolf said. Rapture, the hacker now sitting at Wolf's workstation, brought up a screen filled with the newsfeed of a popular social media platform. The hashtag *#WhoDidIt?* was heavily trending.

"Space aliens?" George asked, reading the screen along with Wolf.

"It's a joke," Wolf said. "To most, but some believe it. Others use it to be funny."

Rapture clicked and sorted.

"Iran is blamed the most," Wolf said, reading the screen. "China second. Russia third. Others are close after that—the American government did it themselves, various ethnic groups, and North Korea."

"That is not ideal. Russia must be blamed. If the American president won't resign, he must be forced to attack. You are prepared for the next stage?" George asked.

Wolf nodded.

They were ready to unleash social media posts from "verified" users.

The users were made up and controlled by the hackers. They had meticulously created them over the past year—kept them updated with pictures of supposed friends, families, and pets; posted memes; and engaged in discussions about movies, books, and politics.

In reality, they were a few thousand pretend people from all walks of life, based mostly in America. They had many carefully cultivated friends and followers and were about to start sharing "the truth" about the attacks on the country.

The hackers also controlled a mass of bots—automated software programs seeded on computers around the world. They would take over the social media accounts of actual users who had been hacked and use those people to spread the lies as well.

"Begin as planned," George ordered.

Wolf tapped Rapture on the shoulder. He changed screens and started clicking with his mouse.

A brief blog post appeared a moment later on a respected centrist blogger's website and was immediately cross-posted under his username on the top social media sites.

Breaking—As Yet Unconfirmed

First off, let me say that I'm still sourcing this information. It has not been independently confirmed, so take this with a grain of salt.

However, my source indicates Secretary of State Wilson has died.

His cause of death will be officially reported as heart failure.

In actuality, he was poisoned and died of exposure to a massive dose of polonium-210.

That's right, dear reader, it looks like Russia (the only source for polonium-210) assassinated our secretary of state.

This obviously begs the question—is Russia also behind the cyberattacks on our country?

More as I get it.

#ItWasRussia #NukeRussia #RussiaDidIt

George's large hand landed on Wolf's shoulder, causing the hacker to jump.

"Well done," George said. "The English is perfect."

Wolf got himself quickly back under control and nodded his thanks.

It better be—we worked for a month on the wording.

Wolf and his team had spent the last year studying popular bloggers, dutifully learning the American idioms and phrasing to make the fake post sound authentic, all while writing short pieces on their made-up centrist blog to give it a solid reputation and a respectable number of followers.

If the ploy worked, the outrage against Russia would build. America would have to attack.

"How long do you wait now?" George asked.

"About five minutes," Wolf said. "More, if the post gains traction right away. Less if it doesn't."

Rapture tapped on the keyboard, pulling up windows in a grid showing the top four social media sites in America.

More typing and clicking showed the report already spreading quickly.

The *#NukeRussia* hashtag trended the most, followed closely by *#RussiaDidIt*.

"Release wave 1M," Wolf ordered. This group of bots controlled the smallest subset of hacked accounts and were strictly middle-of-the-road males of retirement age. They weren't the radicals in wave 1R, the midwestern soccer moms in wave 1W, the liberals in 1L, or the deeply conservative 1C.

"And our fake accounts," Wolf said.

With more clicks, Rapture's system automatically controlled the made-up social media accounts and posted different versions of the discussion blaming Russia, all with the same carefully created hashtags.

The hacker at the keyboard clicked on another window, entered a command, and clicked back to the screen with the four social media site windows.

As they watched and refreshed the windows, the blog report spread organically thanks to some real Americans sharing what they'd read, along with the fake accounts that reposted, commented, questioned, and debated. As a final kicker, the hacked accounts of actual people joined in the discussion.

"Post the confirmation," Wolf ordered, taking full command of the operation now. All he'd needed was the initial go-ahead. The rest was up to him.

Rapture clicked away from the social media screens and pulled up another. This showed the most popular social media site for breaking and in-depth news.

Entering the password from memory, Rapture logged into the account of a legitimate, much-respected national political reporter.

Wolf smiled. The man's login had been hacked by his team two weeks before.

With more clicks, Rapture copied and pasted a prewritten statement into the man's account and posted it.

CONFIRMED by three sources. The secretary of state was poisoned with polonium-210. When asked if Russia was to blame, one source said, "That is the logical conclusion." More to come. #Polonium-210 #BreakingNews #SecretaryofState #RussiaDidIt #WW3

"Release the rest of Wave One immediately," Wolf said.

In a few seconds, hundreds of real and fake social media accounts—all controlled and directed by Rapture from his chair in Dubai—reposted the reporter's news with their own comments added.

- *Did you see this? I didn't want to believe it but look who it's from!*
- *I'll be in my basement waiting for the big one if anyone needs me.*
- *President Heringten is a punk if he doesn't address this immediately.*
- *#NukeRussia*
- *Don't fall for it. The current administration attacked us to keep us in line. #HeringtenMustResign*
- *It's all over now.*
- *This is fake. It's all a lie. #IranDidIt #NukeIran*
- *My sister's friend works at the hospital where #SecState died. Men w/ Geiger counters swarmed the place early this morning. It all makes sense now.*
- *President Heringten must defend our country.*
- *#EconomicSanctions but #NoWar*
- *#RussiaDidIt*

The last hashtag trended, soaring into the thousands as the news spread.

"It is done," Wolf said. "We will manage it, releasing more when needed to keep the news spreading and people debating."

"That is all it takes?" George asked. He sounded awed.

He understands computers but didn't grasp their true power until now.

"Yes and no. The word is out, yes. Not everyone will believe the news until they see it confirmed on television or hear it on the radio. We predict the hacked reporter will hesitate to admit he did not post the story. He will be too embarrassed he got hacked. He and other reporters will contact their sources, who will confirm because they believe the news is already public. We also have the advantage of the news being partly true—Russian hackers were to blame," Wolf said with a grin.

"A lie buried in truth makes it easier to believe," George said.

"Exactly. And now?" Wolf asked.

"Now we let them destroy each other. If necessary, we keep pushing until they do. Then we watch them burn."

107

#RUSSIADIDIT

The Kremlin

Dmitry felt uncomfortable in the spacious, ornate office of the president. Instead of sitting in a guest chair, he stood behind one, hands on the chair back, waiting.

The president had summoned him. Dmitry had just returned from his day trip to western Russia, on the Finnish border, for his recruitment mission.

The most important members of the government had entered the large conference room down the hall, where they would be at work all night, trying to manage a situation spiraling out of control.

The news had first hit social media in America but quickly spread around the world. Russia had supposedly killed America's secretary of state with polonium-210—like back in the old days.

There were also rumors that the Americans had proof Russia was behind the cyberattacks.

The people of the world—at least on social media—seemed to accept the rumors and accusations as fact.

The hashtag #NukeRussia was trending.

It was early afternoon in America. Outside the Russian Embassy in Washington, DC, hundreds of protesters had gathered. People chanted, marched, blew whistles, and carried signs such as "Arrest Nikitin" and "#RussiaDidIt."

This is not good.

The door opened behind Dmitry. He spun to see the president march in, waving at his security detail to leave the room. When the door clicked closed, President Nikitin called to Dmitry as he finished the long walk to his desk in the back half of the huge room.

"Is it true, or are we being played?"

Dmitry wanted to say polonium-210 from one of Russia's old reactors wasn't at all his department but didn't. For whatever reason, the president relied on him more and more. At this point, Dmitry was part young spy chief and part Chief of Staff to the president.

I have become what the Americans would call a fixer.

"We have no solid details yet, Mr. President. However, the accusation is so specific and so easily disproven if false that I believe it must be true. If Secretary of State Wilson was poisoned with polonium-210, it likely came from one of our reactors, yes. The Americans have the technology to test and trace it. We will know for sure when they share their findings with us… and the United Nations, no doubt."

The president sat in his chair and immediately leaned forward, forearms on the wide dark wood desk, his normally composed face flushed red with anger. "Who could have done this? Who is the traitor?"

Dmitry remained standing.

"Our people are reviewing security procedures, background checks, and security camera footage now, Mr. President. As yet, we have nothing, I'm sorry to report."

President Nikitin's eyes bore into him.

He no longer looks like a history or economics professor. He's a predator.

"I have no proof, sir, but in my gut, I feel we're being set up. It has been decades since Russia used that method to kill anyone. I had to research the material and method. It isn't what we do now."

"Suicide" by falling from an open window or off the roof of a building, yes. This? No.

"I agree, but why?" the president asked. "And by whom? The Americans would not do this to themselves, no matter what some of their countrymen believe. They would not sacrifice one of their own. They are not monsters. Is it a member of my inner circle who believes me weak and who is willing to risk a war with America to replace me?"

Dmitry shook his head. "I'm sorry, Mr. President. I don't know yet. But I will get you answers."

I hope I can keep that promise.

"Until we have more information, I will attempt to deescalate the situation with the Americans," the president muttered, leaning back with a frustrated sigh. "Mark my words, Dmitry, someone's head will roll for this. Let us hope it is not mine—or everyone in our country if America retaliates."

If they attack, we will be unable to adequately defend ourselves.

Should America decide to do more than a proportionate response—if they decided to go to war and invade, as they had in Iraq and Afghanistan—they would encounter little resistance from the depleted military whose gear and ammunition had been sold off for vodka and vacation homes.

Dmitry assessed President Nikitin, wondering if the man had it in him to defend the country in the only way that would be possible.

Could he launch a nuclear strike?

And would using that method to save the country completely destroy it instead?

108

ONE WEEK

The White House Situation Room
Washington, DC

James looked down the long table where America's best and brightest sat. He had the directors of the CIA, CISA, NCTC, and FBI, along with the chairman of the Joint Chiefs of Staff, the deputy secretary of state, and a dozen others.

Their aides sat in chairs that lined the walls behind them.

He fumed. Social media was trending with details that should have been kept under wraps for hours longer, if not days.

Who leaked the news?

It would do no good to rant and rave, threaten an investigation, or demand loyalty.

But it sure would feel good.

As much as I hate the leak, this time it might get me where I want to go.

With the world watching and his fellow Americans demanding he act, striking Russia would be supported by many.

How do I retaliate without getting us into a world war?

James took a breath, followed by three more. After the last exhale, he held his breath for a count of four, then repeated the steps.

Some at the table watched. They knew he was taking a few seconds to calm down and focus.

Others busied themselves, giving him the space he needed.

A few were speaking on the phone, checking their laptops, or whispering to people on either side of them.

"Mr. President," the chairman of the Joint Chiefs of Staff spoke up. "We must retaliate. If our enemies feel they can—"

James held up a finger, and the man immediately stopped talking.

He's gone from advising caution to wanting to unleash hell.

All eyes turned to James.

Any time now, President Nikitin.

Chad David, sitting behind James's left shoulder, stood and whispered in his ear. "Mr. President, Russian President Nikitin would like to speak with you."

Timing.

James nodded. "Quiet, people. I have a call from President Nikitin."

All I need is one little excuse. If he gives me that, his country pays for what they've done.

A translator slipped into the room, picked up a phone, and stood near the president, ready to speak into his ear. James pulled a landline phone close as Chad nodded. The people who normally listened to this type of call were ready on muted lines elsewhere.

James picked up the phone and spoke, his voice emotionless—hiding his anger, confusion, and suspicion. He gave nothing away. "Mr. President."

President Nikitin spoke into his ear, sounding earnestly apologetic. The interpreter whispered a rapid-fire, nearly real-time translation. "Mr. President, my condolences on the death of Secretary of State Wilson, along with the rest of your countrymen who were harmed or killed on Wednesday. I am calling to say that, to the best of my knowledge, Russia did not commit the atrocious cyberattacks, nor did we assassinate Secretary Wilson."

He sounds like he's telling the truth—but can I believe him?

"Thank you for your condolences, Mr. President."

How should I play this? Diplomatically? Or should I attack?

James had been considering the question for hours without making a final decision.

He followed his gut.

"I understand what you say, but I have just been encouraged to retaliate against you by one of my senior advisors," James said, keeping his voice steady.

Which also happens to be exactly what I want to do.

"All signs point to Russia—or someone in Russia, perhaps a proxy of yours or a group you may eventually claim is a 'rogue element'—attacking our country and killing our people. What shall I tell those who demand we stand up for ourselves?"

James had to wait as his words were translated into Russian.

Or maybe Nikitin is pondering his response.

"I would ask for your restraint, Mr. President. Give us time to look further into this ourselves, as you are undoubtedly doing. I commit to fully working with you to find the attackers—outside or inside of my country. Will you give us…" The Russian paused. "One week? As you know, I will be at the Middle East Peace Summit tomorrow, but my top people will not rest until they discover who is behind this. I will discuss the situation in person with your vice president in Oman if you would like."

He sounds sincere—and desperate.

It was James's turn to sit silently, considering the possibilities.

Damn it, he's playing this perfectly and not giving me an excuse to retaliate.

After a moment, James spoke. "Please give me thirty seconds, Mr. President. I have a question to ask my advisors."

"Of course. Take the time you need," came the translation in his other ear.

James muted the phone and held the receiver to his chest to be extra careful.

"I want no hedging or BS. Right now, each of you tells me your assessment. How likely is it Russia is truly behind this? Give me a percent."

He looked to his left. The deputy secretary of state looked panic-stricken at going first.

"Um, fifty… fifty percent, Mr. President."

James hid his displeasure.

Nice hedge.

He nodded at the next in line—the chairman of the Joint Chiefs of Staff. "Ninety percent, sir."

Decisive. I like it, even if he's only saying that because he wants to go to war with someone.

He continued around the table.

"Sixty percent, sir."

"Too soon to make the call, but if you need a number right now, I'd go with seventy-five percent, Mr. President."

The lowest he heard was fifty percent; the highest was ninety, from, of course, the chairman.

Lastly, with time running out, James directed his attention to the large speakerphone at the center of the table. "Mr. Addison, are you with us?"

"Yes, Mr. President," Gregory Addison said. "We"—he emphasized the word just enough for James to understand he was speaking for himself, his team, and especially Haley—"would strongly advise delaying any response."

"I need a number, Mr. Addison."

After a delay of several seconds, Gregory spoke. "Five percent chance they are behind it, Mr. President. Or lower."

There were gasps and grumbling from the rest of the men and women at the table. James silenced them with a look. "Would you care to elaborate, Mr. Addison?"

Gregory coughed uncomfortably. "No, Mr. President. I'm sorry, not at this time." He hesitated like he was going to add more but instead finished with one word. "Sir."

Isn't that interesting? What has Haley dug up now?

James had been ready to tell the Russian president to go to hell, hang up on him, and authorize an immediate proportionate response—cyberattacks on military and industrial targets that kept casualties to a minimum.

Instead, he mentally stomped on the brakes.

Of all the advisors, Gregory—and his team, especially Haley—have proven correct over and over. If they think Russia didn't do it, I have to find another way to handle this.

He wanted revenge—and damn the personal threat of the deepfake video being released—but he had to do the right thing.

As much as he hated it, and as hard as he was going to be slammed in the media, backing off was the best option for the moment.

James unmuted the phone. "Mr. President? We will get to the bottom of this together. You have one week—or less, if there is any further indication you," James said, emphasizing the last part and letting his voice go cold, "or anyone in your government is responsible for the attacks on the United States of America."

After waiting a few seconds for the translation, President Nikitin responded. "Thank you, Mr. President. We will be in touch."

James hung up, waited until the translator had left the room, and turned to the silent people around the table.

"You have one week," he said. "Find out who did this. I don't care where the trail leads. I want an answer. As clear as possible... and preferably a unanimous recommendation for the actions we should take."

He swept the room, meeting the eyes of each senior advisor before settling on the chairman's. "In the meantime, I want everything on standby for the retaliatory cyberattacks you presented to me earlier. I also want our active military ready for immediate direct action. If we hit them back and they escalate, we're going to war. And we'll be ready for it if we do."

109

TEA

Ekaterina hated the desert with a passion.

The sun.

The heat.

The dryness.

It was far worse than Los Angeles.

Yet here she was.

So much for my retirement.

Still, this was exactly her type of mission.

No one else to worry about except herself.

Vague parameters from Moscow. "Find out what is going on and fix it."

The closest she'd come to actual orders were, "Find a way to help us convince the Americans we had nothing to do with the cyberattacks."

She saw it in the eyes of Mr. Moscow—Dmitry. He didn't expect her to succeed, but he had to try.

She'd do her best, though—for Russia.

The old Russia, what it used to be. What it meant to her when she was proud of her country despite its many problems.

If by some miracle she discovered who had truly attacked America, she would earn her freedom and an official retirement.

No more hiding in the cabin, waiting for the inevitable poisoned tea or shot in the head while she slept.

She would be free to travel the world if she wanted.

She would go to the United Kingdom.

Alaska.

Seattle.

Sweden and Finland.

Rainy places. Cold places—or at least cool.

Not this desert weather, which wasn't bad yet compared to what it would become in a few months but still felt unbearably hot.

In her cabin, Dmitry had little to offer. "We will fly you to Dubai immediately. The Marina area. Russian hackers disappeared from their jobs working unofficially for us in Moscow more than a year ago. They were eventually traced to a luxury residential, retail, and business tower. They have not been seen since."

She'd arrived in Dubai, checked into a mid-range hotel suitable for her cover as a retired Russian school teacher, and scouted the thirty-five-story building the boy Dmitry had claimed Russian hackers worked in.

The mission was off to a good start, all things considered.

After staking out the back exit of the tower late the night before immediately after she had arrived, hoping to catch the hackers leaving the building but coming up empty, she'd gotten up early and circled the block once before choosing the coffee shop inside the building, next to the front doors.

She had the photographs of the Russian hackers memorized.

Since she was forgoing the outdoor patio, all she had to do now was sip her tea in air-conditioned comfort and watch to see if the men arrived for work through the main entrance.

Time passed.

She enjoyed her tea and the people-watching.

It feels good to be back on the job.

Later in the day, Niko, her driver, fixer, and protegee would arrive from Los Angeles. She would have another set of eyes for searching or a man to stage a distraction, allowing her to slip into the building and go floor to floor—if she had to—until she found the hackers.

Rich businessmen in the traditional long flowing robe-like tunics or stylish Western business suits were dropped off under the covered porte-cochere, emerging from the back seats of their chauffeured luxury cars and SUVs to hustle into the building for meetings or work.

Others left the building, picked up by other fancy vehicles, confirming both her research and Moscow's—the building was a mixed-use office and residential tower.

There were no skinny Russian hackers. No young, geeky men at all.

Still, the day was young, the air-conditioning cold, and the tea surprisingly good.

Ekaterina nearly choked on her drink. The ruggedly handsome black-haired American who had held her at gunpoint in Los Angeles weeks before strolled by outside.

How has he found me again?

Could there be a mole in Moscow?

Her country was corrupt—maybe always had been, she could admit. Many people would gladly take dollars for state secrets.

Of course, there was another possibility.

Have I stumbled upon him?

It made sense for the Americans to send this warrior and his team. They were older than average soldiers and blended in well.

She moved further inside the coffee shop, angling her body away from him, careful not to glance his way as a server took his order at the outside table he had chosen.

With all her experience, she couldn't spot the team members he'd worked with before: the beefy dark-skinned man, the pale bearded man who reminded her of a small bear, or the curvy woman with dimples and long dark hair the warrior had called "Tex."

None of the other patrons seemed like warriors or spies, nor did any of the people she could see on the street.

He could be here alone, or his team could be scattered at locations around the area, keeping watch the same as me.

She couldn't guess how he'd known about the target building and didn't care.

But how could she capitalize on the situation?

The Americans bested me and my team in Los Angeles...

Though her face showed no emotion, inside she smiled happily at her new plan.

I do not need to figure out the situation, infiltrate the building, or find the hackers.

She only had to follow the American warrior, who she decided to nickname "Fox" because of how cunning he was months before.

Ekat only occasionally glanced at Fox as he sipped coffee outside in the sun. In her mind, he had point; he was now in charge of the surveillance.

When he uncovered a lead or slipped away to a different location, she would don one of her two reversible sun hats—giving her four different looks—and tail him until he led her to her targets.

This time she couldn't stop the small, tight-lipped smile as she sipped her tea.

110

INTUITION

Axe finished his coffee from the shop on the ground floor of the target building, then walked around the incredibly wealthy neighborhood, taking in the tall buildings, lush landscaping, and pricy shops.

While he'd flown, the IT geeks and Void had worked their magic. They were convinced a building called the Lux View Marina Tower was the place to investigate.

After arriving late the night before, he'd checked into a hotel, did a quick recon walk, saw nothing, and went back to the hotel to get some much-needed sleep.

He started fresh this morning—with coffee.

His camera remained stowed in his backpack, along with a tripod and various lenses. For now, he was a tourist or a photographer on assignment, scouting out locations, depending on who asked.

He'd wait until sunset to get some pictures of the ocean and wide-angle shots of the skyline. No people. The briefing material Haley's team had hastily thrown together for him indicated taking pictures of people without their consent was a sure way of landing in a lot of trouble.

So for the time being, he had a finger marking a page in a popular guidebook he'd picked up at the private jet terminal where he'd landed and was contenting himself with walking around in awe of the incredible wealth on display.

Police were everywhere. So were surveillance cameras. He also caught drones on patrol.

They take security seriously here.

Axe was glad to no longer be cooped up in the luxury condo in Virginia, but his current situation was daunting.

For the first time in a while, he was on his own again. No team. Not even Haley. Back to being a team of one.

With the severe punishments for carrying weapons in the UAE, Axe had left everything behind, including his pocketknife. It felt strange being unarmed.

The thirty-five-story building Void and the other geeks had identified as the likely target—where it looked like the hacking had been done from or routed through—was a fortress.

There was no way he could get in covertly or in his undercover role as a photographer. He couldn't waltz up and ask if he could wander the building taking pictures.

And finally, with all the police and security cameras, he'd felt like every step was being watched since he'd stopped for coffee this morning.

Axe put the paranoia into a mental box, closed the door, and focused on the mission.

Time to shake the tree. Get in, figure things out, and handle it.

As the day went on, the sun became unrelenting, bringing back his years in the desert. Thankfully, the spring temperature and dry air were perfect. Not too hot—yet. That would change in another few weeks, but for now, walking around the luxurious city was fine.

Axe spent the day wandering. He'd circled the Lux View Marina Tower once already, stretching his legs and doing more recon.

It pays to be prepared.

However, as the afternoon ended, he was no closer to a solution about how to accomplish his mission or even what next step to take.

On instinct, Axe walked past the Tower and turned left at the end of the block, heading up the less fancy street behind the building. To his left, the Lux View Marina Tower's bright white exterior glowed in the lowering sun. Its tall bulk cast the shorter, older, and moderately less luxurious buildings behind it in shadow.

I bet plenty of rich people were pissed off when the building went up, blocking their sun and views.

Axe smiled and nodded at a police officer walking slowly toward him but got only a stare in response.

Axe crossed to a bench directly behind the Tower on the opposite side of the street. He sat and relaxed, taking a load off while he thought through the problem.

The wealthy enter through the underground parking garage or get dropped off in front.

He'd already watched the comings and goings at the front door while enjoying coffee earlier.

Tomorrow, he could rent a car and park it beneath the building at dawn to stake out the elevators—if public parking was even allowed. He'd have to check that out first if tonight's gut instinct didn't pay off.

Axe read a few paragraphs in his guidebook, surreptitiously keeping track of the comings and goings from the rear, non-public entrance to the skyscraper.

Around the world, workers—cooks, maids, private security, all the help keeping rich people living in luxury—always come and go through the back.

Maybe hackers were the same—if they didn't also live in the building. If geeky young men wandered out, he could follow them home and have a nice, long discussion with them in the privacy of their apartment.

Otherwise, Axe would watch for the cooks, butlers, or other hired help. The majority of workers in the country were expats from other countries in the Middle East. Some certainly were treated well, especially those allowed to come to work each day and return to their own apartments at night.

Others, frequently live-in help, were paid poorly, treated worse, and rarely left the residences where they worked.

Those he couldn't help.

But an underpaid, potentially disgruntled worker desperate for a way out—or for extra cash to send home to his family? If Axe could find a person like that, he had thousands in both US dollars and Emirati dirhams —the local currency—in his wallet, tucked into a hidden pocket in his belt, and stashed in the lining of the jacket in his backpack.

Money talks—and makes the world go 'round. I'm happy to pay a source to answer my questions about the building.

An insider might know a way to sneak in or have information to share about hackers living or working there.

It was nearly five o'clock. He hadn't thought to ask Haley what time domestic staff got off work here, but he'd bide his time on the bench, watching and waiting for the hackers—or a perfect target to trade a fortune in dollars for a few honest answers about the building, any interesting activity they knew about, or rumors about geeky young men coming and going.

Axe's skin tingled again like it had all day. He focused intently on the guidebook for several seconds, running his finger along the page as if tracing the route on a map, before glancing up quickly, hoping to catch sight of whoever was observing him.

Across the street, the policeman he'd nodded at earlier stared at him before continuing up the road, walking his beat.

Axe relaxed at the false alarm. He wasn't used to working in cities.

Give me night vision goggles, an M4, a team, and a capture/kill mission in the desert over this.

He'd just have to turn down the frequency of his intuition and the feeling of being under surveillance. In this city, there was no getting around it.

111

GUT CHECK

High Pointe Downtown Condos
Arlington, Virginia

Haley put her head in her hands and sighed. They'd been at it for hours—all day and half the night, ever since she'd opened her big mouth and whispered to Gregory the five percent assessment of whether Russia was responsible for the assassination of Secretary of State Wilson and the cyberattacks.

She and the team had nothing to show except her hunch, which at least was shared by Dave and Nancy, though for different reasons.

"Let's go through it again," she said.

Everyone with her in the living room—Marcus, Gregory, Nancy, and Dave—groaned.

We're burnt out. We need more sleep.

Void and the IT department workers sat at the far end of the kitchen table. They'd slept well and had jumped back into their side of the investigation with enthusiasm.

Tucci watched over Void from his barstool at the kitchen island, shotgun nearby on the off chance Void bolted down the hall toward the condo's front door and the entryway with the elevator.

"Okay, forget that," Haley said. "Gut check. Who do you think did it?"

"I'll go first," Marcus said. He stood from the sofa sectional, picking up Haley's short-barrel M4 and slinging it around his shoulder crosswise on his body, muzzle pointing mostly down. Once Haley had learned he could shoot—and he'd admitted he could handle the M4—she'd passed it over to him for the time being. They'd switch off guard duty with it, backing up Tucci.

"Russia is being set up to take the fall... but I don't know by who. Best guess would be Iran," he said, stopping at the floor-to-ceiling windows to gaze at the darkened city below them.

Haley nodded. Her intuition agreed Russia was being set up. They weren't reckless enough to actually attack the United States and kill people. It had to be a rogue element in the government, which had happened once before, recently. Or another country had coordinated the attacks to make Russia take the fall. But who?

"Dave?"

"I think someone discovered what I did—that Russia's in trouble—and is using that to put them in a bind while furthering their own interests. The data point to China as the most likely... or an element within China. I think China's president is too risk-averse to attack us directly, but a splinter group or a hacker group tired of China being second in the world could do it. But I can't figure how Dubai plays into it," he said, tilting his head to the kitchen.

Haley nodded. Void and the team had made progress, pinpointing a building they thought the hacks may have either originated from or passed through. She'd gotten Axe the message when he'd landed in Dubai.

A hacker collective with a direct-action component might do it.

"Nancy?" Haley turned to look at her, sitting with her back to the windows. Behind her, Marcus stood, still looking out at the city.

"I agree," Nancy said. "I think—"

She was interrupted by Marcus toppling over with a cry of pain, landing upside down on the couch next to her.

Time seemed to slow as Haley noted the hole in the thick glass of the window and the spreading blood on the shoulder of Marcus's dress shirt.

"Get down!" she yelled, diving to the floor. "Sniper!"

Tucci gasped from near the kitchen. "I'm hit!"

Haley grabbed Nancy by the leg and dragged her off the couch before repeating the move with Marcus, yanking him by the uninjured arm.

A quick check showed Dave and Gregory were on the ground near her.

The couch hid their location from the outside, though it wouldn't provide much protection against a high-power sniper round if the person shooting at them decided to open up and hope for lucky shots.

We need it dark!

She crawled on hands and knees to the wall, keeping the couch between her and the window for as long as possible. She launched herself for the switches controlling the living room lights before flattening herself onto the ground.

The drywall exploded an inch from her head, forcing her to move toward the kitchen.

She risked another bullet when she got there, raising up and hitting the long row of switches.

The entire condo was now dark.

"Geeks—behind the kitchen island right now!"

They scrambled her way with the woman—Kaylin—having the guts to grab her laptop and backpack before rushing from the dining room table.

"Tucci? Tell me you're not dead."

"I'm not dead," he said, his voice tight with pain. "But I'm having a shitty week, I'll tell you that."

He can still joke at least.

"Gregory, how's Marcus?" she called.

"Hit in the shoulder," Gregory yelled back. "Bloody, but he's okay for now. What do you need?"

"Everybody, stay hidden from the windows," she called.

Void and the IT geeks joined Tucci behind the island. She low-crawled to them, wondering if she'd get a bullet in the head.

She made it with no gunfire.

In the blue glow of the microwave's clock, the faces of the geeks showed their shock.

Tucci sat with his back to the dishwasher in the kitchen island, hands pressed to his side, bleeding all over the pristine tile floor. "It probably looks worse than it is," he said.

Two down from sniper rounds, taking the shotgun and the M4 out of commission.

Someone had been watching them for a while and had targeted the men perceived as guards.

"Okay, here's the plan," she said. "We'll—"

Down the hall, gunfire came from the front door, followed by the splintering of wood.

The door thudded against the wall as it swung all the way open.

Haley drew her pistol, the move instinctive from hours at the range, and aimed it down the hallway, ready to shoot anyone coming her way.

112

GO

Haley shot the first man in the hallway, hitting him twice in the chest and once in the face before he dropped to the floor, dead.

She got off one shot at the man following him before he stopped and backed up, moving out of sight.

"Kaylin, take Void and the rest of the team," Haley whispered. "Stay low; get to the emergency lines on the south patio."

Given the shots taken at Marcus and Tucci, the sniper had to be set up level with them on a balcony or roof of a nearby building.

"The sniper won't have a shot at you there. Get the rigging on and go over the edge. When you get to the ground, undo the belts. The system will retract, and the next two will go down. But don't wait. You and Void run—and run fast—away from here. Find a public place like a convenience store—"

She paused to shoot at the tango peeking around the corner of the hallway but didn't think she hit him.

"Call 911 and follow their lead. Got it?"

"We're twenty-three stories off the ground," Void said. His voice shook.

That's right—he's afraid of heights. He'll just have to deal.

"Go before I give you to them," she said, using her best Axe voice.

The five of them hurried off.

"I've got the living room access covered," Gregory whispered just loud enough for her to hear.

"Copy."

Movement came from the hallway, but she didn't have a shot.

They're getting ready to rush us.

"Where's the shotgun?" Haley whispered to Tucci. Blood flowed freely from his side though he had his hand pressed hard against the wound, clenching his teeth against the pain.

"On the island countertop, sorry."

She would love to have the firepower of the weapon, especially if she was about to get rushed, but she didn't relish the thought of risking exposure to the sniper to get it.

Still, she could hold the hallway for a while. How long depended on whether they had sent more men than she had bullets.

They thought this was going to be easy once they took out all the guards.

But they hadn't counted on her.

113

THE SNIPER

Downtown Arlington, Virginia

Laying prone on the flat roof of the skyscraper a few blocks away from the condo building, Chinese sniper Meng Chao had no shot.

Watching through his scope, he was mostly blind since the blond woman had turned off the lights.

He could make out movement and shadows inside due to the lights from appliances in the kitchen and ambient light seeping in from the surrounding buildings, but not well enough to target people easily.

His eye never left the scope, though, just in case.

The group in the condo building several blocks away had reacted surprisingly swiftly to his first two shots.

He had hit both of the primary targets—the men guarding the group.

The thick glass windows and variable winds so high off the ground had caused both shots to miss the center mass mark he'd aimed for.

Their men are out of commission. That is good enough.

Unfortunately, the Russian soldiers who were supposed to breach the door had been late by several seconds.

Instead of his shots hitting home at the same moment they broke into the condo, something had delayed them.

If we had comms, this wouldn't have happened.

The whole affair had been poorly run from the start.

After the death of his original team at the suburban restaurant, he'd loaded up his rifle and escaped in the remaining vehicle, heading once again toward Atlanta.

He'd gotten much closer than last time before the team's mission phone buzzed.

New assignment. Pay is doubled. Respond.

The offer of extra money had helped entice him to admit he was the only surviving member of the team, but yes, he was ready, willing, and able to continue the mission.

He had a family back in China who needed all the extra money he could send them.

Meng Chao had met the three freshly arrived Russian special forces members and planned the mission.

They must be dead.

Why else wouldn't he see them rushing into the home?

Meng Chao repeated his sweep from left to right.

The living room—where the first guard had toppled over the sofa as the others dived for cover.

The space between the sectional sofa and the kitchen and dining room. The blond had surprised him, risking herself to rush across the exposed area to turn off the lights in the condo.

And finally, the kitchen island, behind which several people hid, including the second guard.

He caught movement near the kitchen. At least one person had dashed the few feet from behind the island through the doorway at the south side of the kitchen.

No shot.

The distance from him to the target was too great to hit anyone moving fast, especially only a few feet before he lost sight of them. And he didn't have a view—or shot—of the south side of the building.

The doorway led to another room, which he had seen earlier when the lights were still on—an informal, eat-in area with a four-person table and a small balcony with two chairs that looked south through a clear-glass wall of a railing.

There may be a way...

If he relocated to another part of the roof, he might have a shot. It would be difficult, but—

Another person dashed across the open space.

Meng scrambled to his right, desperate to get a better view of what the people were doing.

He could see the shapes of the bodies through the glass windows.

Four people now stood at the door to the balcony. Meng couldn't shoot them—the angle didn't work. He'd have to shoot through the thick glass of the condo and across the length of two rooms.

He thought one of the figures might be the tall, lanky form of the primary target the Russians wanted to rescue—or abduct, depending on how one looked at it.

Dawson, they called him. The hacker.

A smaller figure—the young woman—and the hacker were stepping into some sort of harness.

What are they doing?

The people near Dawson were likely the three men and one woman he had been sitting near earlier.

He figured out what the woman and Dawson were doing.

They're escaping.

Some newer tall buildings in expensive areas of Beijing had self-rescue systems installed. They were simple-to-use automatic rappelling devices that clipped onto an anchor point and safely lowered a person to the ground. All someone had to do was step into a pre-buckled harness, attach a large clip to a bolt sunk into a wall, tighten the straps, and have the courage to step outside and let go.

They would descend at a slow rate, stopping when the person stepped onto the ground and took their weight off the system.

Unless Meng acted quickly, the target would get away.

The team hadn't been large enough to station a person on the ground floor of the building or outside. All three Russians were attacking on the twenty-third floor.

Meng lay the rifle inside the padded, hard-side case, snapped it closed, and ran at full speed to the propped-open door leading to his building's emergency staircase. If he hurried, he might make it to the ground floor, across a few city blocks, and over to the south side of the building in time to follow the hacker—or catch him before he made it to safety.

He focused on the chase and not the bonus money he would receive for capturing the target.

114

THE EDGE

High Pointe Downtown Condos
Arlington, Virginia

The light breeze felt like a gale to Void's frazzled mind.

Standing a few inches outside, away from the safety of the door, made him struggle to breathe.

He recognized the balcony as entirely safe and plenty large, but it felt like his toes were barely touching a tiny ledge and that any move he made would be disastrous.

"I can't do it," Void said.

He swayed, overwhelmed with fear and dizziness, looking past the glass railing and wall surrounding the balcony to the three-hundred-foot drop and the street below.

The second-floor rappel from the prison had freaked him out, but he'd gotten through it with sheer willpower.

The helicopter ride had been bad enough. Crashing had shaken him to the core.

Whatever fear of heights he'd had was exponentially worse after those experiences.

The harness straps bit into his legs and stomach where he'd pulled them overly tight, thinking he could talk himself into being brave.

No way. I'd rather take my chances with whoever the armed men are.

They might be trying to rescue him, not abduct him.

Anything is better than going over the edge of this balcony.

"I can't do it," he said again. He tried to step back into the condo, but the rest of the IT guys—besides Kaylin—blocked his way.

"It's okay," Kaylin said, grabbing his arm and coming to his rescue. "But you have to let the rest of us get away."

She had her harness on and buckled, the flat vinyl lead stretching just inside the doorway to its own anchor point next to his.

Void nodded, feeling less terrified with her strong hand on his arm.

"Good. Step inside and close your eyes so you don't panic when we undo the buckles."

He closed his eyes and walked back into the safety of the small breakfast nook.

"Deep breaths," Kaylin said. "We're going to hold onto your arms, so you feel safer and calm down quicker, okay?"

Void nodded, struggling to get his breathing under control.

The men of the IT team held his arms.

These guys are the best.

One held his waist as Kaylin stood in front of him and touched his stomach above the buckle to the waist strap. "It'll just be a few seconds. You're fine. Keep breathing."

Finally, someone who understands.

Her calming voice sounded nice.

So did her closeness.

Maybe when this is over, we can—

His eyes snapped open as the men he'd been working closely with for the past twenty-four hours picked him up, stepped outside—straight to the balcony's railing—and dropped him over the edge.

"I'm sorry!" Kaylin called. "I'll be right behind you."

He was too surprised, offended, and terrified to scream as the descent line went taut and he slowly started lowering to the ground.

115

THE NEGOTIATION

High Pointe Downtown Condos
Arlington, Virginia

"No one else has to die!" a man's voice yelled from the hallway.

Haley knew that accent.

Russian. No doubt.

Did that change her assessment of who was behind the attacks?

She forced the thought aside for now.

"If we come in, it will be very bloody. Give us Dawson Reite, and we will leave you in peace," the man continued.

Haley's intuition kicked in.

He's lying.

No, that wasn't quite it.

He's... bluffing?

She replayed the chaotic seconds of the hallway firefight.

I killed the first man and shot another.

The one speaking had to be the third guy, who had peeked around the corner.

Three in the hallway—plus the sniper.

A typical four-man team.

The one speaking is in charge... And there's probably one by the elevators watching their backs.

Haley had a horrible thought.

And another in a get-away vehicle on the street as a lookout or to delay the police.

The street far below... where she'd sent Void and the IT team.

"Let me ask Dawson what he wants!" Haley yelled toward the hallway.

She handed her pistol to Tucci and tilted her head at the hall. He nodded and aimed the 9mm toward the opening, his face tight with pain.

Haley popped up, lunged forward, grabbed the shotgun on the far side of the island counter, and dropped back before the sniper could take a shot.

She checked the shotgun, making sure it was ready to fire, and crouched. "He wants to know who you are and why he should go with you," she called.

Not waiting for the answer, she pushed forward, running full tilt for the hall, shotgun at the ready.

"We're here to rescue him, not hurt—"

Haley tracked the man by his voice, leading with the shotgun, exposing the bare minimum of her body around the corner as she fired a round into his chest from five feet.

As he collapsed backward, Haley put a round into the injured—and dead-looking—tango on the ground.

She dropped to the floor as she swung back around the corner, expecting rounds to fly straight through the drywall at her if she was wrong and there were more men in the hall or outside the front door.

No shots followed her.

The only sounds from the other side of the wall were the quiet, desperate, dying sounds of the man she'd been speaking with.

Picking herself up, she poked her head around the corner and took in the scene.

Three dead. No one standing.

The door to the twenty-third-floor hallway gaped open, splintered near the locks where it had been shot and kicked in. It didn't feel like there was anyone out there, but she didn't have time to find out.

"Someone get over here with the M4," she called into the living room. "I think we're clear, but we have to check."

"Coming to you," Gregory said.

"Come over—but I'm leaving."

She didn't wait for a response.

Jumping to her feet, she called as she ran. "Tucci, don't shoot. I'm coming back to you."

"Copy!"

She held the shotgun in the middle of the barrel and made eye contact in the darkness with Tucci. "Switch!"

He held up her pistol, butt first.

They swapped weapons as she slid behind the kitchen island.

Her pistol went into its holster at her waist while she crawled to the drawer to the right of the dual stoves.

There has to be... Yes!

Top-of-the-line silicone oven mitts.

Only the best.

Slipping them on and risking the sniper, she stood and ran straight through the kitchen, past the small eat-in dining table, and onto the south balcony.

The three IT guys leaned over the railing, looking down.

"Get out of the way!" Haley yelled.

Their heads swung back, and they stepped aside.

The two yellow safety lines stretched from the anchor points, over the railing, and down into the night.

She didn't think.

Leaning over the edge, her stomach on the top of the glass wall, she grabbed one of the lines with both hands in the padded silicone gloves, flung herself over the railing, and fell.

I sure hope this works.

116

THE FALL

High Pointe Downtown Condos
Arlington, Virginia

Haley fell.

She squeezed the safety line. The oven mitts kept her hands from burning, but holding on as tightly as she could only slowed her a little.

She plummeted much faster than she had planned.

Trapping the line between the rubber sides of her shoes slowed her from an unsustainably fast descent to one that was merely scary as hell.

Is it enough?

The ground, and a figure at the end of the line, were coming fast. Another figure had already reached the sidewalk.

Void. He's heavier than Kaylin and probably went over first.

"Heads up!" Haley yelled.

Kaylin's head jerked up in surprise. "What the—"

Haley let go of the line with her feet and tried to time it perfectly.

She crashed into Kaylin. One hand slipped from the safety line while she desperately wrapped her legs around the young woman, gripping with all her strength.

"Haley?" Kaylin asked.

"Hi." She grabbed one of the harness straps with her free hand, then the other, her legs tightly holding Kaylin's waist. "You okay? Did I hurt you?"

Kaylin blinked several times, eyes wide, trying to grasp the situation. "I'm fine, but are you insane?"

That's an excellent question.

"Void's in danger," Haley answered. "There might be bad guys on the street."

"You jumped off the balcony…" she muttered.

Their combined weight brought them quickly closer to Void.

"Did you know he was that afraid of heights?" Kaylin asked as they sped toward the ground. "He refused to go so we, sort of, you know…"

"You tossed him over?"

"Not exactly tossed. But yeah, I had the guys drop him," Kaylin said, her voice filled with regret.

"Whatever it takes to accomplish the mission."

Kaylin pointedly looked at the melted red oven mitts clenching the safety harness. "Yeah, I see that."

117

PROMISES

Meng shoved the sniper rifle case under thick bushes next to the building as he exited the emergency stairs.

He hated leaving the weapon behind, especially covered with his fingerprints, but it would slow him down, and he'd be too much of a spectacle running with it.

No matter what else happened next, his sniper mission was over. Police would be converging on the area any second.

But if he successfully captured Dawson Reite, a new part of his assignment would begin.

He ran at full speed south.

Is this worth it? Should I run the other way, go to ground for a month, work my way to Mexico, and get across the border?

He could report that he did his part, but the Russians failed, letting the hacker escape.

No one knew he had a slim chance to capture Reite.

The Russians are probably dead.

He would still get extra money for the work done so far…

But the idea of a big bonus kept him moving.

At the end of the block, he turned, running toward the condo building two streets away.

I was right!

A figure—Reite, he guessed—lay curled on the ground in the fetal position, easy to see in the glow of a streetlight.

Two women—the brave, beautiful blond and the young hacker—knelt over him.

Did he fall? Is he dead?

Police sirens wailed from his left.

He only had two women to contend with—none of the men with guns. Aside from the police cars coming to the area, he faced no threats.

Meng slowed to a brisk walk and pulled his pistol from its holster, concealing it behind his leg. As he passed under a streetlight, he angled his body more to ensure the weapon couldn't be seen by the group ahead.

He had to get closer. Even with his excellent shooting ability, the weapon wasn't effective this far away.

Slowing more, he crossed the last intersection between him and the group huddled on the sidewalk.

Seventy-five feet.

Fifty feet.

The women still hadn't spotted him.

A police car slammed on its brakes halfway up the block at the main entrance to the residential building. After a quick glance its way, Meng ignored the police and focused solely on closing the distance to the women he had to kill.

The blond finally looked up and met his eyes.

"Are you okay?" he called.

Forty feet. Close enough to hit two stationary targets—and miss the hacker.

He stopped, raising his pistol... and noticed the weapon in the blond's hand, already aimed at him.

Two bullets slammed into his chest before he could shoot.

Haley fired a third time, as Axe had trained her and as she'd practiced time and again at the range.

The short man in dark clothes, a pistol in his hands, fell to the ground.

A distant part of her mind cataloged the kill as her main focus turned to sweeping the area for additional threats.

"How did you know?" Kaylin asked, looking sick at the death but sounding awed at Haley's ability to identify the man hurrying toward them as an enemy.

How did I know?

The signs were there. A man by himself making a beeline toward them. The quick glance at the police car up the street—and the lack of curiosity or concern. The way he held his hand behind his leg, hiding the pistol.

"Training and experience," she told Kaylin before turning to the hacker. "Come on, Void, let's go. There might be more of them."

"I think I'd be better off with them—or the police," he mumbled from the ground where he lay. He hadn't moved since they'd maneuvered him out of the harness, letting it retract for the next person to escape the condo.

"No, you wouldn't," she said, shaking him gently. "True, whoever wants you needs you alive, but we don't know what for."

"They could be trying to rescue me. Help me escape."

"Or they could want to interrogate you, torture you until you help them with more hacks, or hold you for ransom."

"Or hold you for ransom while interrogating and torturing you," Kaylin added.

Haley smiled at her.

She's getting into the swing of things now.

"As long as we don't go into any more tall buildings?" Void asked, practically begging.

Haley shook her head. "Sorry, no promises."

118

FLIGHT

Downtown Arlington, Virginia

Haley dragged Void along the sidewalk, hurrying away from the condo building where more police cars arrived around the corner near the front entrance. Void was unsteady on his feet, still recovering from the fright of his life—as well as having to yank up his loose, sagging pants every few steps.

Kaylin followed, looking like she was having the time of her life.

"How did they find us?" Haley asked as she led the two computer geeks across the street and around the corner, hiding them from any other authorities coming to the building.

She stopped and faced Void and Kaylin. "Did they track us from what you were doing online? Or did they find us using traffic cameras or our phones—things like that?"

Kaylin hesitated, deferring to Void, but the poor guy stared off into space.

"Probably from what we did," Kaylin admitted. "The same way we found them in Dubai. Maybe we made a mistake, but they might have back-traced us, narrowing it first to an area, then the building. After that, they just showed up and…"

The gravity of what had happened suddenly caught up with Kaylin. She turned around and leaned forward.

Haley lightly touched her shoulder. "Breathe slowly through your nose and out your mouth. Go ahead and throw up if you have to."

Haley felt fine—she'd instinctively put the feelings of shooting the first three men in the condo, plus the last one on the street, into the box exactly as Axe had taught her.

I'll relive the moments—and pay the price—later. Once the mission is done.

"We have to go to ground. Get away and stay safe. No more putting others in danger," she muttered to herself.

Where can we hide?

"Does whoever is tracking us know who I am—like, my name?" Haley asked. "Or are they just tracking us in general?"

Void blinked several times and focused on her. Kaylin stayed bent over, breathing slowly.

Void shook his head. "It's not personal," he mumbled. "They did the same to us as we did to find them. I must have missed a step. I'm sorry—being in prison and out of the game for a year, I might be rusty."

"So they probably don't know my name? Who I'm friends with, where I've been, my previous missions?"

Void shook his head. "No way. Well..." he hedged. "They could have seen your license plate on the SUV and gotten info from that."

"No," Haley said. "It's registered to a shell company that has no connection to me."

"If you drive it, it has a connection to you."

"Okay, true, but it's a very difficult connection to find. They'd have to hack my law firm, and even then, I made sure they didn't put me in their system. I have a paper file in a cabinet, not anything in their computers. If they actually accessed the law firm, it would end there."

"Then you should be good," Void said. "Just... wherever we go, make it the ground floor, okay?"

Haley nodded. "I have an idea."

If I can get us there.

"But you still haven't explained why they keep coming for you," Haley told him. "Who is it?"

Void shrugged, looking helpless and confused. "I don't know. I'm sorry. I've thought about it and can't think of anyone. I don't have any family. No girlfriend," he said softly with a flick of his eyes toward Kaylin. "A few buddies I hacked with, but they disappeared when I got arrested. None of them would have the pull to do that," he said, pointing toward the condo building two streets over. "What you said before rings true, I guess. They want to make me hack for them. Maybe there's a target they can't get to and think I can."

Haley nodded, pulling together the pieces of a plan. "Kaylin," she said, bending forward next to the still queasy young woman. "How old are you?"

"Twenty-six," she said, slowly straightening up. "I'm doing better now, I think."

Haley kept her face still but mentally shook her head.

She's older than me, but I see her as a kid, just like Void.

"You have a major credit card with some available credit?"

"Yes, of course."

"Great." Haley pulled her phone from her pocket and opened a ride-sharing app. "We're going to the airport to rent a car."

"They might be looking for ride shares from the area," Void pointed out. "I would, if I could break into the company's database, which wouldn't be easy but wouldn't be horrible, either. I'd look for any middle-of-the-night trips out of the area. If I knew you escaped, I mean. Your car would be unavailable, probably."

Damn it, he's right.

Did it make sense to call Gregory and let him take the lead? They could go to the military base an hour to the east and hole up with the rest of the CAG team in safety. No one would attack them there.

Something wasn't clicking for her.

Kaylin mumbled, but Haley didn't hear.

They're out of men.

A team had hit the prison, trying to rescue or abduct Void. She and Axe had killed one in the hallway of the visitor building.

A few hours later, the diner had been hit—probably by the same team.

She, Marcus, Tucci, Axe, and the security team on the roof had killed several of the tangos attacking the restaurant.

The sniper got away—we suspected that.

The same sniper had just shot Tucci and Marcus.

He had a vehicle. The mission isn't over until it's over.

He's the one she had shot on the sidewalk as he came toward them, weapon ready.

The three other bad guys assaulting the condo from the hallway were either part of the original team or new.

Overall, there should have been more people.

There would have been… if there were more available.

It doesn't mean there aren't some on their way to the area or into the country for another attempt.

It depended on whether whoever was calling the shots wanted to continue going after Void or if enough was enough.

Haley clicked on her phone and summoned a rideshare.

We'll have time… and can handle them if they come.

"Same plan," she said. "Rideshare to the airport. Kaylin, you'll rent a car." She turned to Void. "You'll keep helping us, right?"

She let the tone of her voice speak for her. She'd saved his life—again.

Void nodded. "Yes, of course. But if they are good—and so far, they've shown themselves to be—they'll track us again. And send more people."

"Don't worry about that. I'll make it hard to track us, and where we're going, we'll have guards and a distinct advantage over anyone coming our way."

Void nodded, though he didn't seem convinced.

Kaylin raised her hand a few inches. "Question? Why do I rent the car?"

Haley shook her head and smiled, thinking about the vehicles she'd rented for herself and Axe over the past few missions. "I'm not allowed to any longer. The ones I get tend to end up shot, destroyed, or abandoned."

Kaylin stared at her for a second. "Okay, great. I guess."

"Don't worry," Haley said. "We'll get all the insurance coverage they offer."

PART 4

FRIDAY NIGHT - DUBAI

119

THE TARGET

Axe was going to miss the sunset if he didn't break away and head for the beach, but his cover story had to wait.

I'll say I need to take pictures at dawn if anyone asks.

Axe had wandered the area but always kept the rear employee entrance of the Lux View Marina Tower in sight.

Finally, workers shuffled out of the building. They came in ones and twos at first, then in larger groups, talking quietly, heads down.

No one glanced his way. They didn't look around or make eye contact with other people on the street and hurried off in the direction of the nearby metro station.

No... No...No...

Axe didn't pick up the right vibe from anyone. They seemed like workers everywhere, happy to be done with the day's work and ready for a night of relaxation, television, or socializing.

More workers emerged.

Still, none seemed right to Axe.

The exodus slowed to a trickle.

A few people working late who didn't finish their chores.

He watched them all go, wondering about the soundness of his plan.

For ten minutes, no other workers came into view.

If this doesn't work, I'll have to get creative in the morning.

Axe was about to leave his bench when a group of five men, all dressed in clean yet worn casual clothes of dark cotton pants and T-shirts exited.

Four walked close together, not speaking, hurrying away. Their shirts were colorful: red, blue, green, and a dark orange.

One trailed them, hanging back.

Those four don't want anything to do with the last guy.

The man in back was built like Axe, standing around six foot tall, neither thin nor stocky. He had Axe's dark black hair and a black beard typical for workers in the area—though much more trimmed than Axe's. He wore a pair of dark pants, like the men ahead of him, and a dark loose-fitting T-shirt.

He walked with his head down and his shoulders slumped, the picture of a defeated man.

He's having a bad day—or week.

He looked exactly like the type of person who might be open to a life-changing amount of money in exchange for the valuable intel Axe needed.

Axe hesitated. It was a big risk to pick a man out of a crowd leaving a tall building and hope he would not only talk to him but have any useful information at all.

If it costs me some time and money, so be it.

At least he'd have done something other than wander around the block and sit on his rear end for hours.

If this didn't work, there was always tomorrow.

And I'm part of a team. Haley and the rest are hard at work.

They might get him better intel at any moment.

For now, though, Axe would do what was in front of him and see how it played out. Maybe the target he had picked out would know someone else who could help.

Whatever works.

Standing from the bench, Axe stretched, consulted his guidebook, and followed the men—including the straggler—toward the metro station.

A forty-minute ride on the Red Line, sitting one carriage back from his target, brought him to the Centrepoint Metro Station.

Emerging at street level, Axe immediately felt out of place. There were some hotels, but he was no longer in the main affluent tourist area.

This part of the city had far more locals than tourists. Although not poor, it certainly didn't feel like the area he'd been in all day. There were wall-to-wall shops on the street and offices of all types on the second and third floors of the low-rise buildings. Stores sold cell phones and accessories, perfume, and cheaper, no-name electronics. Mid-range restaurants had outdoor seating under umbrellas to shade from the hot sun during the day, and small corner markets offered prepared takeout food.

It reminded Axe of Manhattan.

It's like I left the touristy Times Square and traveled to the lower midtown area.

For the most part, people only glanced at him, though at times he got harder stares from young men.

And he still felt like he was being watched from time to time.

Locals live here. People who have jobs and are doing well... but this isn't the foreign worker section.

Axe had read about the country's work camp areas—dozens of buildings housing expat workers crammed together into small rooms. He hoped the man he'd targeted wouldn't lead him there. He'd never blend in and would have to abandon his plan.

His target—Axe dubbed him Ray because he was similar in build to a friend of Axe's with that name in high school—lagged behind his friends until they were far ahead. He was especially easy to tail—he never looked back or around. Ray kept his eyes on the ground a few feet in front of him and plodded along like he didn't care whether he made it home anytime soon.

After fifteen minutes of walking straight down the main commercial road for the area, Ray turned right onto a less busy street lined with smaller shops and cheaper restaurants.

Axe was back a few hundred yards, so he picked up his pace. He didn't want to lose Ray in this area. Hanging out anywhere on the street would be fine for a while, but he'd quickly attract attention.

This wasn't an area the average American tourist visited.

Axe waited at the corner for the light to change so he could cross the street—no jaywalking here.

Ray was a hundred yards up the side street, which had cheaper stores than the main road and lower-end restaurants with outdoor seating. Five-story buildings lined the road with signs showing they were long-stay hotels with kitchens, like the many "Suites"-style hotels in the United States.

The area had a decidedly middle-class, blue-collar feel.

If I had to guess, I'd say the workers' boss puts them up in one of the low-end residence hotels.

The place would be better than the deplorable worker camp housing, keeping the workers themselves happy, yet cheap enough for a person living in the Lux View Marina Tower to easily afford.

Ray stopped in his tracks as Axe crossed the road.

Uh-oh. Did he notice me on the long walk?

Axe buried his nose in the guidebook for a moment, then glanced up at the street signs on the corner of the road, acting lost.

Out of the corner of his eye, Axe saw Ray step into a hole-in-the-wall market, like a corner bodega in any large city. It would have cheap food to go along with a small selection of groceries.

This could work.

The sun was nearly down. Would Ray return to his apartment or eat his food somewhere nearby?

Farther up the road, Ray's four coworkers were easy to pick out in their bright-colored T-shirts. They sat laughing at a restaurant's large round outdoor table. A fifth chair sat empty.

He doesn't want to eat with his friends or doesn't have the money... or they don't want to eat with him.

To Axe's left, across two lanes of traffic, a center median lined with trees and bushes had a sidewalk down the middle. There were benches every fifty feet, alternating sides of the wide path. Most were empty.

On the far side of the median, two more lanes of traffic ran the other direction. There were no parks nearby as far as Axe could see, and the map in his guidebook didn't show this area in any detail.

He'll go there to eat in peace—away from everyone else.

When the stoplight changed, Axe crossed the road, stopping on the median. He walked, passing the first bench and hesitating at the second. With an exaggerated sigh, he studied his guidebook again, then moved ahead to the third bench, where he sat for a moment and dropped a crumpled bill of the local currency—the dirham—and nudged it underneath.

Then he stood, looked both directions, pretending to be confused and lost, before he walked back to the second bench. He sat without looking up from his guidebook.

Less than five minutes later, Ray walked slowly by and sat on the third bench, fifty feet farther up the sidewalk.

Axe gave him a few minutes to start eating his food before standing again and hesitantly walking toward him.

"Excuse me," Axe called as he approached. "I'm sorry to bother you, but I'm lost. Do you speak English?" he added.

Ray paused mid-bite and nodded.

He looks almost shell-shocked.

Axe walked closer and spotted the money under the bench. "Oh, it looks like some money fell out of your pocket!"

Ray frowned as he finished swallowing his food and looked where Axe was pointing.

In a flash, he scooped up the money and pocketed it.

"Thank you," Ray said. The guy's face was easy to read—a mix of "I can't believe my luck," fear, and desperation.

Don't ever play poker, my friend.

"Could I ask for your help finding this location on my map?" Axe asked, playing the part of a clueless lost American tourist to perfection. "I… I could offer you some money for your time," he said, pulling out a wad of dirhams worth a fortune like he didn't know how much money it was.

Ray wet his lips and forced out a smile. "Yes, I can help. Please, join me."

Axe smiled his appreciation and joined Ray on the bench.

Gotcha.

120

KARMA

Al Mateena Street
Deira District
Dubai, United Arab Emirates

As they sat side by side on the bench, it only took a moment for Ray to show where they were on Axe's guidebook map and explain how to return to the metro station.

"Thank you so much for your help," Axe said, overdoing the gratitude and playing into the stereotype of a stupid American. "Here," he said, pulling two bills off the thick fold of dirhams, pretending to be unaware that he was offering nearly one hundred US dollars. "For your time and trouble—maybe you can buy dessert." He didn't wait for Ray to accept; Axe pushed the money into the man's hands.

"No, no, it is too much," Ray said, protesting weakly.

"It is my pleasure," Axe said, sliding the rest of the money back into his pocket.

He followed a hunch, knowing few foreign workers were allowed to bring their families to the country. "You have a wife? Kids? If there is any left over after dessert, you can buy them a gift."

Ray's face clouded at the mention of his wife. He seemed to withdraw inside himself like the energy had been sucked from his body.

Axe's elation of guessing correctly and hitting an obvious nerve was tempered with his genuine concern for the man.

"Did I say something wrong?" Axe asked. "I'm sorry—I'm sorry. Did she..." He paused and shook his head. "It's none of my business. I apologize for bringing it up."

Axe didn't have to fake feeling horrible. Ray looked like he'd been punched in the gut. He leaned forward, elbows on his knees, and put his head in his hands.

Is he going to cry?

Axe didn't think. He put his hand gently on Ray's shoulder and squeezed lightly. "I'm sorry for... whatever happened."

He was no longer playing a role or recruiting a source. Ray was a human being in obvious pain. Axe couldn't bring himself to exploit the situation. If Ray were a more solid target or had valuable intel, Axe might have forged ahead. But not in this situation. It just wasn't worth it.

They sat on the bench together. Axe said nothing more but offered his presence as another human being who had experienced plenty of loss himself as a source of strength for the stranger.

After a few minutes, Ray sat upright. "Thank you," he muttered.

Axe nodded and removed his hand from Ray's shoulder. "I'm sorry I brought up the subject. I know I'm a stranger, but I have... suffered. Lost people close to me."

Images flashed through Axe's mind of good people gone too early: warriors and civilians, family, friends, and brothers. "I can listen. Or talk. Sometimes, it helps. Even with a stranger."

Axe felt like crap for singling out someone in such obvious pain in order to bribe him for intel.

What was I thinking? The mission can wait. This is too important.

Ray didn't look at Axe or speak for several seconds. Axe waited, knowing what it took to open up old—or new—wounds and talk about them.

"You are American?" Ray asked.

"Yes."

Might as well tell the truth. The man is smarter—and deeper—than I thought.

"A soldier once?"

Nailed it.

"Yes."

"My name is Jamil. I am Afghan. From a village in the east—across the border from Waziristan, Pakistan. Do you know the area?"

The conversation was headed into dangerous territory. Axe knew the area—he'd done ops all over Afghanistan, back in the day.

"A proud, strong people with a challenging life there," Axe answered. "You came here for work and send money home?" he asked, going on the offensive with the conversation.

If I let him keep asking questions, we're going to get into areas I can't discuss.

Ray—Jamil—nodded and lowered his head again.

"And something happened back home... while you've been away?" Axe guessed.

Jamil once again nodded.

"I'm sorry. That is devastating, to be so far away and powerless to help."

"It was my fault!" Jamil whispered, his voice filled with rage and regret.

Axe hesitated. There had been many times he'd felt like he was to blame or listened to the stories of others who believed the same. Usually, it wasn't true. Life—and death—happened. People often accepted blame when they shouldn't or experienced survivor's guilt, which felt just as bad.

Once in a while, though, the tragedy really was someone's fault.

Either way, the feelings of guilt were there. Logical arguments of "It wasn't really your fault" or "You couldn't have known" rarely helped when people felt such raw emotions.

Axe nodded slowly. "I know the feeling," he said and shut up.

The streetlights had come on as they talked. The last light faded from the sky. The stores and restaurants were brightly lit. Laughter and the din of conversation carried on the air from both sides of the street as people enjoyed the pleasant temperature of a spring night.

On the bench, Axe and Jamil occupied a bubble of guilt and grief.

"I betrayed a trust," Jamil said after a long silence. "And..." He trailed off and put his head back in his hands. He mumbled in English. The best Axe could make it out, he thought it sounded like Jamil thought he'd be better off dead.

This guy's in a dark place.

It took Axe a minute of thinking through the possibilities to come up with a guess. Jamil sat with his face covered the entire time, lost in his emotions.

He's over here working for some ultra-rich guy who lives or works in a luxury tower where condos cost millions of dollars.

Axe made an informed guess. "Did your family pay the price for what you did?"

If they aren't paying this guy his salary as a punishment for some minor infraction, I'm definitely giving him enough money to make it right.

"Are they refusing to pay you?" he asked.

I can't save the world, but a few hundred dollars might change this guy's life.

Axe could live with giving up the money. Maybe some good karma would come his way down the road and end up helping the mission.

You never know.

Jamil took a long, shuddering breath and sat up, shaking his head. "No. Nothing like that. I'm sorry, I have burdened you enough. Thank you for your concern."

He continued pulling himself together.

Wait a second. Is this guy playing me?

Axe checked his gut, fighting against his innate cynicism after seeing so much bad in the world.

No. He's for real.

Jamil was dismissing him because the pain had gotten too much—or Axe had gotten too close to the truth.

Axe hesitated for a moment before nodding and standing. "I hope you find peace," he said quietly.

Jamil met his eye and nodded his thanks.

Axe debated asking the questions about the Tower he needed answered but immediately decided against it.

It was one thing to take advantage of an enemy.

It was quite another to use an innocent civilian's pain to further the mission.

I told Haley back at the beginning of all this that I'm not cut out to be a spy.

Axe turned back the way he'd come, heading toward the corner and the long walk back to the metro station. He'd use the time to brainstorm other ways to get intel on the Tower.

"American," Jamil called quietly.

Axe turned, hiding his surprise. Jamil stood and walked toward him. "Your money," he said, offering Axe both the bills for the directions and the crumpled notes from under the bench.

This is a much smarter guy than I thought.

Axe shook his head. "Please, you keep it." He left unsaid the obvious truth—Jamil needed the money more than Axe did.

Jamil hesitated a second before stuffing the money into his pocket. He stepped close enough to whisper. "I am not an educated man, though I was taught English and some Russian. But I know people. I can tell you are an honorable person. I see you have questions for me. Questions you gave up asking to offer me comfort. I don't know how or why you chose me, but I will answer your questions. But not here. We have already spoken too long."

He described a place to meet—an alley a few blocks away where they would have privacy.

"I will go for a long walk later, as I do most nights," Jamil said. "You will return to the metro, then double back. I will help however I can."

With that, Jamil bowed his head, raised his hand in a small wave, and walked away up the road.

Axe turned away as well and walked with purpose to the corner, keeping the surprised relief off his face.

Karma.

121

THE SLIP

Aboard *Mine, All Mine*
Lighthouse Bay Yacht Club
Southampton, New York

Haley sat on the deck of Kelton Kellison's multimillion-dollar yacht that used to belong to his assistant, the domestic terrorist Todd Berkley. The sun wasn't up yet, and the spring morning was cold on the water.

She was bundled in a men's coat from onboard. The red down jacket was a few sizes too large for her, but she didn't care. It was warm, allowing her to sit outside on the covered stern of the boat for her call with Gregory.

"These comms are secure," she told him. They were communicating on their cell phones via the secure messaging and calling app. A similar app had been breached years before by none other than the CIA, their sister intelligence agency, and used to spy on people for years before it came to light. But Void had pronounced the app they used as nearly impossible to break into.

"Good," Gregory said. He sounded tired. Being up all night explaining armed dead guys in a condo you don't own, another dead guy on the sidewalk outside, and two wounded employees who had been shot in the condo by sniper rounds from a roof several blocks away would wear out anyone.

"You're safe?" he asked.

"Yes. Axe's buddies are going to hang out with us for a while."

Axe's former SEAL Team was home from deployment and had time off. They'd jumped at the chance for a spring vacation on a large yacht in a Long Island marina.

Four of them were driving up from Virginia. They would be at the boat soon, depending on early morning traffic. Red, Thor, Ronbo, and Link were coming loaded with their personal weapons, night vision goggles, comms, and enough ammo to fight a war, all in answer to her call for help.

If the enemy came again, it would go as poorly for them as the last two times, but Haley wouldn't have to be the one pulling the trigger. She could focus on doing her intel job—not the work of an operator—for a change.

"Marcus and Tucci are out of intensive care and doing fine," Gregory said, filling her in. "Four EKIA"—enemies killed in action—"including the one on the street. They figure him for the sniper; they found a long gun in a hard case near the building he shot from."

"Copy. No other injuries on our side?"

"Unfortunately, two of the building guards, the doorman, and both front desk staff are dead. They didn't have a chance against a team of soldiers with no compunction against killing."

The poor people working at the building. They were civilians— innocent.

"Of our people," Gregory added, "Nancy and Dave are shaken up. The kids," he added, meaning the three IT men who followed Void, Kaylin, and Haley to the ground using the escape harnesses, "are both freaked out and excited at the adventure. I reunited them with their computers, but they're at a major disadvantage without your friend and his instructions."

"Don't worry about that. We have it covered on our end."

Void and Kaylin were at the spacious galley table, just inside the thick sliding glass door, sitting close together as the hacker instructed the IT woman on the continuing search to find more clues to the attack on the country.

"The authorities?" she asked.

"Handled," was all Gregory said. He didn't elaborate. "What's new on your end?"

She, Void, and Kaylin had only arrived a while before. After renting a car at the airport and driving all the way out to Long Island, she hadn't had much time to hunt for new intel. She drove while Void and Kaylin slept. All she'd had was time to think… which was enough.

"I don't have new intel, but I had a thought," she said, thinking about how to explain her reasoning.

"Go on."

"What happened to the country was horrible, but is that it?" she asked. "Not minimizing the loss and the deaths in any way, understand."

The death toll so far from the car hack, the trains crashing and derailing, and the nuisance hacks of the water plants, power plants, and fire sprinkler systems was an astonishing 1,184 men, women, and children dead.

"I get it. You have a feeling about another attack?"

Haley sighed. She was exhausted, too. "Actually, no. No hunches or intuition this time."

Gregory let out a tired chuckle. "That's unusual."

"Yes."

And I hate it.

"But during the drive, I had some time to think."

She thought she heard Gregory mutter an "uh-oh" under his breath.

Yep—exactly.

"Logically, the upcoming peace summit is a big, fat, juicy target," Haley said. The high-profile event didn't have any connection to the cyberattack on the United States, but if she'd been a terrorist, it was a target she wouldn't have been able to pass up.

"Which is why they chose to host it at a nearly brand-new ultra-luxury resort hotel on top of a desert mountain in the middle of nowhere," Gregory said. "It's naturally secure and well protected. I had the same concern and put in a call to the director of the Secret Service. Absent a salvo of ballistic missiles—which they still might be able to take out with their surface-to-air missile defense network—it's going to be the most secure place in the world for the next few days."

"What about cybersecurity? I don't know, the air handling systems, gas lines, that type of thing?" She didn't have a feeling about the event—it was more of a worry.

I'm turning into my grandmother, worrying about everything.

"Triple-checked," Gregory said.

"Okay," she said, sounding grumpy even to herself. "I just can't get beyond the concern about an attack on the vice president there."

If the deep fake video came out and Uncle Jimmy was suddenly forced to resign, then the VP died in Oman, the Speaker of the House was next in line for the presidency.

And the current Speaker is a putz.

"It's a very safe place," Gregory said. "With the dignitaries and leaders of so many countries attending, it has to be. The resort was designed and built from the ground up to be secure."

It had better be.

Russia's President Nikitin would be there, along with China's premier; Iran's supreme leader; Iraq's newest president; business, tribal, and governmental leaders of Afghanistan; Pakistan's premier; several top members of Saudi Arabia's royal family; Israel's deputy prime minister; Syria's president; and many other Middle Eastern leaders and dignitaries.

All were arriving later today her time—Saturday in Oman.

The VP would be on his way any minute, she guessed.

"This is a historic meeting," Gregory continued. "A chance for everyone to mingle and speak unofficially. No press coverage. Totally private. Lower-level negotiators will work on the big underlying issues that have kept the region from peace for so long, but it's the big guys sitting together, finding common ground, that might make it work."

"After so long, you really think anything will change?" Haley asked, not bothering to hide her skepticism. "These aren't little problems they're dealing with—they're huge."

"I agree. The summit isn't the end—they're admitting it's a first tiny step. Maybe a bond is formed over a meal that a year from now leads to just enough trust for an initial agreement between adversaries. But we must have a presence there. Russia will be flexing its muscles, deepening relationships to better control and manipulate oil prices. That could greatly affect the United States. Plus, the more the countries in the region rally to Russia's side—or China's—the less influence we have."

Gregory paused, and she could just see him taking off his fashionable glasses and running a hand through his graying hair. "The president would call it off if we had a specific threat to worry about. And he'd warn our allies. Maybe our enemies as well, if it wouldn't compromise sources and methods. Face it, Haley, we're stuck with this unless you can be more specific than a general concern."

She sighed quietly. "I don't have it."

Gregory hesitated before speaking again.

"In the past, we've respected and trusted your intuition. If you tell me that's what you have, I'll move heaven and earth to convince the president not to go."

What did he just say?

"Wait. What do you mean, convince the president not to go?"

"Sorry," Gregory sighed tiredly. "Slip of the tongue. I'm exhausted. I meant I'd try to convince the president to not send the VP."

The way he said it made Haley's arms tingle, one of the ways she felt her intuition.

He's trying to tell me something without explicitly saying it.

The clues clicked into place.

The president is going to Oman himself!

"Do you have a gut feeling, Haley?" he asked softly.

He's begging me to say yes.

She couldn't lie. If she said her intuition told her there was a threat and there wasn't, that would be the end. There would be no more trusting her judgment or word. The next time she had a concern, all anyone would remember was this time when she cried wolf.

"Not at the moment," she said, her voice filled with frustration.

There was silence on the line. Haley felt them share an unspoken pact —she had to find out whether there was truly a threat facing the summit... and save the president.

Don't worry, Uncle Jimmy. I won't let you die over there.

122

THE PLAN

James arranged the two business-size white envelopes side by side on the otherwise empty Resolute desk. He'd removed the few framed photos that normally sat next to the phone, shoving them into the lower desk drawer.

Each envelope bore the Presidential Seal in the top left corner in the return address area.

He'd written a large capital "A" on one of the envelopes before sealing it and a "B" on the other.

I hope no one has to open either of these.

The side door to his Chief of Staff's office opened after one sharp knock. "Ready, Mr. President?" Chad asked as he entered the Oval Office.

"Yes, though I wish I could bring you along," James said, standing, pushing the executive leather chair under the desk, and joining Chad to wait for the visitors arriving any second.

"If this goes badly, I'll see you on the other side," James said, his voice low.

"It's been an honor, sir," Chad said, equally quietly.

Three soft knocks came from the main entrance—the door leading to the waiting area.

"Mr. President, the vice president is here," Mary Beth, his tireless executive assistant said, poking her head in.

"Send him in, please. And Agent Monroe when he arrives, please," James said.

"Yes, Mr. President."

The door opened fully, and the new vice president entered.

He looks the part.

At fifty-one years old, he was ten years younger than James, though his face already had stress lines around the mouth and bags under his eyes. He was about the same height at James—six feet, give or take. He had short, straight brown hair in a corporate cut, just long enough to not look like he was recently out of the military. His nose had a small scar across the bridge where it skewed to his left, courtesy of an overzealous sparring partner in basic training.

Vice President Robert Cabreran's face was thinner and more elongated than James's, but they both had the builds of former warriors who still took care of themselves. Still, he looked worn.

Maybe I've kept him too busy.

Robert, a former successful entrepreneur turned governor of a swing state, had little foreign policy experience but plenty of brains. He was also a quick learner and hard worker.

James had sent him around the world since he'd stepped into the role as VP, meeting dignitaries and learning the ropes of international diplomacy. Secretary of State Wilson had been right at his side, an ever-present teacher.

Robert had been the right man at the right time. After the previous vice president's untimely "suicide," James had needed a polished yet innocuous person to slip into the role.

James had wanted someone who wouldn't make waves. A good man who was middle of the road politically.

Robert had served in the National Guard in his younger years, including two combat tours in Afghanistan as an officer in charge of a platoon of grunts.

In the unlikely event he had to step into the role of president, James felt he could trust the man to do the job with the best interests of the country in his heart.

And it may well come to that before this mess is over.

In private, James might have addressed Robert by his National Guard call sign—Razor—but not this morning.

People may write books about this meeting.

Better to have it recalled with the seriousness and formality it required.

"Mr. Vice President, thanks for stopping in before you left," James said, offering his hand.

Robert took it, eyes narrowing.

He knows something is up.

They didn't normally greet with a handshake or use their formal titles.

"Mr. President. Chad," the VP said with a friendly nod to the Chief of Staff. "Last minute pep talk?"

James smiled. "Exactly. Please," he said, gesturing to one of the two couches in the sitting area. "Have a seat." James didn't offer coffee. There wasn't time.

Chad remained standing, but James sat across from Robert for the moment, so they weren't all standing and waiting uncomfortably.

"All packed?" James asked.

"I rarely unpack," Robert said.

"Thanks for putting the miles in for me," James said, genuinely grateful. Running the country, trying to corral Congress, and acting as commander in chief took a tremendous amount of energy. Getting Robert out as the caring, concerned face of the administration domestically and internationally had saved James a lot of time, effort, and jet lag.

Another knock came from the main door, which opened to admit Special Agent Ontrell Greene, director of the Secret Service.

James stood, which caused Robert to stand.

"Director Greene, thank you for coming," James said with another handshake. "Please join us."

James sat on the couch, followed by Greene and the vice president.

Greene sat silently. He was a dark-skinned fifty-five-year-old built like a fire hydrant. He had a wicked sense of humor and was quick with a joke —but not when serious business was at hand. And it didn't take political instincts as good as his to understand a predawn meeting with the president and vice president wasn't the time for laughs—or small talk.

"Director Greene," James started, "the Middle East Peace Summit has to be the prime target on every terrorist's list. Is Vice President Cabreran going to be safe?"

"Absolutely, Mr. President," Greene said. He sat up straight on the edge of the couch, his thick wrists resting on his equally strong thighs. "The location itself is secure," he said in a smooth, deep voice. "We've had people embedded with the on-site security for days. Nothing short of a nuclear strike will get through."

James nodded. "Excellent. What about other security personnel—say, from Iran or Syria—either taking over or selectively targeting people?" James asked. "Like our VP here."

Greene nodded. "Always a concern. But we'll have two people at his side around the clock." He held up a huge hand. "Yes, including in his bedroom while he's asleep. Sorry, Mr. Vice President," he said. "They'll be quiet and will be sitting or standing near the bed."

"That seems... excessive," Robert said, concern in his voice.

"Special circumstances," the agent explained. "Just in case someone tries to come in through the ceiling or a window. Very little chance it could happen, but in the Middle East, on grounds we don't have exclusive control over, that's the plan. We may relax that once you're on-site, depending on the perceived threat level."

"So," James said with a smile, "he's just as safe as if I went myself?"

"Correct, Mr. President," Greene said without the hint of a smile.

James sat back, relaxing, the smile still on his face. "Come on, Fireplug," he said, using the agent's longtime nickname. "If it were me, you wouldn't do anything differently?"

James got a tiny nod from Greene. "We'd use agents who are on your detail already. But not," Greene said, shaking his head, "because you have the A Team and the vice president has the B Team. Only because they know you better—your habits, your routine."

"Things like?"

Greene shook his head. "Not important, Mr. President."

"Humor me." James tried to keep it light, like the request was mere curiosity, but the look on Greene's face showed the man knew the question led somewhere.

"Bathroom schedule and the normal amount of time in there. How quickly you wake up, when you're sleepy, grumpy, talkative, or need some extra space. The little things that make an agent either nearly invisible or seem like a bull lumbering through a china shop, stepping on your toes every time you turn around."

James nodded. "Nothing mission-critical, though?"

Greene didn't speak for a moment as his eyes drilled into James's. "It depends, sir. For example, the secretary of state's security detail caught his collapse several minutes earlier than they might have if they hadn't known his bathroom habits. In that particular case, it didn't end up making a difference, but it easily could have."

James glanced at Chad and got a nod.

"Is there a concern, Mr. President?" Greene asked.

The VP had watched the exchange silently. As James looked at him, Robert's eyes widened, and he shook his head. "This is a bad idea, Mr. President."

He's smarter and more perceptive than I thought.

Greene looked at the vice president for a second, then swung his head back to stare at James.

James nodded at the VP. "I'll be going to Oman and the Middle East Peace Summit instead of you, Robert. I'm sorry."

"Mr. President," Greene said forcefully at the same time Robert voiced the same protest.

James held up his hand, stopping them before they could start. "This is when you both explain why I can't go. We could go round and round for quite some time. You'd both make excellent points, I'm sure. I would pretend to be swayed, you'd feel like you were successful, then I'd lower the hammer. I'd tell you I'm going despite your misgivings. You would try again, harder. In the end, though, I have the single vote in this. So here's what we're going to do. We're not wasting the time. We're skipping all that and moving straight to the point you both say, 'Yes, Mr. President.'"

James stood. The men across from him did the same immediately.

"And we tell no one," James said in a cold, hard voice. "No one. The only people who know are my wife," he said, counting on his fingers, "my secretary, who has instructions to not allow anyone besides Chad here," he said, holding up the third finger, "to speak with 'me'; you two"—two more fingers—"and two agents you designate, who will be my shadows until the reveal at some point in Oman. Robert will join me in the Residence in a few minutes where 'I' will stay, under the weather and saddened by the loss of life from the recent attacks. I'll be working from my upstairs office for the next twenty-four hours."

Both men waited to see that James had finished. They opened their mouths to speak but stopped when James gave them a look.

"'Yes, Mr. President' are the words you're looking for," James reminded them.

Several seconds passed. Robert looked from James to Chad before settling on Greene, who sighed, a look of resignation on his face.

"Yes, Mr. President," Greene said first.

After another second, Robert nodded and spoke. "Yes, Mr. President."

"Excellent," James said. "Robert, I assume you were planning on wearing your overcoat and hat?"

The VP had a cherished, distinctive gray overcoat he wore on most of his trips during the fall and spring.

He also wore a US Army National Guard baseball cap a constituent and fellow veteran had given him.

"Yes, Mr. President. They're both hanging outside in the waiting area."

"Excellent. I'll wear them as a disguise out of the Residence. Greene, Chad here will meet with you in a few minutes to go over the rest of the details after we have another moment alone with the vice president."

"Yes, sir," Greene said and turned to leave.

"Director Greene," James called. The short, stocky man stopped and turned back to face James. "I'm not asking you to do anything illegal or unethical. Your men and women will be protecting me the same way they would the vice president. The usual team here will be doing the same. This is a temporary fake to fool our enemies, not to commit a crime. I need twenty-four hours of your discretion. Trust me when I say I have a very good reason. This isn't a stunt we'll pull again. For this to work, though, you cannot walk out that door and tell anyone, over your radio or in person, besides the two agents who are going to escort me to the limo. Do I have you on my side, Fireplug?"

Greene nodded without hesitation. "All the way, Mr. President, though I'll have to tell at least four agents. Possibly six. They're too good at their jobs to mistake you for the vice president, even in his hat and coat."

James had to concede the point. "Fine. I trust you to be as discreet as possible—and nothing on comms, just in case. Face-to-face only. Thank you. Chad will be right out with more."

The man nodded, turned again, and left, closing the door softly behind him.

James turned to the vice president. "What about you, Robert? When you call your wife tonight, can you lie to her for me? Tell her you arrived safe and sound?"

"Lie to my wife, Mr. President? That is asking a lot."

"Yes, it is."

"Your wife knows," Robert pointed out.

"I told her in person. No comms that could be hacked."

Robert frowned. "I would prefer to call her from here, sir, and explain that I may be out of touch for twenty-four hours while I travel and prepare."

After thinking for a few seconds, James nodded. "You can call from the Residence."

"Thank you, sir."

"Now," James said, then faltered. He'd thought of various ways to explain the situation. The full truth. A partial cover-up. Or go all in with secrecy and "need to know."

"Come over here, Robert," he said, gesturing to the massive desk. "Pull up the chair. Why not? You're me for a while... and you're going to need to be sitting down to hear the rest of the plan."

123

BACK IN BUSINESS

The White House Oval Office
Washington, DC

"My nuclear 'football' case will ride with me," James explained. "I'm still the president. I'm just not where the public—or the rest of the world—thinks I am."

The vice president sat behind the Resolute desk. He looked uncomfortable.

James was in the chair to the side, where Chad normally sat to speak with him.

"I know this is a lot to take in," James continued. "Why don't you tell it back to me in your own words—let's make sure we're all on the same page."

Robert settled into the executive chair, trying to get comfortable but failing.

He's not at all happy with this.

"First, your gut tells you Russia isn't to blame for the recent cyberattacks. You're going to surprise President Nikitin in person at the summit and have a heart-to-heart talk."

James nodded.

So far, so good.

"You also think there is more to the Middle East Peace Summit than meets the eye," Robert continued, "but you can't put your finger on it. You have no intel from the CIA or other agencies to back this up. You're basically going with your gut."

It doesn't sound very good when he says it.

"Yes, that's accurate."

"And last," Robert said, giving James an unhappy look, "you personally are under threat. You won't tell me what it's about, but it has national security implications."

"Yes. Exactly."

Robert leaned forward, glanced at Chad, and whispered to the president. "You can tell me anything. There's no need to keep secrets."

James chuckled without humor and whispered back. "Plausible deniability. The last thing I want is for you to get dragged down with me. You know nothing. That's the truth, and it will be easy to stick to if needed. You can say I confided in you that there was something big, but you didn't know the details. Then you'll react honestly. People can sense authenticity."

James didn't want to tell the man he wasn't a good enough liar yet to survive the storm over the deepfake video if he knew about it beforehand.

"Last thing before we head upstairs," James said.

Robert took a deep breath and looked at—but kept his hands away from—the two white envelopes on the desk.

"Envelopes A and B. They are to remain in my possession at all times and will only be opened if you tell me to."

James waited for Robert to continue, but he didn't.

"Do you—" James started, ready to remind the vice president, but he was cut off.

"Of course, I remember," Robert said, his voice biting. He took a breath and started over, sounding calmer. "Envelope A contains a letter announcing your resignation as president of the United States of America, effective immediately." He glared at James. "You realize I could open this as soon as you're on the plane and start the process to assume the role of president?" Robert asked.

"I do," James said. "But you won't. Now, please, continue. We're running out of time."

Robert frowned but pointed to the second envelope. "B contains a letter invoking the Twenty-Fifth Amendment of the Constitution. You declare you are temporarily transferring the powers and duties of the office to me. I'll deliver this to the president pro tempore of the Senate and the Speaker of the House."

James nodded. "And?"

"If you tell me to open envelope B, I will also immediately order a special prosecutor to look into... whatever is making you invoke the Twenty-Fifth, to leave no stone unturned. And I should pick a real bastard, too—not someone who's going to sugarcoat 'it' or sweep it under the rug."

"You got it," James said, standing from the guest chair to the left of the desk. Robert instinctively stood as well, though not as quickly as he had earlier, when they sat on the couch.

He's already growing into the role.

"Chad will be here to offer guidance. Listen to his counsel, but if it all hits the fan, remember that you're in charge. The buck stops with you, not him."

James offered his hand once again.

They shook.

The moment felt formal.

Monumental.

"Now come on. Grab your coat and hat, and escort me up to the Residence. Chad will talk to Greene, I'll stuff my bare necessities into your briefcase, and we'll get this deception started."

James couldn't help but feel good about the situation.

Yes, we don't know who is after us or why. But I'm back in business, in the field, and on a mission. And that feels damn good.

124

AIR FORCE TWO

"The motorcade is ready for you, Mr.... Vice President," the Secret Service agent outside the door to the second-floor Residence said as James stepped out. "We've cleared the way for you... since we're running behind."

The barely there emphasis on the word "Vice" let James know he didn't have to fake it with these two, but he responded with a simple nod and kept his head down.

The gray overcoat fit a bit tight around the shoulders, and he'd had to adjust the size of the ball cap. Otherwise, James thought he could pass as the VP from a distance.

The Secret Service agents escorted him to the limo, keeping him out of view of anyone besides the other agents.

The ride to the Air Force base at the early hour passed without a hitch, as did his head-down walk up the plane stairs and into the office on the plane.

This only works because of the nature of the peace summit.

The organizers of the event had insisted no reporters be allowed, so Air Force Two—which technically should have been designated Air Force One, since the president was on board—had no press along.

The VP's Chief of Staff and other office personnel were also not invited. And at the last minute, James had informed the deputy secretary of state that he would be needed in DC over the weekend, preventing him from attending the summit.

People would be confused—maybe even suspicious—but the ruse would hold for the short time James needed it to.

Aside from normal staff, like the doctor and nurse who traveled with the VP, the Air Force Two staff, and other Secret Service personnel—none of whom James had to come into contact with if he was careful—it was a much smaller contingent than usual.

As soon as James had taken his seat, the plane started to taxi.

If he was walking into a trap or someone released the deepfake video while he was in Oman, his day would go to hell in a flash.

And he still didn't have a concrete plan of what he'd do once he was there.

But his gut still told him he had to go.

Haley's not the only person who's learned to trust their intuition.

125

THE MEETING

3B Street
Deira District
Dubai, United Arab Emirates

Axe arrived at the designated meeting spot in the dark alley twenty minutes early. No one was out at this late hour.

He slid into the shadows and waited.

The street was dirty and dark, lit only by the glow of televisions coming through thin curtains in the three-story apartment buildings along both sides of the narrow street.

On the ground floor, people parked their cars in open-air carports. Above, each of the tan or white buildings had four apartments per floor. A narrow alley ran between each of the many apartment buildings that filled the neighborhood.

The area looked to be lower blue-collar. People owned vehicles and rented apartments, but everything seemed rundown. The cars were dented and worn, the homes likely small and overcrowded. Still, the people here had jobs, transportation, food, televisions, and decent housing. Quiet, happy voices and laughter came from many of the windows, wide open to catch the cool late-evening breeze.

These are the people that bake the bread, sell the goods, fix and paint homes, and generally run the country.

Axe pressed himself tightly against a pillar in the parking area closest to the alley where Jamil had suggested they meet. He watched silently.

He was out of his element. Anyone who saw him would peg him as not from the area. His clothes, backpack, bushy beard, haircut, and demeanor couldn't be hidden.

I don't blend in here.

Worst of all, he still felt like he was being watched.

Am I paranoid? Or have people seen me walking by?

Probably a bit of both, he figured. As in any tight-knit neighborhood around the world, people looked out for one another. Strangers stuck out and were viewed with suspicion.

Axe positioned his body with the best angle of the street he could get and shut down his energy, going into sniper stealth mode.

It was the best protection he could have. No one would notice him unless they moved into the shadows next to the pillar.

Right on time, Jamil walked up the street, slowed, and stopped ten feet from Axe at the entrance to the alley.

Axe let him wait.

Jamil fidgeted, looked around, and walked slowly up the street.

He's not leaving—he just doesn't want to look suspicious.

After reaching and passing a dumpster overflowing with garbage, he turned and came back toward Axe.

Axe stepped from the shadows when Jamil was still five feet away, not wanting to frighten him.

"Thank you for coming," Axe said in a low voice. "You didn't have to."

Jamil stopped, startled, but calmed down once he saw it was Axe.

"Yes, I did," Jamil replied. "In here," he said, pointing down the alley.

If I'm being set up, the attack will come now.

Axe was unarmed. He'd have to rely on his hand-to-hand skills—or run away, which was the best choice in some situations.

Like in a rough, unwelcoming neighborhood in a foreign country, with absolutely no backup available.

"Why meet in this alley?" Axe asked as he followed the man.

"Many lovers come here. Every apartment is overcrowded. People need privacy."

The explanation eased Axe's mind a little.

The building to the north, like most of the others in the area, had pillars holding up the apartment floors above. This building, though, had its block wall built inside the pillars instead of enclosing them, creating narrow but long openings, like small patios. They passed the first alcove, which already had two figures huddled close together in the corner.

The next was empty.

Jamil gestured for him to stand in the corner. He leaned against the wall, partly blocking Axe's body from view. "I owe you for your support. No one else... none of my friends..."

"You don't owe me. Sometimes it takes another person who has suffered to understand."

Now, how to play this?

Jamil was far smarter than Axe had originally given him credit for.

Do I dare risk the truth?

Jamil also seemed perceptive.

He'll know if I'm lying.

"Do you follow the news? Do you know about the cyberattacks in America?" Axe asked.

Jamil shook his head. "I have had other things on my mind."

Axe nodded. "Of course. My country was attacked using computers," Axe explained, not sure if Jamil would grasp the concept of a cyberattack. "More than a thousand people have died. Many others were injured. My government believes someone in the Lux View Marina Tower helped with or conducted the attacks."

Jamil recoiled as if Axe had struck him. "You... you followed me from my work? Targeted me?"

Axe nodded. "I'm sorry. It was before I knew of your troubles."

Now or never. He attacks, runs, or helps.

"How did you pick me?" Jamil asked so quietly Axe wasn't sure if it was a rhetorical question or if he should answer it.

"Your walk," Axe said, deciding again on honesty. "But mostly because of the men you were with—your coworkers. I could tell they didn't want to be near you. A person like you, I thought, might need a friend."

The truth sounds bad when I say it out loud.

He vowed that once he got through this mission, Haley was doing the spy work, not him.

"Separating the weak from the herd," Jamil mumbled.

Ouch. It sounds worse when put that way.

"I'm sorry," Axe said. "I intended to offer you money in exchange for your help telling me about the building and answering my questions. I didn't know about..." He trailed off. Jamil knew exactly what he meant. "If you have changed your mind, I understand."

Jamil looked up and stared at Axe in the dim lighting from a distant street light, his face grim, eyes hard. "Is this a test? Did Malik send you?"

Axe stared at him in confusion. "I don't know what or who you mean."

Jamil's eyes stayed locked on him, trying to read his face in the dim light. After a few seconds, he seemed to make up his mind. "If you were sent by him, my life is over. Understand that. And my wife's. But I believe you. I will help."

"Thank you."

"What are your questions?"

"I am looking for information about the building—how I could access it. But mainly I need to know if you have seen or heard of any computer hackers. Men, probably. As young as eighteen or nineteen through the early twenties. They would be very smart and would work with computers. There could be as few as three or many more. They might come and go together or stay mostly with one another. They may be Russian—or not. We aren't sure." Axe sighed. "I understand how unlikely it is, but let's talk about the Tower, what you do there, and what you've seen. As we do, perhaps it will lead to a piece of information helpful to me."

Jamil's head tilted. "A group of young men with computers? Like, a secret group?"

"Yes. They would likely hide what they are doing for security purposes."

Jamil nodded slowly, his eyes still locked on Axe. "You have very good instincts, American. On the fifteenth floor, there is a group of such men. They have lived there for a year. None of them have left the building in that time that I am aware of. It is forbidden. It is also forbidden to go into their workspace, which is filled with computers."

Axe's heart pounded. "And how do you know this?"

"I am the one who services the fifteenth floor. I restock their refrigerator and pantry. Bring them meals. Empty the trash. I have seen computers on the desks in their work area as they come and go to the kitchen and their living quarters."

They could be the ones I'm looking for. Or not. But it's a solid lead.

Axe marvelled at the skill, intuition—or dumb luck—that had led him to follow Jamil earlier that night.

"Will you help me? Get me up there?" he asked.

Jamil shook his head. "I cannot get you into the building," he said.

Axe's heart sank.

"But," he continued, leaning closer to Axe in the dark alcove, "if you can meet me on the fourteenth floor, I will help—in exchange for one thing."

"Name it," Axe said quickly, mentally calculating how much cash he had on him and how quickly he could access more.

"You promise to kill the man on the penthouse floor who is in charge of them all... and who harmed my wife."

126

THE GUESS

Deira District
Dubai, United Arab Emirates

Axe kept to the shadows, moving with purpose without hurrying. He didn't want to attract attention in this area late at night but needed to get back to his hotel. There was a lot of planning to do before morning.

The Deira neighborhood had gone quiet as he and Jamil talked. Televisions had flicked off, dim lights had gone dark, and quiet conversations from the apartment buildings had fallen silent.

As Axe walked down the narrow, deserted backstreets, few windows had lights on. A breeze blew small litter around.

Otherwise, the night was still.

Axe had to make it to the main street several blocks ahead before he'd feel more secure. Once on the large road back to the metro station, he'd have a good excuse for being out—he'd gotten turned around and had finally figured out his way.

Anyone catching him in this neighborhood so late would have many questions—none of which Axe had good answers for.

As he walked, his mind reeled at the possibility offered by Jamil. If Axe could somehow find a way to be at the emergency staircase door of the fourteenth floor at 5:55 tomorrow morning, Jamil would let him in.

After that, Axe would go to the penthouse floor and confront the leader of the group.

What he said and did there, he still needed to figure out.

I can't arrest him and can't kill him without proof he's to blame.

Once finished with the leader, Jamil would help Axe on the fifteenth floor, where the hackers lived and worked.

What can I do there? Steal their computers? Kill them? Lock them in a room?

And he had to do it all with no weapons, no backup, and without getting killed or caught.

There are so many holes in this it can barely be called a plan.

Maybe it was time to call in the cavalry.

The problem was the country. Here, money talked. The United States didn't have much pull—certainly not enough to have an otherwise normal rich guy taken in for questioning. Or his employees.

Axe would have to adapt and overcome.

Big problem number one: How can I get into the building and up to the fourteenth-floor stairwell?

Right from the start, he was stuck. There would be security guards, cameras, and locked doors—none of which he was equipped to deal with.

I can't even get started.

And there weren't a lot of hours to make the operation come together.

Maybe Haley, Void, and the geeks can help.

If they could get a door unlocked, he might be able to do the rest.

He couldn't call and talk to them about it while in an area of the city where no tourists should be this late at night.

Plus, he still felt like he was being watched.

Have I been followed all night?

It had gone past the point of paranoia. He was now sure someone had eyes on him.

A police drone?

It sounded crazy, but he'd seen the surveillance drones in action earlier. If he'd drawn the attention of the authorities…

That's not good.

Getting arrested in the United Arab Emirates was no joke.

His cover would stand up to scrutiny, but he had no one to bail him out or come to his rescue.

The US government would help in the same basic way they would for any American, but Gregory wouldn't be calling the president to get him released.

There weren't many times Axe worried about being an unsanctioned asset, but tonight was one of them.

Behind him, maybe a short half block back, a foot scuffed on the ground.

Axe kept walking, pretending to not have heard the near-silent confirmation that someone was definitely trailing him.

Not a drone—but it wasn't paranoia after all.

If it was the police behind him, he couldn't confront them, and running would only make him look guilty.

Killing them was out of the question.

Which left hiding. He'd have to find a place to lose the tail.

A hundred feet ahead, a side street beckoned. Turning would take him away from a direct approach to the main road.

If it's the police targeting me, I can claim I was afraid for my safety and ran away.

That excuse would have to do.

And if a local tough guy or criminal was following him, the real problem came when Axe fought back. An injured local, even an expat worker the police suspected of being a bad seed, would be a big problem. People had undoubtedly seen Axe walking around the area and could describe him. He'd also passed plenty of security cameras on the walk from the metro.

The only workable solution was vanishing.

Time to disappear.

Without altering his stride, Axe turned the corner.

The moment he was out of sight from his stalker, he sprinted ahead, searching for the perfect hiding spot.

A small delivery truck was parked near a green privacy fence that hid a small dumpster. Trash bags filled it to overflowing, reeking of rotting food. Other black trash bags were piled next to it on both sides.

Both the dumpster and under the vehicle are too obvious.

A tree, less than two feet wide, stood in the hard, dry ground five feet from the dumpster.

Risky but doable.

Axe passed the dumpster, took three steps off the sidewalk and melted into the backside of the tree, his shoulder pressed against the trunk. The angle would prevent whoever was following from seeing him. Axe would have to adjust his location as the person rushed by, but it wouldn't be a problem. He shut down his energy, engaged sniper mode, and disappeared.

Footsteps turned the corner and walked slowly down the narrow side street toward him, no longer making an effort to be silent.

They know I'm aware of them.

Assaulting a police officer would get him arrested within the hour. So would harming a local.

There is another way...

He could kill whoever was approaching and hide the body at the bottom of the dumpster.

That's the last resort.

The footsteps came closer. They sounded light, like a person who knew how to move. A police officer or former soldier.

The person passed the dumpster and stopped on the sidewalk near the tree, way too close.

There's no way they can tell I'm here.

They must've thought he was hiding behind the dumpster or among the bags.

I'm fine. They're guessing—right?

127

THE TALK

The American warrior Ekaterina had dubbed "Fox" had good operational skills. As she had followed him from the luxury marina area earlier in the evening, he had blended in better than she thought he would. People glanced his way occasionally, but the way he moved was like water flowing around rocks. He didn't stick out as much as most Americans would have.

Still, he'd been easy enough to keep up with, making no attempts at surveillance detection.

She'd quickly realized it was less because he didn't worry about being followed and more because he tailed a group of workers who had left the Lux View Marina Tower together.

Specifically, one man who had fallen farther and farther behind the rest.

Fox had selected the man to cull from the herd.

Clever, she'd thought. *Recruit an inside man.*

It wasn't her style. She could have played the part of a lost little old Russian tourist lady and snuck into the building.

Or bribed a guard.

Or killed him.

But Fox's approach might work.

Fox had made contact with the building worker on a park bench in the middle of a green space between lanes of traffic, had a long conversation, given him money, and left.

Ekat had almost lost the American after that. He'd done a better job doubling back and making random turns, playing the part of a lost tourist while subtly looking for a tail.

But he was no match for her decades of clandestine surveillance. She'd grown up in Moscow and had worked for years on following people unobtrusively.

He would have outperformed her in the desert or a jungle, but in the city, she was the queen.

After dark, as the street grew quieter, it had been more challenging but well within her abilities.

Ekaterina had watched from a distance as he met his contact from the Tower, huddling covertly in the darkness of a lover's alcove.

She again hadn't been close enough to overhear the discussion.

Now the time had come to confront the man—before he returned to his hotel, where he would disappear into his room. She wouldn't be able to stake out the hallway or watch every exit from the building. Nor could she stay awake all night, hoping to catch him as he emerged, and still be mission-ready when he eventually came out. She wasn't as young as she used to be.

No, it was time for a discussion.

A negotiation.

Or perhaps a fight.

In Los Angeles, Fox had had a team to back him up.

A better, more professional team than she'd had.

Here, she believed, he was alone.

And while he likely thought he could take her in battle, she was equally confident she stood a decent chance of killing him if necessary.

People had underestimated her all her life due to her sex and short stature.

It had given her great pleasure to kill each of them.

But Ekaterina hoped there might be a better way.

For a while, at least. She could decide later what to do when she finished using the American. There was no mercy in her business, even if she was nearly retired.

Ekat frowned for a second, staring at the dumpster behind the tall green privacy wall. There wasn't much light to see by, and the pile of trash bags made a smelly and risky hiding place.

Or would he climb into that mess of a dumpster?

She glanced around. There was no place else to hide, and even the fastest runner couldn't have made it farther down the road.

He must be there.

On the last street, she hadn't wanted to spook the warrior, so she had scraped her foot against the sidewalk to warn him of her presence. But now she didn't want him to rush out and attack. Or shoot her.

No, he wouldn't dare risk a gun in this country, the same as me.

With a slow, deep breath, she decided the direct approach would work best.

Remembering their previous confrontation, Ekat once more raised her hands in surrender.

"Hello again, American," she called out softly toward the dumpster. "It is I, from the coffee shop in Los Angeles. I am unarmed this time. I believe we are working toward the same objective. Let us talk, professional to professional."

128

THE GRANDMOTHER

Deira District
Dubai, United Arab Emirates

Axe's mind raced. He recognized the voice.

That's the little old Russian grandma from LA!

It sounded like she faced the dumpster. As good as she was at following him, his sniper training kept him hidden for the moment.

How long had she been following him? Since the metro?

He'd felt watched all day, from the moment he'd sat down to have coffee outside the Lux View Marina Tower.

Damn it. I blew it. She's been on me from the start.

He had assumed the massive police and electronic surveillance presence had him feeling paranoid when it was probably her all along.

What did she say at the end?

They were working toward the same objective?

He cringed.

She saw me meet with Ray—Jamil. Twice.

He'd really stepped in it this time.

When he didn't come out from the dumpster where she thought he was, the little grandma would eventually leave. He could stay hidden in stealth mode and wait as long as it took…

Except for his deadline. He had one chance at getting access to the Tower, meeting Jamil, and getting the culprits behind the attacks.

If it came to a fight, Axe figured he could hold his own with her, but he wouldn't make the mistake of thinking he could kill her quickly. No one made it to old age as an operator without being extremely skilled... and lucky.

I'd rather not fight her unless there's no other option.

He would take the lesser risk and see where it led.

Fine. You want to talk? Let's talk.

129

THE TRUST

Ekaterina waited expectantly for the man to reveal himself from behind the stinking garbage—or launch an attack.

Neither happened.

Nothing moved in front of her.

Instead, a voice whispered in her ear, startling her so much she gasped.

"It's a small world, isn't it?" the warrior asked.

Goosebumps spread down Ekat's arms as she forced herself to not fight or flee from the American standing directly behind her.

If he'd wanted to, he could have attacked her instead of talking. She would have been at a distinct disadvantage from the start. Though she might still have prevailed, it wouldn't have been easy.

He took the honorable path and gave me an opening—again. Just like in California.

"Shall we talk here, or do you want to walk?" she asked, playing it cool.

"Let's walk," he answered.

Ekat led the way, continuing back toward the street they had turned off. Taking a right at the intersection would bring them to the main road leading to the metro.

The warrior followed close behind her.

"Thank you for not killing me," Ekat began. "Twice in Los Angeles... and just now."

"There was no need."

She nodded. "We don't have much time. I will tell the truth. I ask you to do the same. If I cannot answer truthfully, I will not speak. My name is Ekaterina. Ekat—or Kat for short."

The American hesitated for a moment before speaking. "Alex," he said.

He is not lying. Excellent. We will start small and establish trust.

"From Aléxios—'defender' in Greek."

Alex chucked. "Some names are more fitting than others, aren't they?"

She nodded approvingly.

He is well educated—he knows my name means "pure."

They turned right, staying close to the shadows and away from the occasional streetlight or lit apartment window. Both of them moved silently, instinctively falling into a rhythm of movement as if they had worked as partners for years.

"You were honorable in Los Angeles," Ekaterina said. "You still are. As I said, I believe we are working toward the same goal. Perhaps a temporary alliance?"

"What goal? And why should I trust you? You tried to kill my friend."

Ekat gave a nod and shrug, conceding the point.

"True. I am sorry. The targeting of your friend in the coffee shop was a mission. Orders from higher up. Nothing more. It failed." They walked a few more steps in silence. "I failed."

She let the weight of the statement linger in the air.

"After," she said, "I left America and hid in Russia. I did not tell my handlers or Moscow. I retired from this life."

Another quiet chuckle came from behind her. "They found you."

"Yes."

I will risk the full truth.

"They told me a story of America being attacked—and Russia blamed for it. This was before your secretary of state died and the public discussion on the internet. The man who came to me believed Russia is being framed, as you say."

"Why?"

"Why did he believe? Or why set up?"

"Both."

They skirted another overflowing, smelly dumpster and avoided a dim streetlight nearby, moving in sync without needing to speak.

She was about to confess the part that could get her in trouble with Moscow if the American used the intel against her.

"The truth, you said," Alex reminded her.

"I hesitate because my superiors would not wish me to tell you this," she explained. "But I will. They believe the attacks were orchestrated by Russian hackers who formerly worked for our Red Bear group. Do you know it?"

"Not by that name. A group of hackers technically not affiliated with Russia… but working with or for them. Unofficially?"

"Yes, exactly. Eight of the best disappeared more than a year ago. Another two more recently. The first eight were eventually traced to Dubai. The trail was lost at the Lux View Marina Tower. We believe the hackers went in and either did not exit or escaped in a way we were not able to follow or trace."

She had his interest now.

They neared the brightly lit main street. Even this late at night, the road was busy with cars.

A thirty-minute walk would take them to the metro. She stopped well back from the intersection of the small backstreet and the larger thoroughfare.

For operational security, Ekat wouldn't go straight to any destination. It would take ninety minutes at least to make the trip by staying in the shadows and throwing in counter-surveillance efforts.

"We should not be seen together," she said, turning to take in the large American. "For operational security…"

"And because neither one of our governments would appreciate us talking," he added.

Ekat nodded. "My hotel is not far from the Tower. No security cameras. We share a taxi to my room?"

It was the best she could do.

If he doesn't trust me, this will not work.

She sensed his hesitancy. "Ah. You think it is a trap. No. I am showing you my throat. I will trust you first in hopes you will trust me later."

They locked eyes. It only took a second for him to nod.

He stepped forward, leaving her to follow as he walked to the curb and hailed an approaching taxi.

130

THE NEGOTIATION

Axe used the short taxi ride to look for ways to minimize the danger of working with the enemy—and wonder if he was walking into a trap.

If this is a setup, it's a damn good one.

The tiny Russian sitting next to him couldn't weigh more than ninety pounds. She had pale white skin with deep wrinkles at her mouth and eyes. At her age, her thin, stylishly short brown hair had to be dyed.

She looked like a five-foot tall Russian *babushka*—grandmother—who would live in the apartment upstairs or house down the block and bring borscht over when you were sick.

This particular grandma had also likely killed more people than he had. He could see it in her eyes and sense it in her movements.

She's an operator… but also a straight-up assassin.

"Stop here, please," Ekaterina told the driver before they reached the front of a modest hotel—one a few blocks from her actual hotel.

Tradecraft.

They were in a quieter, less glitzy neighborhood further inland than his four-star hotel.

Ekaterina led Axe in a roundabout path, across streets and doubling back. Both naturally stayed in the shadows without being obvious about it. They finally ended up at the side door of her hotel.

Her room was on the main floor near the side entrance, the second on the left.

Noisy, perhaps, but easy to get into and out of without being noticed.

The room was small but clean, with a queen-size bed and a small desk against the wall with a mesh-backed, wheeled office chair. There was no minibar or other amenities besides a mid-size wall-mounted television. The plug-in cord dangled in plain sight.

"Smart TV," Ekaterina said. "Microphone. Too easily hacked."

Axe nodded as the woman pulled out the desk chair and sat near the window. The curtains were held tightly closed with the clips on two hotel hangers.

She's letting me stay near the door. Smart.

Unless the whole approach really was a setup and her goons were about to burst through the door, trapping him in the room.

Axe turned, putting his back to the wall, Ekaterina to his left and the closed door to his right, ready.

"No one is coming," the grandma said, bending one leg onto the other to unlace her black, thick-cushioned sneaker. She removed it and set it on the floor before repeating the process with the other shoe. "Bottles of water in the bathroom—one for me, please. Clean plastic cups or another bottle for you if you do not trust me."

He hesitated, wanting to believe this was real but still ready for a sudden conflict or a quick jab of sleepy juice into a vein from a goon.

"Please, I am thirsty," Ekaterina said. "I would get it myself but do not want to make you more nervous."

Axe moved to the small bathroom, grabbed two unopened water bottles from the counter, and brought one to the Russian.

"Sit—or not," she said. "But I will speak, then we will negotiate."

She opened the water and drained half of it in a few swallows.

Axe decided to remain standing between the Russian and the door, at least for a while, just in case.

"When I was ten," she started, "my parents were killed in a car accident."

He opened his mouth to offer condolences, but she quickly waved him off.

"There were no living relatives. Since I had been a bright student and excelled at sports, a woman showed up and took me to my new home. A spy school."

Axe kept his face still, but she must have detected something.

"Yes, most of the girls learned the art of seduction. I refused, proved myself in other ways, and forged my own path."

"You killed. At ten?" He tried to keep both his surprise and judgment out of his tone and thought he nailed it.

"No," she answered. "Fourteen. My first operation. It went bad. There was not supposed to be violence." She shrugged, but he could tell something about it still bothered her. "I learned surveillance in Moscow—that is how I followed you so easily today. You are talented, Alex, but I am older and more experienced. You should not be ashamed."

He nodded, conceding the point. He'd been kicking himself for not paying attention to his intuition and conducting at least a few surveillance-detection routines during the course of the day, but he hadn't wanted to look suspicious to any authorities watching, either.

"After Los Angeles, I quit the life of a spy and disappeared. But they found me, as I said." Ekaterina drained the last of the water. "They sent me here because I am not a part of the old guard or the new. Since I retired without notice, they feel I am trustworthy and can get the job done."

"Are you—and can you?" Axe asked.

The tiny Russian woman nodded. "I am. I do not care for their politics or schemes. Who is in control today, who gains or loses power. For weeks, I had a simple life in my cabin, reading books and drinking tea."

She had more to say, but Axe butted in. "Did you enjoy it?"

"Yes—" she said, but stopped, staring at him. A flicker crossed her face.

She's lying.

"Yes, I am lying," she whispered, almost to herself. "I am sorry. I said I would tell the truth." After a pause, she spoke again. "I enjoyed it... much of the time. The quiet, the cold weather. No one giving me stupid, ill-fated assignments and questioning how I did my job. But..."

"You missed the action," Axe filled in, just as quietly. "The sense of purpose."

She nodded with conviction. "Yes. Serving my country. To answer the rest of your question, though—no, I do not believe I can accomplish my mission. Not by myself, and I refused help from the young men I would have been assigned. Gones, you call them."

"Goons," he corrected with a smile.

"Goons, yes. I am sorry—my English is worse when tired or stressed. Together, we can find the Russian hackers, learn why they did this, who is controlling them… and punish them all."

Yep—that's the goal all right. But…

"You and I on the same team? How do you think this would work?" Axe asked. "I still don't see why I should trust you."

She had to have seen both meetings with Jamil. I have the intel—and the power.

Ekaterina needed him more than he needed her.

The grandma smiled as if reading his mind. "You have a plan with your source and believe you can do it all by yourself. Or perhaps with people in America helping." She shook her head. "You cannot."

"How do you know?"

Her head tilted to the side as she considered her answer. After a moment, she shrugged. "Many reasons. But mostly, it is a feeling. Here," she said, touching her lower stomach.

"A gut feeling? Intuition."

She smiled when he said the first term. "Yes. Gut feeling." She took a pen and small notepad from the desk, wrote a few lines, and handed it to him. An email address and a phone number with a code that came from the same secure communication app he used were perfectly printed on the page.

She waved him toward the door. "You go now. Call America. Get help. If you need me, call. I will sleep a few hours and be ready before dawn, when you will act."

How the hell does she know all this?

"It is what I would do," she said, reading his mind again.

"If I don't need help?" he asked, slipping the paper into his pocket.

A sharp, matter-of-fact look. "If you succeed, I will find you, take what I need, then kill you… or die trying."

Well then.

"Thank you for your honesty," Axe said.

Ekaterina stood—slightly less than five feet tall with the shoes off. She gave him a small bow. "Thank you for not killing me in Los Angeles. Now, let me sleep. I will see you in the morning," she said with a twinkle in her eye.

Her confidence threatened to unnerve Axe, but he bowed his head in return and slipped out of the room. He would start an SDR that would throw off anyone trailing him, get to his hotel, and figure out what the hell to do with Jamil, the Lux View Marina Tower, and a Russian *babushka*.

PART 5

SATURDAY MORNING - DUBAI

131

RECKLESS

Dubai, United Arab Emirates

Axe finished trimming his beard using the electric razor in his kit.

He surveyed the results in the mirror, clipped a few errant hairs, and decided it was as close as he was going to get to matching Jamil's beard, as the source had requested. Axe might have a shot at blending in if no one saw him up close. They were about the same height and build, though Jamil's skin was darker and his face narrower. Jamil wouldn't give him the details of the plan, but it was pretty obvious.

He's going to steal a uniform and try to sneak me in disguised as him.

It was a risky plan, but he'd have to deal with it in the morning. There were plenty of other problems to handle before then.

Axe decided to trust that the hotel had no listening devices in the room. This wasn't Russia in the eighties or China today. No one should be interested in him or what went on in his hotel room. His cover seemed to be intact; Ekaterina had claimed no one had followed or been interested in him the entire day and night—besides her, that is.

And it was either that or update Haley from the beach at zero dark thirty.

"It's me," Axe said when she answered.

"Hey," she said.

From that one word, he knew she'd been through more since they'd last checked in.

"What's up?" he asked.

"We're safe," Haley said.

Axe let out a breath he hadn't realized he'd been holding.

"The hackers found us again. Our new friend and one of the IT crew are staying on the yacht," she said. "Tucci and Marcus were hit—there was a sniper on top of another building. They're going to be fine. We're still no closer to solutions, though we're back at work. How about you?"

"I can help a little. The Lux View Marina Tower is home to several hackers—probably eight of them. Maybe ten. They are top Russian hackers gone AWOL from Moscow more than a year ago, two of them more recently. Those could be the ones I spotted in Puerto Rico, I think. Anyway, several of them—eight, my guess—are on the fifteenth floor of the Tower. The person in charge lives on the top floor—the penthouse. He's called 'Malik,' or 'the Malik,' which is an honorific—like how Osama bin Laden's followers called him 'the Sheik.' This guy—Malik—is from a small village in eastern Afghanistan."

"Wow. How did you get all that?"

He didn't want to lie to Haley, but he didn't want to admit yet that he was working with a Russian spy he'd almost had to kill twice only several weeks before—and who may have been behind the attack on the rooftop party of the LA hotel.

Still, it's Haley. I can tell her anything... right?

"A source," he said.

Nope. Can't do it.

"Two sources, actually. Long story. But in the end, I got lucky."

"Luck? Or skill?"

That's an excellent question.

"A little of both, I guess. Can you look into Malik?" He told her the name of the Afghanistan village and other details Jamil had relayed to him, along with what little he'd learned about the Tower the day before. "I'm hoping our new friend can help me access the building."

"Hold on." Haley covered the phone with her hand for several seconds. "Go ahead."

"I need the security system in the Tower shut down for about ten minutes, specifically the stairwell cameras," Axe said.

"He's checking," Haley said. "But there might not be any. If the lobby and parking garage are well guarded, I wouldn't expect cameras. Rich people don't want cameras keeping track of who comes and goes, especially if they use the service elevators or emergency stairs for people who otherwise shouldn't be there."

"Like special friends?"

"Yes, or unofficial business contacts. Government officials. They've made a big public production of cleaning things up in Dubai, but it still has a well-deserved reputation as a safe haven for criminals, drug dealers, and other rich bad guys. There's a lot of bribery, corruption, and illicit deals. As long as you have money, people are willing to look the other way... up to and including at the highest levels."

Axe thought about what he needed to do to make Jamil's plan work. "What about lobby cameras? If there are any, can you disable them for a few minutes? I need to access the emergency stairs from the lobby, and there has to be either a guard near it or a camera."

"I'm guessing a guard—twenty-four seven. People are cheap and easy to pay to look the other way—if you live or work in the building. Again, cameras would be too risky."

Axe sighed. "Is there anything you can do?"

"Hi, yeah," Void said. "We just checked. I mean, we've been working on it for hours, but we checked again. That building is tight. Maybe I could get into its security system, but it would take a ton of work, some luck, and more time than we have. I'm sorry." He sounded sincere.

"No problem," Axe said. "I've got another angle I can try."

It's not what I wanted to do, but it is what it is.

The phone made a noise as Haley picked it up. The quality of the call changed—he was off speakerphone and back on with just her.

"I know that tone," she said. "What's your idea?"

Axe heard a heavy door slide open and *thunk* close again.

She's outside on the stern of the yacht.

"Who's guarding you?" Axe asked to deflect from her question... and because he was worried about them being alone on a yacht with no protection.

"Your old Team," Haley said. "They're back from deployment and happy to spend some time rotating on and off the boat. Red says you owe him, by the way."

"You asked for his help," Axe said with a smile. "Shouldn't you be the one who owes him?"

Haley laughed. "He said you'd say that. 'Not how it works,' he told me to tell you."

Same old Red.

"But you didn't answer my question," Haley said, the seriousness back in her voice. "How will you access the stairwell door? And what's the plan?"

"I can't say."

"What do you mean you can't say?"

"I can't say. That's exactly what I mean."

"No, it sounds like what you mean is, 'I don't want to tell you because you won't like it or approve.'" She sounded pissed.

Damn, she knows me too well.

"Okay, we'll go with that," he said.

"Do you know what you're doing?" she asked.

"I'm shaking the tree and accomplishing the mission."

"Why am I worried? What aren't you telling me?"

"The term 'plausible deniability' comes to mind."

"That's… ominous. Unsettling. And it sounds reckless."

Axe chuckled. "Come on. When have you ever known me to be reckless?"

Haley came right back at him. "Remember that time you launched the van we were in off the side of a hill and turned us into human roadblocks?"

"Come on, that was fun! But okay, aside from that."

"Crashing the SUV into the doorway of the building on St. John."

"We got inside, didn't we?"

She sighed. "And the time you—"

He cut her off.

"Okay, okay, I get the point."

Listing them like that isn't helping me.

"I'll admit, this isn't the most orthodox way of getting the job done, but it might work. And since I probably don't have the juice—or the time—to bribe a guard, it's the only play I have."

"Just don't do anything stupid, okay?"

"Oh, we're way beyond stupid," he muttered, thinking about the many ways working with an enemy—especially a Russian assassin—could go wrong.

"There's still a little time for our friend to poke at the system," Axe said, all business now. "At 0545 hours local—that's 1645 hours your time—I'm going to be in the lobby, accessing the north stairway door. Whatever help you can give me would be great. And… if there are cameras and you watch me, don't worry or even think about anything you see."

"What the hell does that mean?"

"You'll know it if you see it. But then immediately forget about it. Deal?"

They had trusted their lives to each other multiple times. But would Haley go along with being kept in the dark?

After a long pause, she answered. "Whatever you say," she said quietly. "When this is over, though, I want the full story."

"No promises, but I'll try. Okay, with any luck, I'll have more for you in a few hours."

If I haven't been betrayed by Jamil, killed by the building guards or Malik's private security, or stabbed in the back and left for dead by a Russian spy.

132

MALIK

Lux View Marina Tower
Penthouse—Floor 35
Dubai, United Arab Emirates

Gogol stepped onto the balcony and bowed at his brother sitting at the small round table. "Malik."

The sun had yet to come up, though the sky was getting lighter. The cool air had a welcome bite to it.

"Please, sit," Abdul said with a smile through his long, thick beard. "I'm sorry, the coffee hasn't arrived yet. It will be at the same time as always, but I asked you here early. I didn't want us to be interrupted."

He wore another beige *thobe* and a white headscarf with a black headband holding it in place, hiding much of his dark hair.

The outfit contrasted with Gogol's dark Western slacks and white button-down dress shirt.

His brother appeared to be in a good mood.

And why not? The operation is going perfectly.

What they had already accomplished far exceeded what others around the world had done to the Americans.

And what was to come would be the final straw.

Gogol felt pleased and proud.

By this time tomorrow, we will have a new beginning—and I played a large part.

He tamped down his conscience, which rebelled at seeing innocent women and children in America die. He'd had trouble sleeping since the attacks, wondering if they were doing the right thing. An Afghan proverb had been fighting for attention in his mind, and it had taken considerable willpower to keep it from dominating his thoughts.

"If you make two wrongs equal, you won't make either one right."

His eyes flicked away from the view of the dark water and lights of other luxury buildings up and down the coast. His brother was speaking.

"We have much to discuss before I leave," Abdul said.

"Leave?" This was the first Gogol had heard about it.

Abdul nodded, a pleased smile on his face.

He has been keeping secrets—beyond what he has kept hidden from me about our benefactors and those helping plan the overall mission.

"I have a role I have been preparing for my entire life. These last several years, only returning home on occasion, and this stupid display of luxury…" Abdul said, nearly spitting with disgust. "You understand how our village—our entire region—could benefit if this condo was sold and the money dedicated to improving the lives of our people?"

His brother rarely mentioned the subject, but Gogol knew his feelings. "We have accomplished much good by using the trappings of wealth and power," Gogol said. "'Playing the game,' they call it, right?"

His mind flashed to the memory of him standing behind Wolf, watching the computer screen as a family on a street corner in New York was run over by a vehicle.

I gave the orders that had them killed.

Those children would never again play another game.

Gogol forced the thought away, praying his brother hadn't noticed.

Abdul looked at him sharply but continued their discussion. "Playing the game. Exactly. We waste the money here, but it will pay off if we are successful. The ends always justify the means."

He leaned closer to Gogol. "I will go to the site," Abdul whispered, his eyes showing his excitement.

"The risk…"

"Minimal. Someone must be present to be a hero—after," he said, still whispering.

The pieces fell into place.

"You will lead us?" Gogol whispered back, though none of the guards in the room on the other side of the thick sliding door could possibly hear.

"Yes. This will be the last we see each other in this life. It would be too risky."

Gogol processed the realization that this was his goodbye to his brother.

"Your disinformation plan has worked to perfection," Abdul said after a moment, no longer whispering. "America—and the world—blame Russia. Soon, America must retaliate. And because of our video, the American president is either unable to govern effectively or will resign when you release the footage."

Abdul smiled again. "America has been neutered. Their renowned secretary of state is dead. More than a thousand have died in the attacks. Others are injured. Tens of thousands are without power, water, and indoor plumbing."

Abdul chuckled. It sounded evil even to Gogol's ears.

"They have no way out. Soon, Russia and America will be at war. They will start tearing each other apart, exactly as we planned." Abdul seemed to glow with a mix of pleasure and hatred. "We will have our revenge, my brother."

"Our honor will be restored, and justice done," Gogol said immediately. It was the expected answer, and all but a tiny part of him burned with the desire to see it done.

The Americans deserve what has happened so far—and more. So do the Russians.

Most of him believed it.

Once the war started, Gogol and the hackers would fan the flames with other materials they had prepared. They had more fake videos to release, hacks to harm Russia that America would be blamed for, and social media accounts to escalate the situation every step of the way.

"Tonight, there will be few or no survivors," Abdul said, whispering once more. "A tragedy."

His smirk said it would be anything but.

"I will work tirelessly, attempting to rescue people. I will look like a hero. From this, with the other leaders from our country dead, I will emerge as a servant of our homeland. I will unite the tribal areas, business interests, and politicians. The Taliban will fall into place... or be destroyed. Between myself and others like me in our sister countries, we will rule the Middle East and eliminate the corrupt Western influences once and for all."

Abdul smiled with pleasure and excitement. The plan had worked perfectly. The next part would succeed as well.

"You will release the next batch of disinformation as scheduled," Abdul said. "And release the fake videos as you see fit. You will know when to act."

He pushed a thick white envelope across the table. "There are more details here for the next phases. I'm sorry I had to keep much of the rest of the plan from you until now, but it was necessary. Good luck, my brother."

Abdul stood and offered his arms to Gogol, who stood to embrace his brother. "We will see each other again, many years from now, in the afterlife," Abdul whispered in his ear.

"Yes, Malik."

"No, I no longer have the title," Abdul said, pulling away with a proud smile on his face. "You, my brother, are now Malik."

Abdul removed a silver ring from his finger, took Gogol's right hand, and slid the ring on. The viper—the most dangerous animal in Afghanistan and long Abdul's favorite—glared from the top of the ring.

It fit perfectly.

Time seemed to stand still.

In the predawn glow of the sky, Gogol had just received an honor he had never dared dream of.

Malik. Leader of the tribe.

Gogol blinked, feeling the weight of the ring on his hand—and his soul.

His uncertainty and all his concerns vanished in an instant.

The ends always justify the means.

All of the dead Americans, all of the destruction, became worth it in that moment.

The dying women and children no longer mattered.

America and Russia would pay for their past sins.

He felt a fire blaze within him.

I will gladly do all that is necessary to fulfill my duty and serve my people.

After a handshake, Abdul backed toward the balcony door, leaving Gogol standing near the table. "I leave immediately," Abdul said. "You stay here. I have instructed my butler to come in late, giving you peace and quiet to focus, though the coffee will be on time."

Abdul gestured grandly at the balcony, the penthouse behind him, and the sweeping views of the bay and the rich city below them. "This is all yours now, Malik, to enjoy and manage—the legitimate businesses, as well as the ongoing attacks and hacking. Read the instructions I have left for you," he said, pointing to the thick envelope. "Plan your next steps." He smiled at Gogol. "First, though, take some time. Enjoy the coffee and the view. Give thanks for all we have done… and all that is coming."

With a bow, Abdul continued to back away, and left to fulfill his destiny.

Gogol's mind reeled at the sudden change. For years, he had envied Abdul. Emulated him. But he knew he would never be the elder brother, entrusted with so much responsibility, so much control, so many secrets.

In the blink of an eye, his fortunes had turned from second son to Malik. He was now in charge of a vast legitimate business operation—and the equally important organization dedicated to helping Afghanistan realize its true potential on the world stage.

Abdul would lead politically.

Gogol would help secretly from the shadows.

Together, they would be unstoppable.

With the added responsibility and trust placed in him, Gogol's resolve strengthened. The doubts and concerns had vanished, replaced with a certainty deep in his heart.

America must be destroyed. Russia, too. Even if it means their women and children.

He took a few seconds to take in the view—the first rays of the rising sun glinting off the water, the luxury cars already starting to fill the roads below. With a last deep breath of the cool morning air, he sat at the small table, turning his attention to the many pages of instructions for him to read, and hoped the servant with the coffee arrived early.

133

BREAKFAST

Lux View Marina Tower
Main Floor Coffee Shop
Dubai, United Arab Emirates

After speaking with Haley a few hours earlier, Axe had come up with nothing.

As dawn approached, he reluctantly reached out to the Russian and accepted her help.

On the way to the coffee shop at the base of the Tower in the predawn light, he had a last-minute hope when his phone buzzed. Reading the message from Haley, though, his hopes were dashed.

We have no access to the building. Sorry, can't help this morning. Hope the other plan works out. - Malik is a well-known successful businessman in the region. Smart, cunning, and connected. Nothing else yet. Still looking. Good luck.

He entered the coffee shop, which had opened only a few minutes earlier, bought coffee and a snack—home-made baklava—and sat at a table facing the street.

Ekaterina was several tables away, drinking tea. Axe ignored her.

We go with Plan B.

The snack would wait, but he drank his coffee quickly, welcoming the caffeine, and gave Ekat the prearranged signal.

It's not the worst plan in the world.

He just didn't like that it was the Russian's idea and not his.

Axe stood, threw away the empty coffee cup, and moved to the hallway where the restrooms were—and the entrance to the building's south stairs.

Ignoring the security camera mounted on the wall at the end of the hallway, he walked to the men's room door directly underneath and paused in the doorway. He took the large rectangle of baklava wrapped in cellophane and aimed carefully.

This early, right after the coffee shop had opened at 5:30, it had to be left over from the day before. It felt like a brick.

Axe tossed the heavy dessert straight up at the camera.

"The camera is on a..." the *babushka* had paused while explaining her plan on the phone earlier this morning. "A... swivel. That is the word. To aim. One push, it is pointed the wrong way. Security men will think it is a mistake—the door slams, the camera moves. They send a person with a ladder to fix it later when they notice."

The baklava hit the camera, moving it a few degrees but not nearly as much as Axe had hoped.

He caught the treat and threw it again, harder.

The camera moved more this time, tilting to point more toward the wall and less at the stairway door farther down the hall.

How many tries do I get at this before someone notices the movement?

There had to be dozens of cameras in out-of-the-way locations where it didn't make sense to post a guard. Was someone sitting in a guard control room monitoring the cameras in real time, watching this particular security feed? Hopefully not.

Another toss bumped the camera far off from where it had pointed originally. Even with the wide-angle lens, it wouldn't show the staircase door.

Axe skipped using the restroom. He walked back to the seating area of the coffee shop, grabbed a chair near the hallway, unwrapped the treat, and started eating.

Breakfast of champions.

134

NIKO

Lux View Marina Tower
Dubai, United Arab Emirates

The American—Alex—eating the baklava was the sign Ekaterina had been waiting for.

She stood, finished her tea with one last sip, and walked without hurry toward the hallway that led to the bathrooms and the door to the south emergency staircase.

The cardboard to-go cup went into the trash can on the way.

She barely had to stoop to work her fake bobby pins—which were actually carefully disguised lock picks—into the staircase door's lock.

One advantage of being short.

The well-made, high-end lock took her longer to pick than she liked, but less than sixty seconds later, she had the door open.

Ekat sensed rather than heard Alex enter the hallway and come toward her. She held the door for him. As the warrior, he would take over now.

They ascended the stairs as fast as they could silently move, both unarmed but ready for anything.

How many staircases have I used to meet a source, approach a target, or hide?

It had to be hundreds. Over the decades, emergency stairs, dark alleys, and parking garages had been her primary workplaces.

In front of her, the American moved smoothly and quietly.

He is a decent spy, though he clearly dislikes the role. As an operator, he is outstanding.

Ekat would work with someone like him—a killer with conscience and brains—over the many animals she had been assigned to over the years.

Except for Niko.

She smiled at the thought of her frequent assistant, driver, and unofficial protege. After the Los Angeles debacle, she'd given him money and told him to lay low for a month. "I'll be in touch," she'd told him before disappearing in western Russia near the border with Finland, hoping to never see him or anyone else from her former life again. In time, he would realize she was gone and make his own way in the world by getting in touch with Moscow for orders or striking out on his own.

He had taken her call two days before and flown to Dubai immediately, staying at the hotel in the room next to hers, listening at the wall to her conversation with Alex, ready to barge in if she needed help.

This morning, Niko sat at a table in the coffee shop, reading a newspaper and checking his phone from time to time, just another well-dressed, stocky man with a blockish head, small beady eyes, and a surly expression.

She didn't feel bad about not mentioning her backup muscle to Alex.

If he is any good at this job, he noted the man and guessed Niko is with me.

If not… what the American didn't know wouldn't hurt him.

Unless she needed Niko to eliminate Alex, that is.

Then the American would have a real fight on his hands.

So would Niko.

135

6 A.M.

Lux View Marina Tower
Dubai, United Arab Emirates

Axe led the way up the stairs.

"Eighth floor is under renovation," Ekaterina had said when she'd explained her plan. "I called and requested to rent space in the building. We talk, I learn 'secrets.' We will go to the eighth floor and cut across to the north stairs. Easy."

The eighth floor was deserted as promised.

They crossed it and continued up the rest of the way using the north stairs.

Axe and Ekaterina reached the fourteenth floor door with time to spare.

Axe stepped back, giving Ekaterina room to work on the lock in the doorknob.

People could use the doors on each floor to access the emergency stairs, but when they did, they would be trapped in the stairwell by the door locking behind them. For security, they would only be able to exit on the ground level.

If someone controls the entire floor, though, a key might be needed from both sides.

Jamil had said the doors to the stairs were always locked on the fourteenth and fifteenth floors to keep the men on the fifteenth floor from leaving. It would be a technical safety hazard to not have instant access to the fire escape stairs, but there was always plenty of bribe money if a person wanted to keep the doors locked.

A few seconds after she started, Ekat had the door unlocked and pulled open just enough to keep the lock from re-engaging.

Axe glanced at his watch.

Almost time.

Jamil had been clear: Malik's home ran on a specific, tightly organized schedule. Coffee and breakfast at 6:30 sharp. Cleaning the spacious penthouse suite started at 8:15, by which time the boss was in his private office. Lunch was at noon; a snack and tea at 3:30. Dinner began at 6:00.

Jamil himself handled the coffee in the morning. The rest of the staff— besides a butler and the ever-present guards—came in at 8:00.

Axe had to handle the people on the penthouse floor and be finished there and on the fifteenth floor by then or risk discovery.

The Afghan hadn't gone into detail about how Axe might get from the fourteenth-floor stairs to the penthouse and have a chance at taking out Malik. He'd only said he had a plan.

Jamil would help Axe access the fifteenth floor—where the hackers lived and worked—once Axe had fulfilled his promise to kill Malik.

One of the many big problems for Axe kept sticking in his head.

How do I know Malik is the bad guy?

He couldn't just take Jamil's word for it. If Axe could get a crack at the hackers first, ask some questions, and get confirmation their leader was up in the penthouse, fine. He'd go up and bring the bastard to justice —or just eliminate the person responsible for the death and injury of thousands of Americans.

But Jamil wouldn't budge in his demand. Malik first, then the hackers.

Having armed guards and living on the penthouse floor doesn't automatically make you the ringleader of a group of cyberterrorists.

Axe's watch ticked to 5:59. It was time. He would have to figure out the rest as he went along.

Adapt and overcome.

The only easy day was yesterday.

Ekaterina stepped back, staying behind the door as it slowly swung open. Jamil didn't need to know about the Russian woman yet—if ever.

It's nice to have a partner—even if she is technically the enemy. She even brought her own muscle to watch our back.

Axe had spotted the Russian man in the coffee shop and knew it couldn't be a coincidence. He had to be with Ekaterina. But that was a problem for later, once he'd accomplished the mission.

One threat at a time.

136

NO

Axe followed Jamil closely as they hurried down a series of hallways, passing doors labeled "Laundry," "Supplies," and "Mechanical" until they reached one labeled "Kitchen."

"There is direct, nonstop elevator access to the penthouse floor," Jamil explained as they entered a massive kitchen even a professional chef would kill for. It had a huge ten-burner gas stove, four ovens, two large refrigerators, and a walk-in freezer.

A thick, professional-grade cutting board; a meat cleaver with a gleaming, razor-sharp edge; and a long, thin boning knife were already out, ready for the day's preparation.

A rolled ball of butcher's twine was next to the board. One long piece, already cut, lay coiled neatly on the counter.

The kitchen also had a stand-alone pizza oven on the island countertop across from the stove, near the cutting board. The portable, domed item cost an arm and a leg, but Axe had wanted one for the cabin since they had become popular a few years earlier. The propane-fueled oven heated up to over nine hundred degrees and could cook a pizza in sixty seconds.

The oven blazed.

I guess Malik likes pizza for breakfast.

"The direct elevator access is why the building was chosen, I believe," Jamil continued, nervousness plain in his voice. "The other elevator from the parking garage is disabled for all except Malik, who has a special key card." Jamil passed over a blue lanyard with a plastic ID card used to unlock doors. "Take this," he said. "The blue cord is for Friday—one small security measure. As the elevator doors open on the top floor, there will be two guards across the hall. Both are armed with AKs. You will have to get by them, then go down the hall."

He described the way to the correct door, which would lead to a room with a balcony where Malik would be waiting for his breakfast.

"Use the card to unlock the door. There are more guards inside, sometimes by the door, other times not. Two to four guards, armed with pistols and slung AKs."

"What about the hackers? I need them first," Axe said.

"They are on the fifteenth floor. You will return here once Malik is dead. We can use interior stairs—not the emergency staircase—that connect to the fifteenth floor."

"I need the hackers first," Axe said again.

"They are unimportant."

"They attacked my country."

"They did as they were told. Which is better, the soldiers or the commander who gives the orders?"

Axe didn't hesitate. "Both."

Jamil nodded. "For my help, you must kill Malik first. Then his second-in-command—his brother, who works on the fifteenth floor with the hackers. Finally, the computer men. This is the only way. They are bad men. They are the ones to blame for the attack on your country. I am convinced."

Axe had no choice. He had to agree and hope he'd find what he needed for confirmation on the penthouse floor. He'd thought of an idea for that but wasn't sure it would work as well as he hoped.

Adapt and overcome.

"Fine," he said. "I will go to Malik first."

Jamil nodded as they stopped at the kitchen island nearest the blazing pizza oven. A coffee maker was in the middle of preparing a large pot of coffee.

"You will deliver breakfast," Jamil said. "Pour the coffee in right before you leave. Malik demands his coffee very hot." He pointed to a small stainless steel cart nearby. Crisp, ironed white linens covered it except for the sparkling push handle. A beautiful china coffeepot stood next to a white china cup on a matching saucer. A stainless steel cover sat on top of a white china plate with a fork nearby.

"This will allow you to get close enough to the guards to kill them," he said, sounding nervous but not at all hesitant or remorseful.

Jamil removed the round black hat he wore and pulled the long white tunic over his head, laying it carefully a few steps away on another kitchen island. His chest was more muscular than his loose clothes had shown. "Remove your clothes," he said as he kicked off his shoes and pulled down his pants, revealing ordinary tighty-whities.

Axe understood Jamil's plan. They were close enough in build that Jamil assumed the guards wouldn't notice the switch.

"I don't think this is going to be enough of a disguise," Axe said, but he undid the top two buttons on his dress shirt and pulled it over his head before removing his shoes and pants.

"It may buy me a second," Axe continued, "but even with my trimmed beard, the guards will know I'm not you."

Jamil stood in his underwear, his expression going from nervous to petrified. His whole body trembled.

"The clothing and beard are only part of the disguise," he said, his voice shaking.

He stopped Axe from picking up his uniform to get dressed. "Wait. There is one thing we must do first." The words came out in a rush.

The change from focused and committed to abject terror had happened in an instant.

Why is he suddenly losing it?

"My wife…" Jamil started before stopping abruptly. "Malik…" he said and stopped again. He couldn't get any words out.

"What did he do?" Axe asked softly.

"I… I stole from the penthouse to get extra money to send home," Jamil said, the words flooding out. "I was caught. For punishment…" Jamil took a breath. "He had my wife's hand cut off."

The words hung in the air.

Jamil looked like he might collapse from the admission.

Axe regarded him in shock. He'd heard of the ancient practice of cutting off a thief's hand, but it wasn't done much these days… except in some tribal areas or with those who held to the old ways.

Malik is a monster.

"He gave me the hand as a birthday present three days ago," Jamil continued in a whisper. "I wore it on a string around my neck at work as a sign of my betrayal—and a lesson to others."

Jamil's face looked like he'd seen a ghost.

He picked up the meat cleaver with a shaking hand and offered it to Axe.

"The guards will see what they expect to see. Me, in my uniform, delivering breakfast on time as always. Friday's blue security cord. And a fresh hand around 'my' neck—a sign of further punishment."

His eyes met Axe's. "They will never look at your face."

"No," Axe said, his voice firm, refusing to take the offered meat cleaver.

No, no, and no. Hell no. Absolutely not.

"Not like this," Axe said. "All I need is to get into the hallway on the penthouse level. The cart with breakfast and the clothing will buy me the time I need."

Jamil's head started shaking as Axe spoke. "The hallway is too wide. The guards are well trained. They stand far apart to make it harder to attack both at once. You said before—a simple disguise is not enough. They will shoot you dead before you get to either of them."

Having to talk Axe into the horrendous deed seemed to be helping the Afghan. He stood straight and proud, half-naked in the kitchen, and tried to press the knife into Axe's hand.

Axe wouldn't take it. He backed away, shaking his head.

"It is the only way," Jamil whispered fiercely. "And it is what I deserve," he muttered, looking at the floor.

He stretched his left arm out, lowered his body slightly so the arm and hand lay flat, and settled his wrist in the center of the cutting board.

"One cut," Jamil said, "then quickly the pizza oven. I do not know the word in English."

"Cauterize," Axe said automatically. "To stop the bleeding and seal the wound."

Jamil nodded. "Yes."

Axe shook his head again.

I can't do this.

"You are a warrior," Jamil said, not moving from his ready position. "You would give your life for your country. I would give mine for my family. This…" He tilted his head to his left wrist. "This is nothing but what I deserve… and what you need to kill Malik.

Please," he added softly and closed his eyes. His lips moved as if murmuring a prayer.

Jamil held the meat cleaver by the handle, his right hand stretched toward Axe for him to take it.

Axe hesitated, trying to talk himself into it… and failing.

Anything for the mission?

No way.

If I had to do it to myself, yes. But I can't do this to another person, no matter how much the poor guy thinks he wants or deserves it.

"Jamil, no," Axe said gently. "I know you're in pain, but there has to be something else we can do. A distraction. A fire alarm, maybe."

Jamil's eyes opened. He offered Axe a sad smile, though he didn't alter his stooped position that kept his left wrist flat on the cutting board.

"There's always another way," Axe said.

"Not for me," Jamil whispered.

Jamil drew his right arm back, high overhead.

The meat cleaver flashed through the air as Jamil brought it down on his own wrist.

137

THUMP

Lux View Marina Tower
Staff Level—Floor 14
Dubai, United Arab Emirates

The smell of burnt flesh filled the room.

Axe pressed a button, starting up the vent fan above the stove, willing to risk the noise to clear out some of the odor.

Jamil lay passed out on the kitchen's tile floor, the stump of his left arm carefully wrapped with white kitchen towels Axe had used from a stack on the counter and tied off with the white butcher's twine.

Axe hurriedly slipped on Jamil's black socks, white pants, long white tunic shirt, and dumb little black hat. He scrunched his feet into the too-small shoes.

The shoes always give it away.

He'd been on an op where a high-value target tried to pass himself off as a farmer. He had looked the part until Axe noticed the thousand-dollar dress shoes he'd been too cheap to part with.

Dressed in Jamil's uniform, Axe tucked his phone, fake passport, and wallet with bribe money into the pockets of the white pants.

He retraced his steps to reach the north stairs, where he knocked lightly on the door as he pushed it open—Ekaterina had placed a strip of strong tape on the latch to prevent it from clicking shut and locking.

"It's me," he whispered.

Ekaterina moved silently from the hiding place behind the door.

"I need your help," he said. "Jamil chopped off his own hand."

Ekat blinked but said nothing, her expression never changing.

He led the way back to the kitchen.

Ekaterina poked the cauterized, severed hand on the chopping block before kneeling to check on Jamil laying on the floor.

"Brave man," she muttered. "He will be fine," she said, standing.

"Malik ordered his wife's hand cut off and made him wear it around his neck," Axe explained. "It's Jamil's plan for me to get close to Malik."

Ekaterina looked at Axe, then the hand. Her eyebrows raised.

"I'll dress him," Axe said. "Can you…" He hated to ask, but they were in a hurry. "Can you pierce the palm and put the string through?"

"Yes," she said. "I will do this part."

As Axe worked to get Jamil into pants, a shirt, and shoes, he couldn't help but glance at Ekaterina working at the kitchen island.

With the tip of her tongue poking out of her mouth in concentration, she speared Jamil's severed hand with the boning knife.

The cut length of butcher's twine must have frayed. Ekaterina popped the end into her mouth to wet it, then carefully threaded it through the hole she'd made before pinching the ends of twine together and making a simple overhand knot.

She made him stop dressing Jamil to slip the loop over his head, checking the length.

Jamil's hand dangled below Axe's sternum.

This is so messed up. It had better work.

Axe finished with Jamil and stood.

He added the blue lanyard with the pass key around his neck. It rested an inch above the hand.

"Can you take care of him until I'm back?" Axe asked.

Ekaterina nodded. "Go. I will wake him and get to the stairs. We will wait for you."

It was time to leave.

Axe poured the hot coffee into the china pot, then pushed the serving cart toward the kitchen door.

He stopped and backtracked quickly, wiping the blades of the meat cleaver and boning knife on a white kitchen towel. After wrapping each in clean towels, creating makeshift sheaths, he tucked both into the waistband of the pants under the long, loose tunic.

Better than nothing.

He composed himself, thought better of it, and hunched his shoulders, imitating Jamil's posture the first time he had seen him leaving work the night before.

The cauterized hand swung in the air, thumping against his chest as Axe walked, neither slow nor fast, pushing the cart along the route Jamil had explained to him.

138

THE COFFEE

Lux View Marina Tower
Penthouse—Floor 35
Dubai, United Arab Emirates

The middle of an op was not ideal for trying new techniques, but there was a first time for everything. Stepping off an elevator and into view of two experienced guards required commitment to the disguise.

On the elevator ride up to the top floor, Axe decided he would adapt his sniper training to the occasion.

He used the same process as when he needed to vanish, emptying himself of all emotions.

Axe effectively disappeared.

The new technique was allowing his body to radiate energy—a persona based on Jamil.

He slumped further, letting his head drop to stare straight down at the china coffeepot.

The smell coming from it couldn't compete with the cauterized flesh hanging around his neck.

Axe fought not to gag and barely succeeded.

Next, instead of keeping his head and heart empty, Axe let them fill with the emotions he'd seen on Jamil's face.

Fear. Guilt. Shame. Loss. Embarrassment.

And pure, white-hot rage held in check by self-preservation.

A small *ding* came from the elevator.

Axe adjusted his posture, raising his head an inch so the hand could be seen more clearly.

The doors opened.

In the edge of his vision, the guards across the width of the hall were too far away to attack and too far apart to quickly shoot, even if he'd had a gun, exactly as Jamil had said.

Without looking up, Axe pushed the cart forward, careful of the small gap between the elevator car and the floor.

The guards' feet moved.

It worked!

They turned to face away from him.

Axe stepped to the middle of the wide hallway and smoothly turned left like he'd done this every day.

He didn't look up.

Didn't wait for a bullet or a question spoken in Pashto or Dari.

He gave the guards no thought or energy...

And walked right by them.

139

HELP

Axe sensed the alertness as he walked through the door into a large room.

With his head down and shoulders still hunched in shame, he saw the plush carpet and the feet of one guard five feet to his right. Another stood about six feet to his left, and there were more on the other side of the room.

One second, he felt their eyes on him, doing their duty, looking for possible threats.

The next, the energy in the room changed.

Just like in the hallway by the elevator, he sensed the guards' eyes slide off of him and focus on Jamil's dangling hand, pierced through the middle, fresh blood changing the butcher's twine from white to dark red.

An instant later, all attention on him disappeared.

The disgusting smell coming from the hand could have had something to do with it.

The nearby guards shuffled their feet nervously and turned away, just like the two had done near the elevator.

They don't want anything to do with me. It's like I'm marked—or cursed.

Axe had seen something similar during BUD/S. A candidate's energy changed as he started considering giving up and ringing the bell. If he was well liked, a few of his buddies might work their asses off to get him to hold on for a while, to make it to the next break or meal. To not give up on his dreams.

Others, not as personally invested in him, would sense the change. They knew the odds were good the guy was gone. It was just a matter of time.

They would cut ties with him, emotionally and psychologically.

They'd turn away. Ignore him. Pretend he wasn't there.

Anything to keep themselves from getting infected with the darkness of quitting.

Just like the candidates at BUD/S, the guards in the room were afraid that if they got too close, whatever the servant had done to mess up— whatever he'd done to cause him to wear a family member's hand around his neck—would rub off on them.

Superstitious nonsense… but it works for me right now.

Axe plodded across the room toward the sliding door leading to the balcony. One of the cart tires had a tiny squeak that rang through the silent room.

Malik sat with his back partly to the sliding door, focused on a pile of handwritten papers in front of him. From the side, he looked as Jamil had described him, except maybe a few years younger.

Longish dark beard, narrow face, sitting at the balcony table right where Jamil said he'd be. He wore Western clothes—dark pants and a well-pressed white button-down shirt, which was unusual; Jamil had said he most often wore the traditional clothing of men in the United Arab Emirates.

Must have a big meeting today or something.

As Axe neared, a large silver ring with the head of a viper seemed to gleam in the light of the rising sun.

Just as Jamil described it. That's my guy.

Axe still wasn't certain the man was behind the cyberattacks on America.

I can't kill him until I'm sure—no matter what he did to Jamil's wife.

Axe opened the heavy sliding door, carefully pushed the cart outside, then slid the door shut behind him, just as Jamil had said to do.

So far, so good.

Malik didn't look up or say anything as Axe neared the table.

What now?

Still committed to the role, Axe first placed the china plate with silver cover on the far side of the table, figuring if it was him studying important papers, he wouldn't want to be disturbed.

Next came the china coffee cup and saucer, again set on the far side of the small round table.

He picked up the full china coffeepot. The aroma created a craving in Axe's body that pushed past the revolting smell of the hand. He'd gotten ninety minutes of sleep in the last twenty-four hours and could have used another cup of coffee.

He stood, still bent forward, holding the coffeepot, until Malik looked up.

The man's eyes lingered on the dangling hand before they flicked upward to meet Axe's.

"Did you really think you could attack America and get away with it?" Axe whispered, hoping the guy spoke English... and would give Axe a sign.

Surprise hit Malik's face, along with exactly what Axe needed: recognition, anger... and a flash of guilt.

I got you, you bastard.

"You all deserve to die!" Malik said, eyes flashing. He snarled as he rose, lunging for Axe's throat.

Axe pressed his thumb down, opening the large lid of the coffeepot, and flung his arm forward, stopping in time to let the piping hot coffee fly out and scald the man's wide eyes, open mouth, face, and chest.

Malik stepped back, tipping over his chair, pawing at his face, desperately trying to wipe off the dark liquid as he cried out in agony.

Did they hear that?

The heavy sliding glass door must have muffled some of the noise, but the scream had been too loud to miss.

As much as Axe wanted to shove the man over the railing to fall to his death, just to be done with him, he had three or four guards inside to deal with.

If he lands in the street, there will be police up here in no time.

To escape the situation alive, he stepped back, waved his hands in the air, and cried out.

"Help! Help!" he yelled in Pashto. He'd picked up a few words and phrases during his time in Afghanistan years before.

It pays to study the ways of the enemy.

A guard yanked open the sliding door, took in the scene—still not wanting anything to do with the servant with a freshly chopped hand around his neck—and rushed to Malik, who had started wailing.

He's a few seconds away from pointing at me.

Another guard ran onto the balcony and shouted a question at Axe.

Dude, I only know a few words in your language.

Axe held up the pot of coffee, keeping his head down and tracking the second man's progress toward him.

A third guard appeared in the doorway.

Perfect. Let's get this done.

Axe swung the heavy china pot at the nearest guard, smashing it against his face.

Fumbling under the long white tunic, Axe drew the boning knife from behind his back with his left hand.

As the guard's hands instinctively reached for his face and the shard of china stuck in his eye, Axe knifed him in the stomach, aiming upward at the heart.

The guard sagged forward against Axe.

Axe made eye contact with the guard at the door and tried the same trick again. "Help!" he said in Pashto.

The unexpected nature of the attack, combined with the odd request for assistance, caused the man to hesitate. Axe staggered toward him, holding the dying guard in an embrace, leaving the knife stuck in his stomach.

"Help," he whispered as they neared—and pushed the dead weight at the guard.

The smart thing for the guard to do was to grasp the AK slung around his neck and aim it at Axe until he understood the situation better.

He didn't do the smart thing.

He caught his friend, which gave Axe the second he needed to yank the boning knife from the dead guard's stomach and use it to slit the defenseless third guard's throat.

Works every time.

Sensing danger, Axe spun and threw the knife at the guard who had been helping Malik.

He misjudged the distance and the balance of the knife.

Instead of the blade piercing the tango's throat, the knife handle bounced harmlessly off his sternum.

Axe was already digging under the tunic for the meat cleaver when the man reached for the AK dangling across his body.

Bad move.

Axe closed as the tango tried to bring the weapon to bear. He blocked the barrel with his left arm and stepped closer while slashing with his right hand.

The heavy, razor-sharp knife tore deep into the man's neck. Blood spurted from his jugular, dousing Axe.

The tango abandoned all efforts to shoot Axe, clamping both hands to his neck in a futile attempt to stop the geyser of blood.

Axe let him drop and lunged at Malik, repeating the attack with the same results.

Malik fell backward onto the balcony.

He'll be dead in a few seconds.

Axe whirled again, bringing the meat cleaver back and winging it toward the last guard—now standing in the doorway—eyes wide, fumbling for his weapon.

Everyone thinks they're well trained until the unexpected happens and the shit hits the fan.

This time, the hours of practice with throwing knives and axes paid off.

The cleaver flipped end over end and sank into the man's throat with a squelching noise.

Adrenaline coursed through Axe as he checked Malik and each guard, making sure they were dead.

Axe had no doubts. Malik's reaction to Axe's accusation had sealed his fate.

One down. More to go.

Axe fished under his white tunic, now sopping wet with warm, dark red blood from the tangos, and grabbed his phone. He opened the camera app and snapped a series of shots of Malik as he lay on his back, face red from the coffee, hands clutched to his neck, mouth open, a shocked, pained look on his face.

No shots fired. I have time.

Axe used a starched linen napkin to wipe down the handle of the coffee pot, clearing away any fingerprints he may have left behind. He did the same with any other surface he could have touched, from the cart to the sliding door handles. He retrieved both knives, wiping the blood from them on the nearest dead guy's pants.

Axe took two of the guards' 9mm pistols. He left the AKs behind, as they would be too obvious and impossible to hide.

Last but not least, Axe gathered up the papers from the table. Many were sopping wet with coffee and blood splatter, smearing the ink, but Haley and her team might be able to translate what remained. He blotted them carefully, drying them as much as he could before folding them and placing them in the business-size white envelope they had come in.

Time to get the hell out of here.

He had a decision to make—resume the role of defeated servant and try to sneak back past the hallway guards, or go on the attack?

A glance down at his tunic sealed the deal. There was too much blood to pretend he hadn't been in a massacre.

Right. Guns blazing it is.

140

THE PICTURES

Lux View Marina Tower
Penthouse—Floor 35
Dubai, United Arab Emirates

Axe grabbed a small but thick cushion from the couch in the room and bundled it in the crisp linen cloth used to cover the serving cart. He held the bunch of fabric at his stomach, keeping Jamil's hand clear, and prepared for the next conflict.

Once more, he went into sniper mode first before slipping on the emotions of shame and guilt. He added a touch of upset, hoping the lack of the cart, combined with the pile of fabric, would confuse the two guards long enough for him to get close.

Axe slipped out the door into the hallway, head down, shoulders slumped.

He made it down the hallway. Neither guard did more than glance at him before turning away once again.

He shot the first one in the back of the head with the stolen pistol, its sound muffled by the cushion.

The second reacted, but not in time. Axe had to shoot him twice when the first round hit his shoulder instead of center mass.

He left them where they fell. Two missing guards with a trail of blood would be just as bad as finding them dead.

After using the pass card on the lanyard to call the elevator, Axe pushed the only button—for the fourteenth floor—and descended.

The elevator opened into the much less opulent servant hallway.

The rest of the staff would arrive for work in less than ninety minutes. How long before someone discovered the mess on the penthouse level?

Jamil had mentioned a butler, who Axe hadn't seen.

Were there guard shift changes, radio checks, or phone calls and meetings for Malik?

Jamil hadn't known, but he'd believed they'd have at least thirty minutes. From what he'd seen, Malik didn't like to be interrupted during his morning coffee.

But we still need to move as fast as we can.

At some point soon, an alarm would sound.

Ideally, he'd be long gone by then.

Axe hurried to the staircase door, knocked lightly, and slipped through.

Ekaterina emerged from behind the door, taking in the blood on his clothes. "He will live," she whispered with a glance at Jamil.

Axe handed her one of the pistols and a spare magazine, their eyes meeting, agreeing to continue their truce—and trust—even in the presence of weapons that made it easy to betray each other.

Jamil sat on the cement floor of the landing, leaning against the wall at the top of the stairs. His face was pale, and his eyes had the hollow look of a man in shock and extreme pain.

"Is it done?" he managed to croak as Axe crouched next to him.

"Yes. He is dead." Axe took out his phone. Onscreen was the picture of Malik lying dead on the balcony.

He held it close so Jamil could see it. "Now we need your help to get Malik's brother and the hackers who attacked my country," Axe said. "Can you walk?"

Jamil stared at the screen for several seconds before looking at Axe. "I can walk, and I will help. We have gone too far not to. But that is not Malik."

Wait. What?

Axe used his thumb and finger to zoom in on the man's face and held the phone up again.

Jamil shook his head. "That man is not Malik. It is his younger brother, Gogol. The second-in-command."

What the hell?

"He was on the balcony waiting for his coffee, just like you said he would be," Axe said. "He had the ring." Axe swiped to a wide-angle shot showing the silver ring with a viper head.

Jamil shook his head once more, closed his eyes, and leaned back against the wall.

"So where is Malik?" Axe asked, looking between Jamil and Ekaterina, who shrugged.

"I don't know," Jamil said.

Well, damn.

141

THE HAND

Lux View Marina Tower
Floor 15
Dubai, United Arab Emirates

Axe stood at the door to the hacker room after lowering Jamil to lean against the wall until he returned.

"Just the eight men?" Axe asked.

Jamil nodded, then hesitated. "That is how many we cook for. I have seen a group through the door. Five at least. No more than ten."

"Guards?"

"No. None needed. The hackers are true believers, I think. They are not prisoners, though they are locked on the floor. They do not want to leave."

"You'll be all right here?"

Jamil nodded, closed his eyes, and leaned his head against the wall. He was obviously still in a great deal of pain and only holding it together to see the mission through.

Brave guy.

Axe wouldn't let his sacrifice be in vain.

He checked with Ekaterina. Together, they could easily manage all the hackers. Hell, with the pistol, he could do it alone. But he needed intel, which meant at least one hacker had to live. If they were zealots filled with hatred toward America, they might get the idea they could rush him and Ekaterina.

That would be messier than he wanted.

Ekaterina held her pistol and eyed him with a look of amusement in her eyes, like she knew exactly what he was thinking.

How much do I trust her?

Letting him clear the way, making it easy for her to take the hackers and their computers back to Moscow, would be an obvious gambit.

Just because it's obvious doesn't mean I won't fall for it.

His gut told him they were still on the same side… for now.

She won't shoot me in the back of the head. Yet.

"Let's go," he told her. "We'll be right back," he said to Jamil. "Knock on the wall if someone comes, okay?"

Jamil nodded, his eyes still closed as he cradled his left wrist.

"You're wearing that," Ekaterina said as Axe prepared to open the door. It wasn't a question, and her voice held a hint of admiration.

"Yes," he said and offered her a grin. "It can only help, right?"

"Yes," Ekaterina nodded. "After you," she said, her eyes sparkling.

She's enjoying messing with my head—me wondering if I can trust her.

Surprisingly, that only made him trust her more.

Ekaterina opened the door with her free hand, and Axe strode into the hacker room. Once again, Jamil's hand thumped against his chest as he walked.

The large room was mostly empty except for eight rectangular glass tables set up as desks in the middle of the space. Laptop computers sat to one side, but every workstation had a full-size external keyboard and a large external monitor. Seven desks faced the door.

Thin, pale young men sat at each. None of them looked up from their screens as he and Ekaterina marched in.

One desk faced the others. A thin man with close-shaved blond hair sat hunched forward, typing.

As Axe and Ekat moved across the room, the blond turned to glance at them.

This man was several years older than the others—but still young, about twenty-four. He looked like a ferret, with a pointy nose and large, dark eyes.

Emotions played across his face. Confusion. Shock. Fear. And, finally, defiance.

He finished typing without looking at the screen as Axe and Ekaterina neared.

The blond kid stood and faced them, his wheeled desk chair flung back. The other hackers finally looked up at the scene playing out in front of them.

Six were surprised and angry. One, directly in front of the blond's desk, had an expression Axe had seen before.

It came from seeing innocent people killed.

"You in charge?" Axe asked the blond ferret. He stopped a few feet away from the young man, whose eyes had left Axe's face and were glued to Jamil's hand.

The hacker nodded slightly.

"Name?"

"Wolf," Ekaterina muttered.

The hacker's eyes widened as he tore his gaze away from the grisly spectacle of the hand and focused on Ekaterina. He uttered a curse word in Russian that Axe recognized.

Ekaterina's reply—and her accent—caused the other hackers to glance at one another for reassurance.

Axe raised his pistol and aimed it in their direction, not pointing it at any one of them in particular. Most of their heads and bodies were blocked by their giant computer monitors, but he could shoot through them if necessary. "Hands up."

None of them moved until Ekaterina repeated the words in Russian, her tone an odd combination of a grandmother giving a command laced with a sinister promise of extreme pain if they didn't comply.

All eight immediately raised their hands in surrender.

"One by one," Axe said, "you will each disable any login passwords for your computers, but only while she watches."

He was just winging it now, but he had to get the computers into Haley's hands. She and her IT team could dive in and learn all they needed to know about the attacks, from how they were accomplished to what else was planned.

And somewhere on one of the computers had to be the original video showing James Heringten, long before he had a dream to become president of the United States, not killing an unarmed prisoner.

Under no circumstances can Russia be allowed access to any of these computers.

He'd shoot Ekaterina in the head if he had to and worry about the Russian man in the coffee shop later.

Axe glanced at Ekaterina for her to translate, but she shook her head. "They understand. They all speak fluent English."

But they fear you, not me.

"Stand and step away from your computers," Axe said.

Each did.

The mood in the room changed suddenly. Several of the seven young men who had been sitting behind their monitors gasped.

They all stared at Axe's chest.

Ah—now they can see the hand.

He let them take in the gruesome sight and stared at them coldly when they glanced up at him.

"One by one, disable the passwords. Understand?"

This time they nodded right away, eyes wide.

Now they understand English.

"You first," Axe said, nodding at Wolf. Then he addressed the group, unable to resist. "Speak up if you are confused… or if you need a hand."

No one laughed. Not one of the hackers even smiled.

Tough crowd.

142

THE COMPUTERS

Lux View Marina Tower
Floor 15
Dubai, United Arab Emirates

While Ekaterina marched behind each hacker to watch them disable their logins, Axe stepped close to their leader—Wolf.

"Which computers have the deepfake video of President Heringten?" he asked in a low, cold voice.

Wolf hesitated, his large eyes blinking rapidly.

"You don't want me to ask again," Axe said. He lifted up Jamil's hand by the twine and dangled it in front of the hacker's face.

Wolf pulled back. "Only my computer," he said, pointing at his desk.

"The original and the fake?"

Wolf nodded.

Axe had an idea. "What else do you have?"

Another look at the hand stopped Wolf from hesitating. "Other fake videos. Your Speaker of the House. A few more people."

Wolf had gone first to disable the login. The security screen was still on the big monitor.

"Stand over there," Axe said, pointing.

When Wolf could no longer see the screen, Axe quickly entered a password he would easily remember... and that Haley would eventually guess if anything happened to him before he could get the computer into her hands.

Ekaterina returned from watching each hacker on his computer, herding them to line up along the wall nearest the door. "A few have second thoughts about the attacks," she said. "They realized Russia will be next when America re…"

"Retaliates," Axe said.

"Yes. Retaliates."

Wolf frowned and looked at the other hackers.

"Not this one," Ekaterina added with a nod to Wolf. "Yes?"

Wolf muttered another obscenity in Russian.

One of the hackers against the wall spoke up. "We did not know—"

"Bullshit!" Axe said, not able to hold himself back.

The pale young man nodded, his eyes downcast. "We knew but… the women and children… So many hurt and killed…"

"And not the innocent men?" Axe asked, his voice laced with disgust.

The hacker said nothing.

"What will happen to us?" another one of the hackers asked.

"Please don't send us back to Moscow," a third added.

"You want him to send us to America?" the first asked the other. "They will kill us there!"

"Yes, but they will not torture us first," the third young man muttered.

"What happens next depends on how helpful you are," Axe told the group.

Although Russia isn't getting anything, no matter what I have to do to Ekaterina.

Axe moved to his right, getting a better angle on Ekat in case something went down.

The hackers started talking, including Wolf. The entire plan came out. How they had planned and implemented the hacks, escalated the situation using fake social media accounts, and what they had planned to keep the pressure up on America and Russia until they started a full-scale war with each other.

Wolf wrapped it up, looking resigned to his fate. "Something else was coming. I was to receive more instructions. George didn't have the details yet."

"George?" Axe asked. He retrieved his phone and unlocked it before showing the picture of the dead guy from the penthouse floor to Wolf. "Is this George?"

Wolf's shoulders sagged.

I bet he was hoping this guy was coming to his rescue any minute.

"Do you want to end up like him?" Axe asked.

Wolf shook his head.

"Good answer," Axe said. "You're all bringing your computers and coming with me."

Axe turned to Ekaterina, ready to bring up the pistol and shoot her if necessary. "Unless you have a problem with that?" he asked.

143

GO

Ekaterina held the American's gaze, arguing with herself.

It didn't matter what was on the machines. Moscow wanted them, but securing them was not her primary mission.

Yet the traitorous hackers needed to be punished.

She had become cynical over the years. If she took the hackers back to Moscow, they would be interrogated—not to determine their guilt, but to learn how they did the attacks so Moscow might learn from them.

If any hackers are later turned over to the Americans for punishment, they will not be these young men.

There were plenty of others in the Red Bear group who were good with computers—but not at this level. They would "volunteer" to serve their country by admitting their guilt.

"Your country will learn their hacking secrets," Ekaterina said. "Perhaps there is a solution. You take the computers. Learn from them what you can. And these," she said, glancing at the young men hanging on every word, "will get the punishment they deserve. I will handle," she said with a note of finality. She gave Alex a steady look. "You should take the computers and go now."

He stared back at her, knowing exactly what she meant. She would eliminate them, like he did with Malik.

The hackers muttered and looked at one another.

"You don't want to do this," he said.

"No, I do not." She leaned close. "However, if I return them to Moscow, they will not be punished," she whispered, letting the anger seep into her words. "Moscow would use them for offensive purposes." She spoke still softer, so the Russians wouldn't hear. "I love my country but not my government."

There. The truth is out.

The young Foreign Intelligence Services director—Dmitry—believed in the new president, who seemed better than most of the previous ones she had served.

She did not share his optimism.

They are all corrupt. Crooks. Some merely hide it better than others.

"What are your orders?" Alex asked. "Is there any wiggle room?"

"Wiggle room?" She had heard the term before but couldn't remember its meaning.

"Yes. Is there any way you can interpret your orders differently? Do what is best based on the conditions in the field?"

She nodded. "Yes, I have some 'wiggle room.' My brief was to find the hackers and convince America that Russia was not involved in the attacks. I have accomplished my mission, yes? You understand Moscow had no part in this." She frowned at the young men in the room. "They are Russian, yes, but not controlled by my government. They are filth—to harm thousands of innocents." She spoke directly at them. "This is not the way."

All the young men looked at the floor in shame and guilt.

"I understand that," Alex said. "Without you, we would not be here. You accomplished your mission. We do not have to eliminate them or turn them over to Moscow."

She scoffed. "Give them to your government? Your politicians are the same as mine."

"Not all. Not the president."

She said nothing, sure he could read her skepticism.

"And not the people I work with."

"Who?"

Alex hesitated. "No names. It is a small group. Only a few people. And I have a plan."

As he explained it to her, she knew it would work.

The hackers looked on, tense and focused, trying to overhear.

"Agreed," she said after no more than a moment's thought.

It might make me look bad in one way but better in another.

She could live with that.

Ekaterina spoke in English to the line of hackers, explaining what she would do to them in gruesome detail if they disobeyed her or Alex.

The fresh hand around the American's neck helped immensely to convince them of her sincerity.

144

ESCAPE

Lux View Marina Tower
Floor 15
Dubai, United Arab Emirates

All Axe had to do now was get the hackers, their laptops, and the original footage used to make the deepfake video home safely to Haley.

To do that, they had to get away from the Tower and out of the country.

Axe hadn't known if he'd get this far, but he had contingencies in place.

Ekaterina guarded the hackers while Axe collected their laptops. He dumped the contents of two overflowing trash cans on the floor and removed the trash bags. After putting one inside the other, he slid the laptops in, spun the plastic, and tied it in an overhand knot he'd be able to hold with one hand.

That's when the hackers attacked.

Axe sensed it a moment before it happened, but it still caught him off guard when he looked up from the trash bags to see four of the young men running directly at him, their faces filled with rage tinged with fear.

The ferret—Wolf—and two others swarmed Ekaterina.

One of the hackers stayed along the wall, crouching with his hands covering his head.

"No! Stop!" Axe yelled at the ones racing toward him, hoping a commanding tone would do the trick. Axe snatched his pistol from the floor where he'd set it to bag the laptops.

They kept coming.

Ekaterina's pistol cracked three times, followed by thuds.

Axe raised his, giving the hackers a look at their fate if they didn't stop.

They yelled at the top of their lungs, a battle cry that ended abruptly as each took a bullet to the brain and fell, having never gotten within five feet of him.

Three more shots came from Ekaterina as she put a second bullet into each man.

"Don't kill that one!" Axe said, grabbing the bag of laptops and racing over to the wall and the cowering hacker sobbing on the floor.

"I am sorry!" the hacker cried. "I did not hack the vehicles. Only the toilets. I did not kill anyone. I never realized..." he trailed off.

The first part, he's telling the truth. The last part is a big fat lie.

Axe exchanged a look with Ekaterina.

"I need him," he said.

She shrugged. "You will come along?" she asked the hacker. "No games?"

"Yes," the kid said, looking up at them with pitiful eyes. "I am very, very sorry. Wolf typed into our group chat when you entered. He said to be helpful. Pretend to be sorry. He would signal, and we would attack. But I am sorry. I do not pretend. I will help you."

Axe believed him. "Come on, then."

They left the dead hackers where they lay.

Axe carried the bag of laptops as they retraced their steps, hurrying back to the fourteenth floor, to the emergency stairs, and down. He had the hacker—Atom—help Jamil walk while Ekaterina led the way.

How soundproof is this building? Did anyone hear the shots?

No one came to investigate, so he figured they still had some time.

They stopped to hide on the stairs one flight up from the coffee shop while Ekaterina's man—Niko—brought his vehicle around.

Axe went up several stairs to call Haley while Ekaterina watched the hacker, hoping he could actually still trust her.

"It's done," he said without preamble when she answered. "Well, almost. I have one of the hackers. The others—and the man in charge of them, the second-in-command of the operation—are EKIA."

Haley took a second to sort it out. When she replied, she sounded shocked but tried to cover it. "Already?"

"I had help," Axe said.

I'll tell her the story later, in person.

"We can debrief later. Right now, I need to know how much juice we have," he continued. "What can Gregory do? Because I have a big ask."

"We haven't tested it fully," Haley answered, "but my impression is if we have a clear purpose, we can do whatever we want."

She paused and whispered as if that would help prevent their conversation from being overheard if hackers—or the NSA—had managed to crack their comm app. "I know how you operate. Tell me you don't need to deploy a tactical nuclear missile somewhere."

Axe chuckled, grateful for her dark humor. "Nothing like that. I need a fast plane to get from here to where you are. It has to carry me, one guy, plus maybe two more people. On board, I need two or three guards that know what they're doing, have Top Secret intelligence clearance, and will keep their mouths shut forever. Ideally, there's also a trauma doctor or nurse armed with an IV and some seriously heavy-duty pain meds."

"You're injured?" She sounded all business, but Axe detected her concern.

"No. My source. I need all this in Dubai or the surrounding area as soon as possible. My world is going to get very hot in a matter of minutes."

"Final destination?"

"A safe house near wherever you are. A very safe house," Axe said. He sketched out his idea and added the kicker. "I have the hackers' laptops," he said, hoping she'd read between the lines and understand about the deepfake video.

After a pause to think, she did. "Got it," she said.

"Oh—I also have the second-in-command dude's papers, handwritten in Arabic, Pashto, or some other Persian-Arabic script."

"Can you take pictures of them and send them to me?"

"No, it's more complicated than that. They're sopping wet and stuck together."

"Blood?"

"Yes, some, but also coffee. Another long story. They need to be carefully peeled apart and dried out ASAP. Then scanned and looked over for clues about what's coming next. Someone should be doing that on the plane."

"I'll make it happen," Haley said. "Are you mobile? Do you need a vehicle?"

"I have that part handled."

"Okay. Drive south toward…" she trailed off, then gave him directions and coordinates. "I might need an hour. Ninety minutes at the outside, but it will take you at least that long to get there. Does that work?"

"Yes, I think so."

"Good. Oh—do the guards have to be armed? That gets tricky for what I have in mind."

"No. Not if they're mean and know what they're doing."

"Copy."

The hair on Axe's arms stood up as his intuition kicked in.

I bet someone just found the bodies in the penthouse or the fifteenth floor.

"I have to go," he told Haley. "Hurry, okay?"

"Go, but call me again when you can. I have intel about Malik."

Axe hung up as he ran down the stairs, wondering about Haley's news.

"We must go now," Ekaterina said as he raced toward her. "Someone has—"

"Yes, I feel it, too."

"Niko will be here soon," she added as he led the way down the last flight of stairs to the door, using his hip to push the long metal bar that unlatched the door so he wouldn't leave fingerprints behind.

Axe walked into the hallway, followed by Atom, who was assisting Jamil. The servant looked like hell but was up and moving, his arms crossed with the bandaged stump in his armpit.

"Niko is outside," Ekaterina called.

She added a warning in Russian for the hacker. Her tone made Axe shiver.

Glad she's on my side—at least for now.

They paraded through the coffee shop and out the front door. No one glanced their way.

A massive black luxury SUV gleamed in the round driveway of the porte-cochere. The Russian man from the coffee shop earlier sat in the driver's seat, looking at Axe with small dark beady eyes in an otherwise expressionless face.

Axe opened both doors on his side and pushed Jamil into the front.

Ekaterina slipped in, moving more smoothly than anyone her age should be able to, followed by Atom.

Axe swung inside, keeping the bag of computers on his lap. He gave Niko directions, but the SUV didn't move until Ekaterina nodded to him in the rearview mirror.

As Niko pulled forward, three police cars, lights flashing but with their sirens off, raced into the covered circular driveway and skidded to a stop behind them.

145

DESERT RAIN

Gregory woke up with a start, his head on his hands atop the desk. He sat in a tiny office with worn, stained carpet, empty except for the cheap desk, four folding chairs, and a secure telephone. Its glass floor-to-ceiling window looked out onto a large room filled with round tables—a conference space in a little-used area of the military base outside Washington, DC.

His people—those who were awake, at least—worked at the tables.

After the shootout at the condo, the three men of the IT team, Dave, and Nancy had rejoined the rest of the analysts at their temporary location to do what they could.

Gregory rubbed his eyes and picked up the Styrofoam cup of coffee he'd been about to drink before he'd put his head down for a moment of rest. It was cool but not cold.

How long have I been out?

Checking his watch didn't help because he hadn't thought to look at it before resting.

The larger room bustled. When he'd returned to the team, he'd found them hard at work on both the cyberattack investigation and doing their usual job of sifting through the country's intelligence, looking for the next threat.

A dream flitted on the edge of his consciousness.

Something about a storm. Rain. A hurricane, maybe?

A natural disaster of some sort.

It clicked.

Haley.

Gregory reached for his cell phone next to the cup of coffee and brought it close, unlocking the screen to check for messages he may have missed.

Nothing.

The phone buzzed in his hand.

He answered the comms call. "Haley, I was just thinking about you."

"Axe hit the jackpot and needs an exfil," she said, the words tumbling together. "I need you to authorize an immediate 'training mission.' Two helicopters from a Navy ship at the Port of Jebel Ali near Dubai. They'll fly to the desert interior of the UAE, pick up some passengers, and fly to a base in the area, where the passengers will transfer to a jet. All very hush-hush. Time is of the essence here."

Gregory blinked as he processed the request. Nothing about Haley surprised him anymore, and she'd earned his trust. If she needed helicopters in Dubai, he'd authorize them... probably. But he was still her boss, whether she rarely acknowledged the fact or treated him like one. In the end, it would be his ass if his authorization was a bad call, so he had to ask... and he could sense there was something she was leaving out.

"Why two helicopters? How many people is he extracting?"

"Unknown, exactly. Four, maybe, but he also needs guards and a doctor or nurse. I've already worked it out with the Navy, but they won't go without a high-level authorization."

"What aren't you telling me, Haley?"

She let out a frustrated sigh. "Sorry, I'm not trying to hide anything, but Axe is driving toward the desert as we speak. I'll fly the guests to America—he has one of the hackers responsible for the attacks. The other helicopter..."

Here it comes.

"I need it to fly him to Oman. Near the peace summit."

Gregory took off his glasses and rubbed his eyes.

Wow.

"And I suppose you need me to clear all this with the Navy, the United

Arab Emirates, Oman, the Secret Service, and the people in the Oman government in charge of security for the summit."

"Yes. Right away." She paused. "Um, please?"

"Axe found the hackers?" he asked, buying some time while he thought the situation—and request—all the way through. He was fully awake but wasn't sure he'd heard that part right.

"Yes. Sorry, I was about to update you when Axe called. Also, somehow the second-in-command of the operation was taken out. I haven't debriefed Axe yet. But here's the bigger problem—and again, we can get into the nitty-gritty after you authorize the extraction. The guy in charge of the cyberattacks, according to Axe's intel, is Abdul Khan Dagari, also known colloquially as 'Malik' or 'the Malik.' It's an honorific that has a variety of meanings. The most common is something like a tribal leader, only more important than that. It's not like a mayor or governor—it's a wise man people follow because he's important and has it going on. Anyway, get this—he's on the invite list for the peace summit. We believe he's on his way or could already be there."

"Maybe lead with that next time?" Gregory asked, pulling the landline phone over to him. "I've got to call this in."

"I understand, sir, but the... vice president... doesn't arrive for several hours yet. There's time to get Axe into play here—if you call the Navy first."

Haley was right—again. It was hard to be upset with her when she produced results like these.

And she must have picked up on my "accidental slip" about the president going to Oman in place of the VP.

"How certain are you of all this?" he asked, picking up the receiver of the landline and dialing a number from memory.

"Axe says one hundred percent on his end. Malik is behind the cyberattacks. Axe has plenty of proof—a source with direct knowledge, plus one of the hackers, the computers used in the attacks, and some paper documents as well."

A voice on the other end of the landline answered immediately. Gregory didn't bother responding to Haley—she'd overhear his side of the conversation "The is Gregory Addison," he said into the phone, providing his ID and the day's code phrase. "I'm authorizing a training exercise in UAE. Operation..."

"Desert Rain," Haley filled in.

"Desert Rain," Gregory repeated. "Get one bird in the air with the requested personnel. However, no second helicopter. No helicopters enter Oman."

Haley immediately started protesting on the cell phone.

"Haley, there is a no-fly zone for the entire country because of the summit," Gregory explained.

She fell silent.

That shut her up—for now.

He provided another authorization code and a few more details before hanging up the landline.

"The helicopter will be in the air within five minutes, and whatever else you organized is approved except for the helicopter flying Axe to Oman. We have people on-site who can handle it better, anyway. He'd never get close to the resort. Now, give me what you have—from the beginning. Then I'll jump on a conference call with the Secret Service. The..."

He hesitated just long enough so his most perceptive analyst would catch it again.

"...Vice president will need to make the final call about attending the summit."

"Axe has the hackers' laptops," Haley said again.

He didn't get where she was going—he was too tired.

"And the contents of them," Haley continued. "Plans. Solid proof that they were behind the attacks. Evidence. Even videos," she said, putting an emphasis on the last word.

He got it.

The deepfake original!

"Videos?"

"Yes."

"That's very good news," he said.

Well done, Axe.

"Yes, but with Malik behind all this, there has to be more to the story. We're missing something, and my bet is an attack on American interests at the summit. The... vice... president."

"I agree," Gregory said. "I'll make the call. It's too dangerous to attend the summit."

146

THE DESERT

85 Kilometers South of Dubai
United Arab Emirates

The helicopter was a speck in the distance, flying low over the red sand dunes.

Axe stood next to the shiny black SUV. Jamil stood nearby, cradling the stump of his arm, still in pain. Axe had returned the man's hand to him. Instead of holding it, Jamil had slipped the twine over his head to carry it around his neck, saying it was easier that way.

Worry filled Jamil's eyes.

At least he's upright.

In fact, he stood straighter than ever.

He's no longer ashamed. Maybe he feels like he's partly redeemed himself for causing his wife to lose her hand.

"You promised to kill Malik," Jamil said, watching the helicopter approach.

"I haven't forgotten," Axe said. "It will be done. Maybe not by me, but we will do it. America never forgets."

Jamil stared into the desert. "I believe you. However, my wife is now in great danger."

He gave details of where to find his wife and what to say to convince her to leave the village.

"I can't make any promises," Axe said. "But we'll try." He extended his hand. "Thank you for all your help. They will take care of you. Give you medicine for the pain."

Jamil nodded and shook hands. "Please," he whispered. "Save her from that monster."

Axe nodded, but Jamil had already turned away and walked to join Niko—holding Ekat's pistol—and the hacker standing a few hundred feet from the SUV, where the helicopter could land.

Axe moved to Ekaterina. The sound of the helicopter carried across the sand, growing louder by the second. "Do you want to go with them?" he asked. "See this through?"

"You are recruiting me to spy for your country? Or offering asylum?"

He shrugged, offering a smile people called both boyish and devilish. "Either. Both. Whatever you prefer."

She appraised him, eyes narrow. "You could trust me to spy for you?"

"With some things, yes. Others? Maybe—in time."

"No," she said finally, after what looked to Axe like she seriously considered the offer. "Thank you. This is the end of our agreement, I believe."

Axe nodded and offered his hand to her, too. They shook; her small hand had a surprisingly strong grip.

Axe's phone buzzed.

Haley.

Before he said hello, Haley spoke. "Don't get on the helicopter," she said. "You have a new assignment."

She sounds stressed to the max.

Axe glanced at Ekaterina, who was watching the helicopter with a wistful look on her face that vanished when she caught him looking.

"Malik," Haley said, "also known as Abdul Khan Dagari, arrived via his private jet at the Saiq airport in Oman—the one where the world leaders, VIPs, negotiators, dignitaries, and the vice president are arriving throughout the day. His name is on the list of invited delegates from the Afghanistan contingent. He's going to be at the Middle East Peace Summit. Check that—he's probably already there."

"What? How?"

"Doesn't matter. You're mobile, right? There's a no-fly order for the entire country of Oman while the summit is in progress—aside from the pre-approved planes flying in the attendees. I tried to get you there by helicopter, but you have to drive. Go to the town near the resort. I doubt we can get you into the summit, but I'll try. The VP might not even go at this point. Gregory is trying to get him to turn around and come straight home. But my gut tells me having you in the area might help—somehow."

Axe looked at Niko and Ekaterina before turning his back on the grandmother. "I may have a small problem," he told Haley.

"What's the problem? I ran the numbers. You can make it before the VP arrives—assuming he goes—if you leave now. Plus, we figure anything going down will happen at dinner tonight or during the opening speeches tomorrow morning."

Okay, this is awkward.

"I... I'm not alone."

"Who the hell is there with you that's not going on the helicopter?"

The large chopper grew closer, its engine and rotor noise filling the air.

"Call you back," he yelled into the phone and hung up on her.

I'll have to hand off the laptops to a guard on the helicopter and make sure he understands how important they are.

"Ekaterina," he said, turning back to the Russian. She looked at him, her face stoic.

She knows something is going on.

"How would you like to go to Oman with me and try to save the lives of both your president and my vice president?"

For a second, he thought she was going to say no, leaving him with a very difficult choice—force them along, order them into the helicopter at gunpoint, or leave them stranded in the desert.

But after a moment of thought, staring at him, searching for a trick or betrayal, she nodded.

"*Khorosho,*" she said. "Okay. Let us go."

147

THE IDEA

James sat in the small private stateroom of the modified commercial airliner. He'd gotten a few hours of sleep on the couch that folded out into a bed.

After brushing his teeth and cleaning up in the attached lavatory in preparation for what would be a very interesting day, James got a call from Gregory Addison via the plane's sophisticated communication suite.

"We have one of the hackers in custody, sir," Gregory said. "The rest are EKIA, but we have all of their computers. And the issue we discussed Thursday morning?"

The president held his breath, hoping.

The deepfake video.

"Yes?"

"That has been successfully resolved, as far as we know."

"That's excellent news."

"Yes, Mr. President. However, there is another issue," Gregory said. "And sir, your close protection Secret Service agents should be in on the next part of the call."

James put Gregory on hold and called in the two agents who had escorted him from the White House. When they arrived in the room, James put the phone on speaker mode.

"They're here, Mr. Addison," James said. "Please go ahead."

"Mr. President, we believe the person responsible for the cyberattacks is a man named Abdul Khan Dagari—also known as 'Malik.' He is an officially invited attendee of the peace summit as part of the Afghanistan contingent. He is likely already at the resort. We know little about him but must assume he is very dangerous. Our assessment is that he intends to continue to disrupt American interests and harm the country, most likely by coordinating an attack on what would have been the vice president, but is now you—or attempting it himself. I'm sending your agents a photograph of his younger brother, who we're told looks quite similar to him. Aside from this, we have no other information."

An uncomfortable pause followed.

He wants me to turn the plane around—and that's the logical action to take.

"Thank you, Mr. Addison," James said. "We'll be in touch if we need more information."

"Thank you, Mr. President."

He wants to say more, to argue, but he knows me well enough by now to leave it alone.

From their body language, the agents sitting in the two leather swivel seats in front of the small desk didn't like the situation at all.

Then again, they haven't been happy since we left the White House.

They waited for nearly a minute, letting James consider the angles. In the end, though, they couldn't hold back.

"Permission to speak freely, Mr. President?" Stewart, the senior agent, asked. He was in his late forties, fit, clean-cut, with very short brown hair and a tan, weathered face. He was one of the two who had been "in the know" from the start at the White House, personally briefed by Director Greene.

"Of course. Always."

The man nodded his thanks and hesitated a second.

He's going to try to finesse me. Good luck with that.

"Sir," Stewart began, "we in the Service respect you. You're not the typical politician. You've actually been there and done that. Personally, I think you've had many good ideas."

He went to speak, shut his mouth, then forged ahead. "This is not one of them. I'm sorry, but I don't understand how it's either strategically or tactically sound to continue to the summit. Please order the plane to turn around right now. We'll refuel in Germany and go home from there."

James leaned back and put his hands behind his head in a classic power pose. "I hear you. The presence of this guy, the Malik, or Malik, whatever..."

"Abdul Khan Dagari," the other man—Waylan—said, holding up a secure cell phone with the picture of a dead man's face—Malik's brother.

"Yes, Abdul Khan Dagari. His presence is an obvious danger. But life is dangerous—especially your jobs. You chose this. I know neither one of you wants to die—" he held his hand up. "And I'm not saying it's likely. You're looking out for me and the country, not yourselves. I get that. You're going to have to trust me when I say that my attendance at this event is worth almost any risk. I..." The president paused. "You two have been doing this many years. You ever have a hunch, follow it, and have it pay off?"

After a quick glance at each other, they both nodded slowly.

"I have a hunch. I can't explain it, and I won't ignore it. I've trusted my gut for too many years, and it's saved my ass too many times to turn my back on it now. I have to be at this event. We're going in. You and your team will just have to do the best job you can."

He looked each man in the eye. "Would you give your life to protect me and the country?"

Both men nodded without hesitation.

"That's what I thought. And it's basically what I'm asking you to risk doing on this assignment. I don't know what's going to happen, but we'll face it together and hopefully get through it alive. If not..." James shrugged. "We made a choice to serve our great country. This trip will help. We continue forward, understand?"

"Yes, Mr. President," both answered in unison.

"Excellent. Get the photo of the guy's brother out to anyone you need to—it doesn't have to be a secret that we know. Just keep off the comms that it's me arriving until later today when it's revealed to everyone at the summit, okay?"

"Yes, Mr. President," Stewart said, alone this time, while Waylan nodded.

"This is a dangerous mission. I realize the Secret Service is usually in full control of the site, approaches, egress, and more. This is pushing your buttons. I'm sorry. But I learned long ago as a SEAL—we can't control everything. Sometimes we have to embrace the chaos, then adapt and overcome. How copy?"

"Solid copy, Mr. President," Stewart said, standing.

"Embrace the chaos—copy that, Mr. President," Waylan said as he stood.

"Excellent." James smiled and leaned forward. "And if it hits the fan, just make sure I get a weapon before all hell breaks loose. If it's going down, I'm fighting right alongside you."

148

ANOTHER FAVOR

It was going to be a long night. Just one of the small white Styrofoam cups of coffee wasn't going to cut it. Gregory carefully carried three, filled to the brim, back to his tiny temporary office while waiting for Haley to brief Axe and get him on his way to Oman.

Coffee sloshed over the desk in his hurry to answer his cell phone.

"Go ahead," he said.

"Um, I need a favor," Haley said.

From her tone, he knew he didn't really have to ask, but he couldn't help himself. "Am I going to like this?

"Actually, no. Not at all."

"What is it?"

She didn't answer.

"Just spit it out. Rip off the bandage. Get it over with."

"I need a SEAL Team—or a spy—for a clandestine mission."

"Where, Haley?"

Please don't say Moscow.

"Eastern Afghanistan, just over the border from Pakistan."

Okay, worse than Moscow.

The US still had limited ability to conduct clandestine activities in the region, but from the unannounced incursion into Pakistan years before to kill Osama bin Laden to the more recent withdrawal from Afghanistan, it wasn't as simple as making a phone call and sending out the cavalry.

"How far from Kabul?"

"Three hundred kilometers by road but not far by helicopter. Five hundred klicks by car east and slightly north of Kandahar."

"One to ten, how important is it?"

"Ten. It's for Axe's source that broke this whole thing open. Without him, we'd have nothing."

"We already have the information from the source, though, right?" he asked. He hated himself for asking, but looking at the world in this way was part of the job—and one of the pieces of the puzzle he'd have to explain to the president to get authorization for the mission.

Intelligence gathering and analysis can be a cold business.

"We stand by our promises," Haley said, her voice quiet but firm. "America takes care of her own."

Excellent point. Damn it, Haley.

"It's not me this time," Haley said, guessing where his mind had gone. "This one's on Axe."

Fine. Damn it, Axe.

"Timeline?"

"Depends. My hunch is that Malik knows what is coming at the summit or might be in charge of it. If so, he'll live through the coming attack. If he survives, the source's wife in Afghanistan dies."

"We still have some time. I'll see what I can do," he said. "Give me the details."

149

THE RED FLAG

Gregory would have heard by now if the president had turned around to come home.

He's stubbornly moving forward, ignoring the danger.

The Secret Service was the best in the business. With the picture of Malik's younger brother, supplied by Axe, they'd be on high alert and keep him from Malik no matter what.

It's all going to be fine.

Dave and Nancy gave a sharp knock on the glass office door and pushed their way in, laptops in hand. They looked tired—and worried.

Then again, maybe not.

He could feel it. The long day—the long week—was about to get more challenging.

"You're probably going to want Haley in on this," Dave said as he hurried in. His serious tone and worried look made Gregory reach for his cell phone and make the call, no questions asked.

"Haley," he said when she answered, "you're going on speaker with Dave and Nancy."

He hit a button and put the phone on the desk as his two senior analysts sat in the guest chairs opposite him.

"Hi, Haley," Dave said. "We may have a problem."

Nancy gave him a look. "We definitely have a very big problem," she said. "It can't be a coincidence."

Gregory downed the rest of the coffee. "Haley," he said, "let me give them the executive summary of what's happened tonight."

Gregory ran down Axe's success—the capture of the hackers and their computers, the death of the second-in-command of the operation, and the concern that the person behind it all could possibly be a few feet from the vice president. He didn't give them any indication it was actually the president attending. They didn't need to know—even the subtle hints he'd given Haley.

"Okay, Dave and Nancy, why don't you let us know how much worse it is than we thought."

These two usually are pretty steady. If they're worried, I need to be, too.

"That fits in with what we've discovered," Nancy said. "Tell them," Nancy told Dave.

"I wasn't getting anywhere with the cyberattack," he said, "so I switched to looking into the peace summit. Attendees, location, security— you know, the kind of deep dive we do."

Gregory took off his glasses to rub his eyes.

And here we go again.

"He found a reference to a cave at the base of the mountain on which the resort for the peace summit was built," Nancy jumped in, clearly annoyed he wasn't getting to the point fast enough. "We have to call off the vice president's visit."

"A cave or cave system?" Gregory asked. "Is it an opening in the ground where small animals hide or an entire network of tunnels?

Dave shook his head and frowned. "Unknown. It's a vague reference dating back to the seventeenth century in an obscure book I just found online. I told Nancy and we came right in."

"Roads or trails to it? Local building permits, mining rights, or anything that paints more of a picture?"

"No, sir, sorry," Dave said. "But if it's a tunnel system that no one is aware of…"

"Except the bad guys," Haley chimed in over the phone.

"Yes, except the bad guys," Dave said, "that could be very bad. Given enough time, equipment, and manpower, even a small cave could be transformed into a vertical tunnel leading upward to just under the resort."

"Look what the drug cartels have done along our southern border," Nancy added.

"What could be done, though, really?" Gregory asked, pushing to see how far they'd thought it through. "It would take a ton of explosives to bring down the cliff or the hotel, right?"

"True," Dave said. "A tactical nuke might do it. But if in the past year since the resort has been built, they've tunneled up to the basement of the hotel and can punch through at the last minute…"

He left the rest to the imagination—and Gregory's mind went there immediately.

A group of heavily armed men attacking from the basement during the opening night dinner… Or explosive charges planted directly underneath the main room of the conference…

Other possibilities flashed through his mind.

None of them were good.

All involved the security forces, arrayed to protect against intruders approaching from the air or ground outside, outmanned and outgunned by an enemy already in their midst.

"A mining operation like that would have been noticed," he argued, desperately trying to find a hole in the theory.

I do not want to call the president back and ask him to turn the plane around again—right before he's about to land.

He also didn't want to be the one to ignore reality and let the president and the leaders of the Middle East, China, and Russia get killed.

"Besides," Gregory continued, not sure if he was trying to convince himself or his team, "there's a ton of security this weekend. First, the robust resort team guards every inch, inside and out. Then there's the sultan of Oman's security forces. The sultan doesn't want a disaster in his country—he's thrown everything at securing this event. There are also the security teams of each of the heads of state and other rulers, along with the highest-level politicians and most influential leaders from each country. Their security contingent alone must outnumber the attendees ten to one."

"I agree, sir, but it's a red flag," Dave said. "A possibility no one has investigated."

"And with this guy Malik going," Nancy said, "it all fits. There's going to be an attack on the vice president or the entire summit. Somehow, someway, through the tunnel or not."

This is a real possibility.

Before Gregory could speak, an apologetic cough came from Haley. "I sent Axe to the area by car," she admitted.

Gregory resisted pounding his head on the desk.

Damn it, Haley! We're not supposed to have people in the area besides the Secret Service.

"He must be almost there," she continued. "I understand they'll never let him into the resort. Let's route him to look for evidence of a tunnel, cave, or evidence of an impending attack. Just in case the VP doesn't want to back out—or in case we can save the attendees."

"Do it," Gregory ordered. "Tell him to look for anything suspicious, but especially a cave or tunnel system."

There was silence on the end of the line from Haley, like the calm before the storm.

"Do you want to tell them or should I?" Haley asked.

"I… I don't know what you mean," Gregory said. It sounded lame even to him. But it was perfect plausible deniability.

"Fine. I'll say it. Nancy, Dave, the VP didn't go to Oman."

"Haley…" Gregory said, warning her off.

Nancy got it right away and whispered into Dave's ear.

"Oh, no," he muttered.

"All of you," Gregory jumped in, cutting off the discussion. "Excellent work. Now get me more, please. We have a little time until the vice president lands," he said, emphasizing the title. "I don't want to call the president about another threat to the VP based only on a reference in an old book. Work your magic, and get back to me within the hour."

He hung up with Haley as Nancy and Dave left, hurrying back to the table they'd claimed as their workstation.

Gregory would call again if—when—they had something more solid.

And pray that, in the meantime, no attack came.

150

THE COMPOUNDS

Axe sat in the back seat on the right side of the SUV. Niko drove as he had the entire trip. Ekaterina sat in front with him. The passenger seat of the big SUV seemed to swallow her small frame.

Axe had been concerned about crossing the border into Oman, but one look at the little old grandmother in the front seat, traveling with her driver and servant, and they'd been waved straight through.

The updated orders from Haley had vectored them directly underneath the resort, where most of the leaders had already arrived.

He had to find a cave or tunnel, inspect it, and handle whatever threat faced the peace summit.

Just another day at the office.

The afternoon sun beat down on the parched, rocky desert landscape of this part of Oman. It reminded Axe more of the United States' desert southwest of Arizona than the dunes south of Dubai, where they'd put the geeks and Jamil on the helicopter hours earlier.

Mountains surrounded them. There were faded green desert bushes and small trees. The sky was a brilliant blue.

About ten miles back, the well-paved winding road that had brought them around the mountain from the town of Saiq to this area had changed abruptly to a graded crushed gravel road. It snaked its way lower into the valley, which was deserted except for the small group of homes they approached.

The area couldn't be called a town; there were no stores, stop signs, street names, or restaurants. It wasn't named on the GPS map.

There were several large rundown compounds, each surrounded by tall, thick block walls. They didn't look poor, exactly, and weren't abandoned, but it seemed like the people living here were barely getting by. It might once have been a prosperous little community of farmers or people who wanted to live in the desert away from it all yet still be only an hour from the small, wealthy town of Saiq that served the luxury desert resorts at higher elevation.

About a half mile to the northwest, a dark rocky mountain rose abruptly, first at a forty-five-degree angle of scree, boulders, and jumbled rock for hundreds of feet before turning vertical.

Hundreds of feet higher, on the flattened top of the mountain, was the resort hosting the peace summit. Nothing could be seen of it from this far down, but Axe could imagine the elegance, and heads of state, a relatively short distance away but impossible to get to—unless there was some kind of cave or tunnel system, as Haley's team suspected.

Although the SUV's windows were tinted against the desert sun, Axe felt conspicuous and exposed as the big vehicle drove slowly past the buildings.

This has to be the least stealthy target approach ever.

And it was definitely the mission he was least prepared for. He had a pistol with one full magazine plus a half-empty one in his pocket. There hadn't been time or privacy to change, and he hadn't wanted to put Jamil through the trauma of switching clothes, so he was wearing Jamil's stupid white servant's uniform, on backward and inside out to hide the blood splattered on it from the border guards in case they had been stopped. He'd even kept the stupid black hat and cheap, too-small sneakers.

No M4, no body armor.

Worst of all, he had no night vision goggles for whatever cave or tunnels he was supposed to find. He'd begged the helicopter crew for gear, but they had specific orders not to part with any. No one wanted an international incident if the intel was wrong and Axe got caught fully armed with US weapons and equipment. They might assume he was a spy or asset sent to assassinate a dignitary.

Haley had admitted that, technically, he wasn't supposed to be anywhere near here—house rules from the highest levels of Oman, which for security and the peace of mind of all attendees had demanded no country allow any unauthorized operators, spies, or forces in the area during the event.

I'm an unsanctioned asset yet again—along with Ekaterina and Niko.

At least he had the boning knife and meat cleaver from the fourteenth-floor Tower kitchen in Dubai. Both had served him well already.

He had to fight back the image, sound, and smell of what Jamil had done to himself.

There will be time to deal with that after the mission.

"Turn around up there," Ekaterina told Niko, pointing to a dirt pull-off farther up the road. "You will get out quickly," she told Axe. "Find the tunnel. Do your operator duty, yes? Niko will drive me to the scenic lookout."

They had passed a paved parking area halfway down the switchback mountain road, right before it changed to packed dirt. Adventurous wealthy people staying at the area's resorts made the long, slow trip down the road, parked, and hiked on a narrow trail that ran around part of the mountain, right where the lower, less steep area switched to the dead-vertical section of the mountain face.

Her suggestion made sense and was exactly what he was thinking.

Drop me off clandestinely—or as much as driving in a small area like this in broad daylight allows—and distract anyone watching by returning up the road to the overlook.

It would seem like they realized there was nothing to see at the base of the mountain and didn't want to continue on the long, winding loop through the lower desert and back to the city.

"And then?" Axe asked.

"I get out. Stretch my legs. Hike while Niko waits and watches. I will look for the cave entrance up there."

It made sense, though she didn't sound optimistic.

People from the resorts hike this area all the time. If no one has noticed a cave by now, what hope do we have?

They both knew this—nothing had to be said.

The best way to find an entrance to the supposed hidden tunnel was through one of the homes. A compound like this would serve as the perfect cover in which to dig. The occasional truck coming and going wouldn't raise an eyebrow, and powered tunneling equipment could be unloaded in one of the large barnlike structures and put immediately to use. Rock and dirt could be distributed across the inside the compound or hauled away in trucks if there wasn't room for it in the cave system.

"You led the way in the Tower," Axe said. "Now it's my turn."

"Yes, you are the warrior. I am only a spy."

"And an assassin."

Ekaterina tilted her head in acknowledgment of the accuracy of the statement.

He reached around his back, under the tunic, and pulled out the long boning knife and sheath made from kitchen towels and offered them to her.

Ekaterina smiled and shook her head, turning her back to extract a chef's knife of her own.

See—that's the sign of a true professional.

He looked out over the group of homes as Niko slowed.

Tangos could be watching right now, and we'd never know.

"I will find the cave or return here," Ekat said. "I will look for the dead bodies you will leave behind and follow you into the tunnel," Ekaterina said. "You hunt. I will meet you or protect the rear."

Axe hesitated.

Depending on how things go, I might never see her again.

"Thank you for your help at the Tower," he said. "I couldn't have done it without you."

"You would have found a way."

"Not in time."

Once more she acknowledged the truth of his words with a small tilt of her head.

"See you on the other side," he said, wondering if the Russians had a similar sentiment.

She nodded, face serious. "*Uvidimsya na tom svete.* Yes, see you on the other side. And Alex?" Ekaterina's eyes grew hard. "Do not risk the lives of my president and your vice president. Anyone in the tunnel is the enemy. Anyone making tunnel, too. There is no mining here. No gold. If there is a tunnel, it is for an attack. Take no prisoners."

He was sure his eyes were as cold as hers. "My thoughts exactly," he said as Niko turned the vehicle, shielding his side from view of the compounds. When the SUV stopped next to desert bushes and a shallow wash, he paused. "Wait."

Axe thought for a second.

"'All warfare is based on deception. Hence, when able to attack, we must seem unable,'" he said, quoting Sun Tzu.

Ekaterina took a second to translate and consider his idea, then smiled. "Yes. It will work."

Axe took a breath, got into character, opened the door, and fell out as if pushed.

He stumbled and went down to one knee.

The rear door slammed closed as Niko floored the SUV, sending dirt and pebbles flying.

Axe protected his face as the vehicle pulled away.

Let's hope I look like an unwanted worker dumped at the back end of nowhere.

He rose unsteadily to his feet, swaying, his head down, shoulders slumped.

He didn't feel like he was being targeted, but he couldn't tell if anyone had eyes on him.

With a sigh, he glanced up and started shuffling toward the nearest compound.

Might as well start at the beginning.

In his mind, the whole hamlet had to be in on whatever was going on here. They were either complicit or under duress.

Either way, he'd soon find out and be in the thick of the action.

151

OMAN

James watched the desert flash by as the motorcade sped away from the sprawling private airport. On most weekends, it was dedicated to the planes of the rich and famous who flew to the luxury resort.

Today and tomorrow, however, it was reserved exclusively for the aircraft of the region's leaders and their entourages of negotiators, advisors, aides, and security.

The locals never used the airport. It was far too exclusive for anyone living in the area and working at either the Mountain Vista Desert Resort and Spa or one of the smaller yet still exclusive resorts in the area.

The SUVs took the hairpin turns of the road leading up the mountain at breakneck speed, which made complete sense.

This is where I'd hit us if I had an attack planned.

James sat in the back of an armored black SUV with heavily tinted windows instead of the limo he normally rode in, nicknamed "the Beast."

I like sitting up higher like this.

He could see a lot more of the scenery from this height.

Aside from the driver in front, three other men sat in the car with him. A Secret Service agent sat in the passenger seat. One sat on each side of James—Stewart and Waylan again, from Air Force Two.

Neither of the two in front was happy to see him.

The Secret Service had signed off on the VP coming to the Middle Eastern country and the over-the-top security arrangements provided by the host country of Oman.

It didn't mean they liked the idea.

Their inability to be the only security on-site had them further on edge, as did the arrival of hundreds of guests, including leaders of all the Middle Eastern countries—some of which were flat-out enemies of the United States.

James had stepped off the plane and rushed down the stairs with his head down, grateful for the lack of press. The Army National Guard hat screened his face from any distant observers.

The things you can get away with when you rule a country with an iron fist, he'd thought.

He had left the VP's trademark gray overcoat behind in the plane. It would only draw attention in the sun and ninety-degree heat.

The Secret Service had, by prior arrangement, demanded there be no dignitaries or a welcoming committee, so James made it to the third of five SUVs without incident.

The doors slammed shut, and the SUV shot forward seconds later.

The driver noticed first as he glanced in the rearview mirror, his eyes growing big as James waved.

The special agent in the passenger seat swung his head around, and his jaw dropped.

"Surprise, gentlemen," James said with a chuckle.

"Not a word," Stewart growled. "Nothing on the radio, nothing said here. Copy?"

"Copy," both men in front said, though the mood went from professionally concerned to professionally very concerned.

Both men sat up straighter.

They made it up the mountain without incident. There was no press, no protesters, and no cheering fans. It could have been a normal Saturday spring afternoon.

There's nothing to indicate the top men of the Middle East— along with the Russian president, China's premier, and now me—are here.

The lush grounds of the resort were stunning. Palm trees lined the long, smooth entrance road. A narrow fountain at least two football fields long filled the middle of the median between the entrance and exit lanes.

The water sparkled in the afternoon sunlight as geysers bubbled high into the air every three feet.

They sped past tennis courts, an eighteen-hole golf course with perfect green grass—an extravagance in the desert—a bocce ball court, cricket grounds, and a soccer field.

There was a decent-size Ferris wheel in the distance, on the far side of the second group of bungalows.

Desert plants and flowers bloomed everywhere.

It easily outshined every other five-star hotel James had visited as president.

No wonder this place has been so popular since it opened last year.

The special agent in the passenger seat whispered back to Waylan.

"Right now," Waylan answered, "address him as 'sir.' When the secret's out, you can address him as 'Mr. President,' just like normal. Or his code name."

James had originally wanted to be called "Bullseye," but that hadn't gone over well. He meant it in the sense of shooting and hitting the target. The Secret Service thought it tempted fate, as if he was the one being aimed at.

They settled on "Grizzly," which had been the First Lady's suggestion. "You're not like most of the past presidents," she'd told him years before, once the count had come in and they knew he had won. "You're a big grizzly, who's fine until stirred up. Then—watch out."

They continued through the sprawling grounds of the resort. There were forty bungalows for the highest-end visitors, twenty on each side of a four-story main building housing normal guest rooms and suites. All the buildings at the resort were an off-white color to reflect the desert sun.

The bungalows were rectangular and featured narrow but tall windows set deep into thick walls. The front of each had a rounded bump-out James guessed would be the living room, with a few larger square windows. The roof of the villa was a small dome.

The entire resort was an architectural marvel in the region's distinctive style.

At the Secret Service's insistence, with Secretary of State Wilson leading the negotiations, a three-bedroom bungalow in an easily defendable area had been assigned to the VP. The on-site Secret Service detail had camped out there for days.

"Very secure here, sir," the agent in the passenger seat said, loosening up a little. "Locked down tight. Our only real concern is getting to and from."

"Well…" the driver said. He had a slow Texas drawl.

"Yeah. Okay, lots of foreign security personnel with guns, true. But anyone looks at you sideways, sir, and we'll be right there."

"We may all have the same guns…" the driver said.

"But we shoot faster and better, sir," the passenger finished.

"Roger that," James said.

The SUV pulled to a stop a few steps from a bungalow door already held open by a female agent, her eyes constantly scanning the distance.

"There's time to rest or freshen up before the big welcome reception, sir," Stewart said. "We'll get you inside. When is the secret out?"

"I expect it'll happen the moment I take this cap off and leave the room to walk to the reception area," James said. "It sure is going to be interesting."

152

THE BARN

The first door Axe came to confirmed his suspicions. It was relatively new, made of thick, sturdy wood and heavy-duty hinges, with a modern knob and a deadbolt lock. Set in the mortared, sand-color stone walls that seemed to be common to the area, it would open into a courtyard, not the house itself.

He knocked—not too hard, not too soft, hoping the sound would carry into the home.

When no one answered, he let his shoulders droop more in case he was being watched. Turning, he shuffled several hundred yards to the next compound's door and repeated the process with the same result.

Third time's a charm?

He had to walk further this time, moving closer to the base of the mountain slope with each step. The way the group of homesteads was laid out, this compound was the closest to the mountain. If no one answered at this one, he would turn right, move away from the steep incline ahead, and hope he'd find someone home eventually.

Or maybe I'll mantle the fence, drop to the other side, and get this party started.

Before he knocked, he sensed a presence on the other side of the door.

Keeping his body in character, Axe prepared his mind for any possibility, from an old man to a warrior with a weapon.

The door swung open a second after Axe knocked. With his head bowed, Axe could only take in the man in the door from the chest down, but what he saw made him want to reach for one of the knives or the pistol at his waist.

Plain, used workpants—but with sturdy combat boots. A military bearing and energy.

The man's hands were empty but large and calloused.

Axe raised his hand the way he'd seen others do in the region—palm out, then brought to his heart. With his other hand, he gestured to his throat and let out a pained cough.

Will the act—and the outfit—fool him?

The man, who Axe had no doubt was a guard, growled a question. Axe had no hope of understanding the language, but the intent was clear.

Who are you, and what are you doing here?

Axe coughed again, left hand to throat, and sagged forward.

The guard put out a hand, half to stop Axe and half to catch the forward fall.

Axe risked a glance up as he came close. The man's eyes gave him away.

He's a killer.

Unfortunately, Axe's eyes must have clued the man into who—and what—Axe was as well.

The guard reached behind his back, but Axe was quicker.

A hard knee to the groin silenced the man and brought his head down.

A sharp twist of the neck dropped him to the ground.

And now the clock is ticking.

The man had a knife handle sticking out of his waist, not the pistol Axe had hoped for.

Too difficult to explain a gun—and gunshots—I bet.

A quick scan of the interior of the compound showed a low stone house with shutters closed, a few small outbuildings, and a larger two-story rectangular mud and brick building that would have been called a barn back home, though the shape wasn't that of a traditional American barn.

The grayish-tan color blended in with the surrounding hard-packed desert dirt of the compound grounds.

There was no doubt in Axe's mind. That's where the tunnel would be.

If I'm running a mining operation to reach the resort at the top of the mountain, I'm basing it there.

There wasn't much use for stealth now. Anyone seeing a stranger in a servant's uniform inside the compound walls would know he didn't belong. So Axe ran at the grayish-green double barn doors at the end closest to him, expecting a shout of alarm to come at any second.

153

THE VAN

There was no time for Axe to check the compound's main house. For all he knew, there could be a hundred guys inside, gearing up and waiting for the order to attack during the summit's welcome dinner.

Or later tonight, once people are tucked away in bed.

The targets would be dispersed and in secure buildings, but the attackers would have the cover of darkness.

And if they only have a few specific targets, it wouldn't be hard to accomplish their mission.

If he'd had his old Team—or even just Haley or Ekaterina—they could've cleared the house and surrounding buildings first. It would've kept them from having their backs exposed to attack.

He didn't have the team or the time.

I'll just have to run and gun fast enough that no one catches up to me.

Axe gently pushed open the barn door.

Another guard, just inside, was not expecting an intruder. Leaning against the wall in the cool interior of the barn, he glanced at Axe, unconcerned.

Probably expecting his buddy from the front gate. Surprise!

Axe slipped the boning knife into his stomach, pierced his heart, and dropped him gently to the ground.

The guy, with a full dark beard and narrow weathered face, seemed like a warrior, but it was hard to tell for sure with him lying dead and bleeding on the dirt floor of the barn.

This one carried a knife and a cell phone but no other weapons.

Axe unlocked the smartphone with the dead man's thumb and turned off the lock screen security feature so he could access it again later or get it to Haley.

No calls, no texts, few apps. A burner phone.

Despite the blood on the man's dark shirt, it would be a better fit than Jamil's blood-spattered long white tunic.

Axe removed the tunic, stripped the shirt off the dead man, and slipped into the one more suitable for a clandestine operation. He also dumped the black servant hat. The shoes didn't look like they'd fit, so he left them.

Much better.

The barn was nothing special. Aside from a large white delivery van —the kind some people in America had taken to converting to live in for an idyllic "van life"—parked near the rear wall, the building looked ordinary in every way. Lit by a single bare, dim bulb hanging from the center of the ceiling, it had a hard-packed dirt floor and smelled cool and dry.

Rakes, shovels, hedge trimmers, and other tools hung neatly on a grid of two-by-fours affixed to the wall on the left. Old pieces of lumber, from studs to planks, were stacked neatly in a corner.

A small tractor sat on the right, along with various pieces of machinery he thought could be used for grading or packing the ground if a driveway got too rutted or a piece of land needed to be flattened.

Everything looked old but well cared for.

A place for everything and everything in its place.

There was no digging equipment, armed guards, or crates of explosives.

The sight brought Axe up short.

Did I just kill two innocent people—local farmers or ranchers?

The thought made his stomach churn.

The SEALs' old saying came to mind.

"The intel is always wrong."

If he'd taken the lives of civilians…

He forced the thought from his head. If that's what he'd done, he would deal with the guilt and repercussions later. Right now, he had a barn to search.

He covered every inch of the space in ten minutes. There were no false doors and no tunnel openings hidden under the pile of lumber, which was the first place he checked.

The inside of the large van was also empty, with a scratched metal cargo floor and worn seats up front.

Maybe they're digging from inside the house?

He moved to the barn doors, ready to search the rest of the grounds— without killing any more potentially innocent people, if possible.

His feet slowed on their own before his mind fully understood why.

I'm missing something.

He let his eyes roam over the barn's dark interior.

This was the best location for a tunnel, but where was the entrance?

Axe knelt to scope out the room from a lower vantage point. His eyes rested on the white truck backed into the barn and resting near the rear wall.

There.

Although it was dark under the van, the earth there looked different.

He hurried over, got down on his stomach, and slid under the rear wheels.

Wood barn doors—similar to the ones at the front of the building— were set in the ground, painted to match the dark color of the dirt around them.

They can't open upward, so...

Axe slipped the blade of the boning knife into the narrow opening a few inches below the center of the two doors and slid it slowly forward.

What must have been a simple hook and eye latch on the backside popped.

Axe caught the left door with his free hand and immediately dropped the knife to catch the other, keeping them from slamming open and alerting whoever had shut the door behind them that he was coming.

Found it.

Before going in, he checked his cell phone. It had reception, probably from cell towers all over the nearby mountains. Rich people demanded nonstop connection even when they were on vacation.

He typed out a long text and hit send.

Hidden tunnel found. Few guards left behind. Almost everyone is gone. Could be the endgame of a plan. Recommend evacuating the vice

president and informing Oman security about the probable threat.
Advise them I am on-site and going in. Dressed in a dead guard's shirt—
tell them not to shoot me.

He double-checked the phone, making sure it was set to completely silent mode and the message had gone through, then looked down into the darkness.

Now for the fun part.

Axe slipped into the tunnel and climbed down a six-foot ladder leaning against the wall, wishing he had night vision goggles.

154

THE RECEPTION

The Reception Courtyard
The Mountain Vista Desert Resort and Spa
Outside Saiq, Oman

The view was already incredible, but Dmitry thought it would only get more so as the sun set. The resort's location was perfect. Perched on the edge of the flat mountain overlooking a large valley and other, lower mountains in the distance, it felt like he was on the edge of the world. It beat Moscow, and especially his sad tiny old office, any day.

He wasn't here, however, to admire the desert beauty or enjoy the lavish luxury of the resort. He'd come along as President Nikitin's "senior advisor," complete with a fake identity.

Dmitry felt more like the president's Chief of Staff each day, so why not attend? The president used him as a sounding board and seemed to trust his judgment. It was a chance to get out of Russia, into the field, and observe the players his department kept tabs on—and plotted against.

The reception was in full swing. Every important player was there, from kings and princes to heads of state—or the seconds-in-command of a few countries—along with wealthy power brokers, unofficial dealmakers, and high-level advisors and aides.

Some people who looked important weren't; several of those who acted like mere advisors could make or break a deal, whether for a large arms purchase, an increase or reduction in oil production, or a mutually beneficial economic agreement.

Or, as was the supposed reason for the meeting, peace in the Middle East.

Dmitry and President Nikitin stood on the deck of the infinity pool near the edge of the cliff, with a ninety-degree drop straight down to the valley far below.

"This may be more challenging than I expected," President Nikitin muttered as he looked across the large open grass area where the attendees gathered for the late afternoon reception. A few hundred people, many in the traditional *thobes*—the long robes common to the area—milled around talking and laughing.

On the president's left, Saitov Utkin, the foreign minister—Russia's secretary of state—agreed. "They don't know how to react. Did we attack America or not? Should they express their appreciation or avoid being seen speaking with you?"

Nearby, two of the president's large, muscular bodyguards stood, meaty arms crossed, watching the other guests greet one another and mingle.

The bodyguards for other dignitaries kept their distance.

Behind Dmitry, two paces back, President Nikitin's hand-picked translator waited, hands clasped behind him, looking out of place in a less-than-perfectly fitted suit. He could handle English, Arabic, Farsi, and Hebrew.

They had been standing at the edge of the group of dignitaries for ten minutes, yet no one made their way over to President Nikitin to say hello.

"Perhaps the bodyguards are off-putting?" Dmitry murmured from next to the president, more concerned about the intimidating bodyguards hearing than any of the guests.

"Quite right," President Nikitin said. With a gesture, he dismissed the men, who moved several yards away and relaxed their posture.

A few moments later, a man with a long gray beard, wearing an expensive-looking dark cloak-like robe and a black turban on his head, made his way slowly over. Two aides in similar traditional Iranian clothing trailed behind him.

"The supreme leader of Iran," Dmitry muttered without moving his lips. He took a step back as the translator stepped forward, moving to the president's right side, a half step behind him.

This will be interesting.

Pleasantries were exchanged for a moment before the real discussion began. Thankfully, the translator spoke loudly enough for Dmitry to catch most of it.

"Well done with the attack on the Americans," the supreme leader started.

"That was not our doing," President Nikitin replied pleasantly.

"Of course, of course. My mistake," the supreme leader said with a grin and a sparkle in his eyes. "Some hackers, I understand. So difficult to control the youth of today, isn't it?"

"Yes, quite," Utkin said, always the diplomat.

The president and foreign minister let the older man, who had been in power for decades, guide the conversation to various topics, from the striking beauty of the resort to the opportunities for their two countries to work more closely together in the future.

Dmitry listened, taking it all in, and said nothing.

This is how every conversation tonight will go. All pleasantries and vague promises.

Utkin had told the president this. And while Nikitin was desperate to forge new alliances, strengthen old ones, and get a commitment from the other oil-producing countries to reduce production, he had agreed to take it slow and play it cool.

The meeting with the Iranian opened the floodgates. Small groups of men, consisting of a country's leader, a translator, and various advisors or powerful men not in the government, made the trip to the side of the pool to greet the Russian president and make small talk.

Only the second-in-command of China stayed away, stationed on the far side of the grass reception area with several aides surrounding him. He, Nikitin, and the American vice president were the only non-Middle Eastern powers invited—and it seemed that China was not interested in chatting yet.

"Much better," President Nikitin said after another in the long line of mundane conversations about the cooling desert air, spectacular resort... and Russia being unfairly targeted by America for something it "clearly had no hand in," or words to that effect, all said with a raised eyebrow, wink, or half smile.

"But we still haven't—" President Nikitin stopped.

Coming toward them was a man with a stylish dark beard, in his mid-forties, wearing a red and black scarf with a black band and a perfectly flowing *thobe*.

The president stood straighter. This was the man most important of all to Russia's plans—the crown prince and prime minister of Saudi Arabia. With him in their corner, the rest would fall in line. The countries of the region would gradually reduce their oil production. Prices would climb. Russia would earn more from its oil, replenish its depleted treasury, and continue improving its economy—and military might.

Russian weapons would be produced and sold to the players in the area, also making Russia money.

Ties would be strengthened. Russia's influence would improve, and that of America would lessen.

Strong, mutually beneficial relationships would be deepened.

Without him, what Russia needed to accomplish wouldn't be impossible, but it would take a tremendous amount of extra work and luck.

The crown prince was only ten feet away when a rumble of murmuring spread through the assembled guests.

"What is happening?" President Nikitin asked.

One of the crown prince's advisors whispered into his ear. The crown prince stopped and turned to look back toward the resort building and the path to the bungalows.

"Why did he stop? What is it?" the president asked.

Dmitry couldn't believe his eyes as he caught a glimpse of someone entering the reception grounds, a pleasant, relaxed smile on his face.

What?

"Sir, it is the president of the United States of America," Dmitry said.

"You mean the vice president," Utkin muttered, his voice filled with scorn. He'd been opposed to Dmitry coming along.

"No," Dmitry said, keeping his voice neutral, resisting the impulse to put the man in his place. "It is President James Heringten."

And he looks very pleased with himself.

155

THE SURPRISE

"All stations," Stewart had called into his wrist mic as James stood ready inside the bungalow door. "Grizzly," he said, emphasizing the code name, "is on the move toward the reception. Heads up."

James had thought he heard a gasp from the agent on the other side of the door as Stewart opened it, but that could just have been his imagination.

After making sure his tie was straight, James had stepped outside and begun the walk to the grassy reception area between the main building and the pool at the edge of the cliff overlooking the canyon below.

James strolled purposefully on the wide concrete path. The sun wouldn't set for maybe forty-five minutes, but low, solar-powered lamps lighted the path against the coming darkness. As he neared the large courtyard, already filled with a few hundred or so attendees mingling and chatting, he caught several servers and security staff glancing his way.

Agents Waylan and Stewart followed a few steps behind and ten feet to either side of him. They would only jump in if a direct threat appeared or "Malik" moved toward him.

Otherwise, he was on his own. If the VP had attended, the plan had been to have Secretary of State Wilson stick with him. With Wilson gone, the deputy would have come.

James didn't want any of that. Before leaving, the deputy secretary of state had been told he'd be needed in the United States with the president. The "VP" would be fine on his own.

One older man, dressed in a waiter outfit of loose white pants, a white button-up short-sleeve shirt, and a dark patterned headscarf, did a classic double take, his eyes widening in surprise.

James nodded at him and smiled.

There's someone who follows the news, knows what I look like, and that I'm not supposed to be here.

So either an educated, well-informed staff member, an undercover security guard, or a spy.

At an opening between two fountains, unofficially designated as a security checkpoint, two guards looked at each other and hesitated as James approached. He thought they wouldn't let him through, but they nodded to him and stepped aside.

I'm either being watched right now, or they are well trained.

Probably both, he decided.

Conversation at the nearest group of men stopped mid-sentence as the person speaking saw him. The others turned to see what the first was looking at. Seconds passed as they processed the surprise.

A ripple of energy went through the party as others noticed.

This would be more fun if it weren't for the threat of an imminent attack by the mysterious Malik or any of the dozens of guards with automatic weapons in the area whose leaders despise America and me.

The first group of men moved to him, offering their hands and condolences over America's recent losses.

They actually sound sincere.

Then again, at this level of diplomacy, lying was a well-honed skill.

Sincerity is the key. Once you can fake that, you've got it made.

After them, it seemed like the entire group of leaders subtly queued up to greet the surprise attendee.

Across the lawn, near the pool, Russian President Nikitin stood with an advisor and the country's chief diplomat.

That's going to be an interesting conversation.

But first, James had to get through all the well-wishers, get a sense of who was a true friend, and do his best to make connections he could use to further America's interests.

He was flying blind, relying on his memory instead of a stack of briefing notes and an aide to remind him who was who.

He kept his eye out for Malik. He'd studied the picture of the man's dead brother—courtesy of Axe—delivered to the Secret Service. The face was burnt into his memory.

James didn't see him. He could be hanging back—or maybe the intel was wrong.

A quick glance at his watch between people saying hi showed he didn't have long until dinner. A short greeting from the crown prince of Oman would be coming up, then they'd go inside for the summit's opening speech by the sultan himself, followed by a lengthy dinner.

James hoped that he wouldn't be stuck at the boring table.

156

IMMINENT THREAT

Temporary Central Analysis Group Headquarters
Joint Base Andrews
Prince George's County, Maryland

Gregory checked his watch and did the math.

The president should be at the peace summit reception now.

They'd heard nothing from Axe since Haley had gotten a text from him saying he was going into the tunnel he'd found.

That was five minutes ago.

Gregory had kept the line open with Haley so they could communicate instantaneously. It wasn't the same as being in a room together, but it would do.

Dave and Nancy had joined him in the tiny rundown office. Absent another report from Axe—unlikely to come through if he was underground in a tunnel—they had to decide on their own what to recommend to the president.

"Time's up," Gregory said. "Do we evacuate the president or not?"

The president might resist, but if I call the director of the Secret Service—Greene—and say there's an active, specific threat of imminent harm against POTUS, he'll do the right thing and get the president out of there.

The tricky bit was the "active, specific threat of imminent harm." The president was committed to this summit and had broken protocol after protocol to be there himself. A vague warning of a possible danger wouldn't sway him or the Secret Service. The threat from Malik had proven that.

President Heringten would only argue that the potential gains from the event were more important than marginal, nonspecific risks.

Gregory had another minute before he had to make a call of some sort.

They have to at least be informed about the construction of the tunnel.

"Assume a tunnel and or cave system to and under the resort," Gregory started. "Which is more likely—an attack by a bunch of soldiers or a ton of explosives used to take out a specific bungalow, area, or the main building?"

From Gregory's cell phone on the desk between the three of them, Haley spoke up. "Soldiers would be more definite. They shoot people and make sure they're dead. But with all the security for each attendee, it would take a large, heavily armed team."

"There's no defense against explosives, as long as a bomb-sniffing dog doesn't detect them—which they wouldn't, being several feet underground," Nancy said.

"Axe will take care of any bombs," Haley replied. "But against a small army of armed men waiting in a tunnel to surface and start a bloodbath? He couldn't take them all out."

"I agree," Gregory said. "We can't place all our hope on Axe stopping an army. Nor can we know for sure he can get to any explosives in time to disarm them and stop the destruction."

He offered a grim smile to Dave. "Dave, I'm sorry. You're going to hate this. But we've had some success in the past with it. Okay, everyone —gut check. Tell me what your intuition says is more probable—an armed attack or somehow taking down the building. Haley, you first."

"Taking down the building," Haley said immediately. "Arming, transporting, and housing the number of men required to ensure success would be difficult. Someone would have noticed."

"Nancy?" Gregory asked.

"I agree with Haley. I think they've tunneled up right below the main structural supports of the building and created a hole under its footprint. If they blow the supports and the remaining rock and dirt, the entire resort might collapse upon itself."

"Dave?"

"Logically," he said, stressing the word, "if it were my operation, I'd do both." He paused and frowned. "But if I had to trust my intuition, I'd go with what Nancy said. I would excavate a large enough area under the main building—or use a natural cave. Then I'd drill right up near the main structural supports for the building, pack the holes with explosives, and wait until the moment when everyone was assured to be together in one place. Then I'd blow it up and let the whole thing come down like a house of cards."

There was silence in the room and from Haley as they considered the devastating ramifications of the type of attack they were contemplating.

Gregory knew the answer but had to ask one last time before he made the call. "Do we have any proof we can offer to sway the president?"

What we have right now isn't enough to call off the event—or even the president's participation in it.

"Not until we hear from Axe," Haley said after several seconds of silence from everyone else.

Gregory grasped at straws.

There has to be a way to keep the president and the attendees safe.

"Going out on a limb here," he said. "When is the most likely time of attack?"

Nancy and Dave pulled up the detailed itinerary provided to the vice president's office.

"My vote is 5:16 p.m. local time," Dave said after only a second. "The sultan of Oman is a stickler for punctuality and starts his welcome speech one minute earlier. No one would dare miss that."

"Yes," Haley said. "All the high-level people will be there. It would be a slap in the face to not be."

Nancy looked up from the itinerary. "Absolutely. There's no other time except the welcome speech and the first course of dinner people will all be together. Even the closing speech will be skipped by some—they'll have gotten what they need or left early in a real or fake huff."

"From a timing standpoint, wouldn't they need a spotter? An employee, maybe?" Gregory asked.

Dave shook his head. "No need. Not with the sultan. Absent an act of God, his speech will start at 5:15 on the dot."

Nancy nodded. "There's less risk of exposure that way. With all the security, an overt signal might be noticed. Let's remember, too, that Malik has taken great pains to keep his involvement hidden. Without Axe's source and the capture of the hackers, we'd never suspect him. He wouldn't want to send a signal and be noticed."

Gregory had an idea.

It's risky, but it might be the compromise I need.

"I agree," he said. He picked up the landline phone on the desk to call the president's private cell phone.

In the middle of a reception with the leaders of the Middle East?

President Heringten wouldn't be taking calls.

He might not even have the phone on him.

But someone would.

Gregory dialed the number from memory, praying for an answer… and the right words to explain their growing concern about the president's safety.

157

THE LADDER

The Tunnel
Beneath the Mountain Vista Desert Resort and Spa

Axe retrieved the fallen boning knife from the dirt at the base of the ladder and opted to keep it ready instead of the heavier meat cleaver.

Opposite the ladder, a tunnel roughly cut into the ground started due north but curved gently uphill and to the right. There were none of the wooden supports Axe expected, though the walls and ceiling looked like there might have been framing at some point.

The opening was nearly six feet tall and about four feet wide, though the work was rough and showed no finesse.

This was never meant to last—but was constructed to bring in a piece of machinery or crates of a certain size, I bet.

In the distance, Axe caught a dim glow.

So kind of them to light my way.

He stooped, slipping into the tunnel, and silently moved forward.

Axe hugged the wall as he neared the light. He had sensed a presence long before the tunnel curved enough for him to lean to the side and see a bored man sitting on the ground with his back to the wall and legs outstretched, eyes closed.

An automatic rifle leaned against the wall to his right.

The presence of a sentry meant an operation had to be in progress.

Getting close to the man without being noticed might've been possible, but it would take forever.

If Haley's intel was correct—and despite his earlier doubts, it had been so far—Axe didn't have that kind of time.

Axe clasped both hands over the bloodiest part of the dead man's shirt and walked silently forward, head down just enough to keep his face hidden but enough to see the seated guard's reaction.

The man must have been snoozing because Axe closed to within ten feet before he moved.

He climbed to his feet, asking a question that had to be something like, "What's wrong—are you hurt?"

Axe used the knife he'd concealed with his forearm, snapping his hand out to slash the man's throat to keep him from crying out. He stepped in, catching the guard before he fell and lowering him to the tunnel floor.

This guard had no phone or knife, but Axe snagged the AK and one extra magazine.

The tunnel continued to spiral upward into darkness.

The next two lazy guards fell the same way. Axe got close, pretended to be an injured comrade, and killed them with his trusty kitchen knife.

They certainly aren't suspicious or expecting trouble.

It made sense. After weeks or months of no one discovering them as they tunneled, how would someone stumble upon them now?

They don't know how smart Haley, Nancy, and Dave are.

A few minutes later, the tunnel ended abruptly, opening into a small cave with a twenty-foot-high ceiling.

Along a well-worn path, lit by widely spaced dim lanterns sitting on the ground, the cave opened up more into a spacious natural cavern.

A ladder sat against the far wall, leading to a ledge ten feet up. A brighter battery-operated lamp sat on the ground near the opening farther back from the ledge, along with another dim one at the base of the ladder.

There was no guard.

Strange.

Axe waited, extending his senses, but detected no movement, sound, or energy. But the glowing lamp at the bottom of the ladder suggested more than one person was planning on climbing down at some point and needed decent lighting to accomplish whatever task they had planned.

He traded stealth for speed and hurried across the large open space.

Halfway across, a man emerged from a dark opening ten feet to the left of the ladder, tying the drawstring on his pants.

He and Axe saw each other at the same time.

Axe was too far away for the knife, but he had the AK slung across the front of his body, pointed down.

The guard had his AK slung on one shoulder, barrel up like he was marching in formation, as if he had slipped it on when he left his post, never expecting trouble.

Axe dropped the knife, swung the muzzle upward, and fired before the guard could fumble his own weapon into use.

The sound of three shots boomed through the silent cave.

So much for stealth.

As the noise faded, concerned voices yelled from the ledge.

Axe raised the AK to his shoulder and aimed at the opening above the ladder. It looked like another tunnel leading farther upward.

A guard stepped out of the tunnel, yelling for his friend while looking down.

Axe shot him, too.

The man clutched his chest, staggered, and took a dive off the ledge, landing with a *thump* on the rocky ground near the base of the ladder.

Another man came seconds later but held back. He stuck his weapon out, only exposing his arms, and pulled the trigger.

Round after round rained down in the cave as the man "sprayed and prayed."

Axe shot at the AK and the man's arms but missed, though he succeeded in driving the man back as he fired a final burst.

A sharp pain made Axe gasp as a bullet tore into his right thigh.

Another hit him in the back—low, above his right glute.

Ricochets—damn it!

Ignoring the pain, he reached the ladder and climbed it awkwardly, one hand holding the AK.

As he neared the top, the man from the tunnel leaned over the edge. His eyes widened as he saw Axe on the ladder.

They fired at the same time.

The tango missed.

Axe didn't. His bullets slammed into the man's face, dropping him.

As Axe fired, his right leg gave out and slipped off the ladder.

He barn-doored, swinging to the left, and lost his grip.

It took him a second to realize he was falling.

An instant later, he landed hard on his back, followed by his head slamming into the ground.

Axe fought the darkness that threatened to take him away.

No—if I black out now, I'm dead.

With the wind knocked out of him, he couldn't breathe, but he sure as hell could crawl.

He rolled onto his stomach, running on adrenaline, willpower, and a need to survive.

The bathroom area.

He crawled as fast as he could toward the dark opening the first guard had emerged from, sticking close to the cave wall.

No one else shot at him.

His vision swam.

He felt dizzy.

That's another concussion for sure.

Instinct guided him further into the darkness despite the foul odor coming from ahead as he got his breath back.

He assessed the situation. There were a few positives.

I'm not dead, and no one is shooting at me right now.

The cons greatly outweighed the pros.

The gunfire made a hell of a racket.

I'm alone with no nearby backup.

The phone won't work in these caves, so I have no comms.

I'm injured.

The ricochets weren't going to kill him in the next few minutes, but the more blood he lost, the worse he'd feel, and the weaker he would be.

If he couldn't stop the bleeding, it wouldn't be long before he was no longer combat-ready.

And my head feels wrong. That's the biggest issue.

Lying face down near the dark stench of what must have been a natural outhouse for several men for many weeks, if not months, he processed what he had to do next.

Shoot anyone who investigates. Check my wounds. Stop the bleeding. Get my head back together.

Axe sat up, leaned against the cave wall, and pointed the AK back toward where the enemy would soon come for him.

Let them come—it'll save me the trouble.

He fought to keep his eyes open… and failed.

158

THE BLOCK

The Cliffs
Below the Mountain Vista Desert Resort and Spa

Ekaterina halted on the narrow trail that wound its way horizontally around this part of the mountain, halfway up, right between where the steep vertical face met the lower reaches consisting of boulders and scree running to the valley floor another few hundred feet below.

After Niko had dropped her off, she'd followed a well-marked hiking trail from the scenic view parking area.

A few feet to her left, the trail fell off into nothing but the angled rock and desert below.

The brownish-red rock looked solid, but the scree below, along with boulders both large and small that had broken off the cliff, showed it to be crumblier than she had initially believed.

The sun would set soon. She had her cell phone with its tiny light but no flashlight. Being outdoors at night on a treacherous trail wouldn't be her first choice, but the stars and a sliver of moon would be out. She would do whatever was needed to help Alex.

He is a good man. Honorable.

She slowed and craned her neck, looking up at the hundreds of feet of sheer rock to the top of the cliff.

No one could climb that.

The location of the resort was well defended... unless Alex and his team of Americans were correct and there was a cave and tunnel complex somewhere behind the thick rock to her right.

A slight breeze blew, but nothing stirred.

Under any other circumstances, the moment would be idyllic: a chance to take pictures and kiss the husband she'd never had before returning to a luxury resort for a five-course meal.

Instead, she worried about Alex—and accomplishing the mission.

Her president she was less concerned about. After him, there would be another, and another, all versions of the same person—one who thought his way of saving the country was the best but actually just craved power, control, and glory.

A faint *crack crack crack* came from somewhere nearby, so quiet she wondered if she'd imagined it.

That sounded like gunfire.

Could the Americans have been wrong? Was the attack happening already, on top of the cliff, with armed men shooting at the leaders of the Middle East, along with President Nikitin and the American vice president?

The return gunfire a few seconds later—a magazine being unloaded on full automatic—gave her the answer.

It is coming from inside the mountain.

She wouldn't hear it through the rock unless...

Craning her neck, Ekat saw a block of rock, about the size of a refrigerator, jutting from the vertical face of the mountain about fifteen feet above the trail. She rushed forward before turning and looking back. The setting sun allowed her to see better than she would have another time of the day.

The top of the block had detached from the main cliff face over time, leaving a long, deep "V" that started a few feet wide at the top and narrowed at the bottom.

That rock will fall someday. Sooner if given a push.

More gunshots—and they came from behind the block.

Over the years, as it pulled away from the face, a small hole into the cave behind it may have opened.

Examining the slope showed a handhold here and a foothold there.

I can make it.

Ekaterina put her hand on the rock, then one foot, the other hand, and the other foot, stepping up.

She found other small handholds, along with narrow ledges for her feet.

She climbed as quickly as she could, aware that a slip would drop her onto the narrow trail, where she might roll, fall over the edge, and plummet to her death.

Reaching the block, she didn't dare use it to hold herself to the wall inside the "V." It was attached only by an accumulation of dirty, rocky soil.

Behind it, the gaping crack was filled with small rocks and gravel.

Holding onto the cliff face with her left hand, she drew the kitchen knife from its towel sheath at the small of her back.

She stabbed at the loosest-looking area about halfway up the crack.

Gravel and dirt fell away, revealing an opening.

Cool air hit her face.

She stabbed with the knife again, digging more dirt from the opening. After slipping the knife carefully back into its holder, she stuck her right hand into the opening at the top and yanked.

Great chunks of rock and dirt dropped to the trail, rolled off, and careened the rest of the way to the desert floor and the compound of houses below.

A few more scoops made the hole big enough for her to squeeze through. She stuck her arm inside and sought a handhold.

Nothing.

If she could reach a little farther, she could touch the wall.

She leaned to her right, seeking…

The fist-sized rock her left hand clung to snapped off the face.

With both hands unconnected to the rock, she lost her balance.

Her feet started to slip from the small ledge they had rested comfortably on.

In desperation, she planted first one foot, then the other, on the refrigerator rock where it still connected to the face. Her hands sought places to hold and found tiny nubs she could pinch between her thumbs and fingers.

I will not be able to hold on if—

The block tore loose as if in slow motion, creaking and groaning.

With her grip failing, Ekaterina forced her feet into the crack, then her right hip.

She ended up wedged in the crack, her body held in place by the friction of her back and front pressing against the rough surface, her feet on other tiny nubs.

There was enough light to see a few feet inside, so she inched her way to the right, her hand exploring the interior of the rock, pulling, and her feet doing the same until they found footholds.

After a few of these moves, she lost the light and had to proceed in the dark, but at least she had found the cave.

The ground has to be somewhere below.

She angled down, not thinking about how high up she might be.

The crack widened. No longer was she held by the friction of her body partly wedged between two of the interior cave walls.

Her handholds weren't the greatest, and her footholds were worse.

She was going to fall.

Reaching left, right, up, and down, she found nothing with her right hand.

Behind her, the other face was too far away to lean back against.

She refused to cry out as her left hand slipped, putting all the weight on her feet, which also slipped off the rock.

She fell.

An instant later, her feet touched the ground.

Ekaterina was so shocked she simply sat down on the rocky floor.

Allowing herself one deep breath, she stood, dusted herself off, pulled out her phone to use as a flashlight, and moved deeper into the cave.

159

THE WARNING

The Reception Courtyard
The Mountain Vista Desert Resort and Spa
Outside Saiq, Oman

Special Agent Waylan was stressed and unhappy, to say the least.

Standing in the middle of the reception courtyard, staying ten feet from the president as he mingled and chatted up several people who routinely wished "Death to America" in speeches, didn't make for a fun evening.

Other men, just like him and Stewart, stood nearby—the protection detail of the men the president chatted with. All of them were armed—as Waylan was.

Any of them could have orders to take a shot at POTUS.

Waylan wasn't close enough to step in and take the bullet.

If someone went for their gun, he might be able to draw and fire in time to stop the death of the president of the United States of America, but it wasn't a sure thing.

The attacker would die—and his employer would blame it on him being a "rogue element."

There would be worldwide political condemnation against whatever country the killer had been working for, but without proof the assassination had been condoned, life would go on for everyone except President Heringten and the shooter.

Behind the scenes, whichever country had the nerve to do it would be a hero to a bunch of other countries.

Plus, somewhere in the crowd was the guy who was behind the cyberattacks that had killed a thousand people and messed up the lives of tens of thousands more.

Great. Just great.

The gig had been bad enough when the vice president had agreed to attend.

Having Heringten come instead, being a cowboy to what—catch people off guard?—was so much worse.

His head on a swivel, he stayed ready for anything... except the president's cell phone buzzing in his pocket.

Waylan wanted to ignore it. If there was a threat, he'd have heard about it over the Secret Service comms. But few people had the president's private number. There would be a good reason for the phone to ring—and the president would have his ass if Waylan didn't pick up the call.

Maybe it'll be something big enough back home to end this cluster and let us get Grizzly out of this den of vipers.

"Special Agent Waylan on POTUS's phone," he answered softly, holding the phone to his ear with his left hand. His right hand didn't budge from near the sidearm under his unbuttoned suit coat.

"Gregory Addison, Central Analysis Group," the man on the end of the phone said, followed by a series of code words.

This can't be good.

"Go ahead," Waylan said. His eyes continued to scan for danger as he took a few steps to his left to match President Heringten's movements.

"I have a possible threat against the president to report," Addison said. "Is he available?"

"No," Waylan said. "He's mingling, and the reception is in full swing. What's the threat?"

It better not be another warning about Malik.

He and Stewart had seen the man earlier, but he kept to the edge of the crowd, only greeting a few people. He seemed content to stand back and watch. He never approached the president.

"We have new intel," Addison said. "Not enough to pull the president, unfortunately. But we have an asset who discovered a tunnel system into the mountain you're standing on. The assumption is that it leads to a natural cave system. My people found obscure references to it in old books. We're concerned an attack from underground may be a possibility, but we're more worried that explosive charges placed under the main building would collapse it."

Holy shit!

His training kicked in. There were multiple threats against the president and vice president every day—especially each time they ventured from the safety of their offices. Death threats, bomb threats, the works.

Although he didn't have personal experience with Gregory Addison and the Central Analysis Group, he knew they'd been right on the money multiple times in the past few years. They were to be taken seriously.

"What can we do about it?" Waylan asked. "I'll tell him, but he won't budge. We've been trying to talk him out of this from the start, but he insists the summit is important. He says he has a hunch."

"Tell him the specifics of the threat and ask him to leave," Addison said. "Barring that, we believe that the most likely time of an attack or detonation of explosives is when all the attendees are together—5:15 to 5:20, when the sultan of Oman opens the summit with his welcome speech. You should be on high alert then or—ideally—not in the building at all."

"Copy. I'll let him know and hope for the best."

Wayland hung up, returned the phone to his pocket, and spoke into the microphone hidden in his sleeve. "All stations. Threat warning from Central Analysis Group. Possible tunnel or cave system under this whole place. Potential for attack, yet no specifics. They are also concerned about explosives below ground—under the basement. Send the K-9 team down there for another check, but be out of the building by 5:15. That's when there is the most probability for an attack, according to the analysis."

He got confirmation from all stations. After a nod from Stewart on the other side of the president, Waylan moved in.

The president flicked his gaze at him, shook the hand of some guy in a traditional robe that Waylan couldn't help but think had to be a lot like wearing a dress, and leaned his head in.

"Mr. President, sorry to interrupt. I just got a call from Gregory Addison. The Central Analysis Group has intel of a cave or tunnel system under this whole place. They're warning of a potential impending attack. Most likely, he said, is explosives beneath the main building. If that's the case, the most probable time for detonation and or attack is between 5:15 and 5:20. He urges your evacuation. I concur."

The president, to his credit, took several seconds to think it over. A few people nearby noticed; no one approached to interrupt the conversation.

"Did he say where the intel came from?" the president asked.

"Addison said they had an asset confirm the tunnel opening, sir."

The president frowned.

That means something to him—he's taking the threat more seriously now.

"An armed attack seems unlikely," the president muttered, "given the number of guards. It would take an army to make an impact. But explosives... Would the K-9 detect them if they were buried under the basement?"

"Probably not, Mr. President. But I sent the unit back down there anyway."

The president stood straight and looked around the lush courtyard with its green grass, bubbling fountains, and the increasingly stunning sunset, but it looked like he focused most of all on the four-story main building.

After checking his watch, he closed his eyes for a second.

He's making a decision.

The president opened his eyes and leaned back to Waylan. "Pull the K-9 team from the basement immediately. In fact, pull everyone out of the main building—subtly. I'm taking this seriously, but we aren't going to panic. I want to play it both ways. Not only are our lives important, but the lives of everyone here are, too. There's no time to convince everyone to abandon the summit—and this could very well be a ruse to get us to cry wolf. We'd lose credibility and embarrass the hell out of ourselves."

Waylan used the radio to call the K-9 team back and order everyone out of the building, speaking in the quietest whisper he could manage to still be heard over the radio.

"What about you, Mr. President? We have to get you to safety."

"If Addison is correct, we still have a little time. And the safest place to be is outside, surrounded by you and a lot of other guns. No, I have something else in mind."

"Sir?"

"I'm going to make a scene."

160

THE GENERATOR

The Cave
Beneath the Mountain Vista Desert Resort and Spa

The four of them stood in a row near the wall of the cave, directly underneath the west side of the resort. Beside them sat generators. Connected to each was a thick cord leading to large rectangular machines notched into the wall, ready to destroy the great hotel and kill everyone in it—if the devices worked as planned.

The man farthest from Hamid had started his generator early, just to be safe.

The sound of the generator reverberated around the large, low space they had painstakingly excavated beneath the resort's footprint.

What was that?

Hamid had heard something right as the generator's engine caught.

It had to be the echo of the engine.

The man at the first generator offered a relieved smile as his machine ran perfectly. The mission could succeed with only one device, they'd been told; it would just take longer.

And the results would not be as impactful.

The timing must be exact.

The idea had been drilled into their heads over and over. There was no margin for error. But they all feared making a mistake or having a last-minute problem they couldn't fix. If the choice was between nothing—having the mission fail because of them—or being delayed, the delay would have to do.

With one generator running, they would be ensured at least partial success—eventually—even if nothing else worked.

Technically, they should shut down the first generator now and test the others, but a quick check of their watches—comically done at nearly the same time—showed it made sense just to let it run. They'd start the others soon, too. They had plenty of fuel, and in fact, the longer they ran before the devices were started, the more fuel they'd use, making the generators slightly lighter and easier to move quickly out of the cave system.

Nothing could be left behind to show that they had ever been here, aside from the tunnel, which might or might not collapse—Malik's experts had been uncertain.

Hamid and the other men had been more than willing to risk it for Malik and his vision—even though operational security hadn't allowed them to know what the plan was after the destruction of the resort. They were part of a grand plan that would change the Middle East forever.

They were heroes.

Hamid stood closest to the rough opening in the floor where the ladder stuck out. He wasn't looking forward to lowering the generators and the other machinery down with ropes or helping to get it all back to the white delivery truck in the barn. Even with the wheels on the generators and strapping the devices to them, moving everything out would be a challenge. They had the manpower for it—the men guarding the series of ladders below, along with other guards in the tunnel that would be coming up to help.

He checked his watch again.

Almost time.

They would leave all four machines running for the prescribed time before shutting them down and getting out as fast as possible.

With time on his hands until the next step, his mind returned to the sound he'd heard.

It was nothing. An echo.

He couldn't let it go.

"Did you hear shooting?" he yelled to the man standing near him in the blue shirt, who was responsible for the second generator.

"What? No," he yelled back, pointing at his generator. "It's fine since we fixed it."

"No. Gunfire!"

The man looked confused and shook his head. "I can't hear a thing!"

Hamid checked his watch again, torn. His mission was here. He had to start his generator, check the plug-in, and flip the switch on the device. It was a very simple task, but it was his responsibility. The most important one—what they had been working toward for an entire year.

Who could find us here?

No one.

It was only an echo.

Besides, guards had been stationed in the long tunnel just in case.

Still more waited at the final ladders leading to this room.

If every man did his job, the mission would be a success.

He and the other men in the large, low cave would focus on their assignment with the generators and machines.

Above, the resort would come crashing down, killing people without gunfire or explosives.

Everyone would believe the greatest terrorist attack in history was a horrific natural disaster, just the way Malik wanted.

161

RELENTLESS FORWARD PROGRESS

The Cave
Beneath the Mountain Vista Desert Resort and Spa

After coming to again, Axe cut strips from his shirt to bandage the ricochet gunshot wounds, which hurt and bled a lot but weren't as bad as he thought. After that, it was time to resume the mission.

Axe returned to the ladder, ready to take care of business.

His head didn't cooperate. His vision swam. He felt weak and unfocused, stumbling a few times, but the mission had to go on.

He went from seeing double to triple and back to double, but he climbed the ladder again, careful to not put all his weight on his right leg this time. As he stepped from the ladder onto the rock ledge, he staggered, flailing his arms to regain his balance.

Falling again would definitely suck.

He was having a hard time concentrating—another sure sign of a severe concussion.

Been there, done that.

But he hadn't made it through BUD/S and fifteen years on the front lines by quitting when things got tough or when he didn't feel one hundred percent.

Rifle up—and with more magazines in his pocket, courtesy of the dead guards—he inched his way into the next cavern. He had to pause once to vomit when the nausea got too much for him.

Yep. Concussion.

On the opposite side of this opening, another excavated hole awaited. A bright lamp sat on the ground right outside.

Axe rushed across the open space, ready to fire, but there was no one around.

He followed the rough tunnel, walking upward in a tight spiral, in the dark.

They've cleared this area of lamps already, I bet.

He kept moving forward, step by step.

His mind played tricks on him. He couldn't tell if he'd been walking a few minutes or a few hours.

Checking his watch didn't help. He had trouble focusing on the dial.

Screw it, just keep moving. Relentless forward progress.

It wasn't until he saw the bright glow of light ahead that he realized the noise he heard had to be real and not his damaged brain imagining things.

That's a motor... a generator, maybe?

When more started up, he was sure.

Definitely small gas-powered generators.

Why would anyone lug generators this far into the mountain? Could they be used to power mining machinery?

Maybe they're about to break through into the lower levels of the resort.

He didn't have a good sense of vertical distance traveled, but the first carved tunnel system, where he'd eliminated the guards as they relaxed and napped, had taken him a while to navigate. He'd also climbed one—or was it two?—ladders, plus the tight spiral he'd just finished.

But he couldn't think of a reason for the generators.

There was only one way to find out what was going on. He continued forward.

162

FOLLOW

Ekaterina turned off the cell phone flashlight when she saw the faint glow of a lamp in the distance.

She glided forward, silently moving from shadow to shadow, alert for movement, sound, or the sense of another human being nearby.

The two dead bearded men near the base of a tall ladder told her all she needed to know.

Alex has been this way.

The men's AKs had been stripped of their magazines, though both had knives still in sheaths at their waists. She took the knife that had the best heft to replace the kitchen knife still in her waistband. It had served her well, but using it to pound the rock and dirt had dulled the blade.

Armed with the new blade, she lightly climbed the ladder and continued on, following her temporary American partner.

163

THE DEVICES

Hamid started his generator's engine at 4:55—five minutes before scheduled—to let the machine warm up or give him time to make a last-minute repair.

It fired up fine.

The other two men did the same. They grinned excitedly at each other.

The large space—the size of the hotel directly above them—had plenty of air. They were in no danger of being overwhelmed with carbon monoxide from the generators. Certainly not in the short amount of time they needed.

The cavern they'd found and expanded had a low ceiling, though, forcing them to stoop.

Does carbon monoxide rise or fall?

He didn't know—it wasn't something he'd considered or dealt with. He'd used small, simple engines all his life, but never in a wide, low, confined space.

He was about to ask the man at the next generator about the gas when he heard a sound other than the steady rumble of the engines.

Hearing it a second time gave him another chance to figure it out.

Those are gunshots.

And unlike when he thought he'd heard them earlier, these were close. Very close.

It came from the cave below us—at the base of the ladder.

He turned to look at the other three men.

Their faces told him they had heard it too—and identified the sounds the same as he had.

All of them knew gunfire. Each had taken up arms—against Russian soldiers when they were younger and America's soldiers when they had come to their homeland.

Hamid reacted first, reaching down to flip the switch on the squat machine plugged into his generator and pressed firmly into the rock wall where he'd carefully chiseled a perfect opening for it to rest inside.

He imagined he could feel the vibrations from the machines but knew that was impossible. The frequencies weren't in a range for him to hear or feel.

The others did the same before following his lead and drawing their knives.

If the building above collapses early, so be it.

They had a new mission—defend the machinery long enough for the vibrations to affect the structural support of the resort and bring it crashing down.

164

THE KNIVES

The Cave
Beneath the Mountain Vista Desert Resort and Spa

The tunnel had opened into another wide cavern, lit by more lamps than usual.

A guard was on alert, waiting for Axe.

He had fired as Axe edged his way around the wall of the tunnel to recon the area.

Two bullets hit Axe, one above his right pec and another on the right arm.

Damn it!

The wounds burned before Axe could shut out the pain.

At least I didn't get shot in the head.

Axe stuck the AK around the corner, pointed in the general direction of the man who had shot him, and fired three times—covering fire more than anything else.

The man must have heard a faint echo of the earlier gunshots from farther down the tunnel and been ready for him.

And I'm not moving nearly as quietly or quickly as usual.

Axe dropped low, ignoring the pain from his leg, glute, shoulder, and arm, and fired blindly around the corner again.

A flurry of answering shots came back.

Fighting back dizziness, Axe exploded upward, waited for the inevitable pause as the tango's overexcited shooting emptied his magazine, then flung himself away from the tunnel wall.

Three tangos swam in his vision, frantically changing magazines. Only one was real—but which?

Axe shot them all.

They dropped when he hit the real one.

The three dead guards—Axe he was still seeing triple—lay sprawled on the ground at the foot of yet another damn ladder.

He dragged his increasingly lame right leg forward but had to stop to lean against the wall, more because of his damaged head than the fresh gunshot wounds or older ricochet damage.

Come on, not again.

If he could keep it together another few minutes, he was sure he'd finish the mission.

He didn't care much about what happened after that.

Of course, he'd try to make it out of the tunnel, retracing his steps.

He would never give up.

But that mattered so much less than stopping the bombs… or whatever the assholes in the cave and tunnels were doing.

He closed his eyes, offering his messed-up head a compromise.

I'll take a break for a few seconds, get my brain back, then go finish this.

The seconds stretched by. At some level, he was aware of resting longer than he had intended—and much longer than was wise in the middle of an operation, let alone during an assault of an enemy position.

His instincts made him snap his eyes open just in time to see a bunch of men—some hazy and indistinct, others solid and deadly looking—running across the cave toward him, their shadows bouncing crazily off the walls and ceiling in the glow of the lamps.

He shot at them—and what had to be their doubles or triples, because of his damaged brain—but at least a few made it to him when the magazine ran out.

Blades cut into his arm. One came at his face. He wasn't sure if it was real or a hallucination, but he jerked his head back, avoiding getting his eyes slit open.

Moving like he was underwater, he felt the bite of the knife as it slashed again, cutting his forehead.

Blood immediately fell like a heavy rain into his eyes, making it impossible to see.

He took a knife to his left shoulder and caught the hand of the assailant before he could yank it back, holding him close and punching him in the face.

The pain from the wound in his right shoulder and arm made him nearly faint, but the satisfying crunch that came from the tango's nose breaking almost made up for it.

Axe's nose exploded in pain a second later as the man he'd just punched connected with his own blow.

Axe shoved the man away, ignoring the fresh pain in his crooked nose.

He used the pain to fuel his focus. With a quick wipe of the blood from his eyes, he took stock of the situation.

Three bodies bled on the ground. He was reasonably sure they were real.

Two men stood in front of him, advancing with their knives out, blood lust in their eyes. One had a crooked nose that Axe was sure matched his own.

With a snarl, Axe attacked while he could still focus.

Against two inexperienced tangos, he would normally have an advantage.

In his weakened condition, though, it was an even match at best.

At worst, they held the upper hand.

It didn't matter. He had a mission to accomplish, and he damn well wasn't going to let these two stand in the way.

165

THE INTERRUPTION

James calmly worked his way toward the small stage near the resort's main building, moving slowly but surely to the left side of the low carpeted platform. The attendees made way for him with nods and handshakes as he passed. His translator stayed on his heels. Waylan and Stewart were nearby.

James stopped, knees nearly touching the side of the stage, and nodded politely to the sultan of Oman's son—the crown prince. The man, standing six feet away, directly behind the stage, nodded back and returned to flicking through small white notecards.

If the possibility of the building blowing up is another one of Haley's hunches, I'm taking it seriously.

What he was about to attempt would piss off a lot of important people if Gregory's team was wrong.

If the intel was right, however, no one would realize what he'd done.

I can live without credit for saving everyone's asses.

Behind the stage, the off-white main resort building glowed in the incredible sunset.

James checked his watch as the crown prince stepped onto the stage with a nervous smile.

Five o'clock to the second. Punctual, just like his dad taught him.

The crown prince's close-cropped beard was dark, and he wore a white ankle-length tunic over white pants. His turban was orange with a navy-blue pattern.

The microphone squealed for a second with feedback as the crown prince took it from a tall stand.

He cleared his throat and began. He spoke in Arabic. James's interpreter quietly translated. "Good evening and welcome."

The crown prince's voice was deeper than his thin frame suggested, and James could hear the warmth in it.

The kid will make a better leader than his father someday.

The crowd, already quieting down out of respect, watched attentively. The young man—in his thirties—continued speaking. The American interpretor kept pace with a nearly instantaneous translation. "My father has a brilliant welcome speech planned but was generous enough to allow me this smaller stage, prior to the official start of the event, to say a few words. A test of sorts, I suspect."

The crowd around James chuckled in appreciation a second before the interpreter caught up, so James smiled instead of laughing conspicuously late. The sultan of Oman was carefully training the crown prince to take over someday. Rumor had it that the father was strict and had very high standards.

"I only offer an informal welcome before my father's official one. I gladly extend to all of you the hospitality of our country and wish you a weekend filled with progress toward peace."

James joined in the enthusiastic applause that followed the words.

"Now, as you all know, my father keeps a very exacting schedule," he said and checked his watch, "and I have five seconds to ask you to—"

James raised his hand, making his move. "I beg your pardon, but may I say a short word?" he called in a loud voice.

There was a murmur of surprise from the audience as James slowly stepped onto the stage, his hands held up and away from his body, not wanting to get shot on his way to saving everyone's lives.

Behind the stage, two of the crown prince's guards tensed and stepped up onto the platform before glancing to their boss for instructions.

"I know this breaks every protocol," James said quietly, "but please. It is very important to me and my country."

James felt the tiniest bit of pity for the young man who stared at James with a fake smile plastered on his face.

He's frantically trying to figure out a way to say no without making a scene.

The bodyguards moved closer.

James nodded, smiled, and called out, "Thank you!" as he slowly advanced, his hand outstretched for the microphone.

There was perfect silence from the audience as the drama unfolded onstage.

As James stepped closer, the crown prince handed him the microphone reluctantly and took two steps to the side, offering the stage to James.

With the microphone pointed down and his side still to the audience, James whispered to the kid. "I'm sorry," James said sincerely. "Please trust me."

The crown prince spoke English fluently, having earned a degree in England, and would understand the words.

Haley, you'd better damn well be right about this.

If not, the United States had likely just embarrassed the next ruler of Oman, made a new enemy, and gotten a son in big trouble with his father.

James turned to face the crowd, the setting sun hitting him full in the face.

"Thank you, Your Highness," he started, "for generously allowing me to interrupt you. I know we are on a tight schedule," James continued, stalling as best he could without being obvious. "We have your father's speech to look forward to—and I assure you I will not make a habit of stealing the stage like this."

After a few seconds for the translations to come through, there were a few cautiously polite chuckles.

"This is a breach of protocol, and for that," James said, "I am tremendously sorry, Your Highness. But I may be called back to the United States at any moment, and I want to make sure you and the other leaders of the Middle East witness this. As you all know, we have faced a brutal cyberattack that could have happened in any of your countries as well."

James stalled more, detailing some of the death, destruction, and problems facing the United States from the attacks.

When the crown prince started to fidget impatiently at his grandstanding, James had to move on.

"Many in my intelligence teams are convinced Russia is behind this attack," James said, getting to the meat of his plan.

Heads whipped around to catch President Nikitin's reaction from near the pool. He stood stoically, his face neutral.

Next to him, his foreign minister struggled to hold back anger at being called out in such an undiplomatic fashion.

"I have my doubts about this determination," James said. The audience turned back to stare at James. Many looked shocked. Others seemed skeptical.

"In America, we have an expression—'the elephant in the room.' It means there is a large, obvious problem that no one will address because to do so is difficult or unpleasant. I prefer to confront things head-on." James offered a hard smile that he knew didn't reach his eyes. "Perhaps that is from my training and background."

Most in the group knew about James's history as a Navy SEAL who had seen combat throughout the Middle East and other countries during his active-duty days.

"And in the spirit of dealing with the problem directly, I would like to invite President Nikitin to the stage for a brief face-to-face discussion."

James raised his free hand and gestured to the stage. "Mr. President? Please join me for a moment."

166

HOLD

The Reception Courtyard
The Mountain Vista Desert Resort and Spa
Outside Saiq, Oman

Abdul's joy at seeing President Heringten in the crowd instead of the vice president lasted the entire reception... until Heringten stepped onto the stage just as the Crown Prince was about to usher everyone inside the soon-to-be destroyed building.

No!

Rage filled him. America—along with Russia years before—had invaded his country and harmed or killed so many of his people.

Now, its president was putting all his work, all his planning, at risk with a speech.

The devices underground should have just been started precisely at five o'clock. The experts had predicted they would need approximately fifteen minutes of runtime. The resonance created by the frequencies would interact with the resort's concrete, weakening it to the point of failure.

The entire structure had been specifically designed and built to collapse when the proper frequencies were applied—during the summit.

If the attendees didn't hurry into the building, the devices worked better than planned, or the timing was otherwise off, the whole "natural disaster" would fail.

By design, the plan for the destruction of the building required no communication or signal.

He only had a last-ditch fail-safe. A one-time way of delaying the operation.

With a slow, smooth movement, Abdul slipped his hand inside the loose robe he wore and pressed his thumb to the cell phone's round button.

He hated relying on technology. He wasn't familiar with it and didn't trust it.

In this case, however, it had been set up to be as foolproof as possible.

On the phone's main screen, there was one icon—a smiley face. If Abdul pressed it for three seconds, a text would automatically be sent to a man standing several hundred feet below him outside a barn a quarter mile from the base of the mountain.

That man would rush inside, drop into a tunnel, and run—yelling—until he was heard by the first man in the tunnel.

He would repeat the process and signal the next man.

This would continue until word reached the four handpicked, well-trained, intelligent men who manned the generators and devices in a hollowed-out cave directly under the main building.

They would turn off the machines, wait fifteen minutes, then begin again.

Abdul pressed and held the little face until the phone chirped a signal.

It is done.

He figured at least ten minutes before the men stopped the machines. Maybe longer.

Is that quick enough?

The technology was untested on this scale. He had been assured that the building needed several minutes for the vibrational frequencies to trigger its collapse, but the exact timing couldn't be determined.

As the Russian president reluctantly strode to the stage, Abdul could only hope his men stopped the machines in time, the spectacle on stage concluded quickly, and everyone in front of him was soon lying dead inside the resort's grand ballroom, buried under tons of rubble.

167

THE TANGOS

The Cave
Beneath the Mountain Vista Desert Resort and Spa

Axe hated losing, but that's exactly what was happening. The two tangos were beating him. He had done a considerable amount of damage—both of them were nearly dead, just like him—but the facts were the facts.

He was also losing another battle—the one between his willpower and the physical limitations of his body.

The ricochet wounds in his leg and glutes were seeping blood.

Blood flowed freely from the gunshot in his shoulder and arm.

The body is a finite system. Yes, it can be manipulated with the mind into accessing depths it usually refused to tap out of self-preservation. In the end, though, the damage, loss of blood, head trauma, and the sheer fatigue would take their toll. He would move too slowly to avoid a blow or absorb one too many shocks to the system.

His body would shut down.

He wouldn't die right then, but passing out in the cave, with two tangos still conscious, was a death sentence.

Axe had a momentary reprieve. He had knocked down both tangos before crawling several feet away, unable to muster the energy to finish off either or both.

They had all taken a few minutes to recover.

Axe lay face down on the cave floor, struggling to stay conscious. Although his energy was nearly one hundred percent gone, he recognized his chance. As long as he could stay conscious, now was the time to end the fight.

He clawed the ground, moving a few inches closer to the man nearest him, who he'd dubbed Brown for the color of his shirt.

He heard moaning, followed by a sob, and he couldn't be sure if they came from his own mouth or one of the enemy.

Brown struggled, pushing himself up to his knees, then his feet.

Not so fast.

Axe grabbed his ankle and yanked as hard as he could.

It should have pulled the man down, but it barely moved his leg.

Brown scowled at Axe, his face bruised and battered by Axe's fists.

First, he tried kicking Axe's hand away. When that failed, he leaned down and dropped, leading with his fist, hitting Axe's broken nose yet again.

The pain made Axe see stars. He tasted fresh blood and spat it away, rolling sideways again to get distance from the man.

This is really bad.

As Axe rolled away from Brown, who stayed on the floor of the cave where he'd dropped, moaning, a punch from the second guy—Blue— connected with the bleeding wound on Axe's glute, sending sparks of agony up and down his body.

Where did he come from?

There was a good chance, Axe realized, that he had passed out for a few seconds.

He rolled again, barely feeling the press of the meat cleaver handle in his back or the thick, heavy blade safely secured in the kitchen towel sheath at the back of his waistband.

Wait—what? A weapon?

The pistol and the AK were somewhere nearby, but Axe hadn't seen either in ages.

He lost his train of thought as Blue crawled toward him on his hands and knees, looking like an exhausted dog who had chased down a car and caught it yet couldn't eat it—or walk away.

Axe fought to get back to the idea he'd had a moment before.

Something about a kitchen?

No. He had nothing.

Axe reversed his roll, moving as quickly as he could back at Blue, taking the man's arms out from under him. Blue collapsed onto him.

Right where I want you.

Mustering what might be the last of his strength, Axe wrapped the man in a triangle choke and held on, not letting up long past the point Blue went limp.

Axe didn't have the strength left to push the dead man off him. He lay on his back, preparing for a last attack on the other tango.

The added weight of Blue made a rock pushing into the small of Axe's back hurt. In comparison to the other injuries, an errant rock meant nothing, but he still felt its insistent poke against his spine.

A tickle in his mind told him to pay attention to the rock beneath him.

What if it's not a rock?

He snaked his hand behind him, fully expecting to come out with a piece of rock he could use on Brown, but instead he latched onto the handle of a knife.

The meat cleaver!

Brown regained his feet, smiling maniacally, one eye swollen shut, his nose mangled, his two front teeth missing. He staggered toward Axe, holding a long, bloody knife in an overhand grip, ready to drop down on Axe and finish him off.

Brown steadied himself and used his heel to shove Blue's body off Axe.

He spoke, but between the man's busted mouth and the foreign language, Axe got none of it.

It did, however, give him the opening he needed.

With one last, desperate reach into his nearly empty energy reservoir, Axe pulled the meat cleaver from behind his back and swung upward, aiming for the man's junk.

He missed.

The heavy, sharp blade dug instead into the top of Brown's thigh, just below his groin.

Blood spurted as the man howled in agony.

Not what I meant to do, but I can work with it.

Axe's next swing had a fraction of the momentum and a difficult angle, but the knife bit deeply enough into Brown's other leg to also draw a spurt of blood.

See how you like having both femoral arteries cut, asshole.

Brown dropped the knife and collapsed next to Axe, his hands desperately trying to hold the blood inside his body.

Just to be safe, Axe rolled away until he came to rest against the wall of the cave, face down with his cheek on the ground, facing the screaming man rapidly dying of blood loss. With both arteries cut, Axe gave him less than ninety seconds.

Axe started counting, got lost after ten, and had to go back to one.

By five, his eyes were closed.

At nine, the darkness took him.

168

THE DECLARATION

The Reception Courtyard
The Mountain Vista Desert Resort and Spa
Outside Saiq, Oman

James waited patiently on the stage for the Russian president to make the long walk from the pool deck. If the Central Analysis Group's conclusions were correct, he had no problem with the president's slow approach.

Take your time—the longer you take, the better for all of us.

At some point soon, the crown prince would figure out a way to end this spectacle and get the schedule back on track.

Or he might walk over, take the microphone from James's hand, and suggest the confrontation continue after dinner.

He was in a tough spot of not wanting to create more of a scene or annoy his father by making the dinner start late—though from his expression, he was as intrigued as everyone else.

If the building didn't blow up, James's stunt would be the talk of the weekend.

The crowd parted for President Nikitin and his interpreter. His personal protection detail stationed themselves near James's.

Eventually, Nikitin joined James on stage, along with his translator.

James offered his hand to the president, and they shook solemnly.

"Thank you, Mr. President," James said, turning back to the audience, thinking about what he wanted to say, as well as ways to stretch the discussion as long as possible. He didn't dare check his watch to see how much time he'd eaten up, sure that the crown prince would use the gesture as an excuse to jump in.

"Since a few years after World War II," James started, "the United States and Russia have been locked in a struggle. First, the Cold War, where we each drove our economies to the brink of disaster producing weapons and trying to outdo the other."

The Russian president stood stiffly, lips pressed together, stoically enduring the production.

"When Russia invaded Afghanistan, America was on the other side, pouring weapons, ammunition, and billions of dollars into the *mujahideen* to defend Afghanistan from what we saw as communist aggression. Russia and America were, in all but official declaration, at war."

James sought out the Afghan contingent in the audience. "We helped repel the invaders... and later were repelled ourselves."

James let it drop. He'd have time this weekend to deal with the Afghanis and the chaos of their country.

He didn't look to his right, behind the Russian president, to see how the crown prince was taking the long-winded history lesson.

"Fast forward to earlier this week when America was attacked using computers, as I've detailed. What I'm sure most of you do not know, however, is that an online rumor is correct. Secretary of State Wilson was poisoned with polonium-210."

Surprised chatter broke out among the attendees a second after James finished the sentence.

He did nothing to quiet the audience, though President Nikitin's angry demeanor silenced people more quickly than if he hadn't been onstage.

"President Nikitin and I spoke on the phone. He assured me his government had nothing to do with the attacks on my country or Secretary Wilson." James paused. "I believe him."

More whispers followed before eventually quieting.

"However," he said, staring at the Iranian delegation, "we all know how difficult it is to keep some of our citizens from acting 'on their own.'"

Aside from the stone-cold face staring back at him from the Iranian supreme leader, there were a few coughs from people faced with an uncomfortable truth no one liked to discuss. Using proxy forces to unofficially attack one's enemies was a tried-and-true method used around the region and world.

"As I said, I believed President Nikitin on the phone," James said. "I look forward to talking about it with him more in-depth this weekend, as well as discussing with many of you ways that we can prevent the situations that led to Russia invading Afghanistan, or America's own forays into the region that cost so many lives on both sides."

I won't apologize for what was done by past presidents. I wasn't in the room to make those decisions, and hindsight is twenty-twenty.

He had to believe that previous administrations did their best for the country given the intelligence they had at the time, whether it seemed like a mistake, disaster, or brilliant move years—or decades—later.

And if they didn't—if they did what they wanted to do despite it all and damn the consequences, may God have mercy on their souls.

"But I asked you on stage, Mr. President," James said, turning to the Russian, "to hear from you face-to-face and man-to-man. It's so much easier to detect a lie—or half truth—in person, especially when a person is under pressure. I'm sure you would agree. So please, tell me Russia had nothing to do with the attacks—cyber or on Secretary Wilson—and that you have no knowledge of anyone else in your government who did so."

James handed the mic over before the interpreter finished translating. Nikitin took it automatically, eyes locked on James's.

Surprise! Now let's see what you're made of and how good of a liar you are.

The Russian translator stopped speaking into his president's ear and leaned back, his forehead sweaty in the last glow of the sunset and small but powerful footlights helping to illuminate everyone on stage.

President Nikitin raised the mic to his lips and spoke, his voice strong and clear. He sounded more like a college professor turned president.

James's translator hesitantly stepped onstage, then hurried over to stand behind James, whispering into his ear.

"Thank you, Mr. President," the interpreter said as the Russian spoke. "While highly unusual and sure to get us both into hot water with His Majesty the Sultan of Oman, I appreciate your directness. Much agony in the world could be prevented if we said what we needed to."

The president paused. "Then again, we might also have more conflict. I suppose it depends on the parties involved."

James chuckled along with a few others in the audience. Not everyone had a translator who spoke Russian.

"But I will look you in the eye here and now, in front of these witnesses, who no doubt are as good as any at detecting lies and weakness," Nikitin continued.

He waited until the interpreter had finished before speaking again, directly to James.

"The government of Russia had nothing at all to do with the cyberattacks on America nor the poisoning of Secretary Wilson," he said. He seemed sincere and open. "Additionally, to the best of my knowledge, neither I nor anyone I'm aware of was involved in any way."

Here he paused again, as if debating whether to continue. After several seconds, he spoke. "No—that is not completely true. Since the attacks, it has come to my attention that Russian individuals—hackers—may have acted without my knowledge or permission in the attacks."

The members of the audience who could understand Russian or had translators who did erupted into whispered conversations.

President Nikitin spoke over them. "I will be happy to give you the information at your earliest convenience, but there is an active operation to apprehend these criminals and bring them to justice."

James watched Nikitin carefully. He had seen the lie—or omission— on the man's face before he corrected himself.

He doesn't know we already have his Russian hackers... and that we'll get to the truth of what they knew and who they worked for.

"If I have lied or misled, I pledge here and now in front of all of you" —he gestured at the audience—"to turn myself over to the International Criminal Court in the Hague."

More voices erupted at this declaration.

With that, President Nikitin handed the microphone back to James.

Everything he said seems to be true.

The ball was back in James's court.

He stretched out his hand and shook with Nikitin to applause from the audience.

169

THE CHOICE

The Cave
Beneath the Mountain Vista Desert Resort and Spa

Ekaterina hurriedly followed the trail of dead guards and the sound of generators to another cavern with a ladder at the far end.

She crept forward silently to find the American lying face down along the wall to her left. His hand gripped the meat cleaver from Dubai.

Wet blood coated it.

To the right, a man lay dead. Blood saturated the rocky dirt around him.

More dead men lay nearby.

They died defending something.

She rushed up the ladder, not expecting to meet resistance but ready with the pistol the American had given her just in case.

Ducking her head, she entered a large but low space excavated from the rock.

Raised in the city, she felt more comfortable around buildings and crowds, but her training had taken her into basements, tunnels, and the Russian metro. At times, she had been forced to navigate her way out relying on dead reckoning.

This sense told her she was directly under the main building of the resort not far above.

The sound of the four generators reverberated in the space.

Other machines sat in small alcoves carved into the walls, a green light glowing on each, but otherwise they did nothing.

She walked around flipping the switches on the electronic devices, changing the light on each from green to red.

If the enemy died to keep the machines on, they should be turned off.

Next, she stopped the generators, welcoming the sudden silence.

She searched but found no explosives.

Only one conclusion made any sense.

The electronics must emit frequencies to eventually mimic the effects of an earthquake.

The big question she had, though, was whether she had arrived in time. The machines' effect would be cumulative, not instantaneous.

She considered the situation and made her decision. She was one person. Alex was likely dead. If more men came to finish the operation, she would be at a disadvantage.

They could start the machinery, and the American's death would have been for nothing.

She unplugged the cord from the first generator and picked up one end, tipping it so it moved on its two sturdy wheels. She pulled it to the ledge with the ladder.

With a shove, it fell off the small cliff... and landed on a dead guard.

She frowned and vowed to aim better with the next one.

A minute later, the other generators lay broken and leaking fuel in the cavern below.

As Ekaterina climbed down the ladder, an uneasy feeling came over her.

She heard nothing, but the world felt... not right.

Quickly moving to Alex, she stepped on the meat cleaver he held, in case he wasn't dead. She couldn't have him waking up thinking she was attacking him.

Her fingers felt his neck, not expecting to find a pulse but having to try.

At first, there was nothing.

Moving her fingers a few centimeters, she felt it. A steady beat.

Much too slow—but he is alive.

Ekaterina stood, looking at the dead lying around the cavern. Alex had fought bravely.

She considered the size of the American, her own strength, and the challenges of dragging his body so far.

Isn't it better to let him die here on the battlefield than in a long, dark tunnel five minutes from now?

Or... she could put a bullet into the back of his head.

A quick, painless death.

What would she want for herself?

And what did she owe him for Los Angeles, when it would have been easier for him to shoot her—two different times—than let her live?

170

THE EVAC

The Reception Courtyard
The Mountain Vista Desert Resort and Spa
Outside Saiq, Oman

James had used up all the time he could. He'd done everything in his power to delay the attendees from going straight into the building—except for announcing that one of his elite intelligence units had warned him about a possible attack on the resort.

If he went on any longer, the crown prince was going to take away the microphone.

Nothing happened. Haley was wrong.

Better safe than sorry, he supposed.

Or maybe Axe thwarted the attack.

James thanked the crown prince in a low voice, handed the microphone back to him, and stepped off the stage as the last of the applause from the attendees died down.

James would have to spend the next two days working hard to smooth over Oman's ruffled feathers from the protocol-breaching stunt—in addition to working on the rest of the region's leaders to make sure America's interests were kept in mind and Russia didn't make a successful push for whatever they had planned.

I'll work it out. In private, I might mention the intel about a possible attack.

People might not believe him, but he'd win points for creativity.

The crown prince spoke quickly from the stage behind him. James's interpreter translated. "Please, everyone, we have gotten off schedule. My father awaits. Let us adjourn to dinner."

His Royal Highness jumped off the stage and led the way, turning and beckoning to the crowd, hurrying them forward.

As one, the group of leaders—and their entourages—followed him on the long walk toward the main resort building.

James had to smile.

They're hungry… or worried about pissing off the sultan more than he surely already is.

James trailed them with his ever-present Secret Service agents, Waylan and Stewart, on his wings, ten feet away on either side.

The Russian president and his entourage followed at a distance.

A few stragglers, or maybe staff ready to clean up after the reception—James couldn't tell in the dusk—waited by the pool.

As the first of the guests reached the patio outside the building, a low, ominous creaking came from within.

The leaders slowed. After a few more hesitant steps, they stopped.

The four-story resort groaned, sounding like an old man, broken and battered, settling onto an uncomfortable chair.

Silence followed, feeling like the calm before a storm.

The men in the crowd exchanged glances. As a rule, buildings didn't make noises like those.

People whispered, looking at the building.

No one moved closer.

It seemed prudent to wait.

A minute passed, filled with quieter creaks and groans.

The crown prince took several steps forward before turning with a reassuring yet nervous smile to the men waiting and watching behind him.

The ground trembled, feeling like a strong earthquake, and a massive roar filled the night.

A piece of the building fell, narrowly missing the crown prince.

The crowd surged back.

Seconds later, the structure collapsed, a slow-motion spectacle of destruction.

It looked to James like a video of a building being imploded to make room for a newer one on the same ground.

The west side collapsed first, folding in on itself.

For a moment, it looked like the rest of the building would hold. But it too fell, though not as completely as the west side.

Dust swirled. More pieces of debris landed nearby.

A few of the attendees were struck. Those closest pulled farther away from the building's remains.

It happened. Haley was right again.

Stewart appeared at James's side, taking hold of his right arm. Waylan had his left. "We're getting you out of here, Mr. President," Stewart said.

James was half-dragged toward his bungalow and the SUVs parked outside, which, by long-standing protocol, had been ready for an immediate evac from the moment he'd been dropped off.

As they drew closer to the bungalow, the building groaned again, and the west side settled further.

A terrible silence fell across the area before faint screams came from beneath the building.

"There are people inside," James said, wrenching his arms free. "Some of them might be ours. We're going to help." James turned back to the pile of rubble that was once a multibillion-dollar luxury hotel.

Stewart blocked his way, arms out to the side.

"Sir, you can't go there. Too dangerous. You're evacuating right now."

The man wasn't asking—he was telling James how it was going to be.

Screw that. I won't just let those people die.

"Get out of my way. I'm going to help. You can come along or wait here—your choice. But I'm going in."

James walked forward, holding the man's eye, letting him see his total commitment.

At the last second, Stewart stepped aside, cursed up a storm under his breath, and followed James.

"Evac canceled," Stewart called into his microphone, keeping up with James as he started to run. "Grizzly is going in to help. Maintain your stations. And get me a count of all our people and whether any of them are still inside the main building."

James raced toward the danger, yanking off his tie as he went.

Hang on, people. We're coming.

171

THE REVENGE

The Reception Courtyard
The Mountain Vista Desert Resort and Spa
Outside Saiq, Oman

Abdul stared at the collapsed building from the shadows near the pool, not bothering to hide his shock at the timing of the destruction.

What happened?

He fought the disappointment and anger welling inside him.

Years of planning had been ruined because of President Heringten's impromptu performance and possibly—he would have to look into it later —the incompetence of his men in the caves below.

He vowed that their wives and families would suffer if they ignored his order to delay the attack or otherwise acted incorrectly.

For the moment, he was at a loss of what to do.

The idea of sitting through endless speeches and small group meetings as a respected businessman member of the Afghan coalition repulsed him.

He had no need for peace.

He wanted revenge.

First, against Russia, for invading his country when he was a boy.

The Americans, also, for doing the same years later.

Both had come into his country—his home—and killed those they decided had to die. Those they deemed were suddenly the enemy.

Why?

Because they could.

What did his so-called brothers in the Middle East do?

Did they stand united against their common enemy?

Did they evict the Western powers from the land they were never meant to set foot on?

No.

They looked the other way, offered minimal help, or went so far as to make business deals with Russia or America to line their own pockets at the expense of his country's land and people.

There could be no peace until all who had participated or looked the other way were punished.

So much effort. Planning. Expense. And the only ones dead tonight are staff and—if I am lucky—the sultan of Oman.

The American president, who a moment before had been dragged across the yard toward a bungalow by his security detail, turned and ran toward the building.

What is he doing? Helping?

With a start, Abdul realized this was a second chance.

I will kill him and find some way to blame it on the Russian president.

This would be the final push both countries needed to declare war and destroy each other, which had been the first part of the plan all along.

I will salvage this situation myself.

172

THE BULL

The Cave
Beneath the Mountain Vista Desert Resort and Spa

Axe woke slowly, struggling up from the blackness of unconsciousness.

His body bounced and jostled.

He opened his eyes to the confusing sight of a wall moving past him in dim light.

Walls don't move like that.

It took him another few seconds to figure out the walls were stationary. He was moving down a tunnel.

Where am I?

His entire body hurt, but he was alive and felt better than he had…

The thought slipped away.

As he moved his head, the pain nearly caused him to black out.

What…?

His body stopped bouncing, which helped his head immensely.

"You live, yes?" a voice said from above him.

Russian…

He had known a Russian once. An older woman. Short but strong. A wrinkled face and thin, dyed brown hair.

He opened his eyes and saw the woman he'd remembered.

She was upside down.

It didn't make sense. How could she be upside down?

"Your head is injured," the Russian explained. "And you have lost much blood. I bandaged your wounds and stopped the bleeding—for now."

He followed her with his eyes, careful to not move his head from where it rested on... something soft wrapped around something hard.

She continued moving until she was right-side up.

It clicked.

She was standing over me, looking down.

He struggled to sit up.

"No," the woman said. "You are secured to the—"

She said a word in Russian he didn't understand.

"Cart," she said with a shrug. "Not right, but it does not matter. Rest for another moment, then you will climb down a ladder."

Yeah, that's not going to happen.

"We are in the tunnel. You fought many men. You remember?"

The woman's face and voice were familiar, but he didn't remember much. Just...

A mission.

"You're a friend?"

The woman moved around to stand over his head and stare down on him. She lifted whatever his head leaned against, and they were moving again.

"Yes, a friend. You will remember soon."

A chilling thought came to mind.

Am I her prisoner?

He tried to sit up but realized he was tied or otherwise attached to what the woman called a cart.

He relaxed, spent.

A tunnel. I'm in a tunnel.

"Los Angeles," the Russian said. "The coffee shop?"

I'm in Los Angeles?

That didn't seem right. He'd been there a month or two before, hadn't he?

It came to him then.

The old Russian woman—the operator. The assassin.

He instinctively reached for his pistol and came up empty. There wasn't even a holster.

"You remember," the Russian said. "Relax. I am your friend today. You spared me—twice. I will help you now."

After a few more minutes, they stopped.

"You are strong like bull, yes?" the woman asked. "American operator. You fight like a demon. Now you climb down the ladder. I cannot lower you again. Too heavy."

Again? How many times has she lowered me… and how long have I been out?

Axe's head felt horrible when the woman untied a cloth strip from around his waist and helped him sit up.

"A generator," Axe said, looking at what he'd been riding on. "Not a cart."

"Yes, yes. Generator, thank you. Now, climb down the ladder."

The woman pushed the generator unceremoniously over the edge of the short cliff they stood on. It fell to the floor of the cave below with a crash.

Axe felt his face, wincing as he reached his nose. "I think my nose is broken."

"Yes. You look like a Picasso painting."

Axe stared at her blankly, fighting to get his eyes to focus.

"Woman with the nose on wrong," she said. "Never mind. Go down the ladder. Time is short."

"What's the hurry?" he asked as he grasped the top of the ladder sticking up over the ledge. He held tight as he swayed again before managing to make his legs work enough to get them on the top rung.

"Maybe the cave and tunnels collapse. Some small rocks already while you nap."

"I wasn't napping," he said, annoyed. "I passed out, I think."

She waved her hand as he put his left leg on the next rung down, then matched his right leg to it.

The right leg wasn't working properly but he didn't know why.

"Fine. Hurry."

He pieced the day—or was it night?—together based on the fragments he found in his head.

I'm on a mission. I hit my head at some point and have a wicked concussion.

His gut told him this was bad not from only an operational standpoint but because he may have had concussions before.

I'm not operating well because of that. And I think I may have been shot, stabbed, or both.

Plus, his nose was definitely not facing the correct direction.

At the base of the ladder, Axe waited until the woman righted the generator, then lay back on it as he had been before. His head rested on a dirty kitchen towel wrapped around the handle used to push or pull it.

Ekaterina! That's her name.

Ekaterina picked up the end of the generator and pushed him forward. Pieces of it fell off as they moved, but the wheels functioned.

A chunk of ceiling crashed to the ground behind them at the base of the ladder, right where they had been standing.

Ekaterina sped up, grunting with the effort.

"You are better soon? You run?" she asked.

Smaller rocks dropped from the ceiling of the tunnel a few feet behind them.

"Maybe," Axe said, hoping his mind wasn't making promises his body couldn't deliver.

If it means getting out of here before we're buried in a pile of rubble, I can at least try.

Ekaterina stopped the generator, set down her end, and helped him stand. "You strong like bull, yes? We run now." Her tone didn't allow for the slightest dissent.

"Run like bull," Axe said.

He lumbered down the spiraling tunnel, stumbling into the left wall, bouncing off, hitting the right side, and back.

"No," Ekaterina called. "Strong like bull. Run like deer!"

Like a lame deer who's not going to make it through winter, maybe.

He did the best he could, given that his right leg wasn't working the way he expected it to.

They made better time than with him riding on the generator, though.

Rocks fell behind them. A few dropped in front.

But he kept going in what seemed like an endless spiral, praying they'd make it out alive.

173

THE EXCAVATION

The Rear Lobby
The Mountain Vista Desert Resort and Spa
Outside Saiq, Oman

James fought his way into the building, followed only by Stewart, Waylan, and—surprisingly—the interpreter.

They left the rest of the leaders and their entourages staring in shock at the mostly collapsed building—and the four Americans running into the rubble that was lit only by a few emergency lights.

"Here!" Waylan called, picking his way over debris, broken furniture, wood, and the remains of one of the many huge chandeliers that had hung in the rear lobby area leading to the back patio, the grassy area where they'd gathered for the reception, and the pool beyond.

Pained cries came from the far left corner.

This part of the building had only partially collapsed upon itself. Thick wooden beams that had been both decorative and structural lay broken like twigs. Others were splintered and cracked, bent upon themselves, but hadn't split completely.

Where is the ballroom, where the sultan would be?

James had glanced at a map of the resort on the plane to familiarize himself with the layout, but the darkness, dust, smoke, and collapsed walls made orienting himself difficult.

Waylan zigzagged his way over, around, and through the mess with James, Stewart, and the interpreter following.

A few of the hardier—or braver—leaders trailed slowly behind, searching for other survivors.

"Help me lift this," Waylan called. A man dressed in the white-on-white uniform of a server lay next to a partially intact wall. A dim emergency exit sign lit the scene of his legs trapped under wood and drywall.

"Over here," James yelled at the people he heard moving behind him. "We found someone."

The interpreter repeated the words, yelling in Arabic and Farsi, but no one came to their aid.

Waylan, Stewart, and the interpreter hefted a two-by-four. The entire top part of the wall shifted enough for James to latch onto the man's wrists, lean back, and drag him free.

A muffled sob came from further beneath the rubble.

"Lift it higher!" Waylan said as James continued to pull the injured man toward the door.

Two burly men dressed in tight suits appeared out of the darkness behind them.

The Russian bodyguards!

"Ask them to please help," James told the interpreter, who translated.

The two stepped in behind Stewart, Waylan, and the interpreter and grunted, pushing the remains of the wall higher.

"Have you got it?" James asked, rushing forward to grab another wounded server. He dragged him a few feet before hauling him onto his shoulder in a firefighter's carry.

"Yes. Get out of here and go back to the bungalow!" Waylan called.

James carried the man back toward the exterior of the building.

As he navigated his way around the debris, a cry of agony, frustration, and pain came from further to the west, where more of the building had collapsed.

"Help me, please!" the man's voice yelled in lightly accented English.

"I'm coming!" James called. Looking back through the dark haze at figures moving near the entrance, James yelled, "Someone—help this man here!"

He waved. Two figures waved back.

"We will help," they said.

James passed off the injured server to them and turned to race toward where the call had come from.

He struggled over a couch, broken and laying on its back, and stepped over one of the thick wooden beams that had formerly decorated—and supported—the ceiling.

"Here!" the trapped man's voice called again, sounding weaker than before.

"Hold on!" James yelled, using the sound to home in on the location. It came from a room off the rear lobby area.

He stepped through an open doorway into a damaged room. The dim glow from a distant emergency exit provided a bit of light in the space.

A broken wooden support beam lay diagonally across the office, precariously held up on one end by a filing cabinet.

The battery-powered emergency light in the rear lobby failed to reach the far side of the room.

"Where are you?" James called, peering into the darkness.

His combat instincts saved him.

Without conscious thought, James pulled his head back and right, diminishing the force of the blow.

Instead of knocking him out, the surprise punch merely made him stumble back into the wall, dazed.

Years of training kicked in.

James lunged forward. Staying still and waiting for the next blow would be devastating.

He collided with a body and kept pushing until they both slammed into the opposite wall.

In the dim light, James couldn't make out the man's features, but he had a sense of his build and could feel his clothes as they each struggled to get the upper hand.

It has to be Malik.

James ducked in time to protect his nose from a headbutt, but the force of the forehead-to-forehead impact caused both men to stagger.

James used the moment to hook his heel behind the other man's and take him to the ground.

They fought, trading blows.

James was better trained and stronger.

Malik—if that's who it was—fought with rage and intensity, snarling, cursing, and biting at James's neck and ears.

"Why?" James gasped as they crashed around the room, into the desk, knocking over a chair, and slamming into the metal filing cabinet.

The question had the effect James had hoped.

"Because you—" he started, giving James the opening he needed.

While in the Teams, James had trained and sparred daily, including when on deployment or in action. Hand-to-hand skills had to be kept sharp. You never knew when you'd need them.

The informal bouts included a heavy helping of trash-talking, taunting, and name-calling—anything to get under the skin of the opponent and get him off his game.

James had learned to talk while fighting.

Malik, apparently, hadn't. When he started speaking, he moved a fraction of a second slower than before.

James exploited the error, landing an elbow to the man's head, slowing him further.

A chokehold followed, with James's forearm and bicep cutting off the man's air supply.

In less than ten seconds, as the man flailed, bucked, and tossed, trying futilely to shake James from him, he was out.

After a few more seconds to be sure, James changed positions and snapped the man's neck.

The fight hadn't taken long, but there was no time to lose.

James untangled himself from the man, rolling him face down.

His eyes could see better in the dimness now, and a bright light out in the lobby cut more of the darkness.

Someone found a flashlight... and they're coming this way.

The office looked partly intact—aside from the destruction from the fight, along with the beam that had crashed through the ceiling and landed partly on the file cabinet.

There was nowhere to hide the body.

The bobbing of the flashlight came closer.

He had no time to spare, but James had to be sure. He dropped to his knee and turned the dead man's face toward him.

The approaching flashlight gave him just enough illumination to see the long dark beard streaked with gray; the narrow, weathered face; and the dark, lifeless eyes.

He looked like an older version of the face James had memorized—the younger brother.

Definitely Malik.

With no hope of preventing the discovery of the Afghan, James took the only option left.

He stood, pressed his shoulder against the thick wooden beam resting on top of the filing cabinet, and pushed.

It moved, rocking a half inch, but didn't fall.

The flashlight beam neared.

One more push.

James dug in, using every ounce of energy he had left, calling on the hours in the weight room beneath the White House.

The beam swayed again but refused to topple.

White light filled the room, catching James with his shoulder against the beam and the dead Afghan laying on the floor, perfectly positioned to have the beam fall and crush his body.

Busted. Please let it be Waylan or Stewart.

Both of them—and the translator—might keep their mouths shut.

James straightened, ready to deal with the ramifications of his actions.

The flashlight winked off, leaving James blinking in the sudden darkness.

The man moved next to James. "I help," he said in tentative, halting English.

President Nikitin.

James stood side by side with the Russian.

They both bent and put their shoulders against the beam.

"*Odin, dva, tri,*" Nikitin muttered.

Together, they pushed.

The beam moved farther than when James did it on his own yet still didn't topple.

"Again," James grunted. "One, two, three."

They grunted and heaved.

The beam moved, moved still more, and fell with a crash onto Malik's body as both men stepped back.

They stood in silence for several seconds before James turned to Nikitin in the dimness and spoke.

"The man who attacked my country," he said, not knowing the words in Russian and doubting the man would understand in English. "*Vrag?*" he said, pulling the word for enemy out of his memory from months before, when he had thrown himself into studying the language. He wasn't sure he had it right. If he did, he had probably mangled the pronunciation.

"*Khorosho,*" President Nikitin said, sounding like he understood.

"Mr. President? Mr. President?" Waylan's frantic voice called from outside.

"I'm fine!" he yelled. "In here—the office. We found someone!"

"Where, sir?" Waylan said again. A flashlight beam grew closer.

"Over here, Waylan."

Another frantic voice called in Russian. President Nikitin answered and turned on his flashlight.

Waylan burst into the room, flashlight in one hand, weapon in the other.

"Stand down. I'm fine. President Nikitin and I found this man, but he's dead. Are there any others alive?"

Waylan held the flashlight pointed at the ground. Malik's leg stuck out from under the heavy wooden beam.

One of President Nikitin's Russian bodyguards shoved past Waylan. Nikitin called him off, and he stood taking in the scene along with Waylan.

"Yes sir," Waylan said after a second. "We can hear faint cries."

"Thank God. What about the sultan?"

"People are working their way back there now. It doesn't look good, sir. It's in the area that is the most destroyed."

"Damn. Okay, let's help the best we can. And put that weapon away. The only danger in here is being crushed to death, right?"

Waylan didn't smile. "There's still..." He trailed off.

"Malik is no longer a concern," James said, catching the man's eye and holding it.

A long second passed. Waylan's eyes flicked away from James's, landed on the body under the beam, and flicked back. "Yes sir," he said, and holstered his sidearm.

"Mr. President," James said, gesturing to the Russian. "Let's save some people."

Nikitin nodded, getting the gist if not the words.

The bodyguards led as the four of them worked their way into the back lobby, listening for cries from the wounded.

174

GOOD TO GO

The Cave
Beneath the Mountain Vista Desert Resort and Spa

Axe ran—or did what passed for running in his injured state.

"Turn left," Ekaterina called from behind him.

He turned right, knowing at some level it wasn't correct but not putting it together in time to prevent himself from looking like a fool.

"Other right," she said, taking the lead.

They left a large cavern he thought he'd come through before but couldn't be sure.

She led the way, the lamp she carried showing the chamber narrowing. They were forced sideways, sliding along with both the front and back of their bodies touching the wall.

Warmer, dry desert air came from in front of them.

Behind, more rock crashed, sounding like a freight train hitting a wall.

A few minutes later, Ekaterina stopped. "There is a narrow trail below. Two, three meters down. On the other side, a big drop." She turned back to look at him. "Climb down. Don't miss the trail and go over the edge, okay?"

Axe nodded, though he wasn't sure he could promise that in his current state.

Both his right glute and lower leg dripped blood through the cloth bandages Ekaterina had tied in place.

His shirt was soaked in blood from above his pec, near his shoulder. The wound on his arm bled through the makeshift bandage Ekat had wrapped around it.

He blocked out the pain and focused on finishing the mission.

Ekaterina turned off the lamp. The night sky sparkled with stars, and the moon was rising, giving the desert valley a ghostly glow. When their eyes had adjusted to the starlit night, she went out of the narrow opening, smoothly climbing down the rock.

Axe had to rest for a minute. Finally, he mustered his strength and inched his way out of the opening, looking and feeling for handholds.

Move by move, Axe climbed down.

He might have faded out for a few minutes, his body desperately clinging to the cliff while his mind took a break.

It felt like ages later, but finally, he stood next to Ekaterina, who held her cell phone. She looked up at him, concerned. "Well done. Strong like bull, but you are bleeding again. Do not worry. Niko is coming to help."

Axe felt himself slipping away again. The pain didn't bother him so much, but he felt weak.

Lightheaded.

The blood loss.

Whatever strength he'd recovered as Ekaterina let him "nap" was gone.

I will never quit.

He'd rather die than give up.

"Alex, are you okay?" Ekaterina asked from a distance, worry in her voice. "A few more minutes, yes?"

He thought he saw Niko running along the trail in the starlight, but it might have been wishful thinking.

I don't need help. I'm fine.

Maybe lying to himself would give him the strength he needed.

"Good to go," he said and took a step.

He had time for one last thought.

That's strange.

Somehow, the ground was tilting upward.

An earthquake?

That wasn't right. The rock fall had stopped.

In an instant, it clicked.

Ah—I'm falling.

He got his hands out in front of him just in time to protect his face from more damage, then the darkness in his head matched the still, quiet night.

175

FEAR

Aboard *Mine, All Mine*
Lighthouse Bay Yacht Club
Southampton, New York

Haley monitored the situation from the main cabin of the large yacht, desperately searching for news.

Word had come from the Secret Service—the resort hosting the peace summit had collapsed. There had been no explosion, missile attack, or armed assault. One minute the main building stood. The next, it groaned and fell in on itself.

The president was safe but refused to leave. He was digging in the rubble, assisting the rescue efforts, searching for the sultan of Oman and staff trapped inside.

Aside from the building's inexplicable destruction, there seemed to be no danger.

The crushed body of Malik had been discovered a few minutes before.

Axe had not been heard from since his report about finding the tunnel.

Come on, Axe. Where are you?

As if on cue, her phone buzzed—the ID of Axe's burner phone for the mission appeared on her screen.

"Are you safe? What happened?"

There was a momentary pause.

Bad connection?

"This is the handler for Alex?" an older Russian woman asked.

Haley froze for a second.

What's happening?

"Go ahead," she said, keeping all emotion from her voice.

"Alex is badly injured. We will leave the bullets inside; we have no medical facilities. We slow the bleeding, not stop it. We take him to Muscat. A parking garage, perhaps. Transfer him to a CIA ambulance with a very good doctor. Two hours until we arrive. Okay for you? You can arrange?"

Haley locked down her emotions and resisted the temptation to freak out.

Axe is strong and a survivor.

But it could be a trap. Why and for what, she couldn't guess, but...

"Who is this?"

"A temporary friend. Alex and I..." She hesitated. "Met... in Los Angeles."

"You're the Russian grandmother?" Haley asked, surprised.

The woman chuckled, low and quiet. "Not grandmother, but yes. Old lady. He let me live. I help him now, then we are even."

"You helped with..."

"The Tower, yes. And the cave."

So that's what Axe meant when he mentioned plausible deniability.

Could she trust the enemy?

If Axe trusts her, I trust her. For now.

"Go toward Muscat," Haley said. "Call me in one hour—I will have an address."

"*Harasho,*" the woman said.

"And don't let him die," Haley added, not able to hide the desperation in her voice.

Haley heard a Russian man yell and curse in the background. "He is bleeding badly again. I will call in an hour if he is still alive. Goodbye."

The Russian woman's voice had changed from concerned but practical to...

She's afraid.

176

THE HOSPITAL

The Long Island Municipal Hospital
Massapequa, New York

After getting an update, Haley went to the hospital where Axe's girlfriend Connie worked.

Connie deserved to hear the news in person from a friend.

She and Axe had an interesting relationship, but it seemed to work well for them.

They wouldn't see each other for a month or two, then get together for a long weekend at Axe's cabin, Connie's Long Island house, or a beach getaway on the east coast.

They spoke and texted in between, but not while Axe was on a mission.

While they were definitely in love, they each enjoyed their own lives and liked having the space a long-distance relationship provided.

Connie had dated a SEAL before, so she understood the risks that came with Axe's job.

Still, nothing could prepare a person for what Haley had to say.

She flashed her fake Homeland Security badge in the hospital lobby, picked up a visitor pass, and was directed to the third floor, where Connie was at the end of a ten-hour shift.

Haley took the stairs, realizing she was only putting off the inevitable.

Reaching the third floor, she walked slowly down the wide hallway that smelled like every hospital she'd ever been in.

Haley knew Connie well, having taken a short vacation to Florida together with their men a while back.

But she didn't know how the normally rock-steady nurse would react to seeing her or hearing this news.

Ahead, Connie backed out of a room, making a note on a chart.

As she turned, their eyes met down the length of the hallway.

Connie's brows came together in confusion before her eyes widened. Her mouth dropped open in a silent scream.

"No!" Haley called, rushing forward. "No. He's alive!"

Haley hugged the older woman tightly and cried along with her.

"He's going to be okay," Haley said, trying to sound convincing.

"You wouldn't be here if he was okay," Connie said, choking back tears.

"He was hurt badly, but he's getting outstanding care."

"Where is he? I want to be with him."

"I can't—"

"Haley," Connie said, pulling away. "Where is he?"

"I don't know exactly. Far away."

"How is he—really?" Connie asked using a commanding nurse voice. "Don't lie to me. I can handle it."

"The last I heard…" Haley said, choking the words out. "It didn't look good at all."

PART 6

SUNDAY

177

THE ENVELOPES

The White House Residence
Washington, DC

James nodded at the two Secret Service agents outside the door of the Residence and stepped inside, leaving the vice president's briefcase, hat, and overcoat he'd borrowed by the door. It was late enough that the First Lady would be sound asleep.

Feels good to be home.

The VP sat in the living room reading. He stood as soon as James came in. "Welcome back, Mr. President," he said. The bags under his eyes were darker than usual.

The vice president still wore a suit, though not a tie. His white shirt had a few wrinkles—a testament to how long of a day it must have been for him. As always, his brown hair was perfect, though it was hard to mess up such a short haircut.

Ready for work—just in case.

"Thank you, Robert. How was your time?"

"Quiet. I stayed here and read briefing papers. Oh, and prayed you didn't die or invoke the Twenty-Fifth Amendment, leaving me to clean up after your mess—whatever it was. More importantly, what happened over there? What did I miss?"

Where do I start?

"The resort building collapsed, as you've heard. They're calling it seismic activity."

"An earthquake?"

James nodded.

The VP must have seen something in his look. "It wasn't?" he asked.

"As far as anyone knows, that's exactly what it was."

"But we have other data?" the VP asked, not taking the hint to let it go.

James smiled pleasantly and changed the subject. "We rescued the sultan of Oman ourselves before help arrived. The attendees—those well-dressed men, leaders of their countries—joined together to search for the injured... and dead. The sultan was storming his way out of the ballroom when the building collapsed, coming to learn why his precious schedule had been thrown off, ruining his carefully planned evening. That saved his life. The main ballroom where the dinner was going to be held was totaled."

"What threw off the schedule and kept everyone out of the...? Oh." The vice president's eyes widened. "You?"

James shrugged. "At the last minute, I decided to invite President Nikitin onto the outdoor stage to have a showdown. It took just enough time to keep everyone from going into the building before it collapsed."

Robert eyed James skeptically. "Lucky break."

James nodded. "Yep. Very."

That's all I'm going to say about that tonight. Maybe ever, depending on what Gregory Addison and I decide to write up.

The world didn't always need to know every little detail. Being perceived as lucky had its advantages.

A knock came from the door to the hallway. A second later, Chad David stepped in. "Mr. President. Mr. Vice President. Am I interrupting?"

"No," James said, "please come in. The VP was just heading out."

"Yes," Robert said, taking the hint. "Thank you for letting me step into your shoes for a few days. And," he said, removing two white envelopes labeled "A" and "B" from his suit coat pocket and handing them to James, "I imagine you want these back."

James accepted them without comment and shook the VP's hand. "Well done, Robert. And thank you."

The VP left, picking up his items, which James had left by the door.

Chad approached and sat in the offered leather chair across from the couch. "Good times?" he asked, using the SEAL expression that meant the times had been difficult or interesting, not necessarily good.

"Good times," James said, his voice quiet and serious. The two had been through hell and back together. Chad knew him well.

He can tell that I killed someone.

Thankfully, Chad was too polite to ask—and knew that the time wasn't right to hear the story.

"Everyone pitched in to search for survivors," James said. "Maybe the shared experience will unite them where talking and endless negotiations couldn't."

"Here's hoping," Chad said.

James had gotten updates—and the news about Axe—on the long flight back, but he hadn't been able to ask the one question he wanted to know. "How's Haley holding up?"

Chad's eyes stared off into the distance. "I spoke briefly to Gregory Addison on your behalf a few minutes ago. He said she's doing about as well as can be expected."

"And Axe's girlfriend?"

"Connie. The same."

"Anything I can do?"

"Not at this time, Mr. President," Chad said, switching from old war buddy to Chief of Staff as the moment demanded.

They shared a few quiet seconds. They'd both been in Haley's shoes.

Chad stood. "See you in a few hours, Mr. President."

"Wait a second." James opened both the A and B envelopes, removing a blank sheet of paper from each before handing the envelopes to Chad. "You can take these?"

"Yes, sir."

"And the others?"

Chad opened the left side of his suit coat to reveal two identical envelopes poking out of the top of the inner pocket. "The real letters were never out of my sight. I'll take care of them at home. It's still chilly—a good night for a fire. These will get the kindling started."

"Smart idea," James said. "Think Robert suspected that we didn't fully trust him?"

"No, sir."

"You don't think he looked? Held the envelopes up to the light?"

"I think Mrs. Heringten kept pretty close tabs on him."

"I suspect you're right."

"Still, I'm glad you did it that way, Mr. President. You can't be too careful."

"No," James said, recalling the treachery of his last vice president, who had sold his soul to a terrorist in exchange for a shot at being president. "You can't be too careful."

178

THE SUSPECT

Aboard *Mine, All Mine*
Lighthouse Bay Yacht Club
Southampton, New York

Aside from a few very short naps, Gregory had been up for longer than he could remember.

It didn't matter. For once, he felt okay. The expensive yacht—not nearly as large as Kelton's superyacht from when he was a billionaire, but still fancy—had excellent coffee, and plenty of it.

He'd ordered all the blackout curtains on the yacht closed tight. Using the boat as an off-the-books safehouse for an operation only he and the president knew about had been a risk, but it was one they'd been willing to take.

He only knew it was mid-morning on Saturday by his watch and the stubble on his cheeks and chin from not shaving another day.

"Can you make him more sinister looking?" he asked Haley.

In the yacht's large main cabin off the galley, Haley clicked on the laptop's trackpad, manipulating the software they'd discovered on all the Russian hacker's devices. On the screen, the AI-generated face looked meaner. The man's eyebrows became heavier and arched more. Another few clicks made his eyes darker and smaller.

"Perfect," Gregory told her.

Haley had been subdued since hearing about Axe on Friday night. He gave her all the room he could, but she was needed. As Axe had taught them, emotions had to wait until the crisis was over.

Haley sat at one of seven high-end laptops, made in the USA, which were arranged side by side on the large table. The eighth—containing deepfake videos, including the one of a young James Heringten supposedly shooting a prisoner, along with the original, undoctored version—was locked in the yacht's safe.

Kaylin, a member of the Central Analysis Group's IT department, looked up from one of the other computers. "Sir? If you could approve these, I can prep them for release," she said.

He looked over the database of responses prepared to change the narrative away from Russia and toward the "real" culprit, reading each one carefully. Kaylin had done an excellent job matching the fictitious "voices" for the social media accounts made up by the Russian hackers. She'd nailed the misspellings and poor syntax of a few and kept several of the posts already on the laptop for reuse.

- *i new it!!!!! It never made cents it was the russians! #RussiaDidntDoIt*
- *We're not gonna die! Party time! #RussiaDIDNTDoIt*
- *I better not catch my kid doing crap like that online! Hear me, @JoelHfromOhio? #LoneWolf*
- *I told you all. #Scam. It was a false-flag operation. #RussiaDidntDoIt #FalseFlag #TrustNoOne*
- *My brothers highschool buddy was on that op. Totally legit. #GoSpecialForces!!! #LoneWolf*
- *Thank God #NoWar #RussiaDidntDoIt*
- *Don't fall for it. The current administration attacked us to keep us in line. #HeringtenMustResign #Anarchy!!!*
- *Typical liberal BS! #RussiaDidntDoIt #LoneWolf*
- *Typical conservative BS! #RussiaDidntDoIt #LoneWolf*
- *Better parenting is what the world needs! #LoneWolf*
- *#TrustNoOne #DontBelieveTheirLies*
- *What is this all about? I've been hiking and come home to this?!?*

The list when on and on, with at least a hundred similar comments ready to let loose using the hacker's fake accounts, though he drew the line at utilizing the bots to take control of real Americans' social media posts.

"Well done," Gregory told her. She smiled, exhausted but happy, and brushed her dark hair out of her eyes before returning to the list.

He worried Kaylin was getting too close to Dawson "Void" Reite, currently locked into one of the yacht's cabins, but that was a tomorrow problem, not something to deal with on little sleep and a lot of caffeine.

"Atom," the surviving Russian hacker, was locked in one of the other cabins with a Navy SEAL from Axe's old Team. The kid had been helpful, taking them through the hacks that had devastated the United States.

Haley and Kaylin had needed less than two hours to reverse the hacks from the week before, once Atom had shown them how. The rest of the time had been spent prepping for the disinformation campaign.

Fighting fire with fire.

The world didn't need another war, and America certainly didn't want to take on Russia over what was actually not their fault this time.

"Are we ready?" he asked Kaylin and Haley.

Both nodded.

"Okay, start it up. Just like they did it."

The fake blogs would go first. According to Atom, the hackers had created a fake centrist blogger and built up his following.

"Releasing the breaking news," Kaylin said. She uploaded the first report.

Breaking—As Yet Unconfirmed

I have an insider in the FBI. They tipped me off that the hacker responsible for the cyberattacks on the country has been identified. More to come once I get confirmation from other sources. But—get this —according to my source, the suspect is NOT Russian but a "lone wolf" American living in a foreign country (Mexico???). More as I get it.

Gregory sent a secure message on his cell phone. A buddy at the FBI would reach out to a respected journalist and "confirm" the breaking news as an anonymous source.

Haley sent a text to Captain Hernandez, her contact in Mexico's national police department. He would spread the word to reporters in Mexico about an operation he'd been on early this morning—all very hush-hush—about an American hacker and the small house that had blown up as they raided it.

An hour later, rumors were swirling.

"Start releasing the posts on the fake accounts, little by little," Gregory said.

He sent three more texts to government contacts who would "confirm" on deep background that America had identified the hacker responsible for the attacks hiding in Mexico—and that he'd killed himself with an improvised explosive device instead of being taken alive.

Kaylin and Haley pressed a few buttons on the computers.

"Done," Kaylin said.

"That was easy," Gregory muttered.

"The hackers worked for a year," Kaylin pointed out. "We just took advantage of it."

"And, luckily for us, a lot of people will believe anything they see on the internet," Haley added.

Gregory stood and stretched. "You two handle the updates. Push the narrative. I have to get back to the White House for a briefing," Gregory said. "The president will be making an Oval Office speech about this tonight."

179

THE DEBRIEF

The White House Situation Room
Washington, DC

Aside from the morning workouts with the president, Gregory didn't spend much time at the White House. He preferred it that way. It kept him away from office politics and powerplays, making it easy to lead his team and advise the president.

Today was different, however. This afternoon, his presence was essential, given all that had happened in the past week. He stood at the far end of the long conference table in front of the television monitor. The Situation Room was far emptier than usual. Only a few advisors were present—the bare minimum. The National Security advisor, the NCTC and CISA directors, and the directors of the CIA and FBI waited without pens or paper for Gregory to begin. No aides were present. Nothing would be officially recorded.

"Go ahead, Mr. Addison," the president said from his seat at the head of the table.

"Thank you, Mr. President," he began. "In conjunction with the FBI, CIA, Cybersecurity and Infrastructure Security Agency, and others, we have put the pieces together of the events of last week."

In truth, no one had helped his team at all, but it paid to play nice.

"The hackers were found and resisted apprehension, and all but one were shot and killed while attacking an asset," Gregory said, dropping the bomb—the first of many.

He caught the group unaware. There were shocked expressions and at least one gasp of surprise.

"Dubai?" the CIA director asked, looking the least shocked.

Gregory nodded.

A few of the advisors shifted in their seats, preparing to ask questions, but the president raised his hand in a calming gesture. "Let him continue," he said. "But to answer your first question, I personally told him to keep the details confined to his team until now. They were handling things well. The situation was fluid, and I didn't need him getting bogged down writing reports or attending meetings."

The men and women in the room hid it well, but the undercurrent of dissatisfaction came through anyway. A few glanced at Gregory, eyes narrowed.

I made some enemies here today. No one—especially in this group— wants to be scooped, feel out of the loop... or look bad.

Gregory waited until the president gave him the go-ahead nod to resume.

"Thanks to the CIA and their assistance with the extraction," Gregory continued, "the surviving hacker was flown from Dubai to a safe house in the United States, where he assisted my team in reversing the hacks."

"And the social media rumors we're seeing?" the CISA director blurted out, followed by an apologetic look to the president.

"Yes, that's us, at the direction of the president," Gregory answered.

"To address one of several elephants in the room," President Heringten said, "the hackers were, in fact, Russian. However, according to questioning prior to the hackers attacking the asset who tried to apprehend them, they are not affiliated in any way with the Russian government."

"Yes," Gregory jumped in. "They deserted their posts in Red Bear, the hacking collective clandestinely funded and run by the Russian government, though technically an independent criminal enterprise. The remaining hacker confirms this, as does data on the hackers' laptops, which were also collected—and put to use to release the stranglehold on so many of our computer systems in the country."

"The hackers were recruited by one of their own at Red Bear," Gregory said, "a little more than a year ago. They were offered money, of course. More importantly, they were told they could take the gloves off. Russia continually held them back. If they joined this new group, their efforts would no longer be largely theoretical. They would get to actually exploit our weaknesses and enact their best hacks—and see the results. The one who recruited them all was enticed by—"

"Let me stop you there, Mr. Addison," the president said. He turned his attention to the people around the table. "Needless to say, nothing in this room goes any further than this. No notes, no discussions with aides. Take the highest Top Secret classification and add a level, because that's where this is. What comes next, though, is beyond even that. One word of this, and I'll personally see to the complete destruction of whoever leaks it. Clear?"

There were nods from around the table as everyone said, "Yes, Mr. President."

"Gregory?"

"Thank you, sir," Gregory said. "At this point, based on questioning and on-the-ground assessment, we believe there were two people behind this entire operation." He stopped and jumped ahead in his report based on the looks on the faces of a few of the advisors. "Both are dead. We believe it was two brothers."

Gregory worked a laptop in front of him on the table, and a picture from Axe's phone popped up on the screen behind him. "This is 'George,' according to the hackers. His real name was Gogol, from a village in eastern Afghanistan near the border with Pakistan. He interacted directly with the hacker leader and provided all instruction and direction."

The man's pained expression, glassy eyes, and hands clenched to a bloody wound to his neck meant no one had to ask his fate.

"This is his brother," Gregory said as the screen switched to another picture. "Abdul Khan Dagari. Also known as the Malik—or just Malik—which is an honorific for an elder or respected leader, like Osama bin Laden was known as 'the Sheikh.'"

The picture showed a battered Abdul covered in dust, his skull partly smashed in.

"His body was pulled from the wreckage of the peace summit resort in Oman," Gregory said. "He was part of the official delegation as a very well-connected Afghan businessman, though he was based in Dubai—in the same building as the hackers. We believe this man was the mastermind of the operation."

"What was he doing at the summit?" the National Security advisor asked. "Could he have caused the destruction of the hotel?"

"Yes," Gregory said. "We assume he somehow triggered what happened at the resort, but again, we have no proof of this."

With a click on the computer, the screen went dark.

"Additionally, we no longer believe Russia had a hand in Secretary of State Wilson's death," Gregory said. "Though we're still working out how the polonium-210 was obtained and administered, we believe Abdul Khan Dagari and his brother were responsible for this, as well."

"In summary," Gregory said, "our data so far suggest Abdul Khan Dagari planned the operation as revenge for Russia's invasion of Afghanistan during the eighties and the United States' efforts there against al-Qaeda at first and the Taliban in later years. The first part of the plan called for America and Russia to go to war. Presumably, the Middle East would rise in power as the two superpowers spent their time and treasure destroying each other. Using bots controlling fake social media accounts, they would have spread more and more lies, pushing Russia and America to war if we hadn't gotten there ourselves."

"We came this close to retaliating," President Heringten said. "They would have responded because they were, in fact, innocent." The president looked around the room, making eye contact with each advisor one by one. "If any of you have a problem with the Central Analysis Group and Mr. Addison taking point on this and keeping things close to the vest—on my orders—keep this in mind. At the crucial moment, his team was right." After a moment to let it sink in, he nodded to Gregory to continue.

"On the laptops recovered from the hackers, there are fabricated records that would've been delivered to investigative reporters around the world. They would have 'proven' that Russia was behind the cyberattacks on America. Other documents would show that America had used cyberattacks to destroy infrastructure in Russia—which the hackers would have done themselves if the president hadn't already authorized the retaliation. Our two countries would have been pressured into an escalating conflict based on lies."

"And the second part of the plan?" the National Security advisor asked.

Gregory exchanged a look with the president.

We're getting into dangerous territory now.

President Heringten frowned, then gave him a reluctant nod.

Okay, here we go.

180

THE TRUTH

"The second part of the plan," Gregory said, "is in many ways more alarming."

He was greeted with raised eyebrows and looks of disbelief from the assembled advisors.

Gregory clicked on the laptop. The screen behind him filled with eight frames showing screenshots from videos ranging from grainy to 4K.

"These are videos the hacker leader—'Wolf'—had on his laptop hard drive, ready to share when the time was right. The president has classified them as 'need to know.' They will not be shown here."

There were murmurs around the table.

"You can take it up with me if you have a problem with that," President Heringten said.

That silenced the noise.

"The president and I have watched them, along with the Attorney General," Gregory said. "A very small team of forensic computer experts from the Department of Justice has confirmed that none of the videos are authentic. They are what is known as 'deepfakes.'"

Another click brought up a video showing "Atom," the hacker who was brought to America from Dubai, sitting in a small room. A sheet had been hung behind him to disguise his location.

"What about the videos on Wolf's laptop?" a voice—Gregory—asked from offscreen. "What was the plan?"

"When the one with the American president was released, he would resign or be forced from office," Atom said. He looked down in shame. "I didn't know the details, but I understood the American vice president would be dead."

Gregory paused the playback.

"As you're aware," he said, "the vice president had planned on attending the peace summit. This leads us to believe the destruction of the resort hotel in Oman was not caused by an earthquake, though we have not yet ascertained how the building was destroyed or who may have done it. We will keep investigating."

The video played again.

"With Heringten gone and the vice president dead, the Speaker of the House would be in charge," Atom continued. "He would be approached, told about the videos we had made of him, along with others we would pretend to have. He would be encouraged to escalate the war with Russia even more."

"With the president pro tempore—the next in the order of presidential succession—being a member of the opposite party than the Speaker of the House," Gregory filled in, "we inferred that the Speaker would be reluctant to resign or bring to light the blackmail over the deepfake videos. He would likely have ended up in the pocket of the hackers."

He left unsaid what many people in the room surely thought—the Speaker wouldn't have had the guts to do what was right. He would have never voluntarily given up control, no matter what it meant for the country.

"It appears this was a well-planned and executed operation to harm America—and Russia," the president concluded. "One that partially succeeded."

That about covers the basics. Now the fun begins.

Gregory looked around the room. The gathered men and women didn't seem completely satisfied with the report.

They're smart enough to wonder if someone else was involved—that Malik and his younger brother might not have done this all on their own.

"I, for one, have questions," Samuels, the NCTC director and one of the president's favorites, said.

"I'm sure you all do," the president said, holding up his fingers and counting off. "How did Malik get polonium-210? Was there anyone else involved? What was the plan for after starting a war between America and Russia? And what would have happened had the attack on the Middle East Peace Summit succeeded?"

"And what happened over there?" Samuels asked the president point-blank. "Why did you go instead of the vice president, and why the secrecy, Mr. President?" Samuels realized he may have gone too far and held his hands up in apology. "Sorry, sir."

"No, I understand," the president said. "There are many unanswered questions. We have a lot of work to do. We need to keep digging and get the answers, which is why you're being briefed on this. We'll strategize about how to loop in select members of your staff without discussing certain items you've heard today. But we're going to present a united front to the public. A lone wolf hacker hiding out in Mexico was officially responsible for the attacks. As my trusted advisors, however, you needed to know the truth—or as much as we have of it. And to answer your question, I went to Oman because…" The president paused and shrugged. "Honestly, I had a hunch. My gut, which served me so well in combat, told me to go—and to play it the way I did."

The admission appeased Samuels.

The president dropped it.

Gregory said nothing and kept his face blank.

The president isn't going to take the credit for saving everyone at the summit.

Rumors had started about the president's "lucky" decision to confront the Russian president onstage, delaying the attendees' entrance to the building and saving everyone's lives.

He's also not giving me and my team credit—which I'm happy to live with.

Gregory didn't need more accolades—or to have to explain how he had an asset in the area and what Axe had found.

"Unfortunately, with the other questions, this is all we have at the moment," Gregory said.

One hundred percent true, unfortunately.

The men and women at the table considered the information presented to them.

"Now," the president said, "Many Americans want retaliation against Russia based on inaccurate information."

"Hence the social media and news campaign my team started early this morning," Gregory said.

"Exactly," the president said. "I'll do a presidential address from the Oval Office tonight. Mr. Addison and I already discussed what to present, but I need your input. The public doesn't need to know the whole truth. It would complicate our relationship with Russia to hear that the hacker was a Russian citizen but not working for Russia. And if the two Afghan brothers were implicated, it would open another huge can of worms."

Not the least being who killed the younger brother, his guards, and seven hackers in Dubai, which would certainly create an international incident.

And how the older brother managed to get invited to the peace summit —as well as who else might have been involved in an attempted assassination of the leaders there.

For the first time this afternoon, everyone around the table agreed wholeheartedly. Conspiracy theories would form and multiply as it was, but at least they'd be way offtrack from the truth.

For ninety minutes, they debated, asked questions, and planned.

President Heringten, with Gregory's assistance, subtly guided them to the conclusions and story the two of them had already formulated and put into action.

The question of the cyberattacks would be "solved."

The frozen and broken systems were already being repaired.

The hacker—one disgruntled American lone wolf—was dead.

And the whole thing would be swept under the rug without anyone realizing it.

Whatever is best for the country, whether the average American knows the truth or not.

181

THE COVER-UP

The White House Oval Office
Washington, DC

The Oval Office held only the necessary people for the live television broadcast, but it still felt crowded. Between the person behind the camera, the producer, aides, a makeup person, and Chad David standing nearby to assist with any last-minute items, James had a lot to tune out.

"Good evening, my fellow Americans," James began for the second time in two weeks, staring straight into the large television camera directly in front of his desk.

The teleprompter ran, though he didn't need it tonight. He'd written the short speech himself.

"We continue to grieve our lost loved ones from the attack last week. We wonder how safe our country is when someone can reach out via computers and cause us harm without warning.

"And fire burns in our hearts as we demand those responsible pay the price.

"Finally, I can provide an update. Despite last week's claims on social media that various countries—especially Russia—were behind the devastating cyberattacks and the poisoning of Secretary of State Wilson, both were incorrect."

He paused, then started to lie.

"Our intelligence agencies, working with those of other countries, discovered a trail last week and followed it to a suspect in the cyberattacks," he said, telling some of the truth.

Only the Central Analysis Group had discovered a trail.

"Thanks to the quick action of them and our allies, which I cannot name due to security concerns, they tracked down the suspect. Our allied country, in conjunction with authorities from the United States, raided the home of this individual before dawn this morning," James said, repeating the story he, Gregory, and Haley had made up and his top advisors had agreed would be presented to the world as fact.

"However, instead of allowing himself to be captured, the suspect detonated an improvised explosive device. He was killed, though thankfully no police were injured."

James stared at the camera, giving the people watching a moment to digest this information which, thanks to Gregory and his team, many people already knew from social media and carefully leaked reports.

"The suspect was an American from an isolated area of Northern Arizona, not a Russian," James said, continuing with the legend made up about the fictitious man. "We are still working to understand what caused him to commit these acts, and we are confident we will get to the bottom of it.

James paused again as he shifted gears.

"Additionally, it has been confirmed that Secretary of State Wilson died of a heart attack brought on by tirelessly working to advance American interests around the world. No foul play is suspected," he said, lying his ass off.

"And finally, our intelligence agencies have been working day and night to reverse the hacks that caused so much death and destruction. They have been one hundred percent successful. Now, of course, this is after the fact, after we've been attacked. But we will use this information to strengthen our defenses, so this never happens to our country again."

James took a long pause as he brought the short speech to a close.

"Last week, I promised you vengeance. This week, thanks to the diligent efforts of the men and women in our law enforcement and intelligence divisions, I can confidently tell you that, while our investigation is ongoing and all suspects are innocent until proven guilty, in my heart of hearts, I know that we have gotten our vengeance," he said, voice low, quiet, and dangerous as he finally told the truth.

"No one attacks our country and gets away with it."

PART 7

MONDAY

182

ALL THE WAY

Gregory finished his bench press reps and sat up, proud of the progress he'd made. Several months before, he'd practically quaked at the thought of working out with the president. Now he looked forward to lifting weights a few days a week with his boss.

Even if it also involved important informal briefings and hard-hitting questions, like the ones he was getting this morning.

President Heringten—never James, not even in the gym—handed him a towel.

"How was it that my niece stayed in America, surrounded by a team of people, yet still managed to get shot at and add to her already impressive EKIA body count?"

Gregory wiped his face. "She's Haley, Mr. President."

The president tilted his head and gave him a look.

He's getting used to the idea Haley can handle herself—and is a magnet for armed confrontation.

"I didn't want to ask formally," the president said, changing gears. "Especially not in the Situation room yesterday. Just between us, though, off the record, it seems clear more people were behind the attacks besides Malik and his brother."

Gregory nodded. "That's my best guess. Malik seems to have been the mastermind of the cyberattacks and deepfakes, but he likely could not have done it all on his own. And he certainly wasn't the financier or the one who procured the polonium-210."

"There's another person—or people—involved?"

"Yes, sir. A man—or people—behind the curtain, pulling the levers, so to speak. Supplying the money."

"Who?"

"I'm not sure yet, sir, though I'll keep digging."

The president noted his wording.

"Yes, sir," Gregory said. "Later today, with your permission, I'm planning on pulling Haley and the rest of the team off the investigation. There are plenty of other threats out there for them to be on the lookout for, I'm sure. I will take over this analysis."

"Why?"

"We don't know who the person is or where the path will lead, Mr. President. Someone with this level of pull, the amount of money to fund an operation of this size and scope, and the intelligence to nearly pull it off, is likely to be virtually untouchable. Or, if it's a nation-state like Iran, China, or North Korea, it could be a dicey political situation."

The president was silent for several moments. "A situation like that might call for restraint, which is not my niece's strong suit."

Gregory kept his mouth shut.

"Fine. You handle it directly. To appease Haley, feel free to blame it on me. Tell her this," he said, offering a classic quote Gregory recognized.

"Yes, Mr. President. Thank you."

"If the CIA or other agencies figure this out, fine, but my money is on you getting to the bottom of it first," the president said. "When you do, tell me who it is before taking any action." He hesitated. "Between you and me, I owe a favor to the Russian president."

Gregory hid his surprise.

What an interesting thing to admit.

"Yes, sir. However, if it looks like the analysis is going in a direction you won't like? How far do you want me to go?"

President Heringten thought for a second, then spoke, his voice low and dangerous. "We take it all the way, no matter who it is. But we keep it between us and figure out how to handle it together. No one comes after the United States of America—and the world—like they did." There was no doubt he meant it. "Agreed?"

Gregory nodded. He felt the same. "Yes, sir. All the way."

PART 8

TUESDAY

183

THE CABIN

Axe's Cabin
Rural Virginia

Haley used the spare key Axe had given her to unlock the door to his cabin. "In case of emergency," he'd said months before, after a mission, as he'd pressed it into her hand and told her the code to the security system.

She hadn't wanted to take it, knowing what he really meant by giving it to her.

There would only be one reason she would need to come to the cabin without him there.

And here she was.

The place had Axe's smell tinged with a staleness that felt sad—like the cabin had been left behind, forgotten and abandoned.

Haley went around flipping on the lights, banishing the darkness in the rooms but not in herself.

She cracked a window open for a few minutes to get fresh air inside, though the night was cold.

She took a few minutes to get a fire started in the fireplace. It made the cabin feel more alive and helped her spirits, too.

Now it's like when we gathered around after missions to eat and tell stories.

It took a few trips to unload the items from her car, but when she was done, the cabin smelled better, and the fire had a comforting warmth.

After shutting the window, she sat down on the couch and wrapped herself in the old wool blanket draped across the back.

When was the last time I slept?

She couldn't remember. Every time she tried, she ended up staring at the ceiling, wondering if there was anything she could have done differently.

If I'd been with him… Or hadn't sent him there at all…

She lay down, trying not to think about what might have been.

Curled into the fetal position, surrounded by the smell of Axe and the memories of the good times the team had shared in this room, she drifted off to sleep.

184

THE TRUCK

Axe's Cabin
Rural Virginia

Hours later, Haley jolted awake.

The fire had burned down to dull embers.

She heard again the sound that had woken her—tires on the gravel driveway.

Throwing off the blanket, she rushed to the door and stepped outside, flipping on the external floodlights.

Axe's truck pulled to a stop.

Connie sat in the driver's seat.

Haley rushed down the stairs, scooted around the truck, and carefully opened the passenger door. "Hey," she said, staring.

"Hey," Axe said. He sounded strained and exhausted, but he chuckled, shook his head, and winced. "Don't look at me like that. I'm not dead yet."

She choked back a sob.

Seeing him slumped in the truck, obviously in extreme pain, was a memory she'd never shake.

"You look like hell," she blurted out. His head was wrapped in gauze, along with his arm. He had two black eyes, a bandage covering his nose, and multiple lacerations on his face, including a band of stitches across his forehead.

His shoulders were hunched, and his energy was flatter than she'd ever seen it.

"Don't worry, I feel worse than I look," he said, trying to be funny. He turned serious. "Did someone get my camera gear from the hotel in Dubai?"

"Yes, don't worry. It's in the cabin," Haley said, seeing Axe relax at the news.

"Help me get him inside," Connie said as she came around the truck.

"Shouldn't he be in a hospital?" Haley whispered to her.

"None of the injuries are life-threatening, and he wanted to be home," Connie said.

"You know I'm right here," Axe groaned as he worked his body out of the truck. "Whisper all you want, but there's nothing wrong with my hearing."

Axe helped as much as he could, but the women ended up having to half-carry him up the steps and into the living room. He stifled a moan as they steered him toward the bedroom. "No," he said. "Dump me in the chair."

There was no arguing with the pain in his voice.

"You need a pill," Connie said in a tone that was clear they'd had the discussion several times already.

"I hate those things. I just need to rest," Axe said. It didn't come out as angry or grumpy—just a statement of fact. "Grab my pillow from the bedroom, please?" he asked Connie.

She nodded and hurried down the hall.

As soon as she was gone, Axe fixed Haley with a fierce gaze. "I didn't stop it, did I? The resort collapsed?"

Haley nodded.

He thinks he failed.

"Yes, but you helped save everyone. You found the tunnel and reported in. Because of that, the leaders of the Middle East, along with Uncle Jimmy, the Russian president, and the Chinese premier, are alive. And we know it wasn't caused by some bullshit earthquake like they're saying."

Axe shook his head, grunted in pain, and closed his eyes with a frown.

Haley got in his face.

"Open your eyes and look at me."

Axe did, recoiling at her nearness.

"You said your hearing is fine. Listen up. You didn't fail," she whispered. "You succeeded. Do you hear me?"

After a second, he answered. "I hear you."

This time, it sounded like he believed her.

Haley heard Connie come down the hall, stop, and turn around. A few seconds later, the faint sound of water in the bathroom sink came through the walls.

Thank you for giving us a minute, Connie.

Haley collapsed onto the couch. "If I had been there—"

"We both would look like this," Axe finished.

He closed his eyes again. "The doctors say I don't have too many more concussions left in me."

The statement hung in the air.

Axe opened his eyes to meet hers. "All this will heal," he said, waving his hand vaguely at his face and the rest of his body. He pointed at his head. "This is the concern."

Haley searched for the right words.

Does he need me to listen? To be there for him?

Or was it a time to offer a swift kick in the pants?

There would be more talking later. She hadn't debriefed him yet, and the team was due to come over when Axe felt ready. For now, though, she thought she had an answer.

"These are tough times," she said. "You're in a lot of pain and, because of the concussion, your head isn't on straight. But 'In the worst of conditions,'" she started, quoting the SEAL ethos she had memorized and that Axe lived every day, even since he'd officially retired from the Teams.

He worried her for a second when he didn't immediately get the reference, but then recognition kicked in.

"'…the legacy of my teammates steadies my resolve and silently guides my every deed,'" he quoted, the strength in his voice growing with every word. "I will not fail."

He smiled, tilted his head back, and closed his eyes. He looked like he was finally at peace.

Connie moved into the room with quiet steps and gently tilted his head enough to put the pillow behind him.

She sat on the couch next to Haley and took her hand as they watched Axe slip into sleep.

"I know it looks bad," Connie whispered, "and he's not quite himself because of the head injury. But he's going to be fine, I promise. He could have stayed at the hospital, but what he needs more than anything else is you and the rest of the team. You're the ones who can help him heal and get back to normal."

Haley nodded once. The tears were long gone. In their place, she had found a deep resolve.

She repeated Axe's words under her breath. "I will not fail."

PART 9

THURSDAY

185

FAVORS

Haley collapsed into one of the cheap guest chairs in Gregory's temporary office and got right to it. "I need a favor."

"A favor," Gregory said, like he wasn't surprised at all.

"A few, actually."

"Generally, the government doesn't provide favors for people who do their duty."

Haley shrugged him off. "Mr. Tucci's helicopter got shot down saving us."

Gregory frowned. "Doesn't he have insurance?"

"Interestingly enough, his insurance policy doesn't cover deliberately flying into a combat zone."

She could tell Gregory wanted to argue that landing near an American federal prison in Maryland wasn't a combat zone, but after a few seconds of trying to stare her down, he nodded. "One helicopter."

Haley handed him a spec sheet and—helpfully, she thought—a page listing five options her research had showed were similar to Tucci's destroyed chopper.

"Next?" Gregory asked, glancing at the paper and frowning at the prices.

Haley looked at her notes to buy a second.

Now it gets trickier.

"Void," she said, diving in. "Without him, we wouldn't have found the Tower. We would still be lost, and the entire delegation at the peace summit would be dead."

"He's still a convicted hacker. A felon." Gregory's voice had a hard edge to it.

"He was quite helpful."

They stared at each other for several seconds, locked in silent battle.

"What do you propose?" Gregory eventually asked, breaking first. His eyes narrowed with suspicion.

He knows I already have it worked out.

"Time served."

"He served less than a day before you broke him out!"

She had used a classic sales technique. Suggest an extremely costly item first. When later presented with the overpriced real recommendation, it would seem reasonable in comparison.

"Technically," she pointed out, "it was a total of a year before and during the trial, then more time in my custody. He's still on the yacht, guarded by Tex—Mariana."

"Not happening, Haley. What else do you have?"

She hid her smile behind a fake frustrated frown, hoping Gregory couldn't read her true feelings.

"A suspended sentence, but—" she held up her hand to stop him before he could protest. "Two years of supervised probation. And community service."

Gregory scoffed. "First, who would be qualified to supervise a hacker like that, keeping him out of trouble? And what type of community service would he do? Picking up trash along the highway? Or worse—teaching grade school kids how to hack secure corporate systems?"

Haley waited, knowing he'd get there.

"The Movement in St. John with Bec and Cody? No—we're not putting them in charge of Void. Together, they'd take over the world."

Haley let her body slump, acting like she'd been outplayed. "You're right." She bit her lip, pretending to mull over the problem. "What about Kelton Kellison? He's amazing with computers, and his business is up and running again."

Gregory frowned. "It's not well known, but you and I understand how Kellison got into the position he's in now. He tried to destroy another worldwide company, so he could get a tiny bit richer."

"He's changed. Look at the help he's given us recently."

"What would Void do with Kelton… besides wreaking havoc with the computer systems of Kelton's enemies?"

"One, Void wouldn't do that. He's a decent kid at heart. He means well. Two, we'd monitor him twenty-four seven. Third…"

Gregory nodded slowly. "He'd be available to us."

Haley raised her eyebrows. "That's a great idea."

Gregory gave her a "don't play me" look.

"Sorry," she said. "Yes, he'd be available to us. Unofficially, of course."

"Unsanctioned."

"Yes, one hundred percent unsanctioned. Completely off the books."

Gregory leaned back in his chair and stared past Haley, off into the distance. The silence stretched on so long it grew uncomfortable, kept on, and changed at some point to a companionable stillness.

Through it all, Haley waited patiently.

When Gregory returned his gaze to her and leaned forward, she was ready for the question.

"Why?" he asked.

He knows but wants to hear me say it.

"Because Malik wasn't the mastermind of this operation," she said in a low voice.

Gregory offered her a tight-lipped smile and nodded. "Exactly what I think."

He put his hands together, fingers interlaced, and pulled them back toward his body, cracking all his knuckles.

"Approved. All of it."

Gregory handed the paper filled with helicopter listings back to her. "You deal with this. Get me the invoice, and I'll handle it. But as for Void —Mr. Dawson Reite—he has to go back to prison for a few days at least. Maybe a week. At some point, relatively quickly, he'll be released to the custody of Kelton Kellison. I have to figure out the best way to do it quietly, whether that's a commutation of his sentence or some sort of problem with the evidence in his case. Agreed?"

Haley nodded, quite pleased.

Exactly as I figured.

"Also," Gregory said, "I got word this morning. Axe's source—Jamil. His wife was contacted by a CIA resource and extracted from Afghanistan. She and Jamil will arrive in the United States tomorrow. We owe them. I understand they need a place to live and work to do. She's a good cook, and he has experience as some sort of butler, I understand. I wonder where they could fit in."

She saw the play. "Kelton Kellison needs staff?"

I wonder how long ago he thought of that.

"You said he was moving up in the world. Mariana will already be watching Void. She could supervise the entire situation."

Haley didn't know how well Kelton and Mariana were going to react to all this, but she could get them to play ball for now.

"I'll make it happen," she said.

"Great. Anything else?"

"No, I think that's it. Thank you." Haley stood, giving Gregory a final nod and smile before walking to the door.

He called out before she could open it. "Haley."

She stopped and turned.

"The mastermind behind the attacks…"

"Yes?"

"Whoever it is has to be big. An extremely wealthy individual, perhaps. Or a nation-state. Maybe several countries working together. Hell, it could be Russia behind it after all. Only people with high-level connections could have gotten their hands on polonium-210. But whoever did it was very careful. And let's face it, they succeeded in both hitting America hard and protecting their identity."

"Which is why we have to go after them just as hard," she said right back, guessing where he was going.

"We will. But there are plenty of other threats to our country. So for now, hands off. No side hustles. No 'oops, I stumbled upon this in my free time.'" He stood and walked over to her. "I'm dead serious about this. It's need-to-know. As much as you've accomplished, as many secrets as you hold, you do not need to know. Understand?"

Her instincts screamed at her.

He knew my play all along—and this is his.

Gregory had given her everything she wanted in exchange for not looking for the person or people truly behind the attacks.

Haley struggled with her insatiable need to track down the enemy.

"The president and I are in complete agreement with this, and I have a message for you from him," Gregory said. "'Who wishes to fight must first count the cost.'"

I know the quote—Sun Tzu.

She didn't want to let it go, but it was Uncle Jimmy. He was asking her to back off—until they knew the price of taking the fight to the enemy.

Just this once, I might be able to temper my curiosity.

"Promise me that, if the time comes, I get first crack at it," Haley asked.

"Done." Gregory reached past her and opened the door. "Now, go find the next people who are plotting to harm the United States of America—and put a stop to them."

"With pleasure," she said and walked back to her workstation to hunt.

It's what I do.

186

THE THEORY

Temporary Central Analysis Group Headquarters
Joint Base Andrews
Prince George's County, Maryland

Haley settled in behind her desk. For the moment, she had an honest-to-goodness office. No cubicle. She had real walls and a door. It didn't sound like a big deal, but it felt good. Like she'd arrived.

As soon as Gregory found the team a new location, she would be back in a cubicle. She'd relish this while she could.

Dave poked his head in, smiled nervously, and took one of the guest chairs in front of her desk.

"I would have come to your office," she said. He and Nancy shared the one next door.

He shook his head and double-checked that he'd closed her office door.

Paranoid? Nervous? This isn't like him.

She could guess what he wanted to talk about but let him start in his own way.

"We shouldn't just drop the investigation," he said.

"Gregory said specifically—"

Dave interrupted her. "Nancy and I thought the three of us could work together in our spare time…"

Haley shook her head. "No. Gregory said not to."

"But is that what he really meant—or is it just cover?"

She had wondered the same. "No. I think he meant it."

I would expect Nancy to be pushing this, not him.

The frustrated look on his face made it impossible to resist asking a follow-up question. "Why? What do you have?"

Dave shook his head. "Only lots of questions… and thoughts."

"Such as?"

I wonder if they match mine.

"Someone started digging the tunnel at the same time as the construction of the resort. Even with the caves Axe described, it must have taken months."

Haley nodded to encourage him but didn't speak.

"I think this whole thing was planned from the start," Dave said. "The resort was built knowing a peace summit would happen there shortly after it was finished."

That's a paranoid conspiracy theory… and exactly what I think.

"Nancy wants to very quietly check into the dates of construction and planning," Dave said. "Maybe we can also find out when the peace summit was first proposed and by whom. If we knew who suggested the location, we would be closer to learning if the resort was planned to make the summit a kill zone from the very beginning."

Haley shook her head, sticking to her agreement with Gregory. "We can't. Besides, an endeavor like that would take…"

"A lot of planning."

"Yes," she said. "Deep resources. And commitment. It can't have been only about killing the vice president or the Russian president. It shows a desire to throw the Middle East into chaos—or at least take out the current leaders."

"With a complete leadership shakeup," Dave said, thinking out loud, "who would stand to gain?"

There was a long, pregnant pause.

"A lot of groups and countries," Haley said. "But for one…"

"The United States of America."

"America doesn't have the resources to do this," Haley said, bringing herself back to reality. "On the other hand, blaming it on the US would benefit a lot of countries."

"Including Russia."

He stopped there but had more to say.

"But?" she asked.

Dave shook his head. "You're the one with hunches, Haley, not me."

He's full of it. He just hates admitting he's following his gut for once.

"Come on, spit it out," she told him. "It goes no further—well, except for Axe, if you'll let me."

Dave shook his head, sighed, and mumbled, "Why not?" He leaned close to her. "You and Axe only, all right? I haven't even told Nancy yet."

"You've got it."

"Promise."

"Seriously?"

Dave nodded.

"Fine. I promise."

"Thank you. Here it is—this wasn't an earthquake, explosives, or tunneling."

"Then how the hell did the building collapse?"

"Go with me on this," he said. "If the building was designed and constructed specifically to fail, engineers could have purposefully selected materials more prone to vibrations. They could also have omitted other vibration-isolating materials. With proper planning and a tightly controlled construction process, the resort could have been made susceptible to vibrations."

"Like from an earthquake?"

"Or vibration-inducing machinery," Dave said.

She wasn't an expert in building design and construction, but she got the possibilities.

"Okay, what then?" she asked.

"You ever play that game with the blocks? You stack them up," Dave said, demonstrating three long blocks with one hand and three more in the opposite direction with the other. "You take turns pulling a piece out and stacking it on top until the whole thing collapses when one of you pulls the wrong one and destabilizes the tower?"

"Yes, I had it when I was a kid. Loved it."

"We were playing last night with Nancy's niece and nephew. We hadn't seen them in a while and went over for dinner now that this mess is wrapped up. The nephew runs away to get something, stomping across the floor as kids do. The whole coffee table shakes. It's my turn to go, and the whole tower collapses without me touching it. The niece was delighted—she's younger than her brother and hardly ever wins."

"The vibration of the nephew's footsteps shifted things around."

"Exactly." Dave opened his computer and turned the screen so she could see.

"What am I looking at?" she asked.

"First, these are industrial-grade ultrasonic cleaning machines. They convert sound energy into mechanical vibrations."

He clicked on a different browser tab.

"And these are ultrasonic testing machines. They're used non-destructively. These are just two examples of high-frequency emitters. Several machines like this, under the right conditions, near a building's foundation constructed of low-quality concrete, could create powerful vibrations at selected frequencies."

He held his hands up and shook them back and forth quickly. "If the frequency matched the natural frequency of the building, and there was nothing in place to absorb them…"

"The building would come down." Haley sat back in her chair, staring at the far wall, thinking it through.

Dave nodded. "The whole thing—all those dead leaders—would have been chalked up to an accident. An earthquake." He closed his laptop, looking embarrassed at admitting his theory.

He's always been a steady, logical analyst—and now this.

"If I'm right," he said, "someone took a shot at us—at the world as we know it—and failed."

She raised an eyebrow at Dave. "Boy, when you have a hunch, you go all in, don't you?"

Dave shook his head. "It's not intuition. It's data and logic."

She sat forward, her mind already plotting out methods of investigation… then took a deep breath and reined herself in.

"We have to get to work on this," Dave said, his voice still low. "We could—"

"No."

"Haley—"

"Dave—no. We won this round. They lost. And your hunch—sorry, your argument—is based on playing the wooden tower stacking game with two kids at a coffee table after dinner."

"But it fits," Dave said. "I'm not saying it's a slam dunk, but—"

"We have direct orders from Gregory. Although he promised me that if this needs to be looked into, I—we—get first dibs."

Her thoughts raced, looking for holes in his theory and finding plenty. *But…*

"It feels right, though, doesn't it?" Dave asked.

She didn't trust herself to speak for several seconds as she stared off into space, at war with herself. She wanted to dive right in, find the scent of the trail, and put the pieces of the puzzle together.

She also wanted—needed—to honor her commitment to Gregory.

And her uncle Jimmy, the president of the United States of America.

Finally, she made her decision and looked at Dave. "Yes. It feels exactly right."

187

THE THANK YOU

Novo-Ogaryovo
The Presidential Dacha
West of Moscow, Russia

Ekaterina sipped her tea, wondering if it was poisoned.

No one besides the two men in the room and the president's guards knew she was here. Not even Niko, who was somewhere in Moscow waiting for the next time she needed his help.

If the president wanted her dead, she wouldn't leave his compound alive.

Until they killed her, however, she refused to live in fear. If they were going to kill or detain her for saving their lives and preventing a war with America, so be it.

On the couch to her right sat President Nikitin, also sipping tea from the same teapot.

To her left, on a second couch, sat Dmitry, the young intelligence chief who had first approached her less than two weeks before.

Ekaterina had just finished providing her verbal report—the only one she would give. As she and Alex had agreed, some details were kept vague, such as who did what. Others were embellished. But all in all, she told the truth whenever possible.

"The Americans have our hacker," the president said after a sip of tea.

"Only one. The rest received the proper punishment."

The president frowned. "It would have been better if you had returned them here."

"Yes," she said, attempting a contrite tone. "I am sorry."

But not really. You would have been tempted to use them and their hacks, not punish them.

"Why didn't you immediately tell us the Americans had the hacker?" Dmitry asked.

"I was busy, and you two were flying to Oman. I handled the situation and fulfilled my mission."

"Why did you not communicate the possibility of a tunnel or attack on the summit?"

She wondered if they would accept the truth.

"Telling you would have changed nothing," she said. "Would it?"

The president didn't answer. He held up her phone and looked at it again. "This man," the president said, looking at the picture Alex had provided her of Malik's dead brother. "This is the man behind it all?"

How much does he know?

Ekaterina shrugged. "He is the one in the Tower penthouse wearing the ring designating him Malik, the leader." She finished her tea. "I accomplished the primary mission—to show America that Russia did not attack them," she said. "Letting them take the hacker was the only way to be sure of this. Also, I helped save your lives by transporting the American operator and assisting him in the caves."

Ekaterina paused to let the weight of what she had to say next come through. "You're welcome. You may thank me by letting me have my freedom."

"This is the way you speak to your president?" Nikitin said, but it came out more curious than angry.

"You owe me your life. You will do the honorable thing or not. Nothing I say—or how I say it—should make a difference."

They locked eyes for a long moment before the president turned to his intelligence chief and chuckled. "Dmitry, I suspect this woman has faced foes far more dangerous than you or me."

The young spymaster smiled.

Turning back to her, the president continued. "You have earned your retirement. Many times over, I suspect. You are hereby released from service."

There was no fanfare or handshake, though he did gesture at the teapot to see if she wanted more.

She smiled slightly and shook her head.

"Now that you are retired," the president asked, "what will you do? Sit by the fire and read your books?"

So he knows about the cabin and how I pass my days.

She wondered how long she had been under surveillance—whether it had been the moment she left Los Angeles months before, if she'd been noticed crossing the border from Finland, or if someone in her little town had loose lips and mentioned the quiet woman who had appeared in their midst one late winter day.

"That, and other things," she said.

She'd had an idea of offering her services—her skillset—on the open market.

Just the occasional contract. Always for the right client and the right reason. And never against the interests of Russia.

"Perhaps we can call on you from time to time," the president said mildly with a raised eyebrow.

She stared at him and nearly said words she would have regretted. At the last second, she smiled. "Perhaps."

One never knows.

PART 10

SATURDAY

188

THE TEAM

Axe relaxed in the leather chair near the fire instead of his usual spot close to the kitchen. He felt better. His body and head were on the mend.

The cabin bustled with more people than ever. Having members of the team nearby made a huge difference in his attitude. He could practically feel his body and psyche recovering faster with the talking and laughter surrounding him, though he missed several of the usual group.

Mad Dog and Johnboy were still away on a private contract.

Mariana—Tex—was with Kelton, supervising Void and Kaylin, who had become an item.

Jamil and his wife had also moved into Kelton's new Manhattan high-rise apartment.

Happy to hear Jamil's wife got out safe and they're both being taken care of.

He wouldn't be here now if it weren't for Jamil's bravery and sacrifice.

For the first time, Tucci joined the after-action dinner, sitting on the couch and favoring his shoulder where he'd been shot.

He and Marcus, who sat on the other side of the couch, were engaged in a spirited discussion about the pros and cons of various weapons.

They sound almost as bad as a couple of SEALs.

Nancy, from Haley's Central Analysis Group team, had taken charge in the kitchen, bossing around the members of Axe's old Team.

Red, his long flaming beard and hair neater and trimmer than usual, was on pizza serving duty.

Ronbo gathered up fresh beer bottles for everyone.

Thor leaned against the counter, telling a joke that had everyone smiling.

Link poured chips and pretzels into bowls, his huge hands making the party-size bags look like the tiny ones school kids took for lunch.

Connie had gratefully taken a night off from being his nurse and maid. She was out seeing a movie in the nearest large town.

Gregory and Dave helped out in the kitchen as well, gathering napkins and—doctor's orders—serving up salads for everyone.

"Five minutes," Nancy called.

Haley squatted next to his chair, her face strained.

Uh-oh, here it comes.

"Just in case there's no time later," she started, her voice low to keep Tucci and Marcus from overhearing. She shook her head slowly. "While avoiding fieldwork, I still managed to kill five more tangos."

Axe knew what she meant right away.

"It's getting easier to kill, isn't it?" he asked quietly.

She frowned and nodded, her body slumping. "It's too easy now," she whispered.

He thought back to his active service days—or nights, rather.

"It happens."

"I don't like it."

"Good. We shouldn't."

They shared a moment, and she smiled. "Thanks."

Before she could stand, he hit her with his own concern. "With this latest concussion…" He trailed off, unable to say the words.

"Is it time to call it?" she asked. Her voice was kind and supportive, not judgmental.

She won't talk me out of it if I decide I have to get out of the business.

"I don't know yet," he said, telling her the truth.

He'd gone back and forth the last several days.

Dying on the battlefield while saving the country or his team, had a lot of appeal.

So did living a full life with Connie, maybe getting back to taking more pictures—which had often fallen by the wayside with all the action he'd seen in the past months.

"Dinner is served," Nancy called.

"That wasn't five minutes," Haley whispered.

Axe chuckled. "Discussion to be continued," he said.

"Don't get up, Axe," Thor joked as he came from the kitchen and handed a plate loaded with pizza to Haley and one to him.

"I wasn't planning on it," Axe said, taking his plate.

Tucci and Marcus received delivery service as well.

When everyone had taken their seats, Tucci spoke up. "Is this what you guys do after a mission? Eat pizza, drink beer, and tell stories?"

"Pretty much," Haley said, her mouth full.

"Great. Just like back in my day. Well, I got one for you. So no shit, there I was, watching my helicopter—my livelihood—burn in the middle of a Maryland field." He looked down at his plate for several seconds before speaking again. "The end. That's the story."

He hadn't meant it to be funny, but none of the team could hold back their laughter.

Tucci scowled and took a bite of pizza.

"Oh, yeah, and I got shot," he said as he chewed. "I should have stayed back in New Jersey." He looked at Axe as the laughter died down. "You—lose my number."

This only made everyone laugh more, including Axe.

"Hey, maybe you get a minivan," Thor suggested. "Holds lots of cargo. You could make some sweet money driving people around. Those rideshare companies? I mean, it's not a helicopter, but…"

In response, Tucci rubbed his eye with one finger.

Axe chuckled. It hurt to laugh but was exactly what he needed.

Haley finished her first slice and set her plate, loaded with more, on the coffee table.

The woman can sure put the food away.

She wiped her fingers on a white paper napkin and reached into her back pocket, fishing out a folded piece of paper and offering it to Tucci.

"Here are five helicopters. Check them out, go fly them, whatever you do when purchasing a helicopter. Pick the one you want and let me know. It's yours."

Tucci stared at her, suspicious, disbelieving, and excited all at once. "Just like that?"

"Just like that," Haley said. "It's amazing what you can negotiate after saving the world," she added with a nod to Gregory, who raised his bottle of beer.

"I only saved you and Axe," Tucci muttered. "And the hacker kid."

Haley shrugged with a smile. "Yeah. Only."

"To saving the world," Thor said, raising his beer.

"To saving the world," they repeated, clinked bottles, and drank.

"And..." Axe said. He paused and looked down so the others couldn't see his eyes as they threatened to tear up.

Damn mood swings.

The doctors said he'd have stronger emotions than usual until the concussion was completely healed.

He cleared his throat, blinked, and looked up, raising his bottle. "To absent friends."

Let them think I mean all the men we've lost... along with Admiral Nalen, crazy Mad Dog, steady Johnboy, and impulsive Mariana.

He'd see the four of them again soon for the next mission—if there was one.

But there was no telling when or if he'd run into the two he really meant.

I hope you're doing well wherever you are, Ekaterina and Niko.

The two Russians had risked their lives to save his.

Ekaterina had followed him into the caves to back him up.

Niko had carried him along the narrow mountain trail to the SUV.

Both had worked tirelessly to keep him from bleeding out.

At any point, they could have cut and run. It would have been simpler and safer, but they'd stuck around.

May we meet again someday, under quieter circumstances.

He'd buy them a beer and toast them in person.

"To absent friends," the men and women around the room said quietly and toasted again.

Then the bantering stopped for a while as they dug into their pizza—and salad.

Axe took in the room, adding it up.

Tucci and Marcus had gotten shot while pulling guard duty.

Haley had ended up in action, running and gunning.

Add in Ekaterina and Niko—and himself, of course.

Not the usual suspects, but an extremely capable team.

A team of six.

Axe smiled—his mind, body, and heart at peace for the moment.

It might take a few more weeks, but he'd be back at it in no time.

There were risks. One or two more traumatic brain injuries, the doctors said, and he'd be in a world of trouble.

But he wouldn't trade nights like this for anything.

I am never out of the fight.

Author's Note

Thank you so much for reading. Look for *A Team of Seven* next. Visit me on Facebook, Instagram, or sign up for my newsletter for details and updates. (See information below.)

Available now: the excitement continues with *Target: Redacted*, featuring a new hero along with several favorite characters from the Unsanctioned Asset Series.

Target: Redacted

Someone is killing Americans.

The suspect is connected at the highest levels.

Confronting him is impossible.

Still, justice must be served...

Long-retired Navy SEAL Thomas "T-Bone" Marks left the warrior business behind years ago. He's now a happy, small-town teacher—until the wheels come off his world.

A clandestine intelligence agency offers to help Thomas reclaim his life—in exchange for a few days of his time.

More attacks may be coming. Someone must find out the truth before it's too late.

Someone completely off the radar.

Someone expendable—and with nothing to lose.

Someone like Thomas.

If the intel is correct, there must be instant justice.

Without remorse.

Without mercy.

No matter what the costs.

Thomas is back in the warrior business.

He's a man with a mission—whether he's ready for it or not.

Read my latest pulse-pounding, action-packed thriller!

Type this short link into your browser for more details and to order your copy.

https://geni.us/Target-Redacted

(You can also order it from your favorite local bookstore.)

- Get a free prequel short story about Axe's first mission (along with my newsletter). Go to: https://www.authorbradlee.com/operationrapidrevenge
- If you enjoyed the book, please leave a five-star or written review. It helps new readers discover the book and makes it possible for me to continue bringing you stories.
- I'm active on social media, sharing photos (like Axe would take) and writing progress updates. I also occasionally ask for input on character names, plot points, or reader preferences as I'm writing, so please follow me and help out. Find me here:
- Facebook: https://www.facebook.com/AuthorBradLee
- Instagram: https://www.instagram.com/bradleeauthor/
- Note: in *A Team of Six*, I used the names of some real places but fictionalize many details. I also take inspiration from areas but change names and some features to improve the story. My apologies if you live in or are acquainted with one of the areas and think, "Wait, that's not right." You're correct. License was taken in describing places as well as technology, equipment, weapons, tactics, and military capabilities. Where location details, distances, or technical issues conflicted with the story, I prioritized the story.
- Finally, please join me in thanking Beth, Nicole, Crystal, and Mac for their help. The book is far better because of them.

Made in the USA
Coppell, TX
28 June 2024

34060646R00372